I0743596

Dead Man's Tide
The Dangling Carrot
The Big Kiss-Off

DAY KEENE

Introduction by Cullen Gallagher

Stark House Press • Eureka California

DEAD MAN'S TIDE / THE DANGLING CARROT /
THE BIG KISS-OFF

Published by Stark House Press
1315 H Street
Eureka, CA 95501, USA
griffinskye3@sbcglobal.net
www.starkhousepress.com

DEAD MAN'S TIDE
Originally published by Graphic Publications, New Jersey, as by
William Richards, and copyright © 1953 by Graphic Publishing
Company, Inc. Copyright renewed November 6, 1981, by Irene
Keene and Al James.

THE DANGLING CARROT
Originally published by Ace Books, Inc., New York, and copyright
© 1955 by Ace Books, Inc. Copyright renewed December 29,
1983, by Irene Keene and Al James.

THE BIG KISS-OFF
Originally published by Graphic Books, New Jersey, and
copyright © 1954 by Graphic Publishing Company, Inc.
Copyright renewed December 23, 1982 by Irene Keene and Al
James.

"Run For Your Life: Day Keene's Wrong Men" copyright © 2021
by Cullen Gallagher

Reprinted by permission of Day James, executor of the estate of
Day Keene. All rights reserved under International and Pan-
American Copyright Conventions.

ISBN: 978-1-951473-19-8

Book design by Mark Shepard, shepgraphics.com
Cover design by Jeff Vorzimmer, ¡caliente!design, Austin, Texas
Cover art from the Graphic Books edition of *Dead Man's Tide*
Proofreading by Bill Kelly

PUBLISHER'S NOTE
This is a work of fiction. Names, characters, places and incidents
are either the products of the author's imagination or used
fictionally, and any resemblance to actual persons, living or dead,
events or locales, is entirely coincidental.
Without limiting the rights under copyright reserved above, no
part of this publication may be reproduced, stored, or introduced
into a retrieval system or transmitted in any form or by any
means (electronic, mechanical, photocopying, recording or
otherwise) without the prior written permission of both the
copyright owner and the above publisher of the book.

First Stark House Press Edition: January 2021

RUN FOR YOUR LIFE: DAY KEENE'S WRONG MEN

BY CULLEN GALLAGHER

If anything unifies Day Keene's body of work, it would be the sense of breathlessness that pervades nearly all of his work. As Bill Crider remarked on *Mystery*File*, Keene had "the ability to tell a story that hits the ground running and never lets up." Keene's pacing is relentless. His plots typically unwind over the course of one or two sleepless days as characters rush from one situation to the next, one step ahead of the law, and one step behind the conspiring forces that have, undoubtedly, framed them for one murder or another. The "wrong man" archetype is as central to Keene's books as it is to Alfred Hitchcock's movies.

Running is the natural state of being for Keene's characters. As the protagonist of *Dead Man's Tide* reflects, "Man, he decided, acclimated quickly. He felt perfectly cool, as though he'd been hunted and running for years." Keene, born Gunard Hjertstedt, was himself on the run for the better part of the 1920s, criss-crossing the country as a traveling stock company actor and vaudeville performer in the 1920s. And when he settled into a stable job as a radio writer in Chicago in the 1930s for programs such as *Little Orphan Annie* and *Kitty Keene, Inc.*, the demands of daily scripts kept his fingers plenty busy, racing furiously across the typewriter's keyboard.

Keene was arguably even busier in the 1940s, switching from radio to pulp fiction, and relocating first to St. Petersburg, Florida in the first half of the decade, and then to Los Angeles, California, in the second. By my count—consulting three bibliographies: *The FictionMags Index*, edited by William G. Contento and Phil Stephensen-Payne, "The Pulp Fiction of Day Keene" by Steve Lewis on *Mystery*File,* and William Denton's RARA-AVIS listserv—Keene published 266 short stories in his lifetime, nearly all of them in the pulps, and the bulk of them, 250, between 1940 and 1952. Do the math, and that's nearly 20 stories per year, every year, for thirteen years straight, and during those last few years Keene was also producing multiple novels per year, as well. Between 1949 and his death in 1969, Keene moved back to St. Petersburg and then again back to Los Angeles, and published a jaw-dropping 50 novels.

Day Keene's fingers never stopped running—and neither did his characters.

The three works collected here contain two novels of wrong men on the run, and one "right man" whose guilt is the result of his own transgression—a reminder that, perhaps, even Keene's wrong men are not so innocent, and might be capable of that for which they were framed. They are also all "southern" novels, a geographic region where Keene set several of his books. Keene tended to use locations in or around where he had lived—Chicago, Los Angeles, and St. Petersburg.

Originally published in 1953 by Graphic, *Dead Man's Tide* appeared under the pen name William Richards. Keene also used the name for his true crime story "Strangled," which appeared in the November 1951 issue of *Underworld Detective* (a true crime pulp edited by Lionel White before he began his career as a writer). This was Keene's third novel for Graphic, following *If the Coffin Fits* (1952) and *Strange Witness* (1953); he would pen two more for them the following year, *The Big Kiss-Off* (1954), which is also included here, and *Homicidal Lady* (1954). *Dead Man's Tide* would later be reprinted under Keene's own name in 1958 from Avon as *It's a Sin to Kill*.

Leading with a strong opening was a life-long lesson Keene learned from his pulp days, and *Dead Man's Tide* begins with one of Keene's most vivid images: a nude corpse floating in the Gulf of Mexico with an $18,000 ring gleaming in the moonlight. Though it is not directly identified by name, references to Sister Key and a causeway to Palmetto indicate the central location is St. Petersburg, Florida, Keene's residence at the time.

We first meet protagonist Charlie Ames, ex-trumpet player turned charter boat captain, in typical Keene fashion: waking up in a strange location and into a world of trouble he doesn't remember. He's in a strange bed on someone else's boat, covered in lipstick, there's $5000 in his pocket, an empty whiskey bottle on the floor, and the carpet is soaked in blood. The boat's owner, Helene Camden, is missing. Of course, it turns out that it was her body in the Gulf, and Charlie is suspected of murder. His wife, Mary Lou, doesn't believe him at first, but once she starts investigating she, too, is conked on the head, wakes up floating in the water, and finds herself framed for murder. Waking up to murder is such a prevalent motif in Keene's work that he even used it as the title of one of his books, *Wake Up to Murder* (1952). Theme and variation are key to Keene's methodology. A writer of patterns, he frequently reused elements from previous books and stories, reconfiguring them in different (and, sometimes, similar) ways in new works. Recognizing and tracking these motifs is part of the fun and fascination of Keene's body of work.

In fact, *Dead Man's Tide* is itself a reworking of an early story, "Wait for the Dead Man's Tide!" that originally appeared in the August 1949 issue of *Dime Mystery*. The overall trajectory of the story is the same, but with one crucial difference: the genders are completely reversed. It is Mary Lou Ames who wakes up on a stranger's boat, and it is Mr. Camden—not Mrs.—whose body was floating in the Gulf (also, the opening of the short story omits any references to the corpse being "nude" or its "white buttocks"—Keene spiced it up for the novel). The situation of a wife accused of murder, and the husband who at first does not believe her and then must prove her innocence, would reappear in *Mrs. Homicide*, in which a NYPD cop's wife awakens in a stranger's bed next to a corpse; in both cases, the husband winds up framed for another murder during the course of his investigation.

Another of Keene's recurring motifs is strained relationships. Marital discord and spousal distrust are motivating factors in many books, including all three included in this volume, and especially *The Big Kiss-Off*. Another of Keene's paperback originals for Graphic, this one is set on the coast of Louisiana. A variation on the opening of *Dead Man's Tide*, *The Big Kiss-Off* begins with six bodies on a mud flat in the gulf, rotting, waiting for the tide to carry them away and give them a burial at sea. This is what Cain Cade sees as he navigates his boat into his hometown of Bay Parish. Cain receives a hell of a homecoming. His wife, Janice, sold his family home and divorced him while he was a P.O.W. in Korea. Stepping into a bar, the sheriff and his deputy knock Cain cold and deliver a message from local heavy Tocko Kalavitch that Cain better be out of town by noon tomorrow. But waiting back on his boat is a young woman, Mimi Trujillo Esterpar Moran, a stowaway who entered the country illegally in order to find her missing husband, whose last known address was c/o Tocko Kalavitch. Wouldn't you know it, the next day Cain finds himself framed for murder and on the run from cops, gangsters, and immigration officers.

The Big Kiss-Off recycles many common elements from Keene's work during this period. The theme of family land seizure, as well as the Louisiana setting, would reappear in *Bring Him Back Dead* (1956), one of his twelve novels published by Gold Medal, and one of his strongest works. Mimi's last name would appear in the title of his 1959 Zenith PBO *Moran's Woman*. And the issue of a husband's impotency would become a motivating factor in *Seed of Doubt*.

The third work featured here, *The Dangling Carrot* (1955), was originally published by Ace, as one of their "doubles," with Norman C. Rosenthal's *Silenced Witness* on the flip side. This was Keene's third PBO for Ace, following *Mrs. Homicide* (1953), *Death House Doll* (1954), and preceding *Flight by Night* (1956). The title of this book works as both a metaphor and a euphemism—a symbol of the bait that entraps Judge Evan Johns, as well as of his own fears for his waning virility.

Set in an unnamed small town somewhere in Georgia, *The Dangling Carrot* begins with the disappearance of two prominent businessmen. It is Judge Evan Johns's final day on the circuit court before he steps up to the city court. One of his last cases is Dale Chambers, a young woman who works at the local diner and who was caught for speeding. He lets her off with a warning—but he can't get her off his mind. After his wife announces she is going out of town for a few days, Evan arranges a rendezvous with Dale at his lakefront cabin. Their amorous getaway is interrupted when one of the businessmen is found dead in the lake. The more that Evan attempts to help the investigation, the harder it is to hide his affair with Dale, and after someone saps him from behind, he realizes he might be the next murder victim.

The Dangling Carrot diverges from Keene's typical design in that Evan is not a wrong man, and the only running he's doing is from himself and the inevitable—some secrets can't stay hidden forever. Furthermore, unlike the husbands who falsely suspect their wives of infidelity in *Dead Man's Tide, Mrs. Homicide*, and *Who Has Wilma Lathrop?*, the husband here is undeniably guilty of the affair. Ultimately, the reconciliation between Evan and his wife in *The Dangling Carrot* is one of the most poignant moments in Keene's books, which are more known for their frantic pacing than emotional connection. It's an important moment in his body of work, and anticipates a similar denouement in *Bring Him Back Dead*, in which the husband, who had previously blamed his wife for tensions in their marriage, realizes that he is to blame for their alienation.

Keene's characters aren't perfect or idealized. They're average, working class characters. Not extraordinary or special in any way, and I think that helps readers identify with situations and plots that can sometimes seem too fantastic or coincidental. Wrong—or, sometimes, right—his characters ran for their lives, and took readers along with them on wild, thrilling adventures. Try and keep up with them as you read these three novels, and I hope you enjoy them.

—October 2020
Brooklyn, NY

Cullen Gallagher lives in Brooklyn, NY. His writing has appeared in the *Los Angeles Review of Books*, *Paris Review*, and *Not Coming to a Theater Near You*, as well as in the anthologies *Cult Cinema: An Arrow Video Companion* (2016) edited by Anthony Nield, and *Screen Slate: New York City Cinema 2011-2015* (2017) edited by Jon Dieringer. His western fiction appears in the anthologies *Bourbon & a Good Cigar* (2018) and *Time to Myself* (2018), both edited by Scott Harris. He blogs about noir and western fiction at *Pulp Serenade* (www.pulp-serenade.com).

Dead Man's Tide

DAY KEENE

CHAPTER ONE

The nude body lay like a swimmer in the water, face down, one arm extended. A south moon under, breaking through a rift in the clouds, found fire on one finger of the white, outstretched hand. The small fire glittered and twinkled and flared. Even the full force of the outgoing tide surging through the narrow pass, connecting the bay with the Gulf of Mexico, failed to extinguish it. It seemed to be imbedded in the dead woman's hand, a last spark of life in the otherwise lifeless clay.

For a time the body made good progress. It bobbled past the pier of the Beach Club and the swank homes on the rim of the bay. Gripped by the relentless tide, it glided past Bill's Boat Basin and the dozen small bait camps that adjoined the basin. Here and there, on both sides of the pass, lights winked on as commercial fishermen and bait camp proprietors awakened to prepare for another day. A late returning shrimper chugged under one of the high arches of the bridge. Early fishermen parked their cars and rigged their tackle. Neither they nor the men aboard the shrimp boat saw the body.

A small school of porpoise coming up to blow circled the body curiously and swam on.

The body was headed under an arch of the bridge, out into the open Gulf with the next landfall Yucatan, when the tide turned. The moving corpse lost forward motion. It twisted and turned in a small circle, then came to rest against a barnacle covered bridge piling.

Schools of small fish swarmed around it, only to be frightened away as the force of the incoming tide set it in motion again. Much deeper in the water now, only a strand of bleached blonde hair and one white buttock showing, the body floated back the way it had come, back past the boat camps, the boat basin, the sleeping estates, the Beach Club pier, into the even blacker if more tranquil waters of the upper bay.

There the body snagged on a mangrove root rising out of a small sand bar and lost all motion. Schools of little fish immediately surrounded it. The crabs arrived singly and in pairs. It made no difference to them that the spark on the dead woman's finger was a diamond appraised at eighteen thousand dollars.

For long minutes after he'd awakened, Charlie Ames lay looking up through the dark, listening to the suck of the tide, feeling the familiar motion of the cruiser, wishing the foul taste in his mouth would go away.

We'll have bacon and eggs and grits for breakfast, he decided. Perhaps Mary Lou might even whip up a batch of biscuits. When a man worked as hard as he did, he had a right to a big breakfast. Anyone who thought running a charter fishing boat was a lazy man's job was out of his ignorant mind. Especially an old tub like the *Sally*. If it wasn't the bottom it was the engine. If it wasn't the engine, it was a bilge pump, a rotted rudder post, or a leak in the live bait well.

He wished he could buy a new boat. Thinking about a new boat brought back the quarrel with Mary Lou. Mary Lou was hell determined to keep on singing at the Beach Club. She reasoned with feminine logic that if she could keep her job until the end of the season, they would be able to buy a new boat.

Perhaps they could. But meanwhile he'd go through hell. He knew what working in a place like the Beach Club entailed, especially for a girl as pretty as Mary Lou. He'd tooted a trumpet in similar spots all his adult life until his lip had gone bad.

Ames sucked at his lower lip. The singing wasn't so bad. Mary Lou liked to sing. He didn't even mind her acting as hostess. It gave her a chance to wear pretty clothes. It gave her a taste of life, a nibble at luxury he couldn't give her. If only the rich old goats who could afford to patronize places like the Beach Club would keep their hands and their thoughts to themselves. But they never did. Being in Florida seemed to tickle their ancient libidos. The rye and rum and Scotch they consumed came straight from the Fountain of Youth. They thought because they had money and a girl who sang torch songs on a bandstand was also employed to sit at their tables, they could paw and insult and proposition her with impunity.

Some night he'd slug one of them and that would end the matter of Mary Lou working at the Beach Club. Ames felt a twinge of remorse. He was making something out of nothing. He was jealous. Mary Lou was a sweet kid and as straight as they came. He'd had no call to say the things he had.

Ames was tempted to slip out of his bunk and into Mary Lou's and tell her he was sorry he'd said the foul things he had. All she was trying to do was help him.

He resisted the impulse. One thing would lead to another and both of them needed their rest. Mary Lou had probably come in with the dawn. He had a charter party at eight.

The bunk under him dipped as the moored boat swung with the tide. Ames loved the motion. He loved boats. Even before his lip had gone, he'd never been a Harry James. Mary Lou was no Dinah Shore. And blown-out trumpet players and third-rate girl vocalists were a dime a dozen in Florida.

Ames shuddered at the thought. If he hadn't been born in a bait camp, if he hadn't known the Gulf, if he hadn't been able to buy the *Sally*, he'd probably be tooting with a non-union combo in some piney-woods juke joint for five dollars a night and his drinks while Mary Lou entertained the bearded clientele with *She'll Be Comin' Round The Mountain When She Comes*—with both of them drinking too much and snapping at each other because life hadn't turned out the way they had expected.

This way they were at least secure. They had a home of sorts. When the charter business was bad he could always do some commercial fishing. If only he could afford to buy a boat that would attract the better class and higher paying deep sea fishermen.

Ames lay dreaming in the growing light. Say a forty or forty-two foot cruiser. With a Diesel motor and a ship-to-shore phone and a forward cabin in which Mary Lou could stay out from underfoot, even on all-male charter trips.

If only he could raise five thousand dollars, he could at least make the down payment on the type of boat he wanted. He had seven hundred put by. Ben Sheldon had offered him two thousand for the *Sally*. That made twenty-seven hundred. Figuring her salary and tips, Mary Lou had saved nine hundred and eighty dollars. That brought the total to three thousand, six hundred and eighty dollars. The Beach Club would stay open four more weeks. Mary Lou got fifty a week plus her tips. That meant at least another three hundred and a grand total of thirty-nine hundred dollars.

Ames was sorry he'd quarreled with Mary Lou. She was right and he was wrong. She didn't want to work at the Beach Club. She'd much prefer to stay at home and have babies. Except for what she'd had to spend on dresses, she'd saved every penny she'd made toward the boat.

Another thousand dollars would do it.

A tall man, well-muscled, Ames stretched luxuriously on the bunk. It was time to be up and doing. It was time to awaken Mary Lou. But the bunk had never felt softer. Ames was amused. It just went to show what being in love with a boat or a woman could do to a man's mind. The thin pad felt like an innerspring mattress. He bounced slightly and springs gave under him.

What the hell, Ames thought.

He *was* lying on an innerspring mattress and there were no innersprings on the *Sally*.

Ames called "Mary Lou," softly.

There was no answer but the surge of the tide, the creak of the mooring ropes and the swish of the water in the bilge. Ames sat up and swung his feet to the deck. It was carpeted and unfamiliar. The distance between the two bunks was wider than he remembered it. The opposite bunk also had an innerspring mattress and Mary Lou wasn't on it.

The sour taste in his mouth persisted. His head ached. His body felt suddenly hot. The air coming in through the graying portholes was no longer cool. It was difficult for him to breathe. Ames wanted a light. He *had* to have a light.

He felt along the wall for the gasoline pressure lantern that illuminated the *Sally*. The lantern wasn't where it should be. Then his groping fingers encountered a switch and a bright white light pushed the gray of morning back through the highly polished portholes.

He was aboard a cruiser, but whatever boat he was on, he wasn't aboard the *Sally*. This cabin was paneled in mahogany. It seemed to stretch an endless distance to a beveled mirror door.

Ames looked at the bunk opposite the one on which he had been sleeping. A strapless white evening gown lay in a crumpled heap on top of the unrumpled spread, like someone had damn well wanted it off in a hurry. A pair of sheer hose turned inside out and a wisp of silk that was probably a pair of scanties lay beside the dress.

An empty fifth bottle of bonded whiskey rolled between the two bunks with every rise and fall of the cruiser. Over the bunk in which he had awakened, a built-in ashtray was filled with cigarette stubs, half of which were stained with lipstick. The bunk itself looked as if it had taken a hell of a beating.

Ames looked in the beveled mirror door and realized he was nude. He strode toward the mirror, hoping it was the entrance to the head. He was afraid he was going to be sick. He was.

He stayed in the head a long time. The door was mirrored on both sides. His eyes were slightly bloodshot. He needed a shave. His sun-bronzed face and neck and chest were smeared with the same deep shade of lipstick as the cigarette butts in the ashtray. More, the lipstick had been personally and intimately applied.

Ames turned on the tap in the metal basin and splashed water on his face and chest. It failed to erase the smears. The lipstick was indelible.

Nothing had changed when he came out of the head. He was still alone in the cabin. The cabin was still paneled in mahogany. The empty whiskey bottle still rolled between the two bunks. The strapless evening gown and hose and wisp of silk still lay on the unused bunk.

Ames looked and found his clothes. His skivvy and dungarees and sneakers were heaped on a chrome and red canvas officer's chair with his best white cap perched cockily on top of them.

He sat back on the bunk and tried to think. He had a head. He'd been sick. Still, he couldn't remember drinking. At least not heavily. There had been a time. When he'd been tooting a trumpet things like this happened often. Women, both single and married, were, it would seem, attracted to musicians. But it had been a long time since he'd awakened in a strange bed. He no longer drank to the point of blanking out. He didn't do things like this. He hadn't stepped out since he'd married Mary Lou. He'd had no reason to.

There was a small strand of blonde hair on the pillow. Ames picked it from the indentation and subconsciously wound it around a sun-blackened finger as he thought back to the night before.

He'd fished for bait until almost two o'clock. It had been after two when he'd pulled back into the slip in Bill's Boat Basin. He had secured the *Sally.* He'd made certain the small auxiliary motor that furnished a constant supply of fresh sea water to the live bait well had been working.

He had debated turning in or making a pot of coffee. He'd decided to make a pot of coffee. Then what had happened? His head continued to ache. His mouth had never been so dry.

Then what had happened?

He forced himself to think. Of course. Mrs. Camden had hailed him from the pier.

"Ahoy, the *Sally,*" she'd called.

Ames looked at the strand of blonde hair he'd wound around his fingers. Mrs. Camden was a bleached blonde. She was also a successful business woman. Something to do with cosmetics, he thought. A career girl, Mary Lou had called her.

Ames unwound the strand of hair and dropped it on the carpet. Mrs. Camden had been wearing a strapless white evening gown, with no need of any straps. He remembered distinctly thinking that the brittle blonde could give Jane Russell spades and still come out in front.

The big vein in Ames's throat began to throb.

"Ahoy, the *Sally*," she'd called.

He had answered the hail. Mrs. Camden had been drinking but was in full possession of all her faculties. She'd wanted to know how much he would charge to skipper the forty-eight foot Camden cruiser, the *Sea Bird*, down the west coast to the Keys and up the east coast inland waterway to Baltimore. Her husband, Mrs. Camden said, was flying down next week. They both were much in need of a vacation. She'd thought it would be nice if she and Mr. Camden could return via the inland waterway.

That, Ames thought, *is the trouble. The wrong kind of people have boats*. What he could do with the *Sea Bird*.

He looked around the cabin again. He was on the *Sea Bird*. Of course. He recognized the cabin from Ben Sheldon's description of the boat.

"It's the goddamnedest thing inside you ever saw, Charlie," the fat ship's chandler had told him. "It's like a floating luxury hotel."

It was all of that. Ames averted his eyes from the clothing on the opposite bunk and patted at the sweat beading on his forehead. The question was how had he gotten aboard.

There was tangible evidence as to what had happened. Mary Lou was going to give him hell for it. It would serve him right if she left him.

He forced his mind back to the night just past. He'd told Mrs. Camden he couldn't quote her a price offhand, that such a trip would involve at least a month's time and the subsequent loss of a number of parties, that he'd have to think it over.

While they had been talking, she on the pier, he in the cockpit of the *Sally*, the coffee in the galley had boiled over.

Mrs. Camden had asked, "Is that fresh coffee I smell, Captain?"

He had admitted it was and asked her if she'd like a cup. She said she would enjoy a cup of coffee very much, so he'd invited her aboard. They'd sat in the open cockpit. Mrs. Camden had been more drunk than he'd thought. She'd had difficulty forming her words. But outside of exposing a spot of white thigh every time she crossed and recrossed her legs, the brittle blonde had been a perfect lady. Their talk had been strictly of business. She hadn't said or done a thing that remotely resembled a pass.

Ames wished he knew her first name. Feeling like a fool, he called, "Mrs. Camden."

The suck of the tide and the creak of the mooring ropes answered him. He stood up and looked out of a porthole. Morning was gray in the sky. He could see the murky outline of a pier and beyond it, the black silhouette of the spacious Camden beach home rising out of its lush surroundings of phoenix and coconut palms.

There was no doubt about it. He was aboard the *Sea Bird*. The cruiser was moored to the Camden pier. How he had gotten aboard was another matter. Perhaps Mrs. Camden could tell him. But then where was Mrs. Camden? Ames looked back at the hastily discarded evening dress. The big vein in his neck continued to throb. Unless the blonde cosmetic manufacturer had other clothing aboard, she was feeling the cool of the morning.

Ames picked his cap and pants from the chair, put them on and walked aft. The big cabin opened into a smaller second cabin. It, too, was unoccupied. Angry now, he continued aft and stepped out into the canopy sheltered cockpit.

Damn the big blonde for a bitch! She'd gotten him into a peck of trouble. He'd never be able to square this with Mary Lou. Still, how had he gotten aboard? The last thing he remembered was drinking a second cup of coffee in the open cockpit of the *Sally*.

A small eye of light bobbled among the trees and a woman started out on the pier. Ames waited with clenched fists on his hips. The blonde had probably gone for another bottle. Who did she think she was? Since when was she so hard up that she had to shanghai a charter boat captain? He'd give her hell, then he'd crawl back to the *Sally* and try to make his peace with Mary Lou.

"I was making a pot of coffee," he'd say. "Mrs. Camden said she'd like a cup. I invited her aboard. We had two cups apiece." Ames stuck there. Then what happened? He wished he knew. He'd have a hell of a time convincing Mary Lou that he didn't.

The woman hurrying out on the pier was wearing a flowered housecoat. The long skirt of her silk nightgown showed under the flowered material and swished around her ankles as she walked.

When she was still a hundred feet away, she called:

"Mrs. Camden!"

Ames cocked his cap on the side of his head. Whoever the girl was, she wasn't Mrs. Camden. She was some years younger, for one thing. For another, she had black hair.

"Who are you?" Ames asked her.

The girl was holding a flashlight in one hand. She used her other hand to make sure her housecoat was fastened. "I am Celeste," she said primly. "I am sorry if I intrude. But Madame's Paris office is on the trans-Atlantic phone. So would you be so kind as to inform Mrs. Camden they say the call ees ver' important."

The girl wasn't asking a favor. She was making a statement.

Ames shook his head at her. "Mrs. Camden isn't here."

The maid's eyes widened slightly. Her French accent was even more pronounced. "Mrs. Camden is not on the cruiser?"

Ames took off his cap and ran a crooked forefinger around the leather sweatband. His finger came away wet. "No," he told the girl. "There's no one aboard but me."

The girl raised the beam of her flashlight and played it over his chest and face. Her tone was slightly incredulous as she repeated, "Mrs. Camden is not on the cruiser?"

"No."

"Then where is she?"

"I don't know," Ames said.

CHAPTER TWO

He looked up at the girl. The girl looked down at him. The silence between them lengthened. The drip of the condensation from the roof of the cabin grew more pronounced. Somewhere along the rim of the basin an outboard motor coughed anemically a few times, then settled down into a high-pitched whine.

"Oh," the maid said. "I see."

It was obvious she didn't. She clutched her housecoat tighter and switched off the now useless flashlight. In the growing light of morning she looked frightened.

"Oh," she repeated. "I see."

She hurried back down the pier toward the house, glancing over her shoulder from time to time as if she were afraid that Ames was following.

Ames returned his cap to his head. He felt like a damn fool. When he saw the Camden dame again, he'd tell her plenty. There were men on the other piers now. Several of them had seen him. It would be only a matter of minutes before everyone along the waterfront would know he had spent the night just past aboard the *Sea Bird*.

If he'd had the game he didn't remember it. But he'd sure as hell have the name. And when Mary Lou heard about it she'd pack her bags and leave.

He walked back through the smaller cabin to the master cabin in which he'd awakened. The cabin smelled strongly of perfume. The dryness in Ames's mouth extended to his throat. His throat contracted. He was frightened and didn't know why.

He picked the rolling bottle from the floor in the hope there was still a drink in it. There wasn't, but there were a half-dozen unopened rum and whiskey bottles in an open built-in liquor cabinet at the foot of the bunk.

Ames hadn't noticed the cabinet before. One thing was for sure. The blonde Mrs. Camden believed in sinning deluxe. The corners of Ames's mouth turned down. He hoped he'd had a good time. He wished he remembered it.

He cracked the seal of a rum bottle with his thumb nail and allowed a quarter of a pint of rum to trickle down his throat. The rum wet the dryness and eased the constriction. Ames screwed the cap back on the bottle and returned it to the cabinet. The thing was done. There was no use poor-mouthing about it. The thing for him to do was get to Mary Lou and try to explain that he hadn't meant it to happen.

He picked his skivvy from the chair and pulled it over his head. There was a brown splotch on the garment he didn't remember being there. Fish blood probably, Ames thought.

He rebuckled his belt and sat on the chair to slip his feet into his sneakers and a wad of something in the hip pocket of his dungarees pressed into his flesh. He fished it out and looked at it. It was a thick wad of bills folded once. The top note was a fifty dollar bill. So were the bills under it. Ames wet his second finger on his tongue and began to count. He counted to two thousand dollars and stopped. His mouth was dry again. He hadn't enough saliva to wet his finger. Still, over half the bills remained to be counted.

His hand shaking slightly, he refolded the wad of bills and returned it to his hip pocket. The blonde Mrs. Camden had a lot to explain. He debated taking another drink. He decided against it. He hadn't eaten since supper the night before. The one drink he'd taken was roaring in his head.

He stooped and tied his sneakers. The laces of his right one were gummed with some sticky substance. So was the deep maroon carpet on which he was standing. Ames wiped his fingers on his skivvy and strode back to the canopy covered cockpit. Before he attempted to make his peace with Mary Lou, he wanted to talk to Mrs. Camden—now.

The stern of the cruiser was ten feet from the pier. He gave the forward rope slack then pulled on the aft ropes until he could scramble up on the wood. One of the fishermen on the next pier recognized and hailed him.

"Hi, there, Captain Ames."

"Hi," Ames said and walked rapidly down the pier to the palm tree studded lawn of the rambling Camden beach house.

The front door opening off a flagstone patio was closed. Ames walked around to the back of the house. There was a second smaller patio, screened by purple bougainvillea and yellow allamanda. He could hear the French girl speaking. She sounded excited. Ames rang the bell then rapped impatiently on the wood of the kitchen door.

A small gray-haired man crossed the kitchen and looked at him through the screen.

"Who are you?" Ames asked.

The gray-haired man looked frightened. He said, "Go away, please."

Ames rested his weight on one hand. "I asked you a question. Who are you?"

The man wet his lips by gnawing at them. "I'm Phillips."

"Mrs. Camden's butler?"

"Yes."

Ames realized he was breathing heavily, as if he had run a long way. It was an effort for him to speak. He said, "Tell Mrs. Camden I want to see her. And don't give me any crap about her not being in the house. I know better."

The man on the far side of the screen had trouble swallowing the lump in his throat.

"Don't just stand there," Ames said. He felt as if he were shouting. He was. "You heard me. Tell Mrs. Camden that Charlie Ames wants to see her."

The man who'd said his name was Phillips shook his head. "I—can't."

"Why not?"

"She isn't here."

"You're sure?"

"We're positive," Phillips said. "Celeste and I have just finished looking in every room."

Ames's knees felt suddenly weak. He leaned against the jamb of the door. "Don't give me that."

Phillips shook his head. "I'm not giving you anything. Mrs. Camden isn't here. Now go away. Please."

The black-haired girl came and stood beside Phillips. Tears were trickling down her cheeks but she was holding an efficient looking small calibered automatic pistol as if she knew how to use it. She spat a stream of French at Ames. Ames looked at Phillips.

"What did she say?"

"She said if you don't go away she'll shoot."

Ames began to protest. "But—"

Celeste shot a hole in the screen and the steel jacketed slug shattered an ornate urn on the edge of the patio. Ames looked at the urn, turned on his heel and walked up the drive to the road.

The *Sally* was berthed less than five hundred yards away but he could make better time on the road than he could by climbing fences and scrambling under piers.

Morning was full now. The thin stream of cars on the beach road began to thicken. The land itself was merely a quarter of a mile wide spit of sand with the bay on one side and the Gulf on the other. Most of the land on the bay side had been dredged out of the bay.

The pocket of swank homes ended and the hotels and motels began. Porters polished brass and raked the seaweed off the beach. Early rising tourists, their bodies strangely white, yawned out of their fifteen dollar a night motels and plowed doggedly through the white sand to the water.

Look, Maw, Ames thought grimly, *I'm in the Gulf of Mexico.*

The Fisherman's Lunch, The Spot and Harry's Bar were all doing a good business. On the platform of Rupert's Fish House, Matt Doyle and Tom Mercer were weighing in a nice catch of red snappers.

Both men waved to Ames.

"Hi, Charlie."

Ames lifted his right hand. "Hi."

The single word rasped in his throat. He looked at the fingers of his raised hand, then down at the streaks on his skivvy. The streaks matched the brown spot he'd noticed in the cabin of the cruiser. Brown in artificial light, that was. In broad daylight, both the spot and the streaks where he'd wiped his fingers were red.

When he reached the basin in which the *Sally* was berthed, he cut in between Murphy's drugstore and the shipways next door and walked out on the sagging planking. The *Sally* was straining at her ropes. There was no light aboard. The thirty-two foot cabin cruiser looked small and cramped and shabby and incredibly old in comparison to the *Sea Bird*.

To reach the *Sally*, Ames had to pass a half-dozen other charter boats. Those captains with a charter party were readying their gear. Several of them glanced up, self-conscious, but none of his fellow captains spoke. He'd been right about the news spreading. They knew where he'd spent the night.

He jumped down into the cockpit of the *Sally*, opened the cabin door and forgot to duck low enough, as usual, and banged his forehead against the lintel. The blow knocked the cap from his head. The pain felt good. Still wearing a low-cut green evening gown, Mary Lou was sitting on the edge of her bunk drinking coffee out of a thick white crockery cup. A slim brunette in her late twenties, she looked at Ames over the rim of the mug in her hand but didn't speak.

"I'm sorry, honey," Ames said.

He was. If he couldn't square himself with Mary Lou, nothing would ever be right again. There were lots of women in the world but only one Mary Lou.

The portholes were small. It was dark in the small cabin. It smelled of flesh and sleep and freshly boiled coffee and fish. The girl on the bunk continued to regard him with hurt gray eyes.

Ames debated trying to kiss her. He decided it wouldn't be wise. Mary Lou most likely would hit him with the mug she was holding. He pumped up the Coleman pressure lantern and lighted it. The bright glare lighted the cabin but failed to dispel the feeling of grayness.

Ames looked back at Mary Lou. "I don't suppose you slept."

"Some," she admitted. "Not much." She studied his face and cried silently. "You might have wiped off the lipstick."

Ames sat on the opposite bunk. The pad felt thin, hard, familiar.

"I tried to. Look, honey." He put his hand on her knee and Mary Lou slapped it away.

"Don't touch me."

"Okay," Ames said. "You know where I've been?"

"How could I help knowing? It's all up and down the basin."

Ames swallowed the lump in his throat. "I didn't mean it to happen. I don't know it did."

Mary Lou set her mug of coffee on the edge of the galley stove without rising from the bunk. "What do you mean by that?"

Ames's growing panic continued to mount. He had a feeling of wanting to run, looking back over his shoulder as Mrs. Camden's French maid had done on the Camden pier. He gripped the edge of the bunk until his fingers ached. "Just what I said. I don't remember a goddamn thing except drinking coffee with her in the cockpit of the *Sally*."

"That's your story."

"Yeah." The word was more an expulsion of air than a sound. "I'd just come in from catching my bait. I was making a pot of coffee when she came out on the pier and asked me how much I'd charge to skipper the *Sea Bird* down to the Keys then up to Baltimore."

"Mrs. Camden?"

"Yeah. I said I'd have to think it over. Then she asked if she smelled coffee. I said she did. She asked if she could have a cup. I invited her to come aboard and I gave her a cup of coffee. And that's the last I remember."

Mary Lou's eyes continued to look sullen. "Ha."

"I mean it," Ames insisted. His breathless earnestness gave force to his words. "When I stop loving you like I do, when I start stepping out on you, honey, I—" He tried to go on and couldn't.

"You'll what?" Mary Lou asked.

"I just couldn't."

"But you did."

"No," Ames said. He modified his denial. "At least I don't remember it."

"All you remember is drinking a cup of coffee?"

"Yeah."

The corners of Mary Lou's lips turned down as she stood up. She caught the long skirt by the hem, pulled her evening gown over her head and tossed it on the bunk on which she'd been sitting. She was wearing a strapless divided lace bra. She exchanged it for a stout cotton one. She took a street dress from the small locker that served as a joint clothes closet and put it on. Then, while Ames watched her in silence, she shook out her shoulder-length page boy bob and combed it. She opened her purse and powdered her nose and renewed her lips. Her lips renewed to her satisfaction, she dropped her lipstick back in her purse, snapped it with a sharp click of finality, tucked her purse under her arm and started for the door.

Ames asked, "Where are you going?"

A new freshet of tears carved small channels in the powder Mary Lou had just applied. "I don't know," she said. She continued to cry silently. "But I'm not staying here. It's bad enough, this happening, without you lying to me."

"I'm not lying."

Ames caught her skirt and Mary Lou slapped him.

"Keep your hands off me. I suppose you got lipstick on your face and skivvy drinking coffee." There was a small jar of *helene camden* cleansing cream on the shelf that served Mary Lou as a dressing table. She snatched the jar from the shelf and smashed it on the deck. "The blonde bitch would use indelible lipstick!"

A gob of cold cream from the shattered jar splattered the leg of Ames's dungarees. He picked it off, wiped his fingers on his skivvy and returned his hands to the edge of the bunk. He was afraid and didn't know why. The lump in his throat was growing with his panic. He had to force the words past the lump. "On my face, it's lipstick. On my skivvy, it's blood."

Mary Lou turned with one hand on the knob of the companionway door. "Blood?"

"Yeah."

"How do you know it's blood?"

"I know blood when I see it. I've got it on the laces of my sneakers, too." Ames gritted his teeth against an impulse to be sick. "The carpet in the cabin of the *Sea Bird* was soaked with it."

Mary Lou leaned against the door. Some of the sullen look left her eyes. "You're hurt, Charlie?"

"No."

"Then where did the blood come from?"

"I don't know."

"Why didn't you ask Mrs. Camden?"

"I couldn't."

"Why not?"

"She wasn't in the cabin when I woke up this morning."

"She wasn't in the cabin?"

Ames realized he was panting. "No. Just her evening dress and hose and scanties. Inside out. Like she'd peeled them off in a hell of a hurry." He wanted Mary Lou to believe him. She had to believe him. "But I didn't, Mary Lou. No matter how drunk a man gets, he remembers a thing like that. And I wasn't drinking."

"There was liquor in the cabin?"

"Yeah. An empty bottle rolling between the two bunks. And a whole cabinet filled with unopened bottles."

"Mrs. Camden had gone to the house?"

"No."

"How do you know?"

"Her maid came out on the pier looking for her. There was a long distance call. From Paris. The maid seemed surprised when I told her Mrs. Camden wasn't aboard the cruiser. Then, later, when I pulled myself together and went to the house to ask how come, the butler said she wasn't there, that they'd searched every room in the house for her. And both he and the maid were frightened. And the maid shot at me through the screen door."

"She shot at you?"

"Yeah."

"Why?"

"Like I told you before, she was frightened." Ames tried to swallow the lump in his throat and it bobbed up and returned with his Adam's apple. "And that's not the worst of it." He tugged the thick wad of bills from his pocket and tossed it on the bunk on which he had been sitting. "When I put on my dungarees, I found this in my hip pocket."

Mary Lou came back and stood by the bunk. The fat wad of bills unfolded and lay flat. A thick silence filled the cabin. The smell of the sea was stronger. There was a gurgling of water. The mooring ropes creaked with the pull of the tide. An outbound fishing boat whistled for the bridge tender to raise the draw span. The rusted barrier lowered. The warning bells on the bridge began to ring.

"How much is there?" the girl asked.

"I don't know," Ames said. "I counted up to two thousand dollars and I didn't get half through." Mary Lou picked up the top bill. It was faintly speckled with dried blood. She opened her fingers and the bill fluttered back to the bunk. Her voice was small, "Where did you get all that money, Charlie?"

Ames released the bunk and used his hands to support his face. His words were muffled by his fingers.

"I don't know," he said. "I haven't the least idea. Like I told you, it was in the hip pocket of my dungarees when I came to this morning."

CHAPTER THREE

Mary Lou sat on the bunk and counted the bills. "There are five thousand dollars here."

Ames massaged his temples with his fingers. "So?"

"You don't know where this money came from?"

"No."

"You're not lying to me, Charlie?"

"I swear I'm not."

"You found it in a pocket of your dungarees when you woke up this morning?"

"Yeah. In my right hip pocket."

"And you don't remember anything after drinking a cup of coffee with Mrs. Camden?"

"Two cups of coffee."

"Was she carrying a purse?"

"I don't remember."

"Did she say anything about money?"

"Just in connection with me skippering the *Sea Bird* up to Baltimore."

Mary Lou fingered the bills again. "Hmm."

Ames returned his fingers to the edge of the bunk. "Then you believe me?"

"I don't know," Mary Lou said. She studied her husband's deeply tanned face. "You might cheat on me, Charlie, even loving me as you do, or say you do. That's the way men are. It's the way men are made, I guess." Her wet gray eyes continued to search his face. "But I know you're not a thief. And you're worried, aren't you?"

"Yes," Ames admitted. "I am."

"How much blood was there in the cabin of the *Sea Bird?*"

"Enough. The carpet was soaked with it."

"Splattered around? Like there'd been a fight?"

"No. Just on the carpet."

"Do you remember fighting with anyone?"

"No."

"Are there any marks on you?"

"No."

Mary Lou was practical. She blew her nose and said, "Well, sitting here worrying isn't going to get us anywhere. The thing for us to do is to find out where Mrs. Camden is now and have a talk with her, ask her if she knows where this money came from."

She lit the burner under the coffee pot. "Are you too sick or can you keep a cup of coffee on your stomach?"

Ames stood up, indignant. As always, he bumped his head on the low ceiling. He spoke through a blur of pain. "Goddamn it, Mary Lou. I wasn't drunk last night. I wasn't even drinking. Of course, I can keep a cup of coffee on my stomach. I'm not sick. I'm scared."

"Of what?"

"I don't know."

When the coffee was hot, Mary Lou filled a mug and handed it to him. "Drink this. It may help."

Ames gulped the hot coffee. It tasted good. It melted the bitter film in his mouth and dissolved the lump in his stomach.

Mary Lou put the wad of bills under the thin pad on the bunk. "For now. I only wished it belonged to us."

Ames drained the mug and set it in the small sink. "I don't know if I do or not."

He followed Mary Lou into the cockpit of the *Sally*. The condensation had dried. The sun was high enough to be warm. The *putt-putt* of the two cycle motor that supplied water to the bait well reminded Ames he was due to shove off with a charter party at eight o'clock. Ames looked at his watch. It was seven forty-six. His "sports" would arrive any minute. The *putt-putt* sounded like it was laboring. Ames adjusted the carburetor and wiped his greasy fingers on the leg of his dungarees.

"How about my charter party?"

Mary Lou said, "Give it to one of the boys who is not booked. I don't think the *Falcon's* going out."

As she scrambled up on the pier, Ames caught a flash of slim well formed legs and satin soft thighs. His pulse beat a little faster. Most of his headache went away. Mary Lou had a prettier body than Mrs. Camden could possibly have. Mrs. Camden was forty, at least. She admitted to being thirty-five. She was currently working on her fourth husband. He'd had nothing to do with the blonde woman. Ames was positive of that. He hoped.

He followed Mary Lou. Four boats down the basin Shep Roberts was sitting in the cockpit of the *Falcon*. His feet were propped on his empty bait well as he sat squinting under the brim of his dirty white captain's cap at the hopeful fishermen on the high catwalk running the length of the pier that spanned the pass.

Ames asked, "How'd you like a charter, Shep?"

Shep spoke without turning his head. "Ain't got no bait."

"You can use mine."

"How many in the party?"

"Four."

"How much is the charter?"

"Fifty dollars."

"What they want t' fish for?"

Ames said, "It's their first trip out. I figured on taking them out to the grouper banks and maybe tying into a tarpon or two on the way back. There are still a few rolling in Bunce's Pass."

Shep turned his head and spat tobacco juice over the varnished transom of the *Falcon*. "What you want t' git shet of 'em for?"

Mary Lou compressed her lips. "We've something else we have to do."

Shep lowered his feet to the deck and pushed his cap back on his head. "Okay. I'll take 'em. Thanks."

Ames started on up the stringer and turned back.

"Look, Shep."

"Yeah?"

"About last night. Did you see me come in with my bait?"

"I heard you."

"Did you see the Camden woman walk past on her way to the *Sally*? Did you see me walk back with her?"

"That big blonde that owns the *Sea Bird*?"

"That's the one."

The charter captain shook his head. "No. I can't say I did. I heard someone say something about her up at Harry's this morning, but I turned in early last night."

Mary Lou looked at the man in the boat. "If you did see Charlie with her, you wouldn't tell on him, would you, Shep?"

"No," Shep admitted.

Ames guided Mary Lou up the stringer. "I wasn't with her."

"Then how did you get in the cabin of the *Sea Bird*?"

Ames's head began to ache again. "I don't know."

He looked up the basin to where the *Sea Bird* was berthed. There were two men on the Camden pier and one in the cockpit of the boat.

Mary Lou shielded her eyes with her hand. "I don't know the two men on the pier, but the man in the cockpit looks like Sheriff White."

Ames's sensation of motion returned. He felt like he was running. A drop of sweat escaped the pit of his arm and zig-zagged down his side. It was an effort for him to breathe normally.

"Where are we going?" he asked.

"You'll see," Mary Lou said.

Harry's Bar was crowded with its usual early morning rush of charter boat captains and commercial fishermen. Fat Ben Sheldon, the ship chandler, was bellied to the bar. He glanced up as Ames and Mary Lou entered then closely studied his shot glass. A few of the men nodded but none of them spoke. The loud babble of conversation lowered then died away completely.

Mary Lou led the way to the back booth that served as an office to half of the captains operating out of the basin, because there was a phone in the booth.

Ames sank, panting, on the worn leather. "I thought we were going to try to locate Mrs. Camden."

Mary Lou thumbed through the dog-eared phone book on the table. "We are." She found the number she wanted and dialed it.

"The Helene Camden residence," a man's voice answered the phone.

Ames recognized the voice. It was the gray-haired man he'd seen in the kitchen, the one who had said his name was Phillips and that he was Mrs. Camden's butler.

Mary Lou said, "May I speak to Mrs. Camden, please? It's very important."

"I'm so sorry," Phillips said. "But that will be impossible. We've had some trouble here."

"What kind of trouble?"

"Mrs. Camden has disappeared."

"Disappeared?"

"Yes. From her cruiser, the *Sea Bird*. The police are here now."

Mary Lou looked across the table at Ames. "I—see." Her voice was suddenly small. "Well, could you tell me this. Was Mrs. Camden in the habit of carrying large sums of money?"

"Habitually," Phillips said. He asked tardily, "To whom am I speaking, please?"

Mary Lou cradled the receiver, still looking at Ames.

His flesh felt as if it were crawling. The lump returned to his throat. He had to force his denial past it. "I didn't. I couldn't, Mary Lou. Not for five thousand dollars. Not for any amount of money."

Her young face was a mask of fear. She cried silently. "So you say."

Ames sat cracking his knuckles. Mary Lou's fear was an ugly thing between them. This wasn't happening to him. It couldn't be. He'd had nothing to do with the blonde. He certainly hadn't harmed her. Still, there were the five thousand dollars and the blood. And Mrs. Camden had disappeared.

Harry appeared at the mouth of the booth. "You and Mary Lou want anything, Charlie?"

Ames nodded. "Yeah. Bring us a rum and coke."

Mary Lou shook her head. "None for me."

"One, then," Ames said. He found a single dollar bill in the side pocket of his dungarees and laid it on the table. "A double."

Neither of them spoke again until Harry returned with the drink, picked up the dollar and left.

Angry now, Ames said: "Goddamn! You've got to believe me, honey. I—"

"Yes," Mary Lou said. "I know." The fear left her face. All she looked was tired. "All you did was drink two cups of coffee with her. In the cockpit of the *Sally*."

Put that way, it sounded silly. Ames wanted to pound on the table, pound on Mary Lou, *make* her believe him. He closed his eyes and forced himself to think. He'd invited Mrs. Camden aboard. He'd poured her a cup of the coffee he'd just made. They'd had a second cup. And he'd awakened in the cabin of the *Sea Bird*. With the big blonde's evening gown on the opposite bunk, an empty whiskey bottle on the floor and five thousand dollars in the hip pocket of his dungarees.

Ames's anger drained slowly, like water hand pumped out of a bilge. He didn't blame Mary Lou for not believing him.

Still, to the best of his knowledge, what he'd told her was true.

The ship's bell over the door struck metallically as someone opened the door of the bar. Sheriff White's voice was loud in the sudden silence.

"We'll try here, first, Miss," he said. "Take your time an' look 'em over careful."

"What's the idea, Sheriff?" Harry asked.

White told him. "We're lookin' for a man Mrs. Camden's maid, here, saw aboard the *Sea Bird*. She says she's seen him before, that he's one of the charter boat captains, but she doesn't know his name."

"Oh," Harry said. "I see."

Ames pressed his back to the worn leather of the booth, listening to the click of the maid's high heels as she moved along the bar. He wished he could make himself small. He wished he'd gone out on his charter trip. His neck felt stiff.

"Here he is," the maid said. "Sitting een thee back booth with a girl."

A deeply tanned, gaunt-faced man in his early forties, White loomed tall behind her. "Oh. You, eh, Charlie?" he said.

Ames reached for his untouched drink and knocked it over. Mary Lou stood up to save her dress. Ames automatically wiped his wet fingers on his skivvy.

"Kind of a habit, eh, Charlie?" White asked, "I mean, wiping your fingers on your skivvy. Looks sort of interesting from here."

Ames tried to speak. He couldn't. The lump in his throat was too big.

"You're positive, now?" White asked. "This is the man you saw aboard the *Sea Bird* this morning?"

"I am positive," Celeste said.

White laid a big hand on Ames's shoulder. "Okay, fellow. Let's go back to the Camden house. I want to talk to you."

"What about?" Mary Lou asked.

"About Mrs. Camden," White told her.

CHAPTER FOUR

With growing dark and the pull of the tide, the body moved again. The crabs and the small fish scurried away. More buoyant now, it started back up the bay then, caught by the pull of the current on the fringe of Sister Key, it slipped into the swash channel, spun lazily for a moment then floated slowly down Blind Pass, the other exit to the Gulf.

A flight of gulls spotted it and swooped low, only to fly away screaming. A long-legged heron fishing in the shallows of the key regarded it with distaste. A large school of playful crevalle jacks using the swash channel to cross from one arm of the bay to the other buffeted it as they passed and set the body to bobbling. The motion attracted a swimming turtle. He climbed on the floating flesh, rode it for a short distance then lost interest and plopped back into the water.

The arm that had been extended remained so, as rigor mortis became complete. There was a brief flash of fire and color as the last rays of the setting sun sought for and found the ten carat diamond in the ring now imbedded in the swollen finger.

As the body reached the end of Sister Key and began the long journey to the Gulf via this new pass it was exploring, Buddy Cronkite and Tommy Williams, netting mullet out of season, saw something white in the water.

Buddy, eleven years old, said, "Hit's a sick baby porpoise. They always turn white and spotted jist before they die."

Tommy, age ten, was scornful. "Hain't neither," he insisted. "Hit's a daid hammer haid shark."

To prove his superior knowledge, he waded out to the edge of the channel, whirled his weighted circular net and casting it expertly over the body, he drew it back into the shallows.

One of the weights struck the extended hand and the dead woman turned in the water and lay on her back under the stout nylon netting.

Buddy's teeth began to chatter. "A daid hammer haid shark," he whimpered. "Hit's a nekid woman, without no clothes on, that's what."

The net rope went slack in Tommy's hand. The freckles on the bridge of his nose stood out in bold relief against the sudden white of his face. He tried to tug his net free and couldn't. His voice was shrill.

"Well, don't jist stand there. He'p me git my net offen this thing."

Buddy, still frightened, proved he was a year older and wiser. "We won't do no sich thing. We got t' pull hit into the key an' then go tell the sheriff. You got t' tell when you find a daid one. Hit's the law."

Buddy tugged tentatively at the net rope and changed his mind as the bloated body surged toward him. He dropped the rope and splashed through the shallows toward their flat bottomed skiff. "You pull hit in. You netted hit. I'll go tell the sheriff." Tommy secured the rope in his hand to a fish stake and splashed after him.

"An' leave me here alone with hit agittin' dark? No, sir. We'll both go tell."

The room was small and poorly furnished with a desk, a steel filing cabinet, a few straight-backed chairs. Ames had never been so unutterably weary. He sat, acutely conscious of his best white shirt and blue pants, dangling his white cap between his knees, looking at Mary Lou.

Not even Mary Lou believed him. She thought he'd stayed with Mrs. Camden then lost his head and harmed her and stolen five thousand dollars.

White sat back of the desk with the money in front of him. "How you feel, Charlie?" he asked.

Ames told the truth. "Tired."

"It's been a day," White admitted. "You ready to talk yet, Charlie?"

Ames returned the cap to his head. "I've been talking all day."

"And you're still sticking to your story? The last you remember is drinking a cup of coffee with Mrs. Camden in the cockpit of the *Sally?*"

"That's right."

State's Attorney Keely had been in Orlando. This was the first session he'd sat in on. "How much you got on him, Bill?" he asked White.

White said, "Everything but the body." He fingered through the papers on his clipboard. "The lab reports that the blood on his skivvy and that on the carpet in the main cabin of the *Sea Bird* are both B Rh Positive."

"That's Mrs. Camden's classification?"

"We don't know yet," White said. "We're hoping it's one of the things that Mr. Camden can tell us."

"You've contacted him then?"

"This morning. Long distance. He's on his way down." Sheriff White looked at his watch. "He should get in any time." White continued: "We found this money under the pad of one of the bunks of the *Sally*. We found a gun in the head of the *Sea Bird* with two expended shells. Ames's right hand shows powder burns. Mrs. Camden's maid, a French girl by the name of Celeste, has positively identified Ames as the man she saw aboard the *Sea Bird*."

"I admit I was there," Ames said.

Neither man paid any attention to him. "Is the maid still in the station?" Keely asked.

"I think she is," White said. "I didn't know if you'd get back t'night or not, so I brought her in to have her make a deposition." He looked at one of the officers standing against the wall. "See if Mrs. Camden's maid is still here, will you, Harry?"

"Sure thing, Sheriff," the plainclothesman said.

White looked at Ames. "Look, Charlie. I'm just as tired as you are. You know without me telling you that you're in a bad jam. The way I got it over the phone, Camden is the kind of guy who'll spend a lot of money, if necessary, to nail this thing on you.

"You're a local boy. I knew your old man. I liked him. I like you. I like Mary Lou. I'd hate to see you go to the chair. I know what these rich dames are like. I been sheriff twenty years. I could tell you things that would pop your eyes. Up north they may belong t'the D.A.R. and teach Sunday school every Sunday. But when they git down heah they's a lot of 'em throw away their morals with their girdles. They think jist because they got dough they can buy any husky young guy an' for some reason they go strong for charter boat captains.

"You want me t'tell you what I think happened?" White continued without waiting for Ames to speak. "Mrs. Camden's had three husbands. She's married to a fourth. That's the tipoff right there. She was one of them nymphs. And your story about drinking coffee is a lot o' crap. You're a good-lookin' guy, Charlie. You're young. You've been around. Mrs. Camden knew Mary Lou works at the Beach Club until almost four in the morning. She showed up at the *Sally* with a bottle and a yen for you. You got stinkin' drunk together. Then, afraid Mary Lou might come home earlier than you expected, you moved the party to the *Sea Bird*. You had a hell of a time. The condition of the cabin proves it. Then, like drunks will, you got to quarreling. You knew she had a lot of money. You want a new boat. You tried to get her to buy you one. But she was a good business woman and you weren't *that* good.

"She laughed at you an' hit made you mad. You had a tussle. During it, she took her gun out of that little cabinet by the bunk. You tried to take hit away from her an' hit went off twice an' kilt her. You didn't mean for hit t' happen but she was dead. You got scared. You did the first thing that come to your mind. You threw her body overboard, knowin' the tide was runnin' out an' would carry hit out into the Gulf."

Ames said, tight-lipped, "Then I let her maid see me and I picked up five thousand dollars that was just lying around the cabin convenient and went right home and told Mary Lou about it. For God's sake, give me credit for some sense."

Mary Lou leaned forward in her chair. "That much is true. Charlie came directly home to the *Sally*. He gave the money to me. And he wasn't drunk. He was sick."

"How do you know?" State's Attorney Keely asked.

"He—told me he was sick."

White laid the clipboard on top of the money. "Sure. He told you." The elderly sheriff looked back at Ames. "Why don't you use your head, boy, and make this a little easier on all of us, yourself included? I doubt if the killing was premeditated. There was a drunken brawl. During it, Mrs. Camden was killed. Admit that much and I think maybe the State's Attorney will accept a plea of second degree murder." He looked at Keely. "How about that, Sam?"

Thinking of the crowded court calendar, Keely nodded. "I might at that."

Ames shook his head. "I can't."

"Why not?"

"I don't think I did. I mean kill her. I don't even know she's dead."

"No one could lose that much blood as we found on that rug and live."

"Even so. I don't think I had anything to do with her."

"What makes you so positive?"

"You know what Mrs. Camden looks like. I'm married to Mary Lou."

"He has a point there," State's Attorney Keely admitted.

The plainclothesman who had gone in search of Celeste opened the door of the office. "The maid's gone back to the beach, Sheriff. But there's a guy here who says his name is Camden. He says he just flew down from Baltimore. And he has a lawyer named Ferris with him."

White stood up and came around his desk. "Last chance, Charlie."

Ames took off his white captain's cap and ran a finger around the leather sweatband. His finger came away wet. "The last I remember, we were sitting in the cockpit of the *Sally* drinking coffee."

"Show them in," White said.

Camden was younger than his wife. His hair was black. He wore it long. He was six feet two and weighed two hundred pounds. His expensive gray flannel suit was moulded to his body. He looked more like a movie actor than an executive of a cosmetic firm.

White offered his hand. "Mr. Camden?"

Camden gripped the extended hand. "And you, sir?"

"I'm Sheriff White."

"You've located Helene's body?"

"Not as yet," White admitted.

Ames studied Camden's face. He didn't like the man. His voice was too hearty. He showed too many teeth when he smiled. If the black-haired man was grief-stricken, he was concealing it well. Camden lit a cigarette and the office was perfumed with the fragrance of Turkish tobacco. "I was afraid something like this might happen if I permitted Helene to come to Florida alone." He returned Ames's stare. "This is the fishing guide who killed her?"

White said, "Let's say we have considerable evidence tying him in with Mrs. Camden's disappearance."

The man with Camden introduced himself. "Ferris is the name. Tom Ferris. I've been Helene's attorney for years. Sorry if we delayed anything. We took the first possible plane out of Baltimore after receiving your phone call."

White said he was glad to know Ferris and introduced both men to State's Attorney Keely.

Ames looked across the small office at Mary Lou. She was sitting straight in her chair again, pleating her handkerchief. Mary Lou didn't believe him. She thought he'd two-timed her with Mrs. Camden. It showed in the tilt of her chin, the sullen set of her mouth.

Anger began to replace Ames's fear. To the best of his knowledge, the story he'd told was true. He hadn't been drunk. He hadn't made love to Helene Camden. He hadn't harmed her. He didn't know how he had gotten into the cabin of the *Sea Bird*.

White concluded his brief conference with Ferris and Keely and Camden. "So that's the way it stands. We know damn well he done hit. But we cain't even book him until we find the body."

Camden crossed to the chair in which Ames was sitting and stood with his bunched fists on his hips. "All right. Start talking, fellow. What did you do with Helene's body?"

"I didn't do anything with it," Ames said.

Camden's right hand shot out and slapped Ames out of the chair. "Don't give me that. You're not fooling with a small-town sheriff now. You're bucking *helene camden, incorporated.* If necessary, we'll spend a million dollars to see you get what's coming to you."

Ames knelt on all fours on the oiled wood floor. Blood trickled from his slapped lips. He'd never felt so ashamed, so small, so put upon. His anger continued to grow. They had no right to treat him like this. He hadn't hidden a thing. He'd tried to cooperate with White. But no one, especially an over-dressed bag of wind and that was all Camden was, was going to knock him around.

Ames got to his feet slowly. "Don't do that again," he warned Camden. "I don't even know if your wife is dead."

Camden showed his too-white teeth in a smirk. "That's your story. Talk, damn you. Talk."

He struck out again, with his fist this time. Ames caught the blow on the palm of his left hand and hit Camden so hard his head bounced when it struck the filing case. The big man stood glassy-eyed a moment. Then he slid down the steel case to the floor.

"You shouldn't have done that, Charlie," Sheriff White said.

Ames stood with his legs spread, panting. "You've questioned me all day. Now book me or let me go. Like I just told Camden, I don't even know Mrs. Camden is dead."

The plainclothesman opened the door again. "There are two kids here to see you, Sheriff. Young Cronkite and Tommy Williams. They were netting mullet out at Sister Key and—"

White waved him out of the office. "Tell them to come back. I'm busy."

The policeman stood his ground. "I think you'd better see them, Sheriff."

"Why?"

"Because according to their story, they just threw a mullet net over Mrs. Camden's nude body."

CHAPTER FIVE

The harsh white trouble light Sheriff White's men had erected drowned out the feeble glow of the yellow ceiling light in the gloomy packing shed of Rupert's Fish House. From where Ames sat he could hear the juke in Harry's Bar. The box was playing *You Like?*

His set smile was tight. He didn't like. He didn't like what was happening to him. He didn't like it at all, but there was nothing he could do about it.

Through the open doors of the packing shed he could see a steady procession of out-of-state cars carrying carefree tourists to the dog track, the stock car races and the various beach hot spots.

Two hundred yards up the beach, there were music and laughter. There was a moon. There were stars. Boys and girls were dancing. Boys were telling their girls they loved them. Girls were enacting pleased surprise, when they had planned it that way all the time. Life was warm and normal and human.

Here there was nothing but cold suspicion, the white glare of the trouble light, the ring of unfriendly faces, the canvas covered thing in the corner that once had been Helene Camden.

Ames fished a package of cigarettes from his side coat pocket and lighted one. His manacled wrists made the simple act difficult, but he managed. Ames supposed, in time, a man could get used to anything. Or could he? It was hard for him to think. His mind felt battered by the day of questioning. He wished he could change his story, if only to get some sleep, but he couldn't. The last he remembered was drinking a cup of coffee with Mrs. Camden in the cockpit of the *Sally*.

Ames studied the faces of the coroner's jury that Justice of the Peace Gilmore had impaneled. There were: Murphy, who owned the drug store; Jack Hayden and Bill Mayers, fellow charter boat captains; Mack Gore, who fished for old man Rupert; Mr. Thompson, who owned the Siesta Motel. They returned his look coldly. They, too, were male. They, too, had financial troubles. They thought he'd stayed with Mrs. Camden and then killed her—for five thousand dollars.

Ames looked for and found Mary Lou. It was nine o'clock, almost time for her to go to work. She'd changed from her street dress into an evening gown. She looked harder, older, than he'd ever seen her look. She stood just inside the door. A gray wisp of smoke curled up from the cigarette between her red lips, the lips he'd kissed a thousand times. Not even Mary Lou believed him.

That hurt most of all.

There was a thud of heels on the loading platform. Hal Camden and Attorney Ferris entered the packing shed. Both men had changed into light weight suits and two-toned sport shoes. Their faces looked strangely white, compared to the sun-bronzed faces of the local men.

Gilmore crossed the packing shed to meet them saying, "We'll begin with the identification, Mr. Camden."

Sheriff White dropped his hand on Ames's shoulder. "Last chance,

Charlie."

"You said that before," Ames reminded him.

White persisted. "She made a play for you. You lost your head. You got stinking with her. Sometime during the party you quarreled. It wasn't premeditated. You didn't mean to kill her. It just happened." The fingers on Ames's shoulder tightened. "Hell. We're all with you, boy. We know these things happen. You tell it like it was and there aren't twelve men in Palmetto County who'll send you away for more than ten or fifteen years."

Ames looked back at Mary Lou. Ten or fifteen years. Ten or fifteen years away from Mary Lou. He was thirty now. He'd be forty-five when he got out of prison. He'd much rather go to the chair. He said: "The last I remember—"

Sheriff White's voice sounded weary. "Yes. I know. You were drinking a cup of coffee in the cockpit of the *Sally*."

Ames forced a smile. "You're just burned because Camden called you a small-town sheriff."

"That could be," White admitted.

In his capacity as coroner, Justice of the Peace Gilmore lifted the tarpaulin from the figure on the floor of the packing shed. The nude woman was no longer pretty. She'd been in the water too long. Her flabby flesh was bloated. Most of her face was gone. Ames repressed a shudder.

Gilmore folded the tarpaulin. "She doesn't look so good, does she, Charlie?"

"No," Ames answered. "She doesn't."

He looked at Mary Lou, then back at the nude body and felt better. He didn't care how much evidence there was against him. He was damned if he'd been untrue to Mary Lou. The dead woman's thighs were thick and ugly with broken veins. Her big breasts sagged. Her bleached hair was coarse and beginning to show black at the roots. Even allowing for the crabs and water bloat, she wasn't pretty anywhere. A man married to Mary Lou who'd have anything to do with a bag like Helene Camden ought to have his head examined. It would be like getting up from a T-bone steak dinner to gnaw on a stale ham sandwich.

Gilmore looked at Camden. "Well?"

"It's Helene," Camden said.

"You're positive."

"I'm positive. I recognize the hair and ring and certain other physical attributes." Camden knelt down beside the body and tried unsuccessfully to pull the ring over the swollen flesh. "You'll probably have to cut it off. But when you do, be careful with it. That ring's worth eighteen thousand dollars."

He seemed more concerned with the ring than with the fact that his wife was dead.

Attorney Ferris took a paper from his brief case. "I happen to have the insurance policy with me." He offered the paper to Gilmore. "Perhaps you'd care to check the description against the ring, Mr. Coroner."

Gilmore shook his head. "That won't be necessary, Mr. Ferris."

"Attorney Ferris or Counsellor," Ferris corrected him.

Ames felt almost sorry for Gilmore and Sheriff White. Quite a few of the wealthy Northerners who had winter homes on the beach were stinkers, but Camden and Ferris were more obnoxious than most. Both men were smugly superior to the situation in which they found themselves involved. They were treating the sheriff and the coroner and himself, for that matter, like slightly moronic children.

The backs of Gilmore's ears were red as he studied the list of names he'd compiled. "When the counsellor is before the court acting in a legal capacity, he will be accorded any courtesy forms of address to which he may be entitled." Gilmore looked up from the list of names. "Will Miss Celeste Montigny please come forward?"

The French maid walked into the glare of the trouble light.

"You're Mrs. Camden's maid?" Gilmore asked. The maid bobbed her head. "Oui, monsieur."

Gilmore pointed at Ames. "You recognize this man?"

"Oui, monsieur."

"You saw him board the *Sea Bird* with your mistress last night?"

"No, monsieur. I deed not."

"When did you see him?"

"This morning, monsieur. Shortly after daylight. When I attempted to tell Mrs. Camden her Paris office was on thee phone."

"Where did you see him?"

"Een the cockpit of the *Sea Bird*."

"How was he dressed?"

Celeste looked at Ames for the first time. "Hees feet were bare. He had only his pants and cap on."

"What did you think?"

Celeste was candid. "I theenk he ees a very nice looking young man.

So, how you say, virile."

A burst of laughter followed her statement. Even Camden and Ferris smiled.

Gilmore glowered at the spectators crowded into the packing shed of the fish house.

Celeste continued. "But I am also ver' uneasy for Mrs. Camden."

"Why?"

"Because the young man told me she was not aboard thee boat and I knew it was her intention to pass the night there."

"How did you know that?"

"Mrs. Camden told me so. She told me she had a date with a ver' handsome young charter boat captain and they were, under no circumstances, to be disturbed."

"The bitch," Camden said. "The blonde bitch."

"What did you do then?" Gilmore asked.

Celeste said, "I returned to thee house and told Phillips, he ees thee butler, that Mrs. Camden was not aboard thee cruiser. He, too, was ver' alarmed. Together we searched the house. We had just finished when," Celeste pointed at Ames, "thee captain there came to thee back door and demanded to see Mrs. Camden. And I became even more alarmed."

"Why?"

"He had blood all over his small shirt. I told heem to go away. He would not. So I took a gun that ees kept een thee kitchen and fired at heem through the screen door."

"And then?"

"I dialed the operator and asked her to connect me weeth thee sheriff."

"I see," Gilmore said. "Thank you, Miss Montigny." He looked at Sheriff White. "What time did you get this call, Sheriff?"

"About seven fifteen," White said.

"You proceeded directly to the Camden residence?"

"That's right. When I got there the girl who has just testified told me the situation as she outlined it to the coroner's jury, so I walked out on the pier and had a look at the cruiser."

"Would you please describe to the jury what you found?"

"Well, the main cabin was a mess. You could tell right off that there'd been a party in it. There was a woman's evenin' dress an' hose on one of the bunks, like she'd peeled it off in a hurry. Only one of the bunks had been slept in. There was an empty whiskey bottle rollin' between the two bunks. But what concerned me most was that the carpet was sodden with blood and when I examined the head I found a pearl-handled .32 caliber revolver with two expended shells."

"Recently expended?"

"Within a matter of hours."

"What did you do then, Sheriff?"

"I asked the maid to accompany me to see if we could locate and identify the young captain she said she'd seen aboard the cruiser. The first place we went to was Harry's Bar and she picked Charlie Ames out of the back booth."

"He was alone?"

"No. He was with his wife."

"Did he deny he'd been aboard the *Sea Bird?*"

White was fair. "No. Charlie admitted that right off. But he did deny any knowledge of how he'd gotten aboard." The phrase stuck in Sheriff White's craw. "He claimed and still does, for that matter, that the last he remembered he was drinking coffee with Mrs. Camden in the cockpit of the *Sally.*"

"And how far is the *Sally* berthed from the *Sea Bird?*"

"I'd say about five hundred yards, maybe a little more."

Ames buried his face in his manacled hands. His story sounded foolish. He felt like a fool. This was it. This was the big one and he didn't remember a thing about it. He continued to hold his face in his hands as Sheriff White told about finding the money and two other Palmetto City officers testified to three important facts. His fingerprints matched the fingerprints that had been taken from the pearl handle of the gun. A paraffin test revealed that he'd fired a revolver recently. The blood on his skivvy and shoes matched the blood on the carpet in the main cabin of the *Sea Bird.*

I must have killed her, Ames thought. God knew he'd wanted a new boat, for Mary Lou. It had been the first thing in his mind when he'd awakened. Still, how could he have been so stupid about it? And it did seem, unless a man's mind snapped completely, he'd have some vague recollection of first quarreling with, then killing the woman.

Ames looked up as the officer finished and old Horace Lee was called on to testify as to the tides. In the opinion of the grizzled fisherman a body dropped over the side of the Sea Bird at approximately four o'clock in the morning would ride the current out-going tide about as far as the bridge before the change in tides swept it back into the upper bay and into the Blind Pass channel, where Buddy Cronkite and Tony Williams had found it.

That should do it, Ames thought. He uncovered his face and straightened in the chair as Coroner Gilmore called his last witness.

"Now, if you'll take the stand, Mr. Camden."

Camden took his cigar from his lips. "Yes, Mr. Coroner?"

Gilmore said, "You've heard the testimony. And while I have no wish to intrude on your grief or cause you any further embarrassment, the entire circumstantial case developed against Captain Ames rests solely on one fact."

"And that, sir?"

"In your opinion, was Mrs. Camden the sort of woman who would hold an illicit assignation with a man practically a stranger to her?"

Camden looked at the canvas-covered figure on the rough board floor of the fish house. "I'm sorry, but the answer to that question is yes. Helene was a very self-willed woman and given to sudden impulses. She did what she wanted to do, regardless of morals or convention. And as I told Sheriff White a few minutes after I got off the plane this evening, I was afraid something like this might happen if I permitted Helene to come to Florida alone."

"Thank you, Mr. Camden."

"Not at all," the well groomed executive said. He looked along his cigar at Ames. "I realize that this is only a coroner's jury, but I hope they recommend he be held and when he does come to trial that they give the bastard the chair!"

There was a buzz of conversation as Coroner Gilmore charged the jury. It grew as the jury men conferred among themselves. Ames tried to get at his cigarettes again and couldn't. His manacled hands were shaking too badly. He gave up the attempt and sat looking at Mary Lou until Mr. Murphy signaled to Coroner Gilmore that the jury had reached a conclusion. The buzz of conversation died. In the silence that followed the druggist said soberly:

"We find the deceased, Helene Camden, came to her death from two pistol shots fired by Charlie Ames and recommend that he be indicted for and tried for her murder."

Sheriff White pressed his shoulder. "Let's go, boy."

Ames didn't even hear him. He was watching Mary Lou's slim back disappear into the night. Mary Lou didn't believe him. She didn't intend to stand by. She agreed with the coroner's jury.

Mary Lou thought he'd two-timed her.

CHAPTER SIX

The night wind off the Gulf cool on her flushed face, Mary Lou walked down the wooden pier of Rupert's Fish House then down the shoulder of the heavily traveled beach road toward Harry's Bar and Murphy's Pharmacy and the basin where the *Sally* was berthed.

Charlie was in a jam, a bad one. Her personal feelings no longer mattered. So Mrs. Camden had dazzled Charlie with her money and he had lost his head and killed her. So? She couldn't let him down now. She would have to do what she could for him. Charlie would need a lawyer, a good one.

There was a light in the office of Ben Sheldon's Ways. Mary Lou stood a moment watching the stream of traffic, sucking her cigarette to a miniature torch. She also had to call the club and tell them she wasn't coming to work. She couldn't sing tonight. She couldn't pretend that nothing had happened to her emotionally, not if her life depended on it.

No matter what he'd done to her, she loved Charlie. Mary Lou cried a little. Goddamn Helene Camden! Helene's husband had named her correctly. Mary Lou hoped it was hot where she was, a lot hotter than it was in Florida.

There was movement on the platform of Rupert's Fish House. A car door opened then slammed. A pair of headlights flicked on. A police siren wailed petulantly as the driver of the car tried to ease the big cruiser into the steady stream of traffic. A moment later, its red light revolving, scattering cars coming the other way like so many frightened chickens, the police car wailed past the clump of darkness in which she was standing. Mary Lou caught a glimpse of Sheriff White but couldn't see Charlie. Charlie was probably in the back seat. White was taking him in to the Palmetto City jail.

Mary Lou realized her cigarette was burning her fingers. She dropped it in the sand, extinguished the spark with the toe of her shoe and walked in to talk to Ben Sheldon.

A big man in his early sixties, wearing a crumpled white Palm Beach suit, Ben Sheldon looked up from his desk. "I'm sorry, Mary Lou," he said simply.

Mary Lou sat in the chair beside his desk. "Yes. So am I. But being sorry about it isn't going to pry Charlie out of this jam. I've got to get him a lawyer. How much will you give us for the *Sally*, Ben? Cash money. Now. Tonight."

The fat man picked a dead cigar from the ashtray on his desk and chewed on it thoughtfully. "Well," he began, "the *Sally's* in pretty bad condition. The bottom's rotten, for one thing. For another, the engine needs a complete overhaul." He shook his head dubiously. "Now look. I like you, Mary Lou. I like Charlie."

"Get to the point," Mary Lou said. "How much will you give for the *Sally?* Cash money. Now. Tonight."

Sheldon continued to shake his head. "I couldn't go for over fifteen hundred. And I doubt if I can resell her for that."

Mary Lou opened her mouth to remind him he'd offered Charlie two thousand dollars for the *Sally* less than a week before and changed her mind. If Ben didn't buy the *Sally*, no one would. He was right about the bottom being rotten and the power plant needing a major overhaul. It was, she supposed, human nature to kick a man when he was down and Charlie was down.

"I'll take it," Mary Lou said. "Make out a bill of sale and give me the money. I want to go into town and see what I can do about a lawyer the first thing in the morning."

She lit another cigarette and sat with her eyes closed, smoking, while the fat man used two fingers to peck out a bill of sale on an ancient Oliver typewriter. When he'd finished he gave it to Mary Lou to sign and got the money out of the safe.

"Take your time 'bout clearin' out now, Mary Lou. Use the *Sally* t'night an' t'morrow, if you want to, jist as if the *Sally* was still your own boat."

Mary Lou signed the bill of sale and put the money in her purse. "Thank you. You're generous, Ben."

The fat man shrugged. "Business is business."

Mary Lou snuffed her cigarette and walked next door to Harry's Bar to call the Beach Club. Shep Roberts was drinking beer out of a bottle. He caught her arm as she passed him on the way to the back booth.

"I hear they elected to hold Charlie," Shep said.

Mary Lou nodded. "Yes. They just took him into Palmetto City."

An inarticulate man, Shep had trouble with words. He let his actions speak for him. Fishing in the pocket of his stained white dungarees, he laid a wad of crumpled bills on the bar. "He never done hit, Mary Lou. An' here's the fifty for that charter trip I helped him out on t'day. I want you should use it to help hire a lawyer."

Mary Lou studied Shep's seamed face with wet eyes. "Thanks. Thanks a lot, Shep. I won't need the money. I just sold the *Sally* to Ben. But what makes you think Charlie didn't do it?"

"He loves you," Shep said simply. The inarticulate man found words. "Look. Charlie might cut a man to death. He might steal five thousand dollars. He might even shoot a woman. But he wouldn't so low rate you t' be found daid in baid with a bag like that Camden woman. I happen to know how Charlie feels about you."

Mary Lou squeezed his arm. "Thanks, Shep." She walked on swiftly to the back booth and cried in its privacy a moment before she called the Beach Club. She wished she had Shep's faith in Charlie. Unfortunately, all the evidence was against him.

Back on the *Sally* again, she took off her evening gown and lay down on the hard bunk and stared up at the dark, wondering if she were at fault. Charlie hadn't wanted her to work at the Beach Club. They'd quarreled about it time after time. Perhaps it had hurt his pride and that was why he'd done what he had done.

Men were funny creatures. But then, so were women, for that matter.

It was hot and close in the small cabin. She was too restless to sleep. Mary Lou lit the Coleman lantern and began to pack a bag for Charlie. He'd need several changes of underwear and some clean shirts and his shaving things.

She hadn't realized before how few things Charlie really had. What little money he spent, he spent on her. And he'd been such a nifty dresser when he'd been playing with the bands. Of course, it had been his pride. She was still, more or less, in the business, but it had been a hell of a drop for Charlie, from a hot trumpet player in a name band to an unsuccessful charter boat captain.

Mary Lou laid the elephant bank on top of Charlie's clothes. She'd deliver it with the fifteen hundred to him in the morning. She'd ask him to suggest a lawyer. And if what they had saved wasn't enough, she would get more somehow.

Once started packing, she decided to clear out the *Sally*. Ben could have the old tub in the morning. What she couldn't carry away, either Harry or Mr. Murphy would let her store in their back rooms.

The cooking utensils presented a problem. Mary Lou had decided to pack them in a paper carton. There were always cartons in back of the drugstore. She got one and returned to the *Sally*.

There wasn't much to pack. A few pots, a few pans, a coffee pot, four plates, six cups and saucers.

Mary Lou stopped in her packing and looked thoughtfully into the small cabinet. Then she unpacked the utensils and dishes she'd packed.

There were six saucers but only five cups. One cup was missing. She lifted the pressure lantern from its peg and walked out into the cockpit. Charlie had a habit of leaving coffee cups strewn around. Half of the time he left his cup on top of the live bait well, even on the low roof of the cabin. Bu the sixth cup wasn't in the cockpit. Mary Lot closed her eyes. She'd said:

That's your story.

Yeah, Charlie had told her. *I'd just come in from catching my bait. I was making a pot of coffee whet she came out on the pier and asked how much I'd charge to skipper the* Sea Bird *down to the Keys then up to Baltimore.*

Mrs. Camden?

Yeah. I said I'd have to think it over. Then she asked if she smelled coffee. I said she did. She asked if she could have a cup. I invited her to come aboard and I gave her a cup of coffee. And that's the last I remember.

Mary Lou opened her eyes. It was fantastic. Or was it? To the best of her knowledge, Charlie had never lied to her before.

She fought a small wave of nausea. Whatever he'd done, Charlie loved her. And she'd walked out on him cold. She hadn't even told him she was standing by. She'd been ashamed to in front of so many people. She'd been thinking of herself not Charlie. She had allowed her hurt pride to come between. Even when she'd walked out at the end of the inquest, she'd known she was going to stand by Charlie. But Charlie didn't know. Right now he was sitting in a cell thinking he hadn't a friend in the world.

Mary Lou looked down at the black water lapping at the sides of the *Sally*. She wished she was smarter than she was. What if someone had somehow doped the coffee and both Charlie and Mrs. Camden had been drugged? She wouldn't put it past either Mr. Camden or Mr. Ferris. Both of them were cool customers with a bloated sense of their own importance. She knew. She had to fend off the advances of men just like them six nights a week at the Beach Club, younger men who had married or attached themselves to older women. Especially Mr. Camden. He'd have felt worse if his pet dog had been run over. He'd been much more concerned about his wife's diamond ring than he had about her.

Mary Lou forced herself to think. The basin was unlighted. She might have come home any minute. She probably had come home a few minutes after Charlie had left the *Sally* with Mrs. Camden. The easiest way to dispose of a coffee cup one didn't have time to wash thoroughly would be to toss it over the side.

On impulse, she slipped out of the housecoat she'd put on when she'd taken off her evening gown and lowered herself over the side of the *Sally*. The water was cold with night but the tide was slack and there was no pull to it. Here the water was two fathoms deep. She doubled her body into a knot and dived. Her groping hands encountered bottom, nothing more. She broke water, filled her lungs with air and dove again, this time farther from the boat.

There was little debris on the bottom. The basin was scoured by the tides. Mary Lou dived a fourth, then a fifth time. On her sixth dive her right hand encountered a small hard object. She grasped it and kicked her way to the surface. There was no moon. The light from the stars was too dim for her to see the object clearly. Treading water, Mary Lou shook her hair from her eyes and felt the object with both hands. It was the missing cup. At least, it was a cup.

Here was proof of Charlie's story. He and Mrs. Camden had been on the *Sally*. Charlie had made coffee. Then someone had thrown the cup that he or Mrs. Camden or both of them had used over the side of the boat.

Mary Lou swam back to the *Sally* holding the cup carefully in one hand. There were no trailing ropes. The transom was too high for her to reach. She swam ashore and walked back out on the pier, hoping she wouldn't meet anyone. The water had molded her sheer scanties and bra to her body until they were merely an extra layer of flesh.

Back in the cabin of the *Sally* she set the cup on the small galley and examined it as she toweled her body. It was one of a set. It was the missing cup. She could tell because the bowl was glazed and there was a small chip in the handle.

As she toweled her hair, she started to cry and couldn't stop. Charlie hadn't been unfaithful to her. Every word of his story was true. She stopped crying and one corner of her mouth turned down. Someone thought they were a pair of rubes. Someone was playing them for chumps. Just because she worked at the Beach Club and Charlie was a charter boat captain.

She combed her hair and made up and put on her best dress, a combed white wool with a wide hand-tooled Guatemalan belt. She wouldn't wait until morning. She'd take the cup to Sheriff White right away and explain where she'd found it. If Sheriff White refused to believe her, she'd go to the State's Attorney. If he wouldn't listen to her, she'd take a bus to Tallahassee and talk to the Attorney General. It could be that even after its twenty-four hour immersion in the water, the cup would contain some trace of whatever drug had been used on Charlie.

Mary Lou debated how to carry the cup then wrapped it in a dry towel and put it in the suitcase with the elephant bank and Charlie's clothes. On second thought, she took the money from her purse and laid the fifteen hundred dollars flat on the bottom of the suitcase under Charlie's clean shirts and underwear.

One by one, the lights along the shore were winking out as the residents of the bait camps and the small cottages on the pass and the owners of the big houses on the bay called it a night. Only the jukes and the Beach Club were still lighted and would be for hours. She could call a cab from Harry's.

It was late, much later than she'd thought. Night was blending into early morning. The black waters lapping the sides of the *Sally* were beginning to gurgle and spin in little whorls around the creosoted pilings, gathering force and momentum as slack tide ended and the water in the bay began to feel the irresistible pull of the outgoing tide.

Mary Lou fitted a small knitted hat to her still damp hair and took a last look around the cabin to see if she had missed anything Charlie could possibly use. She couldn't see a thing. She could buy him a carton of cigarettes in Harry's with love from Mary Lou.

She brushed at her eyes with the back of her hand. She was damned if she'd cry anymore. The time for crying was past. What she wanted was action on Charlie's behalf. She meant to see that there was some.

From force of habit she locked the cabin of the *Sally*. Both she and Charlie always did. So did most of the charter boat fleet. Not that the tourists stole. But the charter boats were so quaint and the tourists were hell on souvenirs. Shep had caught one trying to lug off his compass.

Mary Lou set the suitcase on the pier and stepped up on the weathered planking. She'd almost reached the T, when she sensed or thought she sensed someone lurking behind a crooked piling.

She lowered the suitcase to the pier. Her voice was small. "Who's there?"

The only answer was the gurgle of the tide and the uniform creak of the mooring ropes of the long line of unlighted charter boats.

It's my nerves, Mary Lou thought. Her nerves were shot. Small wonder. Perhaps she'd have a coke and rum in Harry's while she was waiting for the cab to come out of town. The coke and rum that Charlie had offered her that morning.

She grasped the handle of the suitcase and started on again.

As she passed the crooked piling a white arm holding a short piece of pipe cut through the night in a short but vicious arc. The pipe struck the back of her head. Too stunned to scream, still clinging to the suitcase, Mary Lou fell to her knees and the piece of pipe found her head again.

She continued to kneel in an attitude of prayer. One star of all the millions in the sky grew brighter than the rest. It grew in size and brilliance until it filled the sky. Then the star exploded in a shower of shooting sparks and all was dark and silence.

CHAPTER SEVEN

She was cold. She was tired. She would dive once more, then give it up as hopeless. It was, after all, a fantastic story. It wasn't likely the cup would be on the bottom of the basin.

Mary Lou dived down and down in her quest. Her groping hands were unable to find bottom. The pressure on her chest increased until she felt as if she were being crushed. She opened her eyes on a wet black wall of water. She wasn't diving. She was drowning.

Fighting panic and the invisible force hurrying her along in the wet black void, she forced her body to the surface. Her lungs felt as if they were bursting. She had to breathe.

She broke water and filled her lungs with air. One glance at the black silhouette looming still blacker against the night was enough to tell her she was in the center of the pass not far from the bridge. She wasn't diving for the cup. She'd had it. Someone had knocked her out on the pier and rolled her body into the pass. Mary Lou fought to breathe. Her mind cleared slowly. She brushed her hair out of her eyes with one hand. Whoever had knocked her out hadn't rolled her off the pier. They'd rowed her to the center of the pass. The tide wouldn't have pulled her out of the basin this fast.

She stood a moment treading water, gulping air, glad there was no moon, hoping that whoever had hit her hadn't seen her break water. The back of her head felt numb. Her wool dress was binding her legs. Her wide leather belt felt like it was cutting her in two. She could hear, or thought she could hear, the creak of muffled oar locks. Then the pull of the outgoing tide swept her under the pier. Mary Lou caught at one of the great concrete pilings and the accumulated barnacles tore at her hands. A huge fish cut the water nearby, leaving a phosphorescent wake. She hoped it wasn't a shark. The pull of the tide was too strong. The barnacles were too sharp. Now she was out from under the pier. The tide was hurrying her toward the distant line of white breakers and rip tides, where the swirling waters of the pass poured into the Gulf.

Mary Lou turned on her back and floated until she could breathe normally again. This was the route Helene Camden's body had been meant to travel. But the blonde woman had been dropped two hours later when the tide had begun to slacken. Mary Lou unbuckled her wide belt and let it drop away from her body. She kicked off her shoes then fought her way out of her dress. Now she could swim. She turned on her side. The breakers were closer now. Once the rip tides caught her, she would be helpless. She kicked out strongly, forcing her body through the water, swimming to the right obliquely. If she could bring up on the hook, she could wade ashore from there. Even at high tide, less than three feet of water washed over the bar.

She swam for what seemed hours, not daring to rest or float. She tried a crawl then a side stroke, alternating between the two in an attempt to conserve her strength. Then one of her thrashing arms struck bottom. She was on the bar. Mary Lou lowered her bare feet to the sand and stood a long time, panting, sobbing with relief, fighting the pull of the tide. Then she waded ashore through waist-deep water, pausing from time to time to rest or glance at the sweep of headlights, as an occasional car crossed the now distant bridge.

She didn't know who had struck her. She didn't care. That was for Sheriff White to determine. Only one thing was clear. Charlie hadn't killed Helene Camden. Helene Camden had been killed by a man or a woman willing to kill a second time to cover up the first murder that he or she had committed.

When she reached the beach, Mary Lou sat on the sand until her legs and arms stopped trembling. The sand still retained some of the heat of the day but the night wind was cool on her bare flesh. She got to her feet and walked along the beach, chafing her arms and thighs to warm them. She didn't dare go back to the *Sally* for a dress. She couldn't go into town as she was.

There was a line of unlighted rental cottages on the hook. She cut in closer to them. Most of them had clotheslines strung from their porches to a windblown palm or stunted Australian pine tree. Most of the clotheslines were draped with damp bathing suits. Mary Lou picked one that she thought would fit her and found an almost-dry white terry cloth robe.

She struggled into the bathing suit and zipped it, then put on the white robe. It was damp but it cut off the wind. She could return them in the morning.

The important thing right now was for her to contact Sheriff White and tell him what had happened to her....

There were lights in the lobbies of the hotels, in the Owl Diner, in the railroad station and in the all-night filling station on Fourth Street, but for the most part, Palmetto City slept. The long rows of green benches were deserted. With the exception of an occasional police cruiser and the Street Department crews sweeping and hosing down the streets, there was little vehicular or pedestrian traffic.

There were also lights in the Palmetto City police station. In the small back room of the station, reserved for county use, Sheriff White lighted a fresh cigar as he got to his feet.

His voice was unutterably weary. "Okay. Have it your way, Charlie. It's your story and you're stuck with it. But for my money, the whole affair stinks. I've a feeling we're being diddled." The aged sheriff was indignant. "Why, that smooth son-of-a-bitch of a Camden didn't feel as bad about his wife being daid as I would about losin' a five dollar bill."

"Not as bad," Gilmore said. "And that Ferris fellow is a booger, too. 'Attorney Ferris or Counsellor' he tells me."

State's Attorney Keely grinned. "Well, you told him off, John."

"I did at that," Gilmore said. "But the thing that got me the hottest under the collar was the way Camden acted about the ring. 'You'll probably have to cut it off,' he says. 'But when you do, be careful with it. That ring's worth eighteen thousand dollars.'"

Keely continued to grin. "You saw her. Why else would he marry her but for her money?" The State's Attorney glanced at his watch and picked his hat from the desk. "Well, it's getting on toward five. You boys can kick it around as long as you want to. I'm going home. The coroner's jury voted to hold Ames for trial and there's nothing we can do about it as long as he refuses to cooperate."

"Not a thing," White agreed.

Keely fitted his hat to his head. "I'll draw up a true bill in the morning. When you going to move him, Bob?"

White puffed at his cigar. "After I get some sleep." He looked through the smoke at Ames. "Last chance, Charlie. Once I take you up to the county seat, the chances are you won't leave there again until they take you to Raiford. You're sure now that Mrs. Camden didn't say anything about her husband?"

It was an effort for Ames to speak. His voice was husky with fatigue. "Just what I've told you, Sheriff. She said he was flying down next week, that they were both much in need of a vacation and she thought it would be nice if she and Mr. Camden could return home via the inland waterway."

"Then you invited her aboard for a cup of coffee?"

"Yes, sir."

"Who made the coffee? You or Mrs. Camden?"

"It was already made. I'd made it when I came in with my bait."

"So you had two cups of coffee with her and you don't remember another thing until you came to, nekid in the cabin of the *Sea Bird?*"

"That's the way it happened."

"You do hit to her?"

"You've seen her. You've seen Mary Lou."

Sheriff White pushed his hat on the back of his head. "It's the goddamnedest thing I ever heard. If you're lying you're good at hit, Charlie. But your story jist don't make sense."

In the doorway, Keely asked, "You found anyone yet who saw him board the *Sea Bird* with the Camden woman?"

White shook his head. "Not yet. But that doesn't mean a thing. The boys out on the beach stick tighter than beggar weed on a blue serge suit. Hell, effen half of them had seen him kill her, they'd still swear on a Bible that Charlie was fishing the twenty fathom bank at the time."

Biff Clymer, the desk sergeant, looked over the State's Attorney's shoulder. "Lady to see you, Sheriff."

"Who?"

"Mary Lou Ames," Clymer said.

Keely stepped aside to allow Mary Lou to enter the smoke-filled room. She wrapped her borrowed terry cloth robe around her as though it were an evening cape and walked directly to the chair in which Ames was sitting.

"I'm sorry, Charlie," she said. "I mean about walking out on you. I didn't really. I meant to stand by, honestly I did. Even before this happened. I sold the *Sally* to Ben to pay for a lawyer." Mary Lou's lower lip quivered. "And I put the money in the suitcase with your clothes and the elephant bank and the cup." Reaction was setting in. Her body shook as with cold. "But I don't know if it's still there."

"What the hell?" Sheriff White said.

Ames got to his feet and held her. "Honey."

The terry cloth robe fell open as Mary Lou pressed her cheek to his. "And I believe you, darling. I know you weren't untrue to me. I know you didn't kill Helene Camden."

Sheriff White's eyes traveled slowly from Mary Lou's bare feet up her shapely legs to her skimpy bathing suit and rested on her wet hair.

Keely took off his hat and laid it on the desk. "I knew I should have gone home."

White touched Mary Lou's shoulder. "What are you doing in that get-up? What happened to you, Mrs. Ames?"

Mary Lou told him. "Someone tried to kill me."

"Who?"

"I don't know."

"How?"

"They slugged me with a piece of pipe and threw me in the pass."

"You were wearing that outfit when it happened?"

"No. I was dressed to come down here. But the tide was running out. I had to take off my dress in order to reach the hook. So I borrowed this suit and robe from a line."

"Why?" White asked. "I mean, why were you slugged?"

Mary Lou turned to face him. "I think because I found the cup."

"What cup?"

"The cup Charlie drank the coffee out of."

"I see. And where did you find this cup?"

"On the bottom of the basin, about twenty feet out from the *Sally*."

"You dove for it?"

"Yes."

"Why?"

"Because it was missing when I went to pack the set. There were six saucers but only five cups."

Sheriff White took off his hat and ran a crooked forefinger around the leather sweatband. "You're way over my head, Mrs. Ames. I don't get this at all."

Coroner Gilmore got up from the chair in which he was sitting and offered it to Mary Lou. "What you have to tell us is pertinent to the charge against your husband?"

"Yes, sir."

Gilmore indicated the chair again. "Then suppose you start at the beginning."

Mary Lou continued to cling to Ames. "Thank you. I'd rather stand."

Ames tightened his arm about her waist. "What's this about a cup, honey?"

"Well," Mary Lou began. "Like I said, I sold the boat to Ben. For fifteen hundred dollars. Then while I was packing some clothes for you, I suddenly realized that you'd never lied to me, Charlie, that if you said the last thing you remembered was drinking a cup of coffee, that was the way it happened. Then when I went to pack the dishes, one of the cups was gone."

Keely was frankly skeptical. "So you dove for it in the middle of the night?"

"Yes."

"Why?"

"Because if Charlie was drugged and whoever drugged him didn't have time to wash the cup, the easiest way to dispose of it would be to throw it over the side. And I thought if I found the cup it still might have some trace of the drug in it."

"You found it on your first dive?"

"No. I dove six or seven times."

"And then—?"

"I dried my hair and dressed. And I wrapped the cup in a towel and put it in the suitcase with Charlie's clothes and the money."

"And started down here with it?"

"Yes, sir. But I didn't get here. When I got to the T of the pier someone hit me with a piece of pipe and threw me into the water."

"Was it a man or woman who hit you?"

"I don't know," Mary Lou said. "But for some reason I'm under the impression it was a woman."

"Why?"

"I don't know. It's just an impression. All I saw was the pipe."

Keely looked at White. White returned his hat to his head. "I'll be damned if I know what to think," he admitted. "With your permission, Mrs. Ames."

Gently for so large a man, he parted Mary Lou's matted hair and studied the back of her head.

"Well?" Gilmore asked.

"She's been hit," White told him. "Hard. Were you by any chance wearing a hat, Mrs. Ames?"

"Yes. I was. A small white knitted one. It must have come off in the water."

"It and your hair are all that saved you," White said. "She was struck at least twice," he told Keely. "And both wounds could stand some attention."

Mary Lou shook her head. "Not until you find out if the suitcase is still on the pier. I was afraid to go back alone."

A moment of silence followed. Then Coroner Gilmore said, "At least it's a new angle. Mrs. Ames thinks she was struck by a woman. That French maid who testified, what was her name, Celeste Montigny, is a mighty pretty little piece. What if she and Camden were having an affair and Mrs. Camden discovered it and threatened to cut him off at the pants pocket?"

Some of the weariness left White's face. "You know, you might have something there, John. A small-town sheriff, am I? Come on. Let's all ride out to the basin."

CHAPTER EIGHT

Ames rode in the back seat of the car with Mary Lou on one side of him and Sheriff White on the other. He was tired but he no longer felt bitter. Mary Lou still loved him. She believed him. To the best of his knowledge, he hadn't made love to or killed Helene Camden. This thing would work out somehow.

The lights of Palmetto City dropped behind. The black silhouette of acres of palm trees replaced the orderly rows of small houses wearing scarlet flame vine and purple bougainvillea and yellow allamanda on their pastel colored walls. Patches of sand began to appear. Mangrove rose out of the swamps. The sweet-sour smell of the tide flats was strong. They crossed the long causeway to the beach.

From the front seat of the car, Keely asked, "Did you notice anything strange about the taste of the coffee you say you drank, Ames?"

Ames was truthful. "No. I always drink it without sugar and it's always sort of bitter."

"Were you sick when you came to yesterday morning?"

"Yes. I was."

"You threw up?"

"Yes. For a long time."

"Did you have a metallic taste in your mouth?"

"I did."

"It could have been chloral," Gilmore said.

Keely protested, "But if Camden and the French girl are in back of this, why only drug one cup? How was it introduced into the coffee? And where was Helene Camden all this time?"

"I wouldn't know," Gilmore admitted.

Ames asked Mary Lou how she felt.

"I feel fine," Mary Lou said.

"Your head doesn't hurt?"

"Not much."

"They're minor lacerations," White said. "She was struck jist hard enough to break the skin."

Ames squeezed Mary Lou's hand. "You crazy kid. You might have been killed."

Mary Lou squeezed back. "But I wasn't. I did damn near drown. I thought I'd never make the hook."

White lighted a fresh cigar. "You didn't see whoever it was who struck you?"

Mary Lou shook her head. "No. He came out from behind the piling after I'd passed it. I don't know if he was tall or short or what he looked like."

"He?"

"She, then."

"Your impression is it was a woman?"

"Yes."

"You smell perfume or anything like that?"

"No, sir."

They reached the east side of the pass and the uniformed deputy sheriff slowed down for the sharp turn onto the bridge. Morning was almost full. The catwalk on the bridge over the pass was already lined with optimistic early morning fishermen. All of them looked curiously at the blue and white police car.

"Cut the lane back of Sheldon's Ways," White ordered the driver.

"Yes, sir."

The deputy sheriff did as he'd been ordered and parked the cruiser on the edge of the basin. For a moment no one moved. The wind was from the east. The sweet-sour smell of the tide flats was stronger here. The only sound was the raucous squawking of a flight of greedy gulls fighting over the cut-up trash fish with which the bridge fishermen were chumming the water under their lines.

"The mackerel must be running," Keely said.

"Must be," White granted.

A few of the boats showed lights as the captains with charters got breakfast, checked their bait and went over their gear and tackle.

Sheriff White opened the door on his side. "Well, let's git at it."

Mary Lou looked at the handcuffs encircling her husband's wrists. "Does Charlie have to wear those?"

"Yes," Sheriff White said flatly.

Keely and Gilmore got out. The driver stayed back of the wheel to listen to the crackle of the two-way radio. Ames followed White from the car. He knew what White was thinking now that the elderly man's enthusiasm to prove he wasn't a small-town sheriff was beginning to wear off. Mary Lou's story was too pat, too providential, too theatrical. It was the sort of thing a girl vocalist at the Beach Club would think up to attempt to pry a former hot trumpet player out of a murder rap. It was cloak and dagger stuff. Such things seldom happened in real life. Now that his first flush of enthusiasm was wearing thin, White was reverting to his original opinion. He and Helene Camden had gotten drunk together. They'd moved the party to the *Sea Bird*. Sometime during the night they'd quarreled and he had killed her. So she'd been forty and fat. To a drunken man all women are attractive. Then there was the five thousand dollars. The money was still to be explained. The hell of it was White was a small-town sheriff. Keely was a small-town prosecutor. And while Gilmore might be a capable justice of the peace, he was way over his head in his dual capacity as coroner.

White led the way out on the pier. The battered leather suitcase was still where Mary Lou had dropped it. She opened it with trembling fingers and checked the contents. The fifteen hundred dollars was still under Charlie's shirts. The elephant bank with almost eight hundred dollars in it hadn't been touched. But the towel-wrapped cup was gone.

None of the four men spoke. Still kneeling, Mary Lou said, "Whoever tried to kill me took the cup."

"Why?" White asked.

Mary Lou said, "Maybe he was afraid a laboratory analysis would show some trace of whatever was used to drug Charlie."

Sheriff White's, "Could be," was noncommittal.

Ames could read the doubt in his eyes. *Here we go again*, he thought.

Mary Lou said, "You don't believe me. But there was a cup. I found it on the bottom of the basin, in about two fathoms. And I wrapped it in a towel and put it in the suitcase."

"An' started to town with the suitcase when some someone, you don't really know if it was a man or a woman, hit you with a piece of pipe and rolled you into the basin."

Mary Lou shook her head. "No. They must have rowed me out to the middle of the pass while I was still unconscious. The tide wouldn't have sucked me out of the basin that fast."

"Anyway, after they knocked you unconscious, they took the cup out of the suitcase."

"They must have."

"Why didn't they take the money you got for the *Sally?*"

"I don't know."

Mary Lou's lower lip began to quiver again. Her eyes filled with tears. Ames helped her to her feet. "Easy makes it, baby. Everything's going to be all right. We're just blowing a couple of blue ones." He was sorry he'd used the simile as soon as it was out of his mouth. He didn't like White's reaction. It took him out of the charter boat captain class and grouped him with Camden and Ferris.

"So?" Gilmore asked.

"I don't know, John," White said. "I'll be damned if I do. So Camden and the French maid were playin' house and Mrs. Camden got onto the fact that they were holdin' hands. Camden was in Baltimore when this happened. I checked with the State's Attorney's office there. The maid isn't as big as Mary Lou. She'd have a hell of a time knockin' anyone out, let alone rowin' 'em out into the middle of the pass with the tide at the full. Besides, gettin' back to the dead blonde, Ames admits she boarded the *Sally* of her own free will and *asked* for a cup of coffee. Ames says he'd jist come in from gettin' bait. He admits makin' the coffee hisself. So how did the drug, if there was any drug, get into the coffee?"

Mary Lou's lower lip stopped trembling and thrust out in a pout. "You don't believe me."

Sheriff White's voice was gentle. "Let's put it this way, Mary Lou. So one of your cups was missin'. You *say* you dove over side and recovered it. You say you put it in this suitcase. If the cup had still been in the suitcase, what would it prove? Twenty-four hours in the water would have washed away any trace of a drug. Can you prove *you* didn't throw the cup over side and then recover it in an attempt to make Charlie's story hold up?"

"N-no. But in that case why isn't it still in the suitcase?"

"Because the story sounded better this way. It gives credence to your story about bein' slugged. Can you *prove* that someone slugged you and threw you in the pass?"

"No-o." She touched the back of her head. "But—"

White looked tired. He undoubtedly was. He was, after all, in his early sixties. "You could have hit yourself with almost anythin', Mary Lou. You're young. You love Charlie. An' if a-hittin' yourself on the head a couple of times would save him from the chair, hit would be worth hit to you. Now mind you, I ain't sayin' you're lyin'. It kin be your story is true. But hit's improbable as hell."

A deep silence followed. The gulls continued to squawk. An outboard motor pooped a few times then settled down into a high-pitched drone. Several charter boat captains came out into the cockpit of their boats and looked at the little group on the pier.

State's Attorney Keely inspected the planking around the crooked piling. "I don't see any sign of blood."

"It would seem there would be some," Gilmore said, "if Mrs. Ames was struck as hard as she says she was."

Ames felt Mary Lou's body stiffen in his arms. He tried to hush her and couldn't.

"You're a bunch of goddamn small-town fools," she cried. "You're like all the rest of the local business men. The Chamber of Commerce has you buffaloed. You're willing to let the tourists walk all over you, just so they keep coming down here. And you'll let Charlie go to the chair just because you're afraid of the Camden money."

Neither Gilmore nor Keely said anything.

Sheriff White's voice continued gentle. "Now, honey. You're jist upset. That hain't no way fo' a pretty girl like you t' talk. An' hit ain't so. Effen I thought Camden killed his wife or planned to have her kilt, I'd jug him before he could say Baltimore."

White turned and took his cigar from his mouth as the driver of the parked cruiser hurried out on the pier. "There's another one, Sheriff," the deputy said. "It just came in on the two-way. Cody said the guy was so excited he could hardly make head or tail out of what the Camden butler was saying but that according to what he could get, there's another body floating in the slip where the *Sea Bird* is berthed and the only thing that's kept the tide from suckin' it out to sea is that it's tangled in a mess of rope."

"Who is it?"

"That's what Cody couldn't get. He said Phillips talked so fast and was so excited that he had a hell of a time getting his name and address out of him. Then by the time he'd asked who was dead, the butler had hung up."

The eyes of the group on the pier lifted in unison and looked up the awakening bay and basin. There was a small knot of people on the Camden pier but it was too far away and the morning mist was too heavy for any of them to stand out as individuals.

Keely took off his hat and patted his forehead with his breast pocket handkerchief. "I knew I should have gone home." He glanced at his watch. "I have to be in court at nine o'clock."

"What time is it?"

"Four minutes after six."

White returned his cigar to his mouth. "Well, let's go see. You go first, Charlie."

Ames walked back down the pier. Mary Lou walked beside him, dabbing at her eyes from time to time with the backs of her hands, sobs still shaking her shoulders. "It happened just as I told it, Charlie."

"I know," Ames said.

Ben Sheldon was standing in the doorway of the sleeping quarters adjoining his office. His feet were bare. His only garment was a pair of wrinkled pajama pants. His eyes were puffed with sleep. His fat belly hung over the draw string of his pajama pants.

"What you doin' out heah this early, Bob?" he asked White.

White jerked his thumb up the basin. "Hit would seem someone else is daid up t' the Camden place." He started to get into the cruiser and looked over his shoulder at the fat man. "You hear any commotion out on the pier last night, Ben?"

"No. Not ary."

"You didn't hear a woman scream?"

The chandler shook his head. "No. I didn't hear a thing, Bob."

Sheriff White settled himself in the back seat of the car and looked sideways at Mary Lou.

She stopped crying and said fiercely, "I didn't have time to scream."

"Drive to the Camden place," White told the driver.

It was full morning now. The mist was lifting. The sun rising out of the mangrove swamp on the far side of the bay was drying the condensation on the Camden lawn and streaking the private pier with yellow.

The usual morbid crowd had gathered. Sheriff White sat a moment after the police car had stopped, picking out individuals on the pier. He could see Camden and Ferris and Phillips. Mixed in with the local people he knew were a dozen or more tourists, the men in bathing trunks, the women in bathing or play suits. A fat woman with flabby white legs, wearing tight yellow shorts and a halter, was leaning over the hand rail looking at something in the water.

"You know," White told Keely. "The beach used to be a nice place to live until the tourists and the moneyed snow birds loused it up. Now it's one damn thing after another." He got out and held the door open for Ames. "Okay. Let's go, Charlie."

The kettle drums of fatigue were beginning to play a tympanic solo in Ames's head. He hadn't slept for twenty-four hours. He'd been under a constant strain. He'd been questioned incessantly. He'd been moved from one place to another and then back to the place he'd been first. "Okay. Let's go, Charlie" had become his theme song. Now, with a new angle on which to work, with a possible solution in sight, Sheriff White had decided not to believe Mary Lou.

The muscles in Ames's neck corded. The large veins in his temples began to throb. His jaw thrust out at a stubborn angle. *To hell with them*, he thought. *To hell with all of them!* Cocking his white captain's cap at as jaunty an angle as he could manage, with Mary Lou at his side, swaggering slightly as he walked, Ames preceded White and Keely and Gilmore out on the pier.

CHAPTER NINE

Ferris turned from the rail and nodded begrudging approval as Sheriff White forced his way through the group of curious onlookers staring at the object in the water.

"I must say," the lawyer said, "you got here promptly. We found the body less than ten minutes ago."

"I was jist down the road apiece," White said.

Hal Camden was standing beside the lawyer. He no longer looked like a movie actor. He needed a shave. His eyes were puffed and bloodshot. His expensive silk robe was rumpled. The legs of his pajamas showed under the cuffs of trousers pulled on so hastily he'd forgotten to zip the fly. His overlong hair needed combing. He exuded an aroma of whiskey. "I don't know why," he said plaintively, "everything happens to me."

White ignored him to look over the rail.

Mary Lou gasped, "It's the maid. It's the maid who's dead."

Ames gripped the rail with his manacled hands. At least, they couldn't pin the maid's death on him. He'd been in custody, in the back room of the Palmetto City police station when Miss Montigny had been killed. Perhaps now Sheriff White would believe Mary Lou's story. It would seem obvious that whoever had drugged him had killed Mrs. Camden and murdered Celeste.

The dead girl, fully clothed in a black silk maid's uniform complete with a once frothy, now sodden, white apron and a white ruche in her black hair, was lying on her back with both arms extended. Her sightless eyes were open and staring at the morning sun. There was no blood on her face or dress or any external sign of death.

Ames wondered what was holding her up. Then he saw that the small of her back was resting on the line of an anchor buoy used to secure a nine foot marine plywood dinghy. Her body rose and fell with the movement of the boat.

"Who found her?" Sheriff White asked.

"I did," Camden admitted.

"When?"

"I don't know the exact time. A few minutes before I had Phillips call the station."

"What were you doing out here this time of morning?"

Camden rubbed the stubble of beard on his chin with the palm of one hand. "I'd been going over Helene's personal books with Tom. We'd spent most of the night at it. I went to my room and couldn't sleep. So I walked out here." Camden indicated the body. "And that's what I found."

Sheriff White looked at Ferris. "You're Tom?"

"Tom Ferris. Attorney Tom Ferris," the lawyer said.

"Oh, yes. That's right. You're Mrs. Camden's lawyer. Or should I say counsellor?" White emphasized the word. "What do you know about this?"

A slightly built man, dapper even in pajamas and robe, Ferris stroked his wisp of a mustache. "Nothing. Not a thing, Sheriff. As Mr. Camden just told you, we spent most of the night going over Helene's personal records. When we finished, I went directly to my room and I believe I must have slept an hour or two before I heard Hal shout."

"I was never so shocked in my life," Camden said.

"I kin imagine," the fat woman in the tight shorts sympathized.

Camden continued. "I thought at first Celeste had stumbled and fallen off the pier." He indicated the smashed glass of a square case that held a life preserver. "So I smashed that and started to throw the preserver to her. Then I saw she was dead. At least there was no motion, except what the water imparted to the body. So I shouted for help instead and a few moments later Tom and Phillips joined me on the pier. Phillips and I wanted to recover the body but Tom advised us to leave it where it is."

Ferris continued to stroke his mustache. "That is, I believe, the correct procedure in an instance like this."

"That's right," Sheriff White said. "Did either of you hear her scream any time during the night?"

Ferris shook his head. "No, sir. But she might have. We were quite engrossed in what we were doing and we were working in the library on the far side of the house."

"I see."

Phillips, the butler, cleared his throat. "If I might be so bold, sir."

Sheriff White transferred his attention to the butler. "Yes—?"

"I thought I heard a scream, sir. Well, not exactly a scream. More a sound of distress."

"What time was this?"

"Between two-thirty and three o'clock this morning, sir, shortly after I'd made certain neither Mr. Camden nor Mr. Ferris required my services and had retired to my room."

"Did you do anything about it?"

"I looked out my window, sir. But when the sound wasn't repeated, I attributed it to a gull or a night bird of some kind and retired."

"And that's all you know about it?"

"Yes, sir."

White put his fore and second fingers in his mouth and whistled to attract the attention of the deputy still sitting in the police car. When the deputy came out on the pier, White indicated the body. "Get it, will you, Ken? Better borrow a boat from someone. And don't try to lift it up on the dock. Row it into shore."

"Yes, sir," the deputy said.

State's Attorney Keely rested his elbows on the railing of the pier. "Funny how the body hangs on that rope. You'd think it would slide one way or the other."

"Wouldn't you?" White asked. He looked at Coroner Gilmore. "Call in over the two-way for me, will you, John? Ask Cody to send out another car and four or five men."

Gilmore lighted a cigarette. "Gladly."

Ames and Mary Lou stood holding hands. She said, "This should prove something."

"It should," Ames agreed. "The way I see it, whoever drugged me and killed Mrs. Camden killed the maid."

"Why? Why should they?"

"I don't know," Ames admitted. "You're the sheriff. I'm just a charter boat captain."

Sheriff White looked at Mary Lou. "Were you aboard the *Sally* between two-thirty and three o'clock?"

"I was."

"Awake?"

"Yes."

"Did you hear a scream?"

Mary Lou shook her head. "No. At least, nothing I recognized as a scream."

There was a creak of oar locks as Deputy Sheriff Ken Sayers rowed under the pier in a borrowed boat.

Ferris retied the belt of his robe. "If I may be so bold as to ask, what is Ames doing here? I thought he'd be in a cell in Sweetwater by now."

The curious on the pier crowded a little closer.

"He will by nightfall," White said. After a slight hesitation, White added, "You see, there's been another small development. A little over an hour ago, Mrs. Ames came into town with a very interestin' story about one of her cups bein' missin'. She says she dove overboard an' found hit on the bottom of the basin about twenty feet out from the *Sally*. She says she wrapped it in a towel and put it in a suitcase an' started to bring hit to me. But before she could git off the pier, someone struck her on the haid with a piece of pipe an' rolled her into the pass. She says she came to, jist in time to strike out for the hook."

"The hook?" Ferris puzzled.

A spit of land extendin' out apiece on the Gulf side of the bridge."

"Oh."

Camden ran his fingers through his too-long hair.

"Make sense, Sheriff. It was her husband who killed Helene not Mrs. Ames. Why should anyone want to harm her?"

"Well, her story is that Charlie's coffee was drugged an' whoever drugged hit didn't have time to wash the cup so they threw hit overside."

"Ridiculous," Ferris said.

"It don't stack up too good," White admitted.

"You found the cup?"

"No. All we found was the suitcase."

Her borrowed bathing suit was too tight. The bound edges were cutting into her thighs and breasts. It was difficult for her to breathe. Mary Lou was uncomfortable. She was tired. She'd almost drowned and no one but Charlie believed her. "You," she told Sheriff White hotly, "are a stupid old fool! There *was* a cup. I *was* struck on the head and rolled into the pass. And Charlie didn't kill Mrs. Camden. He *was* drugged and—"

"I know, honey," White interrupted her. "An' the last he remembers is drinkin' a cup o' coffee in the cockpit of the *Sally*."

Mary Lou buried her wet face on Ames's chest.

He stood helpless, unable even to pat her shoulder. "How's for letting Mary Lou change her clothes?" he asked White. "That suit's two sizes too small for her."

"Any time she's a mind to," White said. "There ain't no charge against her." He leaned on the rail beside Keely. "Handle her as little as you can, Ken. Mebbe you might best tow her in."

The deputy knelt in the boat. "That's what I figured on, but she's hung up on the rope somehow." He rolled up his right shirt sleeve.

Hanging onto the buoy rope with his other hand, he reached over and under the bobbing body.

"What's a holdin' her, Ken?" White asked.

The deputy straightened in the boat, blood and water dripping from his right hand. "Goddamn it to hell!" he swore. "No wonder. There was a knife in her back and the haft was hung up on the rope."

The body slipped over the rope, revolved slowly and began to sink.

"Grab her!" Sheriff White shouted.

Sayers grabbed the maid by an ankle, then taking a short grip on the oar he began to scull toward shore with one hand.

"The knife still in her?" Keely asked.

Sayers shook his head. "No. It pulled loose when I freed her. I'll bring her in, then I'll come back and dive for it."

Ames was glad Mary Lou was facing the other way. He stood looking over her shoulder at the dead girl in the water. There was something indecent about death. It was so impartially final. The dead lost all right to personal dignity. They were so much clay, to be handled as such. Being towed through the water as she was, the dead girl's black skirt and lace-edged white petticoat slipped up to her knees, then her thighs, permitting an exposure she would never have permitted had she been alive.

Ames compared her, mentally, with the body he'd seen on the floor of Rupert's Fish House. The dead maid was young and shapely. Her wet flesh was white and firm. Alive, she had been very pretty. He wondered what had happened to Coroner Gilmore's theory of a possible affair between Mr. Camden and Celeste.

The middle-aged fat woman scratched the seat of her tight shorts. "Shameful," she said. "Shameful."

Mary Lou continued to sob.

"You'd better go change into something more comfortable, honey," Ames said.

"No," Mary Lou sobbed. "I want to stay with you."

Ames knew how she felt. The rising sun was making his head ache. The reflected glare hurt his eyes. His weariness returned in a sodden wave of heat. Coroner Gilmore's theory had sounded fine in the back room of the station. Between it and Sheriff White's resentment at being called a small-town sheriff, he had been almost hopeful. But that had been before this new angle had developed. If Camden and Celeste had been having an affair and Camden had killed Helene to keep his hold on the Camden money, it seemed ridiculous to assume the cosmetic executive had also murdered the girl for whom he had killed his wife.

The crowd on the pier moved shoreward, keeping pace with the deputy in the boat.

State's Attorney Keely pushed away from the rail.

"Okay. Let's go, Charlie," White said.

Mary Lou and Ames moved back down the pier with the crowd. Mary Lou wiped her eyes on the skirt of her borrowed white terry cloth robe as she walked. "As soon as I change into a dress, I'll go into town and get a lawyer," she said. "With the seven hundred in the bank in town, the nine hundred in the elephant bank and the fifteen hundred I got from Ben, we have around thirty-one hundred dollars. We ought to get a good lawyer for that."

Sweat beaded on Ames's face and plastered his shirt to his body. A lot of fishing charters, a lot of songs, a lot of work and self-denial had gone into the gathering of their small bank account. It was to have bought The Boat. Now even the boat they'd had was gone. He wanted to tell Mary Lou to skip hiring a lawyer, that she might need the money later on and his fear was a lump in his throat.

"You do that," Ames said. "Go to Judge Barker. I've had him out on fishing trips. He likes me. He'll recommend a good lawyer."

"Judge Barker," Mary Lou repeated.

As he waited for Sayers to beach the boat and the body he was towing, Ames studied Camden's face. Camden was no more concerned, at least externally, with Celeste Montigny's death than he had been with the death of his wife. He didn't look either grief-stricken or worried. He looked like a man with a hangover. Mr. Ferris was much more concerned.

The lawyer waded out thigh deep to meet the boat and made the dead girl decent by straightening her skirt. "I have her, deputy," he said. "You'd better get back and recover the knife if you can. It may be important."

Sayers looked at White. White nodded. "But best strip to your shorts first, Ken. No sense in wetting your uniform. You cut your hand bad?"

"Not bad," the deputy said.

He took off his uniform shirt and undershirt and laid them on the pier. He laid his gun and gun belt and hat on top of them. He took off his boots and trousers. Then gripping the oar with both hands, he sculled back toward the buoy rope on which the dead girl had been balanced.

Ferris waded ashore with Celeste and laid the limp body on the dry sand.

"Poor kid," the lawyer said. "She got a big bang out of life. A shame this had to happen to her."

CHAPTER TEN

Coroner Gilmore knelt beside the body and felt the wet flesh. "I'd say she's been dead for some hours. I haven't the least idea how many. I'll be glad when we have a Medical Examiner. Being a Justice of the Peace is enough of a job for one man."

Sheriff White squatted beside him. "Could you estimate the time, John?"

"Oh, anyway, three or four hours."

"Say between two and three o'clock this mornin'?"

"Yes. Somewhere along there."

White located Phillips with his eyes. "What time did you say it was when you thought you heard a scream?"

"Between two-thirty and three o'clock, sir."

"Did it seem to come from the direction of the pier?"

"I really couldn't say, sir. As I said before, it was more of a sound than a scream."

"A sound of distress?"

"Yes, sir."

"Like how?"

"Well, like someone had started to call 'Help' and hadn't time to finish the word."

"Would you say it came from outside the house?"

"Definitely, sir," Phillips said.

"How come you were up so late?"

The butler permitted himself a smug smile. "There was the inquest on Mrs. Camden, remember, sir? It was after one when we returned home. And by the time Celeste and I had set out sandwiches and whiskey for the gentlemen, it had reached the hour I mentioned."

"Celeste helped you set out the night lunch, eh?"

"Yes, sir."

"You returned to the kitchen together?"

"Yes, sir."

"Then you were the last one t' see her alive?"

The butler's smug smile grew smugger. "No, sir. Whoever killed her was the last to see her alive, sir. I do know this much. It was Celeste's custom to walk out on the pier for a last cigarette before she retired. She said the Florida moon reminded her of the south of France."

"Did she walk out on the pier last night?"

"I presume so."

"And a few minutes later you heard an unfinished call for help but you didn't bother to investigate."

Phillips' smile faded.

Camden said testily, "For God's sake, stop picking on Phillips. He had no reason to kill Celeste."

White turned his faded blue eyes on Camden. "Do you know anyone who did?"

"No."

Gilmore finished his examination and washed his hands in the bay. "As far as I can tell without undressing her, she was stabbed only once. In the back. On the left side. About where her heart would be. But I'll get Doc Hendry to do a post."

"You do that, John," White said. He continued to squat on the sand beside the dead girl, looking like a gaunt and guileless Buddha with long white drooping mustaches. "Oh, by the way, Mr. Camden. A-speakin' of the inquest. Before I forget."

"Yes—?"

"Your wife was quite a wealthy woman, wasn't she?"

"Very."

"In her own right?"

Camden picked at the stubble of beard on his unshaven jowls. "Yes."

"The money come to you?"

"Unfortunately, no."

White stood up. "Why not?"

"Because I was fool enough to sign a pre-marital agreement. All I get is twenty-five thousand cash, her jewelry and the Florida property."

All, Ames thought. He'd been watching Sayers dive for the knife. He turned and looked at the rambling beach house rising out of the palm tree studded lawn. It reminded him of a picture he'd once seen of Harry James' and Betty Grable's California ranch house. The house was worth at least fifty thousand dollars. Camden claimed the ring imbedded in his dead wife's flesh was worth eighteen thousand.

Plus the cash he'd mentioned, Camden hadn't done too badly. Even after taxes, ninety-three thousand dollars would buy a lot of Scotch and other things.

Mary Lou turned with him. "All."

"A pity," Sheriff White sympathized. "Who gits the rest of the money?"

Camden told him. "The stockholders."

"The stockholders?"

"Of *helene camden, incorporated.*"

Ferris wrung water from the skirt of his robe. "You see, *helene camden* was her life. Helene started it on nothing and built it up to the multimillion dollar business that it is. And she confided in me many times that even after her death she wanted the business to go on as a sort of monument to her."

"I see."

Ferris continued. "While Helene was very self-willed and at times impetuous and unconventional, she was a smart business woman. I know. I've been her personal lawyer for fifteen years. Even her insurance, some two hundred and fifty thousand dollars' worth, goes to the corporation."

State's Attorney Keely whistled. "There must be a lot of money in cosmetics."

A wry smile tugged at Ferris' wisp of a mustache. "There is. You know the old bit of doggerel, Mr. State's Attorney. 'Little pats of powder, little dabs of paint, make the homely girlies look like what they ain't.'"

White had been studying the girl on the sand. He looked from her to Camden. "You didn't happen to walk out on the pier last night, say between two an' three, did you, Mr. Camden?"

Camden's plump cheeks mottled with anger. The hands thrust into the pockets of his robe formed fists. "Oh, for God's sake!"

Ferris said, suavely, "I'll answer that question, Hal. I've been expecting this line of questioning to develop ever since the inquest last night, when I happened to notice Sheriff White comparing Celeste with Helene. I think I know what's in his mind."

"Mind?" Camden snorted.

Sheriff White sucked at the end of one of his mustaches. "That's right interestin', Counsellor. What's in my mind?"

Ferris said, "Celeste was a very pretty girl. She was young, vivacious. You resent the fact that you've had to arrest one of your own for Helene's murder. You'd much rather pin Helene's death on some damn Yankee who merely winters in Florida. Helene was a smart business woman but she'd been around a long time. She was beginning to sag here and there. So you're wondering if it wasn't possible that Hal had been having an affair with Celeste and if Helene hadn't caught him at it and threatened to divorce him. In that case, it would be very possible for Hal to want to see Helene dead. It would also be possible theoretically, that, having killed Helene and knowing that Celeste knew, Hal would get the wind up and kill Celeste to make certain she couldn't give evidence against him." The lawyer lighted an expensive Turkish cigarette. "Unfortunately for your supposition, Hal was in Baltimore when Helene was murdered."

"Yes," White admitted blandly. "I know. I checked on both of you."

Camden's face became more mottled. "Oh, for God's sake," he repeated. "How stupid can you get? Sure, I made a play for Celeste. Helene lighted wherever her fancy struck. If she could play house with fishing guides and the like, I didn't see why I shouldn't hold hands with the maid. But I got as far with Celeste as you're going to get with your nasty insinuations. She was a good kid, playing it straight. And all I got for the pass I made was my face slapped."

Ferris' lips formed a thin straight line, broken only by the oval cigarette. It was obvious he was keeping his temper with an effort. "And last night Hal was with me from the time we left the inquest until approximately four-thirty this morning, a full hour and a half after the elastic time limit your erudite Justice of the Peace, acting in a capacity for which he is not qualified, has set as the time of Celeste's death."

Gilmore dried his hands on his pocket handkerchief. "Well, I guess that tells me off."

"So it would seem," White said. He had trouble with the word. "What's erudite mean, John?"

Gilmore said, "Well, when I graduated from Stetson, erudite was from the Latin *eruditus*, past participle of *erudire*, to free from rudeness; polish; instruct; *e*—out, plus *rudis*—rude. Characterized by wide knowledge of a bookish kind; learned."

Ferris gave him a sour look.

Half of the crowd had remained on the beach. The other half had returned to the end of the pier to watch Deputy Sheriff Sayers dive for the knife that had been in the dead girl's back. The group on the end of the pier cheered.

"Ken must have found the knife," Keely said.

"He must have," White agreed.

The deputy sculled his borrowed boat back to the beach.

"You got it, eh?" White asked.

"Yeah," Sayers panted. He squeegeed water from his body. "But it took fourteen dives. There's a soft marl bottom out there." He picked a knife from the forward thwart and handed it to White.

It was an open clasp knife with a yellow bone handle and a five inch blade, of the type known as Fisherman's Luck.

"It wasn't lucky for her," Sayers said.

Ames wet his lips as he looked at the knife. Mary Lou felt his body stiffen. "What's the matter?" she whispered.

"It's my knife," Ames whispered back. "The one I always keep in my tackle box."

"How do you know?"

A lump formed in Ames's stomach. "I filed my initials on the handle."

Holding the knife by the tip of the blade, Sheriff White studied the bone handle. "C.A.," he read aloud. "That would be Charles Ames or could be." He looked at Ames. "This your knife, Charlie?"

The lump in Ames's stomach moved up into his throat. He was frightened and didn't know why. He couldn't have killed Celeste Montigny. He'd been in custody when she'd died. "It looks like my knife," he said finally. "But anyone could have gotten at it. I seldom lock my tackle box."

Still holding the knife by its tip, White laid it on the dead girl's skirt. "Well, it's a cinch you didn't kill her."

The curious crowded even closer to get a better look at the knife. Ferris lighted a cigarette from the stub of the one he was smoking. The pungent tobacco smelled heavy and somehow out of place in the clean crispness of the rising sun.

"No," Ferris said softly. "That would seem to be an impossibility." He studied Mary Lou's face. "But if I may make a suggestion, Sheriff, an angle does occur to me."

"What?" Sheriff White asked.

Ferris continued to study Mary Lou's face. "Mrs. Ames is obviously in love with her husband. Celeste was your best witness against him. Celeste testified at the inquest that Helene told her she had a date with a handsome young charter boat captain and they were under no circumstances to be disturbed. Celeste also placed Ames aboard the *Sea Bird* the morning Helene was killed. Without her testimony, all your other evidence against him is circumstantial."

"So?"

Helene Camden's lawyer continued. "So Celeste's death is, to say the least, very providential for Ames." Ferris' wry smile appeared again. "Think it over, Sheriff. Ames admits the knife is his. He says he kept it in an unlocked tackle box aboard his own boat, I presume. That fact alone, coupled with Mrs. Ames's fantastic story about diving for a cup and having been struck on the head by a mysterious someone who tried to murder her by rolling her into the pass, would lead me to believe that just possibly Mrs. Ames knows more about this than has been brought out so far."

"I see what you mean," White said.

"Now wait a minute," Ames said. "Don't try to involve Mary Lou in this."

Ferris was smug about it, "I don't think much effort is necessary. A knife is a woman's weapon, Mrs. Ames had access to your knife. She knew Celeste's testimony would send you to the chair." Ferris' voice turned cold. "So Mrs. Ames waylaid Celeste and stabbed her, then she invented this mythical someone who she claims attempted to kill her in the hope the local law would assume the same party killed Celeste."

White tugged at his long mustaches. "Now, that's a right interestin' theory, Counsellor." He turned his faded blue eyes on Mary Lou. "Women in love are hell. They do the damnedest things, also some mighty dumb ones."

Mary Lou pressed against Ames. Her eyes were frightened. "No. Don't believe him, Sheriff White. Someone did try to drown me. A woman. And I didn't kill Celeste. I couldn't. I couldn't kill anyone."

"That's your story," Camden said.

Ferris continued coldly. "Celeste is dead. If the knife hadn't hung up in the rope, she'd be out in the pass by now, possibly following the same path Helene's body took, possibly washed out into the Gulf where it would never have been discovered and the only actual witness against Ames would have mysteriously disappeared."

"It sounds to me," Camden said.

Mary Lou pressed even harder against Ames "No!"

Ames wished he could comfort her.

Celeste wasn't the only one who'd been stabbed. Someone had a knife in him, in Mary Lou and now they were beginning to twist the blade.

Ferris? Camden? Why?

He knew Mary Lou hadn't killed Celeste. It would never occur to her. She was incapable of the physical act. Still, if Sheriff White followed Mr. Ferris' line of reasoning, only one thing could happen. White would arrest Mary Lou on suspicion of murder. A coroner's jury would find that the maid had come to her death at Mary Lou's hands and would recommend she be held and tried for murder.

The sun was high now and hot. Sweat beaded on Ames's face. He couldn't allow that to happen. Not to Mary Lou. He wished he was smarter than he was. He wished his head would stop aching. His awakening in the cabin of the *Sea Bird* seemed a thousand years ago. Ames felt as if he'd been swimming through slime and seaweed ever since, and now, at the end of his swim, he was being forced to climb a glass wall.

Ames studied the faces of the two men. Ferris, he decided, was just being a lawyer. He was just shooting off his mouth showing how smart he was. But Camden's utter lack of emotion was too casual. The widowed cosmetic executive was too unconcerned.

Ninety-three thousand dollars was a lot of money. Celeste had been a very beautiful girl. So Camden had been in Baltimore when his wife had died. He had been on the scene of the crime when Celeste had been stabbed. He said he'd found her body. Ames wished he could talk to Camden alone in a locked room for five minutes. So his wrists were manacled, he'd use his feet.

Without moving his head, the former trumpet player looked from Camden to the foot of the pier where Deputy Sayers' gun was still sandwiched in between Sayers' undershirt and uniform trousers.

Twin drops of sweat escaped the pits of Ames's arms and zig-zagged down his sides. His tired mind raced on. Ferris was right about White. The elderly sheriff was strictly small-town. White would follow the path of least resistance: If he and Mary Lou were both locked up, neither could help the other. The little money they had wouldn't hire two lawyers.

Ames's pulse beat a little faster. On the other hand, if he could get his hands on Sayers' gun and make a break, perhaps come back later and talk to Camden, it might be worth the gamble.

What had he to lose? Neither he nor Mary Lou had a chance as things were.

CHAPTER ELEVEN

The rising sun grew hotter. The sweet-sour smell of the tide flats lessened as the incoming tide began to lap at the sloped sides of the bay. The crowd of mixed locals and tourists moved in closer until they formed a tight little semi-circle around the group on the shore. The fat woman in tight shorts explained to a newcomer:

"They think the girl in the bathing suit done it. It was her husband who killed the Camden woman, see? And the maid was a witness against him."

"Kin you 'magine," the newcomer said. "Who's the young man in his shorts, the one sitting in the row boat?"

The fat woman was proud of her knowledge. "He's the deputy sheriff who dove for the knife. When they moved her it fell out, see?"

Phillips brought a sheet from the house and covered Celeste with it.

Sweat blurred Ames's eyes. He saw Shep Roberts and Ben Sheldon in the crowd. The fat man nodded. Roberts merely looked at him.

Sheriff White rolled his dead cigar between his lips. He sounded unhappy about it. "You make sense, Counsellor," he admitted. "Of course, there's the five thousand dollars we found under the mattress on Ames's boat. The butler fellow, there, or mebbe it was the maid, said that Mrs. Camden was in the habit of carryin' large sums of money, but lessen you got the serial numbers money is hard to trace. Ames could claim he won it in a crap game or at poker. They's always a game goin' on. The charter boat captains an' fishin' guides an' commercial fishermen would rather gamble than fish." He dropped his dead cigar on the beach and ground it into the sand with his heel. "No. Come t' think of it, without Miss Montigny's testimony we ain't got much of a case against Charlie."

State's Attorney Keely started to say something and changed his mind.

Sheriff White looked at Mary Lou. "What you got t' say, Mary Lou?"

Mary Lou's eyes narrowed. "Don't you look at me that way."

"You didn't stab her?"

"No. I never even spoke to the girl."

Camden repeated what he'd said before. "That's your story."

White turned to Gilmore. "You call in like I asked you, John?"

Gilmore nodded. "I did. Cody said he'd send out a car and some boys. They should be here any minute."

Ames took a step toward the pier then two more steps.

Camden came out of his alcoholic lethargy. "Watch him," he said sharply. "Ames is trying to sneak away."

The wash of the tide had carried the rowboat in which Sayers was sitting about ten feet closer to the pier than it had been when Ferris had taken the body from Sayers. The youthful deputy stood up and walked through the ankle deep water. "Hey. Nix, fellow," he called. "Don't give us no trouble." Ames quickened his pace, the crowd giving way before him.

Ames was passing Shep Roberts now. Gilmore called, "Stop him, Shep."

"Stop him, yourse'f," Shep said.

There was a note of alarm in White's voice. "Get him, Ken," he called. "Quick. The damn fool is after your gun."

The deputy splashed through the shallow water at an angle and came out on the hard sand of the beach between Ames and his objective. "Hold it right where you are, Ames," he cautioned. "Blowing your top ain't goin' to do you a bit of good."

The deputy attempted to grip one of Ames's manacled arms. Ames twisted sideways and brought up his arms. The chain that joined his wrists caught the deputy under the chin and snapped his head back.

Sayers staggered and sat down. Ames slipped the gun out from between its sandwich of clothes and held the butt with both hands. His manacled hands were so wet with sweat the heavy gun almost slipped from his fingers.

It was an effort for him to speak. "Let's stop right where we are," he panted.

The tight little knot of men hurrying after him stopped as if they were rooted to the sand. The fat woman began to scream. Sheriff White said, "You're makin' a big mistake, Charlie."

"I'll chance that," Ames said. "Give Mary Lou the key to these things."

"And effen I don't?"

Ames was frank with him. "I don't know," he admitted. "I don't know what I'll do." Sweat trickled down his face. "But I wouldn't chance it if I were you, White. I didn't kill the Camden woman. Mary Lou didn't kill Celeste." His throat was sore with the effort of speaking. "I've taken all I can. I just can't take any more."

From a safe distance, Ferris asked, "Are you going to let him get away with this?"

"He won't get far," White said. "Remember? We're out on the beach. If he does get away, all we have to do is block the causeways." He looked back at Ames. "Better lay that gun down, Charlie."

Ames shook his head. "No. Give Mary Lou the key."

White took the key to the handcuffs from his vest pocket and gave it to Mary Lou. "You'd best talk to him," he told her.

Mary Lou took the key with fingers that shook so badly she almost dropped it in the sand and walked over to her husband. "You shouldn't have, Charlie," she said. "We haven't done anything wrong."

"That's the idea." Ames said. "Stand to one side of me and see if you can get these things off." He added, "Please. Believe me. I know what I'm doing."

Mary Lou did as she was told. She got the key in the lock of the left cuff and unlocked it.

Ames allowed the cuff to swing free. "That will do, for now. Put the key in my pocket and head for Sheriff White's car."

Sayers was back on his feet. His eyes on the gun in Ames's hand, he walked a few steps through the sand toward the man backing away from him. "You'll never make it, Ames. You'll have to shoot me first."

Ames continued to back toward the big blue and white police car. "I'd put on my trousers if I were you. Your underpants are showing."

Sayers bunched his muscles. "I think you're bluffing," he said. He took three quick steps forward and fell on his face in the sand as Shep Roberts thrust out his foot.

The grizzled charter boat captain was apologetic. "Oh. Excuse me."

Sayers sat on the sand and cursed.

"That's a goin' to cost you time, Shep," White said.

"I've done a lot of time," the charter boat captain said meekly. He continued apologetic. "Hit gives me time to catch up on my settin'."

A small laugh rippled through the crowd.

Red-faced with anger now, Camden said, "This is ridiculous. You may be afraid to stop him but I'm not. He killed my wife. His wife killed Celeste."

He took half a dozen quick steps toward Ames, the skirt of his robe flapping in the wind. Ames fired a shot into the sand at his feet and the cosmetic executive stopped as if he'd run into a wall. The blood drained slowly from his face leaving it fish-belly white.

"Then, on the other hand," Shep said.

The crowd laughed again, louder now.

It was a twenty minute run from Palmetto City to the beaches. Ames could hear a siren far away as the car for which Gilmore had called sped toward the scene. Ames opened the door of the cruiser.

"Get in," he told Mary Lou.

"I'm going with you?"

"For apiece," Ames said.

Mary Lou got into the car.

Ames slipped in back of the wheel, resting the barrel of the gun on the rolled down window while he felt for the ignition switch.

Still sitting on the sand, Sayers jeered. "Ya, ya, ya. Go ahead and start it, fellow. The keys are in my trousers."

The disappointment was too great. Ames thought he was going to faint.

"Better call it off, Charlie," White said. "The other boys will be here in a minute. Lay the gun on the seat and come out with your hands up."

Ames sat a moment, sweat dripping down his face.

Her voice small, Mary Lou asked, "What are you going to do, Charlie?"

"Make a run for it," Ames said. "We haven't got a chance this way. White's as dumb as Ferris thinks he is. Is the suitcase on the back seat?"

"Yes."

"Is the money Ben gave you for the *Sally* still in it?"

"Yes."

"Open it and get me two hundred dollars. No. Better make it three."

Mary Lou knelt on the seat and opened the case. "Why don't you take it all?"

Ames spoke without turning his head. "No. Three hundred will be plenty."

Mary Lou peeled some bills from the flat roll.

"Stuff them in my pocket," Ames said. "Use the rest for a lawyer. Do like I told you before. They'll have to let you make a phone call. Call Judge Barker. Ask him to recommend a lawyer."

Mary Lou began to cry. "I wish you wouldn't do this, Charlie."

"I wish I didn't have to."

"They'll hunt you down. They'll shoot."

Ames opened the door on his side. "That's a chance I'll have to take." The germ of an idea began to gnaw at his mind. "About that business on the pier. I mean you being slugged. Are you sure it was a woman?"

"No."

"Could it have been a man wearing woman's clothes? Could that have been what gave you the impression it was a woman?"

"It could have been."

Ames wanted to kiss her good-bye. He'd never wanted anything so badly. It might be the last chance he'd ever get, but he didn't dare to turn his head. Sheriff White's right hand was in his capacious coat pocket now. The chances were he had a gun in that pocket.

Ames stepped from the car to the drive. The wail of the oncoming siren was louder now. A hundred feet away, on the beach road, a steady stream of morning traffic was flowing south toward the causeway that led into Palmetto City and north toward the causeway that led to Seminole Rocks.

"Good-bye, honey," he said.

"Please, Charlie," Mary Lou sobbed.

Ames backed away from the car and down the drive, stiff-kneed. The tight little knot of men who'd been held at a distance by the gun quickly surrounded the car. Sheriff White leaned against the front fender. His voice continued gentle, like a father reproving a headstrong son.

"You're bein' very foolish, Charlie."

Ames continued to back to the road. "I didn't kill Helene Camden. And Mary Lou didn't kill Celeste."

"Let the law prove it."

"The hell with the law," Ames said.

He turned and ran for the road. As he did, there was the sound of a shot behind him. A small geyser of shell erupted, as a bullet dug a hole in the drive a half-inch from his left foot.

"That's once," Sheriff White called.

Still running, Ames glanced back over his shoulder. His left arm extended as if for balance, his right arm cocked, White was holding a short-barrel revolver with its muzzle pointed to the sky. Ames started to shoot back and couldn't. He didn't have anything against White. Instead of shooting, he cut across the lawn to gain the dubious protection of a Phoenix palm.

A second shot severed a palm frond so close to his right ear that

Ames could hear the whistle of the bullet as it passed him.

"That's twice," White said.

"Please, Charlie," Mary Lou shouted. Her voice was hysterical with fear for him.

Ames wiped the sweat from his eyes with his left hand and ran for the road. Several drivers, intrigued by the sound of shots, had stopped their cars. Ames wrenched open the door of a Buick Roadmaster driven by a gum-chewing youth.

"What gives, pal?" the youth began. Then he saw the gun and the dangling handcuff and stopped chomping on his gum. "Now wait a minute, fellow."

Ames thrust the muzzle of the gun against the youth's side. "I haven't time," he panted. "Get me out of here. Fast."

The boy looked at the gun and depressed the accelerator of the car. The big machine leaped forward and around the car in front of it. "You have the gun," he said.

Ames doubted that White would fire a third time. He would be afraid of endangering the driver. There was no third shot.

The wail of the siren grew fainter. The youth drove well and fast, weaving in and out of traffic. They passed the new realty development on Frenchman's Creek then the road to the Seminole causeway. Beyond that point there were few cars on the road. The bay side was heavily fringed with mangrove. There were a few cabbage palms and sea grape on the Gulf side. Between them, with the exception of an occasional small house, there was nothing from the bay to the Gulf but the road and a vast expanse of sand and sea oats.

The young driver began to work on his gum again.

"What they want you for, fellow?"

Ames told him. "Murder."

The youth swallowed and was silent.

Ames added, "But you've no reason to be afraid. All I want from you is the ride." He fished a package of cigarettes from his pocket and used the lighter on the dash.

The driver glanced at him sideways. "I make you now. Your picture was in the morning paper. You're the charter boat captain who killed that rich broad."

"So they say," Ames said.

The phrase reminded him of Camden. He wanted a talk with Camden. He meant to have one as soon as it was dark, if he wasn't interrupted first. Ames wiped his face with the sleeve of his coat. Meanwhile, there was the day to pass. He'd have to hole up somewhere. He couldn't run the roads. The road he was on dead-ended. The causeways were blocked by now. He was stuck on the narrow spit of land that extended eighteen miles from Palmetto Point to Cat Cay Pass with the Gulf of Mexico on one side and Boca Grande Bay on the other.

"I suppose," the youth said, "you know this road dead-ends in about five miles."

"Yes. I know," Ames said.

He found the key Mary Lou had dropped in his pocket and unlocked the handcuff on his right wrist.

The youth hesitated, asked, "That true what it said in the paper about you?"

"What did it say?"

"That you used to play trumpet in Honey Boy Evans' band."

Ames rode, fighting waves of fatigue. *That was long time ago*, he thought. *A thousand years ago*. "Yeah," he said aloud. "I was with Evans for three years. Why?"

"I beat skins for Maxie Ambler," the youth said. "We just finished eight weeks at the Jockey Club in Miami. Now we're laying off one, then opening at the Sky Room in Tampa. That's how come I'm over here. Me and the canary are shacked up on the beach. So help me. She'll never believe me. I just came out for a bottle of cream."

Ames wasn't really interested.

The youthful drummer asked, "What happened to you? I mean this charter boat business."

"I lost my lip," Ames said. "A geek tried to beat it in with the butt of a rifle on Iwo. And I guess he did a pretty good job. Oh, I can still blow a horn, but I can't cut the hot stuff."

"A shame," the youth sympathized. "You must have been pretty good if you played with Honey Boy."

"I got by," Ames said.

He rode, eyeing the fringe of mangrove and the tops of the tall trees rising out of the bay behind it. It could be he could hide out on Pine Key if he could reach it. He knew the island like he knew the deck of the *Sally*. He doubted if White would search the upper bay, at least immediately. The sheriff would concentrate on the causeways, then comb the beach foot by foot.

Ames said, "Stop right there where you see that clump of sea grape, will you, please?"

The driver braked in front of the clump of sea grape. "Know something, fellow?"

"What?"

"You're a hell of a killer."

Ames followed the younger man's eyes. When he had unlocked the handcuff, he'd laid Sayers' gun on the seat between them. It was still lying on the seat. "Yeah. I guess I am," Ames admitted.

"That and saying please."

Ames made certain no other cars were in sight then got out and stood on the shoulder of the road. "Anyway, thanks. Thanks a lot, Skins."

"Think nothing of it," the youth said.

He maneuvered the car in a sharp U-turn and drove back the way they had come. Standing in the shelter of a clump of sea grape, Ames watched the big car out of sight. His choice of a car to commandeer had been the only break he'd gotten since he'd awakened in the cabin of the *Sea Bird*.

He doubted if the youthful drummer would go to the law. In the first place, most musicians were basically good guys. In the second place, by his own admission, the drummer was shacked up with the band's canary and neither of them would want any publicity.

Ames tried to light another cigarette and couldn't. Reaction had set in. His hands were shaking so badly he couldn't bring the lighted match to the tip of his cigarette. He let the match wave itself out. Then when the trembling had subsided, he waded the field of chest high sea oats to the fringe of dark green mangrove rising out of the shore of the bay.

Breathing became less of an effort. For the time being he was safe. More important, he was in a much better position to help Mary Lou than he would be in a cell in Sweetwater jail.

CHAPTER TWELVE

Ames parted the mangrove and looked out over the water. The upper bay was twelve miles wide at this point, but the tall trees of Pine Key were less than half a mile from shore. A flock of great white heron were feeding in the shallows. Three hundred yards down the bay toward the Seminole Rocks causeway, a fisherman in a rowboat was fishing the trout flats off Mermaid Point.

Even at high tide, except for the swash channel and possibly a few pot holes, the deepest water between him and the island would be only chest high. He could walk most of the way. Ames undressed slowly and laid his rolled clothes on a tangle of aerial roots. The silence was complete and drugged with heat. He tried again to light a cigarette and succeeded. He stood ankle deep in the water, smoking, letting the sun beat on his bare body, absorbing the silence. The heat of the sun felt good. Some of his tension left him. He realized he hadn't eaten for hours, but he wasn't hungry. He'd been under too much of a strain, he was still under too much of a strain for food to be important.

Now that the drug had worn off and he was no longer jumping at shadows, he was satisfied in his own mind that he hadn't killed the Camden woman. He hadn't done anything to Helene Camden but give her a cup of coffee. More, despite the derogatory remarks her husband had made about her morals and the fact that her maid had testified that Mrs. Camden had confided in her that she intended to spend the night with a handsome young charter boat captain, Mrs. Camden had been a lady. She hadn't made one improper suggestion or said one improper thing. All she had wanted to know was how much he would charge to skipper the *Sea Bird* down to the Keys and up the east coast inland waterway to Baltimore.

More, this thing had been planned for some time. The coffee itself had been drugged before he put out for bait. It had to be. He'd made the coffee himself and there had been no one aboard the *Sally* but himself and Mrs. Camden.

Now she was dead and he was accused of murder. It failed to make sense from any angle from which Ames viewed it. If someone had killed Helene Camden for gain, why had they put five thousand dollars in the hip pocket of his dungarees? And if it had been Celeste who had slugged Mary Lou and rolled her in the pass, why had Celeste been murdered? By whom?

Ames's head began to ache again. He knew a moment of sadness when he thought of the *Sally*. It had been a good boat. It had earned their bread and butter and an occasional sirloin steak. He and Mary Lou had had a lot of good times aboard her. Now the *Sally* belonged to Ben Sheldon. Ben had bought her for fifteen hundred dollars, five hundred dollars less than Ben had offered him.

Ames wondered about Sheldon. Despite his age and fat, the ship chandler was a ladies' man. He had been married four or five times. He always had some girl on his string, the girl usually young and married. Still, Ben wasn't particular. The fat man played the field and, alive, Helene Camden had been pretty in a brittle blonde sort of a way.

Ben had access to the *Sally*. He could have drugged the coffee and rowed or carried Ames to the *Sea Bird*. Ben could have killed Helene Camden. But if they were telling the truth about Mrs. Camden, she wouldn't attempt to defend a non-existent virtue to the point of losing her life. Nor would Ben leave five thousand dollars in anyone's pants pocket. It was a toss-up which Ben loved most, the opposite sex or money.

Ames reached for his clothes and stood with his right hand raised as a thick-bodied snake slithered along the dry roots and showed Ames the cotton in its mouth. Ames eyed the snake thoughtfully.

"Your great grandpappy caused a lot of trouble, fellow," he told it. Then picking up the bundle of clothes, he cocked his white cap on the back of his head and waded out into the water.

The herons, standing on one leg, put their other legs down and flapping their great wings, moved on to less crowded fishing waters.

Ames waded thigh deep watching the man in the boat off Mermaid Point. The fisherman was casting the other way. Even if he should turn, Ames doubted that the man could see him. He was three hundred yards away. The sun would be in his eyes. Regardless, he would have to chance it.

Twice he stepped into pot holes. The first time he saved his clothes from getting wet by holding them over his head with one hand, while he swam with the other. The second time they got wet. After that, Ames carried the roll under his arm. There would be plenty of time for them to dry after he reached Pine Key. Night was hours away.

He came to the swash channel and swam it.

At one time, before netting in the bay had become illegal, a netting outfit had based their operations on the island. There were still a half-dozen weathered cypress drying racks, with shreds of rotted net still clinging to them, rising from the shore. There was still a palm-thatched cabin of sorts. Ames put on his shoes and his shorts and walked past the crumbling cabin into the shade of the tall trees that had given the island its name.

There was little underbrush. Pine needles crackled under his shoes. Squirrels scolded in the trees. Birds cheeped and twittered.

Ames knew a feeling of peace. He would be safe on the island until nightfall. A wry smile twisted his lips. He would be safe unless Skins had gone to the law, unless the fisherman or someone else had seen him across the half-mile of water.

He located a cluster of small trees growing in a circular formation that formed a natural shelter. From this vantage point he could still see the bay and he spread his clothes on the ground to dry.

There were three cigarettes left in his package. He opened it to dry in the sun then sat with his back against a tree, watching the distant causeway through his green screen of pine needles. The causeway was so distant that the cars crossing it looked like toys. Beyond the causeway was the lower bay and pass and bridge and basin. He'd come a long way in his commandeered car. It was a long way back. He returned his attention to the fisherman. The man was still casting and obviously having good luck. Ames envied him.

The sun was warm on his bare body. He closed his eyes and tried to think. There had to be some solution. Neither he nor Mary Lou had killed anyone. Somebody was throwing off on them.

Ames started back at the beginning. Mary Lou had been singing at the club. He'd just come in from catching his bait. He'd put a pot of coffee on to boil. Mrs. Camden had hailed him from the pier.

Ahoy, the Sally, she'd called.

Ames's chin lowered until it rested on his chest. His clenched fingers relaxed. The sun beat on his bronzed face, unfelt. His head rolled on the trunk of the tree against which he was sitting. His white cap fell off, unnoticed. His chest rose and fell with his breathing. Drugged with fatigue, he slept....

It was dark. He was cold. A particularly vicious mosquito was boring into his thigh. Ames lifted a hand to swat it and sat with his hand raised as a powerful white light swept over the tops of the small trees under which he was sitting and an unfamiliar voice forced its way into his sleep-sodden mind.

"Now he tells us," the voice said.

Ames's neck was stiff. His back felt as if it were broken. He was cold and at the same time his whole body was on fire. He put his raised hand on the small of his back and sat erect. Full consciousness returned slowly.

He could hear the throb of a marine motor. The white light swept the trees again. A second voice said: "For my money, the old Joe is nuts. Ames is out of the country by now. He wouldn't be chump enough to stick around and he had plenty of time to get across the Seminole Rocks Causeway before the boys could block it."

"Funny none of the boys have located that Buick."

"Yeah," the first speaker said. "It is. You'd think the guy would come forward. Just one of those breaks, I guess. It must have been one of the boys on the waterfront. Those damn fishing guides are all outlaws at heart."

Still another man laughed. "Oh, it's not that bad. They were just born too late."

Ames began to gather up his clothes, pausing from time to time to rub his bare flesh with his calloused palms. His body was aflame with bites. The mosquitoes and the sand flies had probably been working on him since dusk. He put on his pants and shirt and coat and looked through his screen of needles. He could see the running lights of a launch and the vague silhouette of four or five uniformed figures.

"Is there an anchorage here?" one of the officers asked.

"I doubt it," another one answered. "We're going to have to wade ashore. I tell you what, Sam. Pull on for another hundred yards or so. As I recall, there are some old drying racks and a cabin on the west shore. And that's where old Joe said he saw someone in a white cap wade ashore."

Ames felt for his cap and found it. Of course. He'd been too tired to think straight. The fisherman had seen his cap. White was visible for a long distance.

There was a throb of power as the launch moved on but the officers' voices were still plainly audible.

"The damn hog," one of them said. "He must have had fifty trout on that string, all of them two pounds or better. Then he had to eat supper before he read his paper."

Ames got to his feet. The fisherman had seen him but hadn't put into shore until late afternoon or early evening. When he'd read of the break in the evening paper he'd called the sheriff's office and reported he'd seen a man wade ashore on Pine Key, a man wearing a white captain's cap. Ames realized that he'd automatically put his cap on his head. He took it off and put it under his coat. He didn't want to leave it on the key. It would be proof that he had been here, that he was still in the vicinity.

The officers' voices were fainter now. "This will do, Sam," the deputy in charge said. "You other guys make sure your lights are working and the four of us will fan out and comb the island while Sam circles it to keep Ames from taking to the water. But watch out for snakes. And keep your guns in your hands and your lights away from your bodies. If the bastard is on the island, remember, he has Ken's gun."

There was a splashing in the water then a crackling of pine needles. Smaller white lights began to stab through the trees. Sleepy squirrels began to scold and birds to cheep and flutter. Ames was glad for the small noise they made. He parted his screen of needles and walked down to the shore.

The first of the stars were beginning to appear but the moon had still to rise. The night felt like hot black velvet. Pine Key was fair sized. It would take the police launch at least five minutes to circle it. He could see the white spotlight probing through the trees on the far side of the island. When the launch passed him again, the light would pin him against the shore like a butterfly on a collector's board, unless he was on its far side.

He waded out into the water, taking great care not to splash but unable to do anything about the phosphorescent ripples caused by his moving legs. The water came to his knees then his thighs. He waded on until it was chest deep, wondering why he wasn't frightened. He wasn't. Man, he decided, acclimated quickly. He felt perfectly cool, as though he'd been hunted and running for years.

The launch was nosing around the far end of the island now. He could see the running lights on the prow showing green to starboard and red to port. A wry smile twisting his lips, he quoted from maritime regulations: "From right ahead to two points abaft the beam on their respective sides, to be visible at least one mile." But maritime regulations said nothing about the powerful spotlight that was mounted on a swivel. And now the officer in the launch was wising up. He was sweeping the water to starboard as well as port.

Ames wished he could do something about his cap. He ducked under water, filled the cap with a scoop of sand and left it on the bottom. When he broke water again, the launch was less than fifty yards away. He crouched as low as he could, with only his face visible, ready to duck with the sweep of light.

Before it was necessary a gun yammered on shore and the deputy in the launch tried to spotlight the sound.

"You get him?" he called.

"Hell, no," the deputy who'd fired answered. His voice was shaky. "But I got a goddamn diamondback that must be six feet long. He was coiled back of a log and I almost stepped on him."

"You wanted the job," the deputy in charge said. "Wait until you're sheriff. Then you can sit on your can and let someone else do the dirty work."

"I should live so long."

"You won't if you step on a six foot diamondback. Watch it, the rest of you guys."

The launch was past Ames now, its powerful light sweeping the drying racks and the cabin. He waded a few more steps and began to swim. The gun in the pocket of his coat felt like it weighed ten pounds. The coat bound his arms but he was afraid to stop and take it off. The next time the launch came around the island, he wanted to be out of range of the spotlight. Next time there would be no diversion.

He lifted his head in the water and located the Seminole Rocks Causeway lights. They were a good five miles distant. The basin was nine miles beyond the causeway. Ames decided he would swim a few hundred yards more then cut in toward Mermaid Point. There was a small bait camp around the bend. Most bait camps left their boats unattended after seven o'clock. Possibly he could borrow a rowboat. He would be safer on the water than on the beach.

His sneakers were weighing him down. He tried to unlace them and couldn't. He'd knotted the wet laces too tightly. More, he was in swash channel now. He could tell by the feel of the water. It was deep. There was a current and the current was working against him.

Ames realized his breathing was labored. He turned on his back and tried to float. The effort was only partially successful. His weighted feet wouldn't stay up. His wet coat and the gun dragged him down. He turned in the water and swam on doggedly, trying to cross the channel so he could wade ashore. He hoped he was swimming in the right direction. There was no light on the point and he was too low in the water to see the distant lights on the causeway.

His breathing became more labored. His chest began to hurt. It was an effort to move his arms, to kick. He lowered his feet and tried to touch bottom. He couldn't. The water was still seven or eight feet deep. Attempting to navigate the bay at night was an entirely different matter from during the day. In the daytime you could tell the depth of the water by its color.

He changed from a crawl to a side stroke and there was a muffled but steady throb in his submerged ear. It sounded like an underwater exhaust and the slow turning of an idling screw.

Ames knew panic. The deputy in the police launch must have seen him. He stopped swimming and raised his head. The unlighted stern of a cruiser rose out of the water less than ten feet away. Ames tried to read the name of the boat and couldn't. It was too dark.

"That you, Charlie?" Shep Roberts called softly.

Ames swam toward the side of the cruiser and a muscled arm reached over the side to help him scramble aboard. Ames stood wet and dripping in the cockpit of the *Falcon*.

"What you doin' here, Shep?" he panted.

"A-lookin' for you," Roberts whispered. "I heered that Bob White's boys were a goin' t' search Pine Key, so I thought I'd kinda mosey down this way in case you were on it."

Ames leaned against the live bait well, still fighting for breath as the grizzled charter boat captain, running without lights, eased the cruiser slowly up the swash channel toward the deep channel leading under the bridge of the Seminole Rocks Causeway. All Ames could think of to say was, "I thought they were going to jail you."

He could feel Roberts grin in the dark. "They did." He seemed proud of the fact. "Leastwise they took me in an' Gilmore fined me twenty-five dollars for obstructin' an officer in the performance of his duty." He pressed a pint bottle into Ames's hand. "Here. Take a shot of this. It'll be good fo' what ails you."

Ames uncapped the bottle but didn't drink. "I didn't kill her, Shep. And Mary Lou didn't kill that French girl."

"Hell!" Roberts said. "I know that. I wouldn't be here ef I thought you had." He deliberated a moment. "Mebbe I would. They's a lot of women that need killin'."

CHAPTER THIRTEEN

The waiting, the long hours of waiting, was hardest. All she could do was dream. Mexico City and a dark-eyed virile young caballero. Rio de Janeiro. Cairo. Cannes. The world was wide. It was also her oyster, complete with pearl. Now all her troubles were over. She would never have to worry about income or keeping up a front again. True, there was one male fly in the ointment. But once the fly had served its purpose, it, too, could be disposed of.

The night wind cool on her cheeks, the waiting woman lifted her head and listened to a police siren wail its way down the beach road. Muted by distance, the siren sounded like a disappointed hound baying after an elusive fox. That's what the police were—hounds. Stupid hounds moving in a circle, chasing their own wagging tails.

If only they would capture Charlie Ames. The young charter boat captain was far from dumb. So was his snip of a wife. With her trained musician's ear, she'd detected the one false note in the score. Neither Ames nor his wife knew a thing, still they knew too much. And a little knowledge sometimes was a dangerous thing. So was the love of a man for his wife.

The waiting woman paced the floor of the unlighted room. The most important thing right now was to turn Helene Camden's tangible and intangible assets into cash. The thought amused her. She laughed. The fly could be depended on for that. The fool. He thought she loved him.

Meanwhile, it was nice to dream....

Still running without lights, Shep Roberts swung in toward shore and held the *Falcon* alongside the last of the unlighted row of commercial fishing boats extending out from the Rupert Fish House pier.

"You sure you know what you're doing, Charlie?"

"No," Ames admitted. "I'm not. But Camden knows more than he's telling. He has to. He's been too unconcerned, too smug about the entire affair."

He started to pick a cigarette from the package Shep had given him and returned the package to his pocket. Sheriff White might or might not have a stake-out on the Camden house, but he was almost certain to have left one on the *Sally*. And the *Sally* was less than a hundred yards away.

"Well, it's your neck," Roberts whispered.

"Yeah. It's my neck." Ames's wet suit and shirt and shorts and sneakers felt cold and clammy. He wished he had a change of clothes. He wished this whole thing hadn't happened. He wished, instead of having to confront Camden, that he was just coming in with his bait, that he could put on a pot of coffee and sit down to wait for Mary Lou to get through singing at the Beach Club.

"You're sure Mary Lou is still in Palmetto City, that they haven't taken her up to Sweetwater?"

Roberts shook his head. "No. I ain't sure. But she was, the last time I heard. Up to six this evenin' they hadn't even held the inquest on the maid. Your bustin' away fixed that. White swears he's agoin' t' git you effen he has t' comb the whole county inch by inch."

"He may at that," Ames said.

He was sorry he'd taken the two drinks he had. He hadn't eaten for so long he couldn't remember the last time. The two drinks had hit him hard. He could feel the whiskey roaring in his head and he wanted his head to be clear.

"You wouldn't have any coffee, would you, Shep?"

"I got some cold in the pot. You want me to heat it up?"

"No. Cold will do."

Shep disappeared into the cabin of the cruiser and reappeared with a mug of cold coffee. Ames drank it, studying the shore line. Lights showed in the back doors of Harry's Bar and Murphy's Pharmacy, in the Fisherman's Lunch, in The Spot. There was a light in Ben Sheldon's office. The fish house was dark. He couldn't tell if the Camden house was lighted. He thought it was. He thought he could see a dim light through the trees.

Ames drained the cold coffee in the mug and handed the mug back to Roberts. "Well, thanks. Thanks a lot for everything, Shep."

"Forget it."

Ames climbed up on the rail and stood with one foot on the rail of the *Falcon* and the other foot on the rail of the last commercial fishing boat in the line. "You'd better get back to your berth. They'll throw the book at you, Shep, if they find out you helped me."

"Let 'em," the aging guide whispered. "I'll read it whilst I'm a-settin'. I've always wanted t' read a book." He restated his position. "No. Like I tol' Mary Lou in Harry's. I've known you man and boy, Charlie. You got disappointed in what you wanted to do for a livin'. You could 'a' let it make you bitter or uppity like some folks I could name. But you didn't. You settled down t' cut bait or fish. You've been jest one of the boys. An' like I tol' Mary Lou last night, you might cut a man t' death. You might steal five thousand dollars. Hell. Who wouldn't? You might even shoot a woman. But you wouldn't rate Mary Lou so low as t' be found daid in baid with a bag like that Camden woman."

Ames squeezed his shoulder. "Thanks, Shep."

Roberts called after him softly, "I'll be right here effen you want to come back the same way."

The Rupert outfit was a large concern. Most of the fleet was in. There were fourteen boats of varying sizes nosed to the long wooden pier. Ames considered climbing up on the pier. It was unlighted. He could make much better time on the pier than he could by scrambling from boat to boat. On the other hand, if there was a stake-out in the cockpit of the *Sally*, he would take a chance on being seen. A moving man would be dimly visible against the sky line. He rejected the idea. It didn't matter how long it took him to reach shore. He wasn't going anywhere.

Some of the boats were rubbing fenders. There were wide gaps of deep water between others and Ames had to haul on their creaking mooring lines until his wet clothes lost their clammy feeling and became drenched with sweat. His long sleep had rested him. The coffee had helped tone down the whiskey. He felt fine physically.

If only he could beat or frighten the truth out of Camden!

So Celeste was dead. So Camden hadn't been having an affair with her. There had to be some other woman involved. It had been a woman who had tried to kill Mary Lou. At least, that was Mary Lou's impression. Now that he'd had some rest, Ames was able to think clearly. He could see things in their proper proportions.

Upon his awakening the cabin of the *Sea Bird* had showed all the touches of a woman's fine hand: the beaten up bunk he had occupied; the strapless gown lying in a crumpled heap on top of the un-rumpled spread on the opposite bunk; the hose turned inside out; the sheer scanties lying beside the dress; the empty whiskey bottle rolling between the bunks; the smears of lipstick intimately and personally applied.

The stage setting had almost convinced him he'd been untrue to Mary Lou. It would convince any man. Only a woman could have staged the scene, a woman who had been a participant in many similar scenes. In other words, a bitch.

Ames hauled the boat in which he was standing close to the next one nearer shore and scrambled over the rails.

His mind raced on. Camden was a ladies' man. The Florida beaches swarmed with his type every season—young, good-looking men who had married older women with money. Young men who drooled over the contents of the bobby-soxers' bikini bathing suits while they danced studied attention on their own sagging meal tickets.

Only Camden had tired of his bargain. If he lived with the blonde career woman for another thirty years, all he would get under the terms of their pre-marital agreement was twenty-five thousand dollars, his wife's ring and the Florida communal property, the whole amounting to ninety-three thousand dollars.

Ames added an item he hadn't taken into consideration before. There was the *Sea Bird*. The *Sea Bird* was registered out of Tampa. That added to the list of things Camden would inherit. Even at a forced sale, the forty-eight foot, Diesel-powered, all mahogany luxury cruiser would bring twenty or twenty-five thousand dollars. That built the total of what Camden stood to gain to one hundred and thirteen thousand dollars.

The corners of Ames's mouth turned down. One hundred and thirteen thousand dollars minus the five thousand that had been stuffed into the hip pocket of his dungarees to make certain that the sacrificial goat would be burned.

Ames wished he could talk to Mary Lou for five minutes. Possibly she'd seen Camden at the Beach Club with some other woman. Sooner or later, all the cheating couples on the beach dropped into the Beach Club for a quick one. It had been one of the reasons why he had objected to her singing there. Ames stopped to pant for breath. There was only one more boat between him and the shore now. He eased himself up on the pier and bear-crawled the rest of the way. He'd been right about the possibility of there being a stake-out on the *Sally*. Sheriff White had left a guard. Ames could see the red glow of a cigarette in the cockpit of the boat he had formerly owned.

Stopped by the wall of the fish house, Ames stood with his back pressed to the unlighted building, his arms outspread, his palms pressed flat to the wood, as he visually reconnoitered the Camden grounds and the intervening piers. As far as he could tell by starlight, there was no one on any of the piers. The Camden house was lighted. He could see the white glow of a lamp throwing a path of light between the smooth boles of the royal palm trees in the yard.

Ames sidled around the corner of the fish house, away from the deputy in the cockpit of the *Sally* and started to jump off the loading platform when he smelled the fragrance of a good cigar. The fat ship chandler saw him at the same time that he saw Sheldon. Sheldon was sitting on the edge of the platform, obviously studying the Camden grounds.

Ames thrust his hand into his right coat pocket. His throat constricted with disappointment.

Sheldon said, "I'll be damned. I thought Bob White's boys had you holed up on Pine Key. The last I heard, some fish hog reported seeing you wade ashore. Anyway, a man in a white cap."

It was an effort for Ames to speak. "What are you doing here, Ben?"

"Studying the *Sea Bird*," the fat man said. "Nice lines in her, huh? I've been wondering what Camden would take for her. If he's pushed for ready cash, as I hear he is, could be I can get her cheap."

Ames gripped the butt of the gun in his pocket. He was interested in only one thing. "Well, what are you waiting for? Why don't you yell for the law?"

Sheldon took the cigar from his mouth. "Why should I? What am I, a cop?" He fished his handkerchief from a capacious side coat pocket and wiped his face and the back of his neck with it. "Believe me, I have enough troubles of my own."

Ames wished he knew what to do. The fat man was a development he hadn't expected. He wished he knew if he could trust Ben. It could be Sheldon was telling the truth. He could be studying the *Sea Bird*. He could be watching the Camden house for some other reason. He could be waiting in the dark of the fish house loading platform for some woman who had no right to meet him.

Sheldon broke the brief silence that followed. "Look, Charlie. I'll make a bargain with you."

"What kind of a bargain?"

"I haven't seen you, you haven't seen me." He returned his cigar to his mouth. "You mind your business, I'll mind mine."

"You won't yell for the law?"

"I answered that one before."

"I can trust you?"

Sheldon spoke around his cigar. "I don't know what else you can do. You're in a bad spot, boy."

Ames realized he was panting. "Yes. A bad spot." He hesitated, asked, "You think I did it, Ben?"

"You mean, kill Mrs. Camden?"

"Yes."

The fat man shook his head. "No."

"You know who did it?"

"I'm studying on it," Sheldon admitted.

Ames stood a moment longer, uncertain just what to do, then he jumped from the loading platform and walked, stiff-kneed, along the edge of the basin. When he reached the next pier he looked back. Ben

Sheldon was still sitting on the platform of the fish house. Ames could see the glowing tip of his cigar.

Ames ducked under the pier and walked on. There was a dry rustling on the sand as a swarm of fiddler crabs scurried out of his way then stood on the rims of their holes waving their pincers at him. He passed two more piers. The next one, with the railing, jutted out from the Camden grounds. At the end of it the *Sea Bird* rose and fell gracefully in the small wash of a passing runabout.

Ames turned and looked back at the dim silhouette of the fish house. If Ben Sheldon was studying the *Sea Bird*, the ship chandler had good eyes.

Ames began to sweat again. He wanted to turn back, but the only way he could go was on. The tide washed higher here. He had to wade through knee deep water to get under the Camden pier. On the far side of the pier, he stood on the lip of the bay and studied the palm studded lawn. There was no sound, no motion, no tell-tale cigarette glow. This was the one place White wouldn't expect him to come.

He crossed the sand where Celeste's body had lain and made his way cautiously across the lawn, moving from shrub to shrub, keeping out of the path of light made by the lamp in the window.

There was a huge red hibiscus bush in one corner of the open patio. Ames stood behind it and looked into the lighted living room. Camden, dressed in gray flannel slacks and a green silk sports shirt, was sprawled in an easy chair. There was a half-filled bottle of whiskey on the end table and, standing beside the bottle of whiskey, the framed picture of a woman.

Ames's pulse beat a little faster. He tried to see the woman's face and couldn't. The glass reflected the lamp light and formed a glare that blotted out her features. He returned his attention to Camden. Camden's too-long hair was combed, he was shaved, but the expression on his face hadn't changed. He was still completely unconcerned. So his wife was dead. So?

Ames left the shelter of the bush and walked around the house. The living room was the only one lighted. He looked in the carport next. Helene Camden's flashy convertible and the Ford station wagon that Phillips had driven to the inquest were gone. It could mean that Ferris and the butler were in town. Ames hoped it did.

He tried the back screen door. The door was unlocked and it opened under his hand. He stood in the dark kitchen a moment, listening. The only sounds he could hear were the faint whirring of an electric clock and the almost as faint purr of traffic on the beach road.

He walked through the kitchen and down a long hall with closed doors on both sides. The hall angled right and opened into a large sunroom that, in turn, opened into the living room.

Ames stood in the doorway a long time before Camden saw him. When he did, the other man got to his feet and stood in front of his chair. It was an effort for him to stand. He had trouble focusing his eyes. He was drunk, much drunker than he looked. He was also very amused.

"Well, whash you know," Camden said, finally. "If it isn't Helene's homicidal boy frien'. So they got you, huh?"

Ames lighted a cigarette, sucked the smoke deep into his lungs and exhaled slowly before he spoke. "Where's Ferris and the butler?"

"Gone into town," Camden said. "T' make arrangements 'bout Helene an' Celeste." His amused smile turned slightly uncertain as his eyes searched the dark sunroom behind Ames. "Where's the police with you? Where's Sheriff White?"

Ames crossed the room and pushed Camden back in his chair. "I'm certain I wouldn't know."

The framed picture was facing the other way. Ames picked it up then set it down again. He'd never been so disappointed.

It was a picture of Helene Camden.

CHAPTER FOURTEEN

Camden tried to get out of the chair into which he'd been pushed. Ames pushed him back.

"Sit still. I want to talk to you."

"Where're the police with you?" Camden repeated.

Ames shook his head. "There aren't any police with me."

Camden licked at his whiskey-puffed lips as he digested the information. "There aren't any police with you? You're all by yourself?"

"That's right."

Camden reached for the bottle on the end table and Ames took it out of his hand. "Uh-uh, you've had enough."

He kicked an ottoman up to the chair and sat facing the other man. "Who's your girl friend, Hal? That is your first name, isn't it?"

Camden continued to try to see past Ames. "Yesh. Thash my name. My name ish Hal."

"All right," Ames said. "I'm waiting."

Camden looked at him stupidly. "For what?"

"The name of your girl friend."

"What girl friend?"

"Oh, for God's sake," Ames said. He slapped Camden's face, hard. "You're not that drunk or are you? Okay. Let's start all over. Who killed Helene?"

"I'm pretty drunk," Camden admitted.

Ames repeated patiently, "Who killed Helene?"

Camden's stolid face brightened. "You did."

Ames slapped him again. "That's a lie!"

Camden felt his face. "You hit me."

"I'll hit you again. With my fist next time. *Who killed Helene?*"

"The hell with you," Camden said. He got to his feet and added with drunken dignity, "You got no right in here. You got no right t' question me. You're nothing but a dirty killer." He took a few uncertain steps away from the chair.

"Where you think you're going?" Ames asked.

Camden answered with drunken determination, "I'm goin' to call the police."

Ames stood up. "Oh, no. Not until I'm through with you. You've put me through hell. You've involved my wife in this thing. Now it's my turn. Who's the other woman?"

"What other woman?"

"The woman who killed Helene and pinned it on me. The woman who tried to kill Mary Lou. The woman who did kill Celeste."

Camden brushed Ames's hand off his arm. "Go away. I don't know what you're talkin' 'bout."

"I'll bet."

Ames realized that his fingers were clenched into fists and that he was breathing through his mouth. He opened his fists and forced himself to breathe normally. He couldn't afford to lose his head now. He had too much at stake and this was his last chance. Unless he could get Camden to talk, he was sunk.

Camden staggered on toward the other side of the living room. Ames walked with him, studying the cosmetic executive's face. The big man wasn't pretending he was drunk. He was drunk. He'd probably been drinking hard ever since his plane had landed at the

Tampa airport. More, he hadn't been too bright to begin with. His utter lack of concern was as much stupidity as it was absence of emotion. Helene Camden hadn't married him for his brains.

Ames remembered something Ben Sheldon had said. When he'd asked Ben what he was doing sitting in the dark, the fat man had told him, *Studying the* Sea Bird. *Nice lines in her, huh? I've been wondering what Camden would take for her. If he's pushed for ready cash, as I hear he is, could be I can get her cheap.*

Ames said, "Sort of convenient your wife died when she did, eh, Hal?"

"Mr. Camden to you," Camden said.

"But it was convenient?"

"Thash my business."

There was a phone in a niche in the wall. Camden attempted to lift it from its cradle and Ames pushed him. "Uh-huh. Not until we get through talking."

Camden's plump cheeks mottled with anger. "Goddamn you," he swore. His big fists flailing air, he rushed Ames.

Ames gave ground. Then coldly deliberate, he smashed a hard right to Camden's jaw that stopped the big man as if he'd run into a wall. Camden's eyes glazed. His knees sagged. He knelt on the floor, then fell face forward and lay with one arm extended.

Ames rubbed his fist with the palm of his other hand, fighting a desire to be sick. He hadn't meant to hit Camden so hard. All he'd wanted to do was keep him away from the phone and perhaps sober him a trifle. Now Camden wasn't going to tell him anything.

He squatted on the floor beside Camden and lighted another cigarette from the stub of the one he was smoking. Camden *had* to talk. Ames realized his hands were shaking again.

He slapped Camden's face lightly. "Hey, you."

The big man continued to lie motionless. Ames felt Camden's pulse. It was steady. The amount of whiskey he'd consumed was contributing as much to his unconsciousness as the blow. Ames pulled the unconscious man to a sitting position.

"Hey, you," Ames repeated.

Camden snored in his face for answer.

Ames wiped his sweaty hands on his wet pants. The lump was back in his throat, his throat was constricted. Camden *had* to talk. Otherwise the hell he'd been through was for nothing.

He fought the limp body over his shoulder in an abortive version of a fireman's carry. It was all he could do to stand up. Camden was a larger man than he looked. He weighed at least two hundred pounds and his bulk wasn't fat, it was muscle. Ames stood a moment uncertain, his legs spread, under the weight on his shoulder. Then he walked across the living room to the unlighted hall and opened the first door he came to.

The dark room was faintly scented with the fragrance of expensive perfume. Ames felt for and found the wall switch and flicked it on. The room was huge, with twin beds against one wall. The robe Ames had been wearing that morning was lying across one of the beds. The other bed hadn't been slept in.

He closed the door behind him and stood a moment looking at another larger framed picture of Helene Camden. It was standing on the "Mr." side on an expensive looking "Mr. and Mrs." chest of drawers and was inscribed

To Hal
With All My Love
Helene

In her day, the owner of *helene camden, incorporated* had been a very pretty woman. Even in the fairly recent picture, she was still attractive. A lot of her own products had gone to make her so, but there was a certain coldness to her face and eyes that detracted from her charms. She'd been a woman who'd known what she'd wanted and gotten it one way or another. Mary Lou had called her a bitch. It could be she'd been one. Ames thought of the bloated body he'd seen on the floor of Rupert's Fish House and shuddered. She was nothing now and he was tagged for it.

He crossed the parquet floor of the bedroom and opened the bathroom door. The bath was as large as most living rooms. There were two stools with a colored tile wall between them. There were two basins, a huge sunken tub and a separate glass-enclosed shower stall. It was the first time Ames had ever seen anything like it. Attorney Ferris hadn't been exaggerating when he'd told Sheriff White there was money in the manufacturing of cosmetics. Even the ceiling was tiled.

Ames slid back the etched glass door of the shower stall and lowered Camden to the tile. The big man continued to snore. Ames ripped off Camden's shirt. He leaned him against the wall in a sitting position. Then turning on the cold water, he adjusted the needle spray so it played on the face of the unconscious man.

Camden kept snoring a few more minutes, his rubbery lips blowing out with every exhalation. Then he stopped snoring and his mouth began to work. He swallowed a mouthful of water and sat up gagging.

"What the hell?"

"It's good for you," Ames said. "I've swallowed a lot of water tonight."

Camden got to his feet and tried to get out of the shower.

Ames pushed him back under the spray. "Not quite so fast. I want you sober when we go 'round again."

He stood poised, waiting for Camden to try to bull his way out of the shower. Camden started to and changed his mind. Instead, he stood rubbing the cold water into his hair and face and chest.

"I thought I remembered seeing you," he said. "I would pick tonight to get drunk."

Most of the thickness was gone from his voice. He took off his sodden slacks and tossed them in a corner of the shower. Stripped to a pair of jockey shorts, he continued to massage the cold water into his body. A minute passed, two minutes, three. Ames turned off the water. Camden ran his fingers through his hair. He stepped out of the shower and toweled. Finished, he tossed the towel aside and stood glowering at Ames.

"All right. I'm sober. Let's have it. What are you doing here?"

Ames leaned against the tile wall. "Looking for information."

"What sort of information?"

"I want the name of your girl friend."

"What girl friend?"

"The one who killed Helene or arranged to have her killed."

"You're crazy. You killed Helene."

Ames shook his head. "Uh-uh. I was just the goat. Some woman arranged that scene in the cabin of the *Sea Bird*. The same woman tried to kill my wife and did kill Celeste."

Camden seemed sincerely puzzled. "What the hell are you trying to hand me, Ames?"

"I'm not trying to hand you anything. I suppose you were in love with your wife."

"No. Not particularly," Camden admitted. He squeegeed water from his wet hair. "Helene was a pretty good joe, but I can't say that I was in love with her. In fact, I was quite relieved when I heard that one of her messes had finally caught up with her. You can stomach some things just so long. And I've been fed up for a long time with being *Mr.* Helene Camden.

"So you plotted to kill her."

Camden shook his head. "Make sense, fellow. I was in Baltimore when Helene died."

"Then you had your girl friend kill her."

"There you go again. What's this about a girl friend?"

Ames fought back a feeling of panic. There *had* to be some other woman involved. Camden had to have guilty knowledge of the murder of his wife.

"You don't have one, I suppose?"

"I have several. Like I told that Cracker sheriff, if Helene could play around with punks like you, I saw no particular reason why I should sit home and knit."

"These girl friends are in Florida?"

"No. In Baltimore." Camden walked toward Ames slowly. "But all this is beside the point. You're supposed to be in custody."

Ames backed out into the bedroom. "That's right. I'm the goat. But I won't be when I leave here. I know damn well I didn't kill Helene. I had nothing to do with her."

"The evidence says different."

"The evidence was rigged."

"So you say."

Ames tried a new tack. "I suppose you don't need money."

"I always need money."

"And now you have it."

"That's right," Camden admitted. "Not as much as I'd like, but when I sell the house and the boat and Helene's ring and collect what's due me from the estate, I should have a nice piece of change."

Ames swallowed the lump in his throat. Camden wasn't acting like he'd expected him to act. Either the man was a consummate actor or he had nothing to fear. He stopped backing and stood his ground. Down on the beach, when the maid's body had been recovered, Camden had denied having an affair with her. He naturally would deny such a thing. But he and Celeste could have plotted together. Celeste could have killed her mistress and arranged the scene to which he had awakened. Her surprise and fear on learning that Mrs. Camden wasn't aboard the *Sea Bird* could have been part of the act, as was the shot she had fired through the screen.

Camden was amused. "Now what's going through your bird brain?"

Ames told him. "Celeste. I think you were lying when you told

White you weren't having an affair with her."

"I suppose you can prove I was."

Ames shook his head. "No." He glanced at the framed picture of Helene Camden. "But if you were, I can imagine what her reaction would have been if she found it out. She'd have cut you both off from the trough before you could open your mouths to deny it."

Camden was even more amused. "And then I stabbed Celeste for fear she'd lose her nerve and give the game away."

"Yes."

"No," Camden corrected him. "You forget. Tom Ferris alibis me from the time the inquest ended until an hour and a half after the time of death set by the local coroner."

"It didn't take long to stab the girl. You could have said you were going to the bathroom." Ames lost his self control and threw a hard right to Camden's face. "Talk, goddamn you, talk."

Camden caught the punch on the palm of his hand and swung a hard left in return that rocked Ames back on his heels. "I've nothing to say," he said. "But thanks for sobering me up. I don't like people who take punches at me. So I'm going to beat your face in. Then I'm going to turn you over to the law." He accompanied the statement with a series of short rights and lefts that drove Ames back against the chest of drawers. "It was a good try, fellow, but it isn't going to work. If you think you can bluff me into sticking out my neck, you're crazy."

Ames fought back desperately. He hadn't meant this to happen. He'd meant to be at the wheel and Camden had taken the play away from him. He weathered the flurry of blows and fought his way out of the corner into which Camden had backed him.

The big man might have married Helene for her money, but he wasn't a coward. He continued to bore in, taking all that Ames could give him.

Ames took a low left to the groin to give a hard right to the jaw that caused Camden to gasp with pain and sent him reeling back into one of the twin beds. The bed caught his knees and he fell back on it. Ames was on him before he could get up, beating at his face with both fists.

"Talk. Admit you killed your wife or had her killed."

Camden's head rolled from side to side. Blood ran out of his mouth. Ames got to his feet and stood panting, looking at the motionless figure. Now it all had to be gone through again. And time was running out.

He wiped the blood from his own nose with the back of his hand. The silence in the room hurt his ears. He'd been through too much. It had gone or for too long. And he was still right where he had started, trying to climb a glass wall.

The throb of a motor attracted his attention. Ames opened the bedroom door and walked down the hall to the kitchen. The lights in the carport were on. Attorney Ferris was getting out of Helene Camden's car. The lawyer lit a cigarette and walked toward the kitchen door. Ames backed down the long hall.

When he reached the master bedroom he looked in. He'd done a better job on Camden than he'd realized. The big man was still unconscious, his once handsome face battered to a pulp.

From the kitchen Ferris called, "Hal!"

Ames walked on into the sunroom, an ugly thought nagging at his mind. Even if Camden were guilty, even if he'd been having an affair with Celeste, it still didn't explain how Celeste could have drugged the coffee in the cockpit of the *Sally*.

"Hal," Ferris called again.

Ames walked on through the living room. He didn't want to talk to the lawyer. It wouldn't serve any purpose. He'd done all he could. The best thing for him to do was to go into town and surrender. He'd been a fool to make a break. He wasn't smart enough to solve this thing. He was just a blown out trumpet player turned charter boat captain and, more recently, goat for a killer. This was one of those bad breaks a man got. He'd have to take whatever a jury gave him while the guilty party went free. He'd been outclassed, outthought, out-smarted.

He couldn't run any further. He'd run as far as he could. Still, there was Mary Lou to consider. She was depending on him. He couldn't let her down.

Ames's headache was back again. Blood persisted in dribbling from his nose. His jaw was sore where Camden had punched it. He took another step toward the front screen door and stopped in the middle of his stride, the short hairs on the back of his neck tingling, as he realized that he was walking through the dark. The living room was no longer lighted. *Someone had turned off the lamp. Someone was in the room with him.*

Back in the unlighted hallway, standing in the doorway of the lighted bedroom, Ferris had discovered Camden. "For God's sake,

Hal," he gasped. "What's happened to you?" Ferris' voice grew fainter as he entered the bedroom. "Hal!" He repeated, "Hal!"

Ames drew his almost forgotten gun from his pocket. His head turned slowly from side to side as if it were on a stiff swivel. Now that Ferris had stopped shouting, the only sound in the living room was the rasp of his own uneven breathing.

Ames's head continued to swivel from side to side. "Who's in here?"

There was a faint swish of silk. Something soft and almost soundless fell on the floor to his left. Ames turned and fired at the sound. He was aware instantly that he'd been tricked. The silk object was a thrown pillow and whoever had thrown it was behind him. He turned again and a hard round object that felt like a piece of pipe thudded against his head.

He tried to raise the gun and couldn't. His whole right side felt numb. Pain opened his fingers. He dropped the gun and fell on his hands and knees thinking, *This is what happened to Mary Lou.*

The swung pipe descended again, striking his shoulder. Ames cried out in pain but kept moving. The third blow struck his upper arm. For a moment Ames thought it was broken.

He forced himself on and fell against the screen door. It gave under his weight and spilled him out onto the patio. He got to his feet and ran. As he did, the gun he had dropped began to yammer almost hysterically, spraying the night around him with lead. Even after the cylinder was empty, the firing pin continued to click metallically against the empty shells.

Ames raced on across the lawn. At the edge of the water he stopped and looked back. The living room was still dark. No one had pursued him. He stood for a long moment waiting for the lights to come on and for Ferris to shout for the police.

When nothing happened, Ames was pleased. He felt better than he had at any time since he'd awakened in the cabin of the *Sea Bird.* He'd been on the right track, but he'd been pounding on the wrong man.

So now he knew.

Ames spat out a mouthful of blood. Then ducking under the Camden pier, he walked back the way he had come. Halfway back to the fish house, he spotted a bobbling flashlight and the vague outline of a running man. Ames pressed his back to the bole of a water-killed palm and waited for the man to pass him.

He could have reached out and touched him. It was one of Sheriff

White's boys, possibly the deputy who'd been staked out on the *Sally*. The deputy ran a few feet, then stopped and listened before running on again. Ames waited until the deputy reached the Camden pier before he moved on.

Ben Sheldon was no longer sitting on the loading platform of the fish house, but the fragrance of his cigar lingered. Ames looked across the basin at the *Sally*. There was no glow in the cockpit. The deputy he'd seen had been from the *Sally*. There would be more in a few minutes. A distant siren was wailing down the beach road. Tight little knots of men were gathered in front of Harry's Bar and The Fisherman's Lunch, looking up the road in the direction from which the shots had come.

He decided to chance the pier and crouching as low as he could, he walked along the line of bobbing fishing boats.

Shep was waiting where he'd said he would be. He cast off as soon as Ames had jumped down into the cockpit. "Whereabouts now?" Shep asked.

Ames leaned against the live bait box, filling his lungs with air as he watched the shore recede. He knew what he wanted to do before he talked to White. He knew what he had to do before anyone would believe him. The roads and the causeways would be blocked, but the waterways were always open. The charter boat crowd and the commercial fishermen were always coming and going, at all hours of the day and night. Ames fingered the three bills in the still wet pocket of his coat. "How much gas you got, Shep?"

"Both tanks are full."

"Think you could make Tampa by tomorrow morning?"

"Effen they ain't moved the channels since the last time I was there." Shep swung the wheel over, hard. "You want t' go t' Tampa?"

"I'll give you a hundred dollars if you'll take me."

"Put it."

"It's a tough trip at night. You may rip the bottom out of your boat."

"Could be," Shep admitted. "We're apt t' get some wet then." Still running without lights, he cut in his other motor. There was a surge of power. The *Falcon* knifed through the dark water under the draw of the bridge across the pass and headed for the open Gulf, where some ten miles out, it could pick up the deep water channel running past quarantine into Tampa sixty miles away.

Ames's jaw was still sore. His arm hurt. Blood kept trickling from his nose. He wiped his nose with the sleeve of his coat and lighted a cigarette with fingers that still shook. "Thanks."

"Jist don't mention money," Shep said. "You concerned in that shootin' back there?"

Ames nodded. "Yes."

"On what side?"

"I was shot at."

Shep leaned out to spot the bell buoy marking the shallows off the hook. "Figured that. Who was a-doin' the shootin'?"

"I'm not quite certain," Ames admitted. "But I think I know how to find out." He braced himself against the rock of the boat as it knifed through the rip tides where the waters of the Gulf of Mexico joined those of Boca Grande Bay. "Look, Shep."

Shep turned on his running lights. "Yeah?"

Ames wiped salt spray from his face. "If you wanted to use a man for a fall guy and get him from where he was to some other place without him raising a fuss or anyone seeing him—"

"Yeah?"

"How would you go about it?"

"This happens in a boat?"

"Yes."

"It's night?"

"Anyway it's dark."

The grizzled guide debated his answer. "Well, first I'd talk nice t' him. I'd git him real interested in somethin'. Then when he wasn't watchin' I'd put somethin' in his whiskey or his coffee or whatever he was drinkin'. An' when he was snorin' good, I'd lower him over the side into a dinghy I'd brought with me an' row him right where I wanted him. Why?"

"That's what happened to me," Ames said.

CHAPTER FIFTEEN

The sidewalks of downtown Tampa were crowded with work-bound office employees, store clerks, minor executives and professional men. A steady stream of cars, three abreast, filled the streets. There was a continuous shrill of police whistles and a blare of automobile horns as the Latin-American citizenry acted as midwife to the new day being born.

Ames bought a morning *Tribune* from a boy on the corner of

Franklin Street and moved on with the crowd. Palmetto City was a tourist town. It depended on its winter visitors for the bulk of its living. Tampa was a city. It had been a city when his grandfather had embarked from Port Tampa for Santiago de Cuba during the Spanish-American war. It had shipyards and cigar factories and heavy industry. Rusty and sleek freighters, banana boats, tankers, even a few passenger ships were warped into its docks from ports all over the world. It had an international airport serving the islands of the Caribbean and Central and South America. As much Spanish as English was spoken on its streets. There was a wide-awake feel to the town, unusual this far south. If it were possible for him to find out what he wanted to know, he could buy the information in Tampa.

There was a small restaurant in the next block. Ames sat at the crowded counter and ordered eggs and ham and buttered grits. The first thing he had to do was buy some clothes.

If Sheriff White had alerted the Tampa police, they would be looking for a charter boat captain wearing a tieless white shirt, a blue serge suit, white sneakers and a white cap. His cap was on the bottom of Boca Grande Bay. Ames studied his clothes. Otherwise, he answered the description.

He read the paper while he ate his breakfast. He was big news even in Tampa, rather Helene Camden was. A reproduction of the framed picture he'd seen in the Camden living room took up a quarter of the first page. Most of the story was a re-hash of what he'd read in the Palmetto City paper Shep had had aboard the *Falcon*. Only one item was new. He read the *Tribune's* version of the shooting on the beach with interest. It quoted Attorney Tom Ferris and Hal Camden verbatim.

According to Hal Camden, Ames was crazy. He had appeared out of nowhere and started to beat on Camden in an attempt to make Camden confess that he had killed his wife or had had her killed. Camden was virtuously indignant. He had loved his wife very much. He had no reason, financially or otherwise, to want to see her dead. He had put up as good a fight as he could but Ames had beaten him unconscious.

Ames skipped on to Attorney Ferris' version of what had happened. Ferris said he had been in town making arrangements for the bodies of Helene Camden and Miss Montigny to be shipped north. He had returned to find Camden unconscious and Ames standing in the middle of the living room with a revolver in his hand. The gun was identified as the revolver that he, Ames, had stolen earlier in the day from a negligent county trooper. According to the direct quotes, there had been a terrific fight. Ferris claimed he had twisted the gun out of his hand and emptied it at Ames as he ran. The attorney had then waited in the darkened living room for the police to arrive, fearful that Ames might have a second gun.

There was no mention of Phillips, the butler, or of any third party in the living room. Ames felt his battered head. Nor was there any mention of a piece of pipe.

He read on down the story. There were the usual wild reports. He had been seen in Bradenton and Fort Myers and as far south and east as Miami. He was believed to be headed for Cuba. It was thought he was still holed up somewhere on the beach. The county and state police were searching all the islands in Boca Grande Bay. As yet no inquest had been held on Miss Montigny and Mary Lou was still being held in Palmetto City jail on a charge of suspicion of murder. The only statement by Sheriff White was the usual police bromide to the effect that his office was making progress and expected to make an arrest any moment.

Ames paid his check and walked up the street to a large department store. Even a few minutes after opening time it was crowded. No one paid any particular attention to him.

He bought a pair of cuffed fawn-colored slacks, a gabardine shirt to match and a pair of two-toned sports shoes. In the drugstore across the street he bought dark sun glasses and one of the long-billed fishermen's caps that all tourists purchased but that none of the local fishermen wore.

There was a bar on the next corner. He changed his clothes in the men's room and washed the salt spray from his hands and face. Disposing of his old clothes was a problem. He solved it by stuffing them under the papers in the unemptied trash barrel. Then he put on the dark sun glasses and looked at himself in the mirror. With the exception of his permanent tan he looked as much like a northern tourist as he could expect to look. He was glad there'd been no picture of him in the paper. He still looked like Charlie Ames.

He located a barber shop next and bought a shave. The barber was filled with the Palmetto Beach story and voluble, a Spanish mine of misinformation. The barber knew Palmetto City well. He and his family swam on the beach every Sunday weather permitted and as God was his judge, everyone knew that Palmetto Beach had the best climate in the world. He would like to live on the beach if it weren't for the sand flies and the mosquitoes and if he could make a living there.

He also knew Captain Ames ... well, not exactly knew him, but a very good friend of his, one Carlos Garcia, a waiter at Los Novedades, had chartered Ames's boat, the *Sally*, several times and Carlos said that Captain Ames was one hell of a swell fellow.

Ames remembered Garcia. A rotund little man with a pleasant smile, he would have made a good fisherman. As Ames recalled, he'd had Carlos out three times.

The barber continued. He'd also seen Mrs. Ames once when the local bartenders' union had thrown a binge at the Beach Club during the off-season, of course, when prices weren't so high. Mrs. Ames or Mary Lou, as she was known at the Beach Club, had sung for them. She was one *muy bello nino*, a beautiful babe, if there ever was one. It was the barber's opinion that Camden had shown her too much money and she had been *falso* with him and Ames had attempted to get even first by staying with and then killing Mrs. Camden. Anyone could see it was a crime of passion. He felt sorry for Captain Ames and he, for one, was glad the goddamn moneyed tourists stayed the hell away from Tampa. They always loused things up. Who did the goddamn-yankees think they were? All this with an Ybor City accent Ames could have cut a loaf of Cuban bread with.

He was glad when he was shaved. He put his change in his pocket and glanced at his watch. It had stopped at eight o'clock, probably the morning before when he'd stepped in the pot hole off Pine Key.

It was ten by the barber's clock. He asked the barber if he could use his phone book and thumbed through the classified section until he came to the heading, Credit Reporting Agencies. There were half a dozen firms listed, the nearest one on Franklin Street not far from where he'd bought his morning paper.

The barber tried to be helpful. "You find what you want, fellow?"

"Yes. I think so," Ames said.

He walked slowly back the way he had come. There were fewer people on the sidewalks now. The shrill of whistles and blare of horns had ceased. A white capped policeman was standing on the corner of Franklin. He looked Ames full in the face, then yawned and looked away. Ames walked on. He was beginning to sweat again. His luck so far had been too good. He couldn't expect it to last.

He had no illusions. He was free on borrowed time. Fifty people on Bayshore Boulevard had seen Shep dock the *Falcon* and a hatless man in a blue serge suit and white sneakers scramble out onto the pier. The *Falcon* was documented out of Palmetto City. The name Palmetto City was painted on its stern in only slightly smaller letters than its own name.

If White had alerted the Tampa police, one of them would hear of it and contact White. He and Shep were known to be good friends. Plainclothes detectives would trail him from the pier to the greasy spoon where he had eaten breakfast. The waiter would remember him vaguely.

Yeah. A big guy who needed a shave.

He would be traced to the department store. The clerk would remember selling him the fawn-colored slacks and a shirt and shoes. The clerk in the drugstore might or might not remember him, but the man back of the bar in which he'd changed clothes would. The trash barrel would be emptied. The police would find his old suit.

A fresh fear nagged at Ames's mind. For all his volubility, the garrulous barber hadn't once mentioned the gash on his head. True, he'd washed his hair in salt water and removed all the blood he could, but that hadn't healed the skin. The blow of the pipe had left a bad laceration. He could feel it. Perhaps the barber had known who he was and that was why he'd talked as much as he had.

The feeling of stiffness returned to Ames's neck. He swiveled his head and looked over his shoulder. The policeman he'd passed was still yawning, at the plump stern of a pretty girl now. No one seemed to be following him. He walked on and up the stairs under a swinging second floor sign reading:

SOUTHERN CREDIT ASSOCIATION

Reports & Collections

The office was at the end of a short hall. Ames opened the door and walked in. An attractive girl in her late teens was sitting behind the receptionist's desk in a small outer office.

"Yes, sir?" she smiled at Ames. "What can we do for you?"

Ames took off his long-billed cap. "I'd like some credit reports. You are affiliated with the National Associated Credit Bureau?"

"We are." The receptionist poised her pencil over her pad. "What is your name, sir?"

"O'Hara," Ames lied. "James O'Hara, of Asheville and Miami and more recently of Palmetto Beach." He built up the mythical character he'd created. "I'm planning a rather large real estate development on the beach, one that will run well into six figures."

The girl was properly impressed. "I see." She added, "I also see, according to the papers, that you're having quite a bit of excitement over there."

Ames waved the statement aside as immaterial. "I'm interested in a credit rating."

The girl was all business again. "Yes, sir."

Ames continued. "I would like a thorough character report and credit rating on two men and one manufacturing company. One of them is local to the beach. Two of them are in Baltimore. Money, within reason, is no object, but time is of the essence. I'd like this report today, as soon as it can be compiled. Can such a thing be done?"

The receptionist said he'd better speak to the manager and ushered him into an inner office, where an alert looking young man sat at a desk literally surrounded by filing cases and out-of-town phone directories. She introduced him as Mr. George and Ames repeated what he had told the girl.

"You want this report today?" Mr. George said when Ames had finished.

"That's right."

The credit man rubbed his chin. "That could be quite an order."

"I realize that."

Mr. George continued to rub his chin. "The local man shouldn't give us any trouble and I have the connections to get any information that is available on the other two. But a rush job like this is going to cost you money, sir."

"How much?"

"You want a detailed report?"

"No. A general will do."

"Then say fifty dollars apiece. A hundred and fifty for the three."

Ames counted the money on the desk.

Mr. George stopped rubbing his chin. "Fine. I'll get right to work. Where do you want us to deliver this report, Mr. O'Hara?"

Ames considered saying he would wait in the outer office but was afraid that the suggestion might make Mr. George suspicious. He named one of the better hotels in town. "You can reach me at the Flamingo."

Mr. George wrote—Mr. James O'Hara, Flamingo Hotel—on his

pad, then looked up at Ames again. "And the two men and the firm on whom you want the reports?"

Ames took a deep breath and told him. "Ben Sheldon of Palmetto Beach. The other man is Thomas Ferris, an attorney-at-law who practices in Baltimore."

"And the firm?"

"*helene camden, incorporated*, also of Baltimore."

Mr. George wrote the three names on his pad. To him, they were only names. "That does it, Mr. O'Hara. I'll send a boy over to your hotel with the reports as soon as I can compile them."

Back on the street again, Ames realized that perspiration was standing out on his forehead in pearl-like drops. He wiped them away with the tips of his fingers and walked slowly in the direction of the hotel he had named. He was glad he had taken three hundred dollars of the fifteen hundred that Ben had given Mary Lou for the *Sally*. Without it, he would have been sunk. He might be anyway. Maybe he was crazy. Maybe he was being a fool. Maybe he was merely prolonging the agony for both himself and Mary Lou.

A half-dozen shallow stone steps led up to the lobby of the hotel. Ames walked up into the cool lobby and knew the same feeling of peace that he had known on Pine Key. As he passed the cigar counter on his way to the room desk, the picture of Helene Camden looked up at him from an early edition of the Tampa *Evening Times*.

Ames dropped a quarter on the counter and folded a paper under his arm. The room clerk was politely impersonal. Ames registered as James O'Hara of Miami and in lieu of baggage, paid for the room in advance.

There was a cool looking lounge off the lobby. Ames sat at the bar and drank a beer before going up to his room. As he drank it he glanced over the front page of the *Times*.

The search for him had intensified and spread. The Coast Guard had been requested to search for an unnamed boat known to be captained by a friend of his. Neither Shep nor the *Falcon* were named in the newspaper report, but it was only a matter of time now. The police knew both names. The net was closing in.

There was also a small one column picture of him, taken while he'd still been tooting a horn for a living. Ames studied the picture. He looked like a sap. His hair was too long. His ears were too big. His face was too fat. His white dinner jacket was moulded to his body. He looked a little like Camden, only he'd been married to a horn.

He was almost glad the Jap had mashed his lip. He liked the water. So he didn't make much money, he was happier than he had ever been or he had been happier until this thing happened. If he ever got out of this scrape he'd never complain again. What's more, Mary Lou was through with singing. The hell with a better boat. He'd make all the living from now on if he had to fish for trout with a handline.

The barman was less voluble than the barber but interested in the case. He tapped the picture of Helene Camden.

"Know something, mister?"

"What?" Ames asked him.

The barman confided, "She's been in here lots of times."

"She has, huh?"

"Yeah. Lots of times. Sometimes with her husband, sometimes with a big fat older guy, but mostly with some young punk she'd just picked up for you-know-what."

"How could you tell?"

The barman shrugged. "When she was with the punks, she always paid the check, see? I guess she was one of them nymphs, huh?"

"It could be," Ames admitted. He was utterly tired of Helene Camden. He wished he never had to hear her name again, but even if what he thought proved true, he still had a long net to haul. There were a lot of small angles and one major one that he had no way of proving.

He picked his change from the bar and rode the elevator up to his room. The clerk had given him a room on the top floor. Ames stood in the window looking out over the city for a moment then turned as the room phone tinkled. He was almost afraid to pick it up.

"This is Southern Credit, Mr. O'Hara," the crisp voice on the other end of the wire said. "This Helene Camden you want the report on. That's the woman who just got herself killed over on Palmetto Beach?"

"Yes," Ames said. "It is."

"You want the report on her or on her firm, *helene camden, incorporated?*"

"I want a report on her firm."

"I see," Mr. George said. "I just wanted to be sure. Sorry to disturb you, Mr. O'Hara."

Ames's knees felt weak. He cradled the phone and sat on the edge of the bed. Now he had something new about which to worry. The phone call could be on the level. It could be a stall. Maybe the credit man had just seen his picture in the *Times* and was checking for the police. A hunted man had so many things to worry about. Everything was suspicious to him.

Ames lay back on the bed but couldn't rest. He took off his shirt and kicked off his shoes. It didn't help. He got up and paced the floor. Either way he was hooked. He had to stay where he was. So he was playing a long shot; it was the only hope that he and Mary Lou had. He was tooting his own little horn in a big time combo and he had to play it by ear. The other two members of the band had written the arrangement.

Ames walked from the bed to the window, then back to the bed, then back to the window again.

It was going to be a long day.

CHAPTER SIXTEEN

Camden's face was a multi-colored thing of battered flesh. He refilled his shot glass and resumed his staring out the open casement window.

There was an unreal quality to the night. It was like a too-vivid scene on a penny post card, the kind printed for the tourist trade to send back to Des Moines or Minneapolis or Montpelier, the cards to arrive in the middle of a blizzard with the temperature hovering on the wrong side of thirty-two degrees. *Having a wonderful time. Wish you were here.*

Tonight the stars hung low and the sky was filled with them. A south moon under rested lightly on the feathery fronds of the tallest palms rising out of the Camden grounds. The lawn was sheer black velvet ornamented with twinkling fireflies. The air was warm and scented with the fragrance of orange blossoms. The purr of the traffic on the beach road was a soothing sound in the distance.

"Pretty, huh?" Ferris asked.

Camden looked at him sourly. "I can't eat 'pretty.'"

"No," Ferris admitted. "You can't."

"Supper," Phillips announced, "is served."

"The hell with it," Camden said. He left the window and sprawled in an easy chair.

Phillips stood uncertainly in the doorway.

"We'll eat a little later," Ferris told him.

"Yes, sir," the butler said. His leather heels made a solid sound down the long tiled hallway.

Camden gulped the drink in his glass. "You're positive that five hundred dollars is all that Helene has in her personal checking account?"

"I'm positive," Ferris said. "I called the bank, didn't I?"

"But where did the money go?"

Ferris spread his hands. "There you have me. But you know as well as I that Helene had expensive tastes. She spent a lot of money."

Camden refilled his glass. "No one woman could spend that much."

Ferris hesitated then said, "I don't want to ride guard on you, Hal, or attempt to tell you your business, but I'd lay off that stuff if I were you. You know what happened last night."

Camden shrugged. "It wouldn't have made any difference. I couldn't have licked the guy if I'd been cold sober. He was too much for me. I still don't see how you got that gun away from him."

Ferris stroked his wisp of a mustache. "I suppose I was just lucky."

Camden touched his battered face with the tips of his fingers. "Believe me, fellow, you were. He was hell determined that I was going to confess that I had killed Helene."

"Ha," Ferris laughed. "That's funny."

A bell chimed musically in the rear of the house. Phillips' heels made their solid sound again. "Who now?" Camden asked, as the butler passed through the living room.

"I'm certain I wouldn't know, sir," Phillips said. He turned on the light in the patio and looked through the screen door. "Yes?"

"I'd like to see Mr. Camden if I can," Ben Sheldon said. "Tell him it's about the *Sea Bird*. I'd like to make an offer for it."

Phillips turned and said, "It's a Mr. Sheldon, sir. He's calling about the *Sea Bird*."

"I heard him," Camden said, impatiently. "Don't keep him standing out there under that light. The mosquitoes will eat him alive. Tell him to come in."

"Yes, sir." The butler opened the screen door. "Come in, Mr. Sheldon."

Immaculate in a freshly laundered white linen suit, the fat man took off his panama and stood just inside the door rolling a fat cigar from one side of his mouth to the other.

Ferris was disappointed. "I hoped it was the police. I hoped they'd caught Ames."

Sheldon spoke around his cigar. "They ain't got Charlie yet, eh? He's putting up a good run for it."

"And all so needless," Ferris said. "They had him once. If White hadn't been so stupid he'd have kept him."

Sheldon was philosophical about it. "Those things happen."

Camden pointed to the bottles and the glasses on a tray. "Fix yourself a drink if you want one."

Moving lightly for so big a man, Sheldon crossed the room to the tray. "Thanks. I don't mind if I do. I'll take one on the rocks."

Camden waited until Sheldon had sloshed whiskey on the ice cubes in his glass. "Now, what's this about the *Sea Bird?*"

Sheldon settled himself in a chair before he spoke. "You know my business?"

"I do. You're the local ship chandler."

"That's right. I also do a little yacht brokerage on the side. You going to keep the house?"

"No."

"Then I imagine the boat is for sale."

"It is."

"Good," Sheldon said. "I'll give you eight thousand for it."

Ferris hooted. "You're out of your mind, Sheldon. The *Sea Bird* cost Helene fifty thousand dollars."

The fat man looked at the lawyer over the rim of his glass. "So what? The Taj Mahal cost a couple of million, maybe even more, but I wouldn't give you a hundred dollars for it. Boats as large as the *Sea Bird* are a drug on the market. Very few people have the kind of money it takes to support a forty-eight foot Diesel-powered cruiser. About all I could do with it is rip out all that fancy stuff and convert it into a commercial fishing boat or possibly sell it to some local captain who wants to attract the higher class charter boat trade."

"Make it ten thousand," Camden said.

"Well, ten then," Sheldon agreed.

"Sell it to him, Tom," Camden said. "Make out bill of sale right now."

Ferris got to his feet. "You're out of your mind Hal," he said hotly.

Camden answered as hotly. "Why wouldn't I be?" Under the pattern of multi-colored bruises left by Ames's fists, his face was haggard. "I marry a bag like Helene. I fetch and tote and put up with her for four years, expecting that when she does die, I'll come into around a hundred grand. And what do I come out with? An empty bank account."

"Oh, I wouldn't say that," Sheldon said. "This house comes to you, doesn't it?"

"Yes."

"It's worth fifty thousand dollars."

"It's worth sixty-five and it's mortgaged for sixty, leaving me five thousand dollars. Hell. I owe my bookie more than that."

Ferris attempted to soothe him. "Now, just take it easy, Hal. We'll find some money somewhere."

"Where? We've checked her personal bank account. We've checked her stocks. We've checked the firm's account. And there isn't a dime anywhere. All we've found are withdrawals and sales. It's almost as if Helene expected to die and cashed in everything then hid the cash."

The fat man said placidly, "A shame. Well, my offer still holds."

"And I accept it," Camden said. "At least, it will give me some cash to go on. Have you a bill of sale, Tom?"

The lawyer opened a brief case lying on the desk. "I imagine I have. I think you're being very foolish, but it's for you to say. After all, you're Helene's heir." He found the printed form and uncapping his fountain pen, he began to fill it in.

Sheldon took a fat wallet from his pocket and counted fifty and one hundred dollar bills on the end table beside his chair.

Camden watched him fascinated. "There must be money in ship chandlering."

"I get by," Sheldon said.

All three of the men were too engrossed in what they were doing to notice the screen door open. Glancing up from the form he was inking, Ferris saw him first. "Oh, my God," he said quietly. "You."

"That's right," Ames said as quietly. "According to the account I read in the paper, you were such a hero last night I thought I'd come back and let you take another gun away from me."

Sheldon stopped counting and wet his thick lips with his tongue. "The cops are looking for you, Charlie."

Ames leaned against the wall next to the door. "Cops are always looking for someone. It's part of their profession, I suppose. How about it, Ben? Feel like talking?"

The fat man started to get to his feet and sat back as Ames lifted the gun in his hand. Sheldon laid his wallet on the money on the end table and mopped his face with his handkerchief. "You nuts or something, Charlie? Stop pointing that gun at me."

Camden looked from the fat man to Ames. "Are you always this way, fellow? Like I told you last night, make sense. What has Sheldon to talk about?"

"You didn't know that Ben was one of your wife's lovers?"

"No, I didn't."

"That's not so," Sheldon said. "Sure I took Helene out a few times, but we were just casual acquaintances. Neighbors on the beach, you might say."

"Let's tell that to Sheriff White, Ben," Ames said. "Are you sure you didn't persuade Helene to turn everything she had into cash and then kill her for the money and pin the blame on me?"

"I'm positive," the fat man said. He struggled to his feet. "Don't even think that, Charlie." His huge body quivered with indignation. "Why, I wouldn't do such a thing. I tell you what. Let's get Sheriff White out here and let him decide between us."

"You didn't slug Mary Lou and roll her into the pass?"

"No."

"You didn't kill Celeste because she became suspicious of you?"

"No."

Camden looked from one man to the other. There was something theatrical about the accusations and the denials, as if Ames and Sheldon had memorized their lines. It was like watching a little theater group, a not particularly good one. "I don't get it," Camden said.

"I do," Ferris said. Some of the color returned to his face. "All right. How much do you two want?"

From the unlighted sunroom, a woman's voice said, "It won't work, Tom. This isn't a shakedown. They know and I doubt if Ames can be bought. Money wouldn't do him any good in the spot he's in."

It was an effort for Camden to turn his head. "You're dead," he said thickly. "I saw your body."

Helene Camden patted his cheek as she walked past him into the room. "No, darling. The old bag is very much alive. But you won't have to do any more fetching or toting for your money. I'll take care of that angle." The blonde woman pointed the gun she was carrying at Ames's belt buckle. "All right, Ames. So you aren't the dumb Cracker I thought you were. So you're a hep ex-trumpet player. Let's hear that gun thud on the floor."

Ames was holding the gun at his side. He opened his fingers and allowed it to fall to the floor.

A long moment of silence followed. The resurrected cosmetics manufacturer used her free hand to smooth the lapel of the smart traveling suit she was wearing. Her fingers were unsteady. Her smile was brittle.

"A pity this had to happen. I thought I had everything worked out so nicely."

Ames said, "A hundred dollars a week and a two hundred dollar bonus. That is, if I get the *Sea Bird* up to Baltimore in three weeks."

Helene Camden continued to smile. "Wise guy," she said sweetly. "Believe me. You went out like a light. I had a hell of a time getting you into the dinghy and an even more difficult time getting your clothes off after I got you aboard the *Sea Bird*."

Camden stared at his wife. "You're not dead."

"No, darling. I wouldn't think of dying, not with over a half-million dollars in the boodle bag." Phillips had followed the blonde woman into the room. She motioned to the gun on the floor. "Pick it up, Phillips. And if any of the gentlemen in the room, with the exception of Mr. Ferris, even looks like he'd like to leave, don't hesitate to shoot."

Phillips picked up the gun and took a position against the wall. "No, Mrs. Camden."

The full import of what was happening finally sank into Camden's alcohol-fogged mind. "Well, I'll be a son-of-a-bitch!"

"You're all of that, Hal," Helene Camden said soberly. "Any man who'd assume his wife's name instead of insisting on using his own is a pretty weak sister." She sat on the extreme edge of a divided divan and laid the gun she was holding on the coffee table in front of the divan. "Not that it matters now."

"No," Camden said. "Not that it matters now. And the woman I identified as you?"

The blonde woman shrugged. "A fool I picked up in New York. It took me some time to find her, but then I've been planning this thing for some time. Besides, you didn't really identify me. You identified my ring. You were so eager to get your hands on the hundred thousand or so dollars you thought you were going to get, you'd have identified any blonde of my approximate weight and size." She patted at her hair and the trembling of her fingers was more pronounced. "But all that doesn't matter. What does matter is what do we do now?"

"Yes," Ferris agreed with her. "What do we do now?"

CHAPTER SEVENTEEN

The silence in the room lengthened until it became almost unbearable. Ames could feel sweat trickling down his sides. He'd been under too much of a strain too long. He felt light headed. It was an effort for him to stand. He spread his feet and leaned his weight against the wall.

Helene Camden studied his face. "What tipped you, Ames?"

"You," Ames told her.

"How so?"

"You've seen the girl I'm married to."

Her eyes narrowed slightly. "You'll pay for that."

Camden was incredulous. "You've been in the house all this time?"

"Most of it," the woman admitted. "Except for several little excursions that became necessary."

Ames said, "It was you who slugged Mary Lou."

Helene Camden lighted a cigarette and spoke through a veil of smoke. "That's right. It worried me when Tom told me she'd walked out on the inquest. I thought she might have spotted some loophole that we'd failed to cover, so I walked over to see what she was doing." She brushed the veil of smoke aside. "Who'd ever think the little fool would miss one cup?"

"We only have six," Ames said.

It was as if the blonde woman hadn't heard him. "For all I knew, it might retain some traces of chloral."

Camden asked, "And Celeste?"

Helene made a gesture of annoyance. "That was a pity. I liked Celeste. But I was too excited over what I'd just had to do to Mrs. Ames that I forgot to lock the door. And when Celeste came into Tom's room to turn down the spread and top sheet she found me lying on them, naked. She wouldn't take money for her silence. She said she was going to the police. I'd taken the knife from a box on the *Sally*, intending to use it on Mrs. Ames, but I decided it would look better if she drowned. I still had it in my purse. So when Celeste turned to leave the room, I used it on her." She returned her attention to Ames. "Then when our captain made his dramatic escape, the police barricaded all the roads and I couldn't get off the beaches without being recognized." Her voice was plaintive. "The way I originally planned it, I intended to be a long way from here by now."

Ferris no longer looked dapper. His face was lined and haggard. "So what do we do now?"

Helene shrugged. "There's only one thing we can do. We'll come to that in a moment." She looked back at Ames. "I made another mistake last night. I shouldn't have tried to knock you unconscious, but you were getting too warm to suit me. I wanted you in custody so the police would lift the barricades and I could get out of here. You knew last night?"

"It made me wonder," Ames said. "Slugging a woman and slugging a man are two different things. You had enough strength to hurt me but not quite enough to knock me out. Then keeping on pulling a trigger after a gun is empty is a woman's trick, a hysterical woman's. When I read in a Tampa paper that Ferris claimed he'd grabbed the gun and shot at me, I knew I'd been right in what I'd done."

"And that was?"

"Spent a hundred and fifty dollars on three credit reports. One on Ben and one on you and Ferris. Ben came out okay. I wish I was worth what he's rated at. But all Ferris had was his yearly retainer from *helene camden, incorporated*. And *helene camden, incorporated* was bankrupt. It owed several hundred thousand dollars in back corporation taxes and import duties. There was even talk of criminal prosecution. What tangible assets there were had been liquidated recently. So then I knew what had happened. You'd cashed in what you could and gotten out while the getting was good."

"That's right," Helene Camden admitted.

"You and Ferris have been planning this for months. I don't know where you got the woman you killed or who she was. I do know that posing as a benevolent party, you brought over quite a few displaced persons to work in your cosmetic plant. Possibly she was one of those."

"You know a lot."

"You'd be surprised," Ames said earnestly, "how detailed a credit report you get for fifty dollars. Anyway, once you'd brought her down here, you planted her in the cabin of the *Sea Bird*, then went into your act with me." He mimicked a woman's voice. "'Oh, is that coffee I smell? I wonder if I might have a cup.' Then when I went in to get the pot to pour a second cup, you fixed the dregs I'd left in the cockpit. You've already explained about Mary Lou and Celeste. And that I think ties it up."

"So it would seem," Helene Camden said.

Camden looked at the gray-haired butler covering the group with the revolver Ames had dropped. He sounded shocked. "My God. Don't tell me you've been sleeping with Phillips too."

Helene laughed. "No, dear. All Phillips is interested in is money. He was to have gotten a substantial sum, sufficient for him to retire on." The aged butler glanced at her sharply and she corrected herself. "He is to get a substantial sum. It's Tom who's been the real boy friend for some time. For the same length of time the firm has been on thin ice. I've had to borrow from Peter to pay Paul. And then there were those goddamn taxes and unpaid import duties. We were afraid we might have to pull something like this sooner or later and we thought you'd make good window decoration and you did. You were just dumb enough to think I was crazy about you because I allowed you certain marital privileges."

Ames looked at Ferris. "There are all types of pee-eyes, it would seem."

Ben Sheldon asked, "And now?"

Helene Camden regarded him thoughtfully. "You shouldn't have stuck your neck into this, Ben. I rather liked you. So you're sixty; you're all man. And I've been a little afraid of you. As I recall, on several of our dates I let slip that I was in a bit of a financial jam."

"Yes," the ship chandler admitted. "You did. That's why I thought Camden might be pushed for cash and I could get the *Sea Bird* cheap, but I never figured anything like this."

Ferris patted the perspiration beading on his face. "So?"

The woman shrugged. "There's only one thing we can do. The way we planned this thing only one death was involved, but we're in so deep now that a few more black marks against us can't possibly matter. You know what we have to do. But how to make it look logical? You're the lawyer. Think."

Ferris poured himself some liquor and drank it neat. "All right. Here's the story. Ames came back with Sheldon to put the pressure on Hal. They forced him to sign the bill of sale for the *Sea Bird* for a fifth of its value then attempted to take back the token money. Hal put up a fight and was killed. Fortunately, Phillips and I heard the shot and were able to avenge him. It isn't much of a story, but I think we can sell it to that dumb Cracker sheriff."

The screen door opened a third time and Sheriff White walked in followed by a half-dozen of his deputies. Mary Lou followed the deputies and stood at the screen door.

"Might be you could an' then again mebbe not," White said. He glanced at Phillips. "Don't try to pull the trigger of that thing, fellow. Ef you do you'll look worse than that blonde woman we picked out of the water. You'd be surprised what twelve or fourteen lead-nosed slugs can do to a man's face. They're most as bad as crabs."

Phillips lowered the gun to his side, then his shaking fingers released it. His face began to twitch as if he were going to cry.

White pushed his hat back on his head. "The same goes for you, Mrs. Camden. You rich folks give me a pain where I'm too much of a gentleman t' tell you." He picked the gun from the coffee table and dropped it in his side coat pocket. "Hell. Me and John and Sam have had this thing figured out for some time, ever since we checked with Baltimore. I've been honin' t' make an arrest all day." He glowered at Ames. "But what with Charlie a-swimmin' an' aboatin' all around the waterways, I was afeared he'd git his silly self kilt an' I wanted him alive t' testify against you." White was indignant. "So I had t' wait 'til he called up from the Flamingo Hotel in Tampa, his voice so awed you'd think he'd jist discovered the Book of Genesis."

His face even more haggard and lined than it had been, Ferris said, "You've been outside all this time?"

Sheriff White nodded. "With a tape recorder pushed up to one of the windows a-takin' down everythin' that was said. I thought it might simplify things at your trial jist in case you should git absent-minded and not be able to recall some of the deetails."

Helene Camden began to cry.

"You're two bodies too late," White told her.

One of the deputies picked up the gun that Phillips had dropped. Mary Lou snuggled her hand into Ames's.

"Hi, mister."

Ames squeezed the hand in his. "Right back at you, missus."

Unable to control himself any longer, Sheldon asked, "How did I do, Bob?"

"You took your part off good," White assured him. "But I've still half a mind t' jug you for withholdin' guilty knowledge. You knew Mrs. Camden was havin' money troubles an' if you'd 'a' spoke up at the inquest like you had a right to instead of figurin' how t' make a fast ten thousand dollars by buyin' the *Sea Bird* cheap, it might have opened a line of testimony that would've saved us a lot of trouble."

"I'm sorry," Sheldon said.

"You should be."

Helene Camden stopped crying and wiped her eyes. She looked from Ferris to Phillips then back at Ferris. "We aren't any of us talking, understand? If we can have that damned recording barred, all the evidence against us will be circumstantial. And I have a half-million dollars to fight this thing."

"I understand," Ferris said. He didn't sound too hopeful.

Sheriff White took off his hat and sat on the other half of the divided divan. "Now there are one or two little things I'd like to clear up before I take you into town."

Ames wasn't interested. He wanted to be alone with Mary Lou. "Before you start, Sheriff," he said, "I wonder if—"

White turned his faded blue eyes on him. "You wonder what?"

"Is there any charge against me?"

White debated the question. "N-no," he decided. "I guess not."

"And Mary Lou?"

"No. I never did think she kilt that maid. I was jist holdin' her in protective custody."

"Then is it all right if we go?"

"I don't see why not."

Ames gripped Mary Lou's arm and started out the door, and realized he had nowhere to go. Mary Lou had sold the *Sally* to Sheldon. He turned back and looked at the fat ship chandler. "How's for selling me back the *Sally*, Ben?"

"What'll you give?" Sheldon asked.

"The fifteen hundred you gave Mary Lou."

"Well, I dunno," the fat man said. "The *Sally's* a mighty good boat. Seems to me I ought to make some profit. I can get three thousand for her easy. Maybe even thirty-five hundred."

White was an old man. He was tired. He, too, had been under a strain. "Goddamn!" he exploded. "Stop hagglin' so I kin git on with my business. Sell him back his boat for what you paid for it or I'll still jug you for withholdin' pertinent knowledge."

The fat man sighed. "Okay. Fifteen hundred dollars."

"I'll give you the money in the morning," Ames said.

He closed the door behind them and he and Mary Lou walked down the drive to the beach road without once looking back. The crescent moon was higher in the sky now but the stars hung just as low.

Neither of them spoke again as they walked down the beach road toward the basin. Two fellow charter boat captains were standing in front of Harry's Bar. The news had spread. Both men grinned at Ames and touched their caps to Mary Lou. "Hi, Charlie. Evenin', Mary Lou."

Ames and Mary Lou returned the greeting then cut in between Murphy's drugstore and the Ways of Sheldon and went out on the sagging planking of the pier. The night was lovelier on the water. The basin reflected the moon and stars. The tide was running in and the *Sally* was straining at her mooring lines. Ames had never seen anything more lovely, with the exception of Mary Lou. He jumped down into the cockpit and lifted Mary Lou down.

He followed Mary Lou into the cabin and as usual forgot to duck low enough and bumped his forehead on the lintel.

It was cosy and intimate in the small cabin. Ames sat on the edge of his bunk watching Mary Lou move around the little galley, measuring coffee, looking to see if there were any cookies. Some day they might, or they might not, have a bigger boat. It was, Ames decided, immaterial. They had something much more wonderful. When the chips had been down both of them had believed in and trusted and tried to help the other.

Mary Lou came and sat on the bunk beside him. "About that five thousand dollars, Charlie. The money that was planted on you."

Ames slipped his arm around her waist. "What about it?"

"Do you think Sheriff White will give it back to you?"

"I doubt that. I doubt it very much," Ames said.

Mary Lou played with his fingers. "Well, I was just thinking. Do we *really* need a bigger boat, Charlie?"

"No," Ames admitted. "We don't. The *Sally* will do us for years. But what are you getting at, honey?"

Mary Lou said, "Well, they were kind of snippy at the club because I wouldn't work night before last, so I told them where they could put their job. And I told them that went for next season, too."

Mary Lou continued. "Even after we give Ben back his fifteen hundred dollars, we'll still have fourteen or fifteen hundred dollars. And if we don't have to save for a new boat—"

"What then?"

Mary Lou continued to play with his fingers. "Well, we aren't getting any younger, Charlie. We've been married for five years. And if we're ever going to have any children—"

In the deep silence that followed, the creak of the mooring ropes and the suck and gurgle of the tide were plainly audible.

Mary Lou raised her face. "Well?"

"Yeah. I see what you mean," Ames said.

He kissed her lifted lips then stood up and blew out the lantern and further words were unnecessary. The coffee and the Camden affair were forgotten as the night and their love filled the cabin.

THE END

The Dangling Carrot
DAY KEENE

CHAPTER ONE

Sam Langley was a mild-mannered man whose life outside of his business had resolved itself into a set routine of bridge several evenings a week, the usual service club lunches and dances and a rare day in the woods or on the lake. His mysterious disappearance evoked considerable alarm—for several reasons. One was the fact that the wealthy manufacturer of ceramics was the second prominent local businessman to disappear in a period of less than three months.

According to the story told to Lieutenant Eagan, the forty-two year old manufacturer and Mrs. Langley were playing bridge with the Hammonds when the continuous howling of a dog annoyed Langley to a point where he rose from the table in the game room with the avowed intention of "Shooting that damn hound."

Both Mrs. Langley and the Hammonds attempted to dissuade him. Langley, however, was adamant and taking an automatic pistol from a drawer in the game room, he opened one of the French windows leading out onto the lawn and strode into the night in the general direction of the howling.

A few minutes later Mrs. Langley and the Hammonds heard three shots. They waited for Langley to return. When he didn't, at Mrs. Langley's request, Mr. Hammond attempted to locate his host. But the other man could not be found. There was only his unfired pistol and an ominous pool of blood on the concrete apron of the garage to prove he had ever existed.

That was at nine o'clock on the evening of the eighth. Judge Evan Johns was not notified. There was no reason he should be. He was a magistrate, not a policeman. Besides, until he assumed the new office to which he had been elected, murder was not in his province.

The morning of the ninth dawned warm and clear. A soft wind blowing up from the south caressed the tops of the taller pecan and chinaberry trees, a playful wind that paused from time to time in shepherding great flocks of fleecy clouds across the sky to swoop down into the tree-shaded streets of Clay City, population twenty-six thousand, to whistle at the girls and swirl their full skirts into a reasonable facsimile of Marilyn Monroe standing on top of a New York subway grating.

Judge Johns awakened, as usual, at exactly seven thirty and lay for a long moment enjoying the spring air, orienting himself to the new day. He had gone to bed early. His night's sleep had been unbroken. He felt fine. He wished that, just once, Lou would get up and eat breakfast with him. Time was when she had. Time was when she had gotten his breakfast. But there had also been a time when Lou, maintaining twin beds were immoral, had insisted they sleep in a double bed; but that was a long long time ago.

A tall man just turned forty with his temples beginning to gray, lean-faced, with a whimsical smile that had endeared him to the electorate, Johns felt mildly puzzled as he showered and shaved. The little things he and Lou once had cherished had fallen away until now really nothing much mattered. After fourteen years of marriage they were only husband and wife. Even their most intimate moments had become a matter of habit.

Johns attempted to be philosophical about it. The fuzz on the sweetest peach wore thin from constant nibbling. A man couldn't expect ecstasy to last forever. Or could he?

When be finished showering and shaving he put on a clean shirt and a fresh white linen suit. He wanted to look his best. He owed the boys that much. When court convened at nine o'clock it would be the last time he would preside over city court, the last time the seemingly endless procession of traffic law violators, habitual drunks and wife beaters, chronic brawlers and perverts and petty thieves, would ever parade before him. The thought pleased him. If he had done well by the people, the voters of Hess and Clay and Calhoun counties had done well by him. It wasn't every young lawyer who rose to the circuit court bench.

Johns wiped the steam from the medicine cabinet mirror and studied his face as he knotted the black string tie he affected. Not that he was so young as he had been. The years were beginning to show. The lines in his face were deepening. He had almost as many white hairs as black. It had been twelve years since he had returned to Lou and Clay City. That had been in the Spring of '43, after he had been shot down over El Alamein during the all-out attack on Rommel in October of the preceding year. At the time he'd felt very bad about being washed out so early in the biggest show he would ever see. His smile turned a trifle smug. But, as matters had turned out, he'd been very fortunate. The minute pieces of flak the Air Force doctors had been unable to remove from his legs and upper body seldom bothered him, except just before a rain. And by the time the last of the boys in the local bar association had been separated from their various branches of the service he had already taken down his shingle and been elected judge of the city court. The pay wasn't spectacular, but it was ample for his needs, or had been.

His tie knotted to his satisfaction, Johns looked, hopefully, into the bedroom to see if Lou was awake. She wasn't. Her unsupported breasts sagging under their film of silk, she was still lying on her back blowing minute bubbles at the ceiling. He wondered as he walked down the stairs to the dining room, as he wondered a hundred times, how Lou could possibly sleep with two dozen metal curlers in her hair and her face smeared with grease or muscle tone, or whatever it was she used.

Hattie Belle had his orange juice waiting. The juice was tepid and filled with seeds. His eggs were underdone, his bacon and toast just this side of being burned, and the buttered grits were soggy.

Johns was tempted to speak sharply to the maid but Hattie Belle came in Lou's department. And, according to Lou, what with all the new factories moving into Clay City to take advantage of the mild weather and the surplus of low-priced labor, and social security and unemployment compensation, even indifferent maids were difficult to come by. Still, if the food continued to be as bad as it had been for the last few months he would have to take to eating his breakfast in one of the restaurants on the courthouse square.

Still hungry, Johns was reaching his broad-brimmed Panama from the hat rack in the front hall when Lou yawned her way down the stairs. She'd put on a shapeless wrapper. Her bare feet were thrust into scuffs, the pom-pom of one of them missing. Combined with the grease on her face and the halo of metal curlers, the unbelted wrapper trailing out behind her gave her the appearance of a creature from another world.

Women, Johns thought, were strange people. They painted their finger and toe nails. They spent hours at their dressing tables and in beauty salons and dress shops consciously making themselves beautiful for strange lecturers at the Woman's Club, for the women with whom they played bridge, for the butcher, the baker, the banker—for everyone except their husbands.

"I'm glad I caught you," she yawned. "Leave the car for me, will you, Evan? I have to pick up the tallies and the favors for the Chamber of Commerce luncheon."

"Of course."

"And please don't forget."

"Forget what?"

"We're playing bridge with the Hammonds tonight."

"Again?"

"We haven't played with them for two weeks."

"I just made a remark."

"Well you didn't need to be so sharp about it."

Johns shrugged and stooped to kiss Lou goodbye. Still miffed, she turned her face away. "You'd better not. You might get grease on your suit. And the cleaning bills are high enough as it is."

Still yawning, she scuffed down the hall to the dining room. Johns opened the front door and stood on the porch a moment debating between calling a cab and walking the five blocks to the combined city hall, police station and magistrate's court.

The day decided him. As he walked down the tree-lined street he tried to be angry with Lou, and couldn't. It was as much his fault as hers. Somehow they'd gotten into a rut, a rut bounded by household bills and paved with bridge at the Hammonds and the Heeleys and service club dances and Carreno Club musicals. Lou, at least on the surface, hadn't even been very enthused over his election to the circuit court bench. All she had said was, "That's nice. How much more will it pay?"

Johns wondered what had happened to his days in the woods and on the lake with Lou enthusing, on his return, over a brace of quail or a stringer of small mouth bass. He wished, just once, for a period of forty-eight hours, with nothing more important than each other. He and Lou could do as they once had done, lock the doors and disconnect the bell and spend an entire week-end just proving how much they loved each other. Or perhaps pick up a bottle and drive out to the lake and get slightly high and wind up swimming naked in the moonlight, content just to touch each other, to pretend there was no one in the world but them. Johns thought wistfully of the lake. He and Lou hadn't used the lake cottage in years. For all the good it did them he might as well put it on the market. Still, it was a link with the past, with brighter, happier, days.

He was practical. Perhaps he expected too much of life. Lou was thirty-seven. He was forty. Mature people didn't cut such didoes. It would be unseemly for a circuit court judge to behave in such a manner. On the other hand it had been fun and surely even after a man reached forty there was more to life than an occasional quick thank you, ma'am, making a fourth at bridge and listening to bosomy sopranos sing music he didn't understand and wouldn't appreciate if he did.

The warm air was filled with the subtle fragrance of green growing things. Cordial greetings of, "Good morning, Your Honor," followed him down the street. Johns' mood brightened as he walked. Next week it would be different. Once he ascended the higher bench he would have plenty to interest him. The trivia to which he had listened for years would be a thing of the past. A circuit court judge had power, the power of divorce and separation, of depriving men and women of their liberty for long periods of time, the power of granting life, of sentencing men to die. He had assumed great and grave responsibilities. Johns hoped he could live up to them.

"Judge not lest ye be judged," the Good Book said. And judging was his business.

After the bright clean freshness of the morning, the antiquated building housing the city court smelled like a sour old man, of stale tobacco smoke and lost hope and faulty plumbing. He would be glad to move into his air conditioned office in the new county building.

A uniformed patrolman was coming out the door. "Good morning, Your Honor," he greeted Johns. "For the last time, eh?"

"For the last time," Johns agreed.

A drunk was yelling in the tank. Sergeant Mercer was booking a vagrant. Johns crossed the worn wooden floor to the stairs leading up to his courtroom and stopped in front of Lieutenant Eagan's open door. The small office was crowded with men. He could see Doctor Avers, the coroner, Hal Terrill, the head of Identification, Jim Kelly, the police reporter on the *Courier*, County Sheriff Bodin and the various plainclothes detectives of the local force detailed to Homicide.

Johns walked into the office. "What's up?"

Jim Kelly told him. "It seems we have another one on our hands, Your Honor."

"Another what?"

Lieutenant Eagan polished his rimless eye glasses with a piece of tissue. "You haven't heard then, Evan?"

"Heard what?"

Eagan returned his glasses to his nose. "Sam Langley disappeared last night."

"You're kidding."

"I wish I was."

"What do you mean he disappeared?"

"Just that," Sheriff Bodin said. "According to the story they tell, him and Mrs. Langley and the Hammonds were playing a rubber of bridge in that big game room of his when the howling of some stray dog annoyed Langley and he took a pistol from a drawer and walked out to shoot it, anyway frighten the dog away. And that was the last they saw him."

Johns lit a cigarette. The story had all the elements of a rib. "You boys aren't by any chance pulling my leg because this is my last day here?"

"So help me, Judge Johns," Kelly said soberly. "It's just like Sheriff Bodin told you. 'I'm going to shoot that damn hound,' he tells Mrs. Langley and the Hammonds. A few minutes later they heard three shots. Then when Langley didn't come back Hammond went out to look for him. But all he could find was Langley's unfired pistol and a big pool of blood on the concrete apron of the garage."

Johns blew smoke through his nose. "Well I'll be damned. You say his pistol hadn't been fired?"

Terrill who doubled in ballistics said, "And hadn't been fired in years."

"You're positive?"

"I'm positive."

"Maybe Sam just walked out."

Lieutenant Eagan scoffed. "And left a quarter of a million dollar ceramic plant behind him. Uh uh. Anyway there is the blood."

Doctor Avers explained, "The body of an adult man contains about five litres of blood. That's roughly five, point, two, eight quarts, and while I have no way of ascertaining for certain I'd say there's at least a gallon spilled on the concrete back of the Langley garage. And no man can lose that much blood and live."

"It's the same type as Sam's?"

"I just checked with the blood bank," Kelly said. "AB Rh positive."

Eagan put his feet up on his desk. "And here's something else for you to think about while you're dishing out fines and thirty days this morning, Evan. Why didn't whoever shot Sam leave him where he fell? And how did they get him away? Carry him piggy-back? The neighbors on both sides of the Langley's say they heard the dog and the shots but both of them swear they didn't hear a car."

Johns sucked on his cigarette. "A real cutie, eh?"

"A cutie," Kelly agreed. "Good for circulation, but rather tough on the widow. Just like Tom Harper ten or twelve weeks ago. Only in this one Lieutenant Eagan has even less to go on. 'I'm going to shoot that hound,' Sam says. Then there are three shots, none of them fired by him. And when Hammond gets out there, say in four or five minutes, none of them are quite certain just how long it was before Hammond went out to look for Langley—presto—abracadabra—open sesame—Sam's gone."

"How's for trading jobs, Evan?" Lieutenant Eagen asked.

Johns looked at his watch. If court was to convene on time, he was due in his chambers in two minutes. "No, thank you," he refused the offer. "I'm afraid it's your headache, Jack. But remember that starting next week I'll be on the circuit bench and when you find whoever killed Sam, if he is dead, I'll throw the book at him."

"That's a big help," Eagan said.

Johns walked on up the stairs. He felt bad about Langley. He and Sam hadn't been really close for years, but they'd gone to the same grade and high school and in years past, as young men, they had hunted and fished together. In fact hunting and fishing had been Sam Langley's big passion. In fact, if he remembered correctly, at one time Sam had seriously considered reentering the government service as a forester or, failing that, buying a fish camp on the lake, just to be close to nature. But his father had changed all that. Langley senior had died and left Sam the ceramic factory and Sam had met and married Ella Townsend and in due time had become enmeshed in much the same dull routine of service clubs and bridge and the economic necessity of making a living in which he, himself, was entangled. Only Sam had made more money in one year than he made in ten.

There was only one bright spot in the picture. The Hammonds would, undoubtedly, be too shaken by their experience to play bridge and would call off their date with Lou and himself. Johns made a mental note. If they did, he would have a talk with Lou, a serious talk. He would try to find out just what had happened to them and what could be done about salvaging their marriage.

CHAPTER TWO

Johns' chambers on the second floor were small and hot and as smelly as the rest of the building. He snuffed his cigarette in the clean ash tray on his desk and washed his hands in the yellow-stained wash bowl behind the woven rattan screen.

Judging from what he'd heard in Eagan's office, the Langley case could cause considerable trouble. As Jim Kelly had pointed out, Jack had even less to go on than he'd had in the Harper case. And the Harper case was still in the unsolved files and would probably stay there.

Harper, too, had disappeared mysteriously. Johns reviewed the case as he dried his hands on a clean towel. At eight o'clock one morning Tom Harper had kissed his wife goodbye and left for his feed and farm implement store. The next Mrs. Harper had heard of him had been two weeks later when a trouble shooter for the power company had looked down from the high line pole, which he had climbed, and had spotted the metal top of a sedan in fifteen feet of water a few feet out from the ramp of the old ferry that had conveyed cars across the river before the new bridge had been built. The car had been Harper's new Buick purchased only the week before, its windshield starred and pierced by gunfire and four high-powered deer rifle slugs in the back of the front seat. But Harper hadn't been in the car.

The case was a sticker. Tom seldom drank to excess. And even if he had been stinking drunk he wouldn't have driven his car off the old ferry ramp. Tom had been born in Clay City and had known all the back roads like he knew the lines in the palm of his hand.

Nor was suicide a possible solution. Tom had no reason to take his life. He had a profitable business and a wife and two married daughters whom he adored. Besides, a man couldn't very well kill himself by shooting himself with a rifle through the windshield of his car, then, dead or dying, drive his car into fifteen feet of water.

The Sam Langley case coming as it did on top of the still unsolved Harper mystery was bound to cause political repercussions. Johns was glad the election was over. It could be, since he was one of the boys, the electorate of Hess and Clay and Calhoun counties wouldn't have elected him to the circuit court bench.

Hal Cass, clerk of the city court, opened the door of the chamber leading into the courtroom. "Whenever you're ready, Evan."

Johns refolded the towel and hung it back on its rack. "Anytime you are."

"You hear about Sam Langley?"

"Jack told me on my way in."

"A honey, eh?"

"To put it mildly. Anything new on the docket today?"

Cass moved his head from side to side. "The usual. Except Willie is back with us."

"Not Willie Jones?"

"The same."

"Don't tell me he got drunk and cut someone."

"That's how his arrest card reads."

"This is the fourth time, isn't it?"

"The fifth."

Johns made certain his string tie was straight. "I suppose I'd better give him ninety days this time. But by rights I should bind him over."

The clerk of the court shrugged. "The way I get it from Denny, once they sew him up the other boy will still hold shine without leaking at the stitches. But one of these mornings Willie is going to sober up and find himself in serious trouble."

"One of these mornings."

"All set?"

"Let's get it over with."

Standing in the doorway of the chamber, Cass nodded to the bailiff waiting in the courtroom, and the bang of a gavel was drowned out by the sound of people getting to their feet as the bailiff intoned the routine mumbo jumbo that preceded Johns' taking his seat. This morning, his last morning in the lower court, Johns was wryly amused. In the eight years he'd sat in magistrate's court the only words he'd ever heard clearly were:

"... is now in session, the Honorable Judge Evan Johns presiding."

Johns walked out and sat back of the desk on the slightly raised dais. Most of the benches in the small courtroom were occupied with dependents and their relatives, traffic law violators in the main, with God only knew how many drunks and brawlers, unable to raise bail, waiting in the bull pen. It was going to be a long session. It would, today of all days. He would be lucky if he finished the session by two o'clock. It would be three by the time he'd eaten lunch, and he'd hoped to spend the afternoon superintending the transfer of his law library and other personal possessions to his new air-conditioned chambers in the county building and, possibly, get in a few holes of golf.

The over-done bacon and underdone eggs and soggy grits were heavy in his stomach. The mild unpleasantness with Lou still rankled. He hadn't meant to be sharp with her. All he had done was make a remark.

"Call the first case," he said.

The defendant, a middle aged man, was charged with failure to yield the right-of-way, with a resulting collision. "How do you plead?" Johns asked him.

"Not guilty," the man said.

"Let the defendant be sworn."

With one hand on the worn Bible Hal Cass offered him, the man swore to tell the truth, the whole truth and nothing but the truth, and Johns listened with half of his mind as the arresting officer moved the magnetized miniature cars on the courtroom blackboard, the other half of his mind still wondering about Sam Langley.

It was a shame about Sam. A self-effacing man in his early forties, the ceramics manufacturer hadn't been a man to make enemies, certainly not an enemy who hated him enough to bait a trap with a howling dog, then pump three bullets into his body. And why, as Jack Eagan had asked, had whoever killed him carried Sam's body away? Why not leave it where it had fallen?

Johns realized the officer had finished his case and the defendant was offering a defense. It wasn't much of a defense. Johns heard him out patiently, asking a pertinent question from time to time, then found the man guilty.

"Twenty dollars and costs. The clerk will call the next case."

The endless procession continued, most of the cases involving minor traffic violations; driving too fast for conditions, failure to observe an authorized stop sign, speeding forty miles an hour in a twenty-five mile zone, unlawful parking, improper state license tag, driving under the influence of liquor, making an improper left turn, unlawfully emerging from a parking space.

Few of the defendants were represented by counsel. Johns continued to listen with half his mind, siding with the arresting officers in most of the cases but occasionally suspending a fine when circumstances seemed to warrant it. He was hot. He was bored. He wished he had a glass of bicarbonate of soda. He would be glad when this last session was over. In circuit court it would be different. There he would have to be on his mental toes every minute of the time, debating the finer points of the law, overruling and sustaining objections, listening to lawyers who knew their business and attempting to guide jurors who didn't. He was looking forward to Monday.

Cass called, "Willie Jones." The door of the bull pen opened, and a huge Negro boy shuffled out and stood in front of Johns' bench. Johns listened to the charge, then asked:

"How do you plead, Willie?"

"Not guilty, sir, Your Honor," Willie said. "At least not all the way guilty. All I do is cut the other boy a little an' he make a swipe at me first. The only difference is he forgot t' duck an' I didn't."

There was a snicker of laughter from the spectators in the courtroom. Willie was a welcome relief from the run-of-the-court traffic offenses and Johns, himself, had difficulty keeping from smiling. He glanced at the record card on his desk as the arresting officer made his case against Willie. Cass had been right. This was the fifth time that Willie had been brought before him. He really should give him ninety days. Still, when he was sober, Willie had a good work record. He also had eight children. And if he threw the book at Willie, Miss Simpkins of Welfare would climb his back. When Willie was tucked away, Welfare had to support his family.

"Did he give you any trouble?" Johns asked the arresting officer.

"No, sir," the officer said. "Willie walked out to the car by himself and sang all the way to the station."

"I don't go for t' git drunk, Your Honor," Willie offered. "I bin workin' hard all day an' I jist stop in this place on my way home for a beer an' hit kind of creep up on me. But I was jist sittin' there mindin' my business, havin' a drink or two, when this other ol' loud-mouth boy starts t' argufy. Then he makes a swipe at me an' I take out my knife an' swipe back."

There was another subdued burst of laughter. Johns tempered justice with common sense. "That swipe is going to cost you thirty days, Willie, the thirty days suspended conditional to your good behavior. But if I were you, I'd stay away from whiskey. If you don't, one of these mornings you're going to wake up in bad trouble. Knives and whiskey don't mix."

Willie was contrite. "Yes, sir. Thank you, Your Honor, You doan eveh see me back here again."

"Call the next case," Johns said.

"Miss Dale Chambers," Cass called.

Johns studied the girl with interest as the arresting officer, a youth by the name of Williams, opened the gate in the railing for her.

Miss Chambers was new to Clay City, at least new to him. Johns tried to decide if she was pretty. He decided she wasn't. The planes of her face were too square, her cheek bones too high, her gray eyes set a trifle too far apart for perfect symmetry. She was vital rather than pretty, with silken straw-colored hair worn in a long page boy bob and a long-legged, slim flanked, full bosomed body that exuded sex with every movement she made. Johns moved uneasily in his chair. Pretty or not, the girl did something to a man. At least she did something to him. He wondered what she was charged with. He hoped it wasn't solicitation. A body like hers should be used and treasured by one man. The thought of her prostituting it made him slightly ill.

"Thank you," she thanked Williams. "Thank you very much."

Her smile was as nice as the rest of her. Johns set back in his chair, relieved. Whatever the charge against her was, it wasn't solicitation. Now that the girl had come closer he could see she was just a girl, not more than nineteen or twenty, and her wide-set gray eyes were still filled with the innocence and the wonder of it all, the joy of just being alive.

The youthful officer blushed to the roots of his crew cut. "I'm certain you're welcome."

Cass read the charge against her. "You are charged with driving seventy-five miles an hour in a thirty-five mile zone."

"How do you plead, Miss Chambers?" Johns asked.

Her smile still hovering on her lips, standing so close to his bench he couldn't help but admire the powdered cleft that separated the two peaked spheres with which her stiffly starched shirtwaist was filled, the blond girl looked up at Johns. "I guess I'm guilty," she told him. Her accent was strictly Deep South, a lot farther south than Clay City. "Leastwise if the officer says so. He should know." Her smile widened. "But, so help me, Your Honor. Not that I'm excusin' myself. But I didn't know that ol' beat-up second hand car of mine could *possibly* go that fast."

The spectators left in the courtroom laughed. Johns didn't even attempt to restrain his smile. After the dull stuffiness of the morning there was something fresh and intensely vital about the girl, a wholesome vitality, like a cleansing spring wind blowing across the lake. He, suddenly, wanted to prolong the case, if just to look at Miss Chambers. "How about that, Williams?" he asked.

The youthful officer didn't seem to know what to do with his hands. "Well, she was doing seventy-five, Your Honor. I clocked her for four blocks. But there wasn't anyone else on the road. And like Miss Chambers just said, I don't think she realized she was going so fast."

"What leads you to that conclusion?"

"Because she tooted at me."

"She what?"

"Tooted. You know. With her horn."

"Where was this?"

"Out on the lake road, just inside the city limits. In front of Chuck's hamburger place. I was sitting in the cruiser taking a coffee break when I heard a car coming pretty fast. Then I see this '48 Plymouth go by. And Miss Chambers looks out the window and waves and toots her horn at me."

"So you chased her in the cruiser?"

"Yes, sir."

Johns was amused. "And just why did you wave and toot your horn at the officer, Miss Chambers?"

The blond girl considered the question. "I don't rightly know," she admitted. "But I'd just been paid. An' it was such a nice night. An' I was feelin' good. An' he looked kind of cute sittin' there. An', well I just tooted."

In the laughter that followed, Johns asked, "Had Miss Chambers been drinking, Officer?"

"No, sir." Williams was emphatic. "Not a drop. And she was a perfect lady. She pulled right over on the shoulder of the road and stopped as soon as I beeped my siren."

"And now you're sorry you stopped her."

Williams was even more embarrassed.

Johns returned his attention to the girl. "How long have you lived in Clay City, Miss Chambers?"

"Nine months, going on ten."

"With your parents?"

"No, sir. By myself." She wasn't asking for sympathy. She was merely making a statement. "You see my mother an' father died when I was just a little ol' yard baby down in Natchez an' kin folk took me in t' raise until I was fifteen. But I've been on my own since then."

"What kind of work do you do?"

"Wait table mostly."

"And where are you working now?"

"At the Elite Cafe."

"That's that new restaurant on the courthouse square, isn't it?"

The girl bobbed her head and Johns decided she was a natural blonde. The roots of her hair were as light as the gently curled ends. For some reason the knowledge both pleased and excited him. "Yes, sir," she said. "It is. Like I said, I came up from Natchez almost ten months ago an' I've been workin' there ever since."

"How much do you make a week?"

"Two dollars a day an' tips."

"Have you ever been arrested before?"

"Once." Miss Chambers amended her statement. "Well, I wasn't exactly arrested. But I did get a ticket for over-parking an' I had to pay a dollar."

In the burst of laughter following her confession, Judge Johns noticed that Jim Kelly had entered the courtroom and was talking earnestly to Cass, and for the benefit of the press he banged his desk with his gavel. "It is customary for this court," he said soberly, "to fine speeders one dollar a mile over the posted limit. In your case that would be forty dollars, Miss Chambers. But seeing as you are comparatively new to Clay City and Officer Williams has testified he doesn't believe you realized how fast you were going, a conclusion in which I agree or you wouldn't have attracted attention to yourself, I fine you forty dollars and suspend the fine."

The blond girl was puzzled. "Does that mean I do or don't have t' pay?"

"You don't. At least not this time."

The girl smiled her slow smile. "Thank you. Thank you very much, Your Honor."

"But don't let it happen again."

"No, sir, Your Honor. I won't."

Johns watched her through the gate and down the aisle and to the door of the courtroom. In the doorway she turned and smiled again, the fingers of one hand closing on a small palm. Then the swinging door hid her from sight.

"Call the next case," Johns said.

Hal Cass came over to the bench instead. "You'd better recess for a few minutes, Evan," he whispered. "Kelly tells me Ella Langley is downstairs raising hell because Jack and his boys haven't been able to find Sam's body."

"What has that to do with me?"

The reporter joined Cass at the bench. "Nothing, actually. But Mrs. Langley thinks that because you and Sam were friends and you are the new circuit court judge that maybe you can do something. And Lieutenant Eagan asked me to ask you, as a personal favor to him, to come down to his office and see if you can't quiet Mrs. Langley before she blows the roof off the station."

"I see," Johns said. "Of course."

He recessed court for fifteen minutes and Kelly walked through his chambers and down the stairs with him. "Holding out, eh, Your Honor? Hiding your light under a gavel?"

Johns was puzzled. "What do you mean by that?"

The reporter shrugged. "Nothing. Except every male in town except you have been eating the Elite Cafe out of supplies hoping the big-chested little blonde will give him a tumble, and all she's put out is checks. But she takes one look at you and those big gray eyes of hers light up like she is Mrs. Tom Edison the night he discovered the first incandescent bulb."

Johns was inwardly pleased and not a little amused. "I'm afraid you're exaggerating."

"Exaggerating? I saw the way she looked at you. The way you looked at her, for that matter." The reporter sighed. "A shame."

"What's a shame?"

"That this is your last morning in city court."

"Why?"

"Because after all these months I just discover how to save the paper a fine when one of the traffic boys picks me up for being a little heavy-footed."

"How?"

Kelly illustrated the alteration with his hands. "Just grow a pair of whatcha-ma-call-ems like she has. Geez. I'd give a week's pay just to look at them. You know how I mean."

"Get your mind out of the gutter," Johns reproved him. "Miss Chambers seems to be a very nice young woman."

"I'm certain she is," Kelly sighed. "At least no one in Clay City is able to boast otherwise. And God knows we've all tried."

CHAPTER THREE

With her eyes red and puffed from weeping and her hair disheveled, Ella Langley looked even older and less attractive than Johns remembered her. She was sitting in Lieutenant Eagan's chair, touching her nose from time to time with a wisp of lace as she laid down the law.

"Well, don't just stand there staring at me. You're supposed to be police officers, aren't you? Why doesn't one of you do something? Why don't you find my husband? At least find his body. A man can't just walk out of his house and disappear. Sam has to be somewhere."

Johns drew up a straight back chair and sat beside her. "Please. Get a hold of yourself, Ella. I'm certain that Lieutenant Eagan and his men are doing all they can."

The woman's painted fingernails dug into his forearm. "Thank God you're here, Evan. Make them do something to find Sam."

"I'm certain they're trying to," Johns said. He thought a moment, then added, "How were things between you and Sam, Ella?"

"What do you mean, how were things between us?"

Johns pursued his trend of thought. "You hadn't quarreled recently?" It was a delicate subject. He worded his question as delicately as he could. "What I am getting at is this. Sam had no reason to 'stage' a disappearance, did he?"

"Don't be silly."

"He had no business worries?"

"None. At least none he discussed with me."

"Your home life was harmonious?"

"Of course."

"There was no other woman in his life?"

Ella Langley wiped her tear-reddened nose with the wisp of lace. "Now you're being insulting, Evan. You know Sam and I have been happily married for fifteen years."

"Yes. I know," Johns said. "But sometimes outside pressures cause men to do strange things. And while Sam made a great deal of money at it I happen to know that he wasn't particularly happy in the ceramics business."

Ella Langley sniffed. "No. He wanted to be an outdoors man. He wanted to be a thirty-two hundred dollar a year forest ranger or run a smelly old bait camp. But I talked that nonsense out of his head years ago."

"Yes. I'm certain you did."

The wife of the missing man continued, "Sam's life was bound up in his home and his business and me." She seemed to be trying to convince herself of the truth of her assertion. "We were very happy together."

Jack Eagan ran his fingers through his thinning hair. "Yeah. I see what you're getting at, Evan," he said. "The same thought occurred to me. And if Sam just walked out I could explain the three shots Mrs. Langley and the Hammonds heard by him carrying a second gun. But I can't explain away the blood."

Doctor Avers repeated what he'd said earlier. "No man could possibly lose that much blood and live."

"And it checks out as Sam's type?"

"AB Rh positive."

"Talk, talk, talk," Ella Langley said. "That's all I've heard since nine o'clock last night. Can't you get it through your thick heads that Sam may be lying somewhere dying?" She got out of the chair in which she was sitting and pounded on Eagan's desk with her fist. "Why doesn't someone do something?"

Lieutenant Eagan attempted to explain that all leaves had been cancelled and every available man on the Clay City force was working on the case, but Ella Langley didn't even hear him.

"You're nitwits, stupid nitwits. All of you. A man can't just walk out of his house and disappear. There's a killer loose in this town and you all know it. First Tom Harper, now Sam. And if you don't find Sam today, now, this morning, within the next few hours, I'm going to get on the phone and engage the best private detective agency in Atlanta."

Eagan was slightly nettled. "If it will make you feel any better, Mrs. Langley, you do just that."

"I intend to," Ella Langley said. "As soon as I get home." She added, vindictively, "Then I'm going to phone the governor and tell him that law enforcement, per se, has completely broken down in Clay City, that you're all either crooked or afraid of your own shadows."

Eagan watched her out of the office, then apologized to Johns. "I'm sorry, Evan. I shouldn't have sent Kelly up for you. But I thought maybe you could do something with her."

"That's all right," Johns said. "We're all in this together."

"Ah," Kelly said. "Our new circuit court judge is a far sighted man. Right now he's thinking of four years from now."

"That's right," Johns admitted. "Also of Sam Langley. Sam and I haven't been close for years, but he was a nice little guy. And for the life of me I can't see why anyone would want to kill him."

"Me, either," Eagan admitted. "Or, even if we could explain away the blood, why he should want to walk out? Sam had just about everything a man wants of life. A nice home. Plenty of money. And an attractive wife. I mean that. She looks like hell today but I've seen Mrs. Langley with her war paint on and when she wants to be, she's still a very pretty woman."

Kelly rested one hip on Eagan's desk. "That gives me an idea."

"What kind of an idea?"

"How about turning what Judge Johns said around? Maybe there's another man."

"It's worth thinking about."

"It happens every day in the week," Kelly said. "There's one just came in over the I.N.S. wire. About some forty year old woman in St. Louis and her twenty-five year old boy friend. Only they fed her husband rat poison."

Johns nodded. "In a screwball case like this anything is possible." He got to his feet. "Well. I'll be glad to be of any help I can. You know that, Jack. But right now I've some more fines to dish out." He paused in the doorway of the office. "And while I'm not trying to tell you your business—"

"Yes—?" Eagan asked.

"If I were you, I'd check all angles. Sam's current financial status. The possibility of there being another woman. The possibility of Ella's having a lover. You questioned the Hammonds, of course?"

"For hours."

"Did either of them notice anything unusual before Sam picked up that pistol and walked out to shoot the dog?"

Lieutenant Eagan glanced through the notes and reports on his clipboard. "N-no. Except Hammond did say that Langley seemed preoccupied all evening. You know, like he was day dreaming or was concerned with some business problem. Then there was the bridge hand he laid down when he went out to shoot the dog."

"What about it?"

"It was one of those once in a life time deals, one spade short of being a perfect hand."

Doctor Avers was incredulous. "And instead of playing it, he walked out to shoot a dog?"

"That's the way we have the story."

"Funny," Johns said. "Damn funny."

He walked back up the stairs. God and God only knew what the end of the matter would be. Clay City wasn't big enough to be a real city. Still it was too large and too sophisticated to be considered a small town. And while its waters ran still, they ran deep. He, personally, knew enough, if the laws were enforced as written in the statutes, to put half of the prominent people, in town, himself included, in jail.

First Tom Harper. Now Sam Langley.

Johns paused in his chambers briefly, considering phoning Lou and asking her to go out and stay with Ella Langley. Then he remembered, in time, there was some unpleasantness between them, something concerning the Woman's Club. Lou would probably refuse to go and Ella wouldn't want her company.

He disposed of the remaining cases on the docket as rapidly as he could, but it was almost two o'clock by the time the last case had been called. He was hot. He was tired. He was hungry and not entirely pleased on returning to his chambers to find Lou waiting for him. The woman from Mars was gone and Lou looked cool and fresh and well-groomed in a light weight summer suit.

The discord of the morning was apparently forgotten as she lifted her face to be kissed. "Isn't it terrible, Evan?"

"You mean about Sam Langley?"

"What else? I almost died when I heard about it on the ten o'clock newscast. Have the police found out who killed him?"

"So far they haven't even found his body. And Ella's been raising hell with Jack."

Lou lit a cigarette. "She would."

Johns washed his hands in the bowl back of the screen. "What brings you downtown? I thought you were going to pick up the tallies and the favors for the Chamber of Commerce luncheon."

"I did that hours ago."

Johns peeked over the top of the screen. Lou had something on her mind, some favor she wanted to ask. He'd lived with her long enough to know. As he toweled his hands he said. "All right. Let's have it, Lou. What is it?"

She snuffed her cigarette. "Well, something has come up. Would you mind very much, Evan, if I fly up to Atlanta for a few days? I won't be gone more than four days at the most."

Johns hung the towel on the rack. "What's doing in Atlanta?"

"The tri-state convention of the Woman's Club. And the girls want me to be our delegate."

"Since when?"

"Since May Gordon called me this noon." The smile on Lou's face turned smug. "You may remember I told you I was supposed to be our delegate but that clique she runs around with pulled a fast one and elected Ella. But now, with this happening, of course she can't go."

"I see."

"And May said the girls wanted to know if I would go in her place and I said I would. You aren't angry with me?"

"Why should I be angry with you?" Johns sat back of his desk and dated and numbered a check. "How much money will you need?"

"Oh, say two hundred dollars. No. You'd better make it three."

"That much? I thought you said you'd only be gone four days."

Lou was hurt. "Well, I may have to do some entertaining. And you wouldn't want me to be cheap about it, would you? After all you are a judge of the circuit court. And some day you may want to run for State's Attorney."

"That's in the distant future."

"Well, you're a good party man. You could be nominated. And the husbands of some of the women who will be there are very influential men. Besides, I may see a dress or two I like."

Johns shrugged and wrote a check for three hundred dollars. Lou didn't ask for much. If she wanted to go to Atlanta, it was all right with him. They could have their talk when she returned.

Lou folded the blotted check and put it in her purse. "You're a sweetheart, Evan. I can just make the bank if I hurry." She kissed him lightly. "See you either Monday or Tuesday, darling. I don't know just which day I will get back."

Johns watched her out of his chambers, then filled in the stub in his check book. Time was when he had bought Lou a two dollar bunch of flowers, and she had stripped down to the buff and spent the entire night thanking him. Now, after fourteen years of marriage, she didn't even have time to tell him whether she intended to take a taxi or leave the car out at the airport.

For some reason the incident depressed him. The money didn't matter. It was as much Lou's as it was his. But somewhere along the way he and Lou had lost something, something very beautiful and intimate and, seemingly, very fragile.

Cass came in to say goodbye. "It's been nice working with you, Evan."

"It's been nice working with you, Hal."

The clerk of the city court was practical. "But I can't feel too badly about the change. It's a step up for you, a big one. And one of these days I'm going to boast I used to be clerk of the court for the State Attorney General."

It was, Johns thought, odd both Lou and Hal should have mentioned the same subject within a matter of minutes. Perhaps it was an omen. On the other hand, he didn't want any state or federal job. Somewhere along the line, with what he and Lou had lost, he'd also lost his ambition. What he really wanted to do was to stop sitting in judgment on his fellow man and hang out his shingle again and be a small town lawyer; a lawyer with time to fish and hunt and play golf and, yes, make love to his wife.

"Well, you know what they say," he told Cass. "South of the Mason-Dixon line, if you believe in God and the Bible, keep your mouth shut and your bowels open, and vote the straight Democratic ticket—you can't go wrong in politics."

Cass laughed at the old gag. "You going to clear out your personal stuff this afternoon?"

"Either today or tomorrow. Right now I'm going to eat. See you around, Cass."

"I'll be here." the clerk of the court said. "Unless this business about Sam Langley, coming as it does on top of the Tom Harper affair, costs us all our jobs in the next election."

"That's four years from now."

Johns descended the stairs a second time. The same, or another drunk, was banging a tin cup against the steel bars of the drunk tank. The aged building smelled as badly as it had that morning. He was glad to be leaving it for good.

Lieutenant Eagan's door was open but the group of men who had been in the office were gone. Johns felt sorry for Jack. If no progress was made on the Harper case and Sam Langley's body wasn't found it wouldn't be too many days before the *Evening Courier*, if only for the added circulation it would bring, would join Ella Langley in screaming for Eagan's scalp. And Jim Kelly would write the story, because it was his job.

He was almost out the front door when the desk sergeant called after him. "Just a minute, Your Honor."

Johns turned in the doorway. "Yes—?"

"Mrs. Johns said for me to tell you she will leave the car in the garage and take a cab out to the airport."

"Thanks," Johns thanked him.

He had done Lou an injustice. Lou hadn't been deliberately thoughtless. She'd just been excited over having been chosen delegate to the tri-state convention. It was, after all, quite an honor to represent a club as big as the Clay City Woman's Club, even if she had been second choice, even if Sam Langley had to die for her to inherit the delegate's mantle.

The clock in the court house tower boomed twice as Johns walked down the street toward the private club at which he usually dined, nodding when he was recognized exchanging pleasantries, stopping from time to time to shake an offered hand. The sense of well-being he'd had when he'd awakened that morning returned.

The afternoon was as nice as morning had been but the wind had risen slightly and the girls in their light spring outfits were having even more trouble with their skirts, one sweet young thing in particular. As Johns walked behind her admiring her poise and the portions of her lithe young body exposed by the playful wind, perhaps because she was blonde, she suddenly reminded him of Miss Dale Chambers and he was no longer amused. What was it Kelly had said?

Every male in town except you has been eating the Elite Cafe out of supplies hoping the big-chested little blonde will give him a tumble and all she's put out is checks. But she takes one look at you and those big gray eyes of hers light up like she is Mrs. Tom Edison the night he discovered the first incandescent bulb.

Johns' masculinity was flattered. The reporter's inference that the blond waitress had been attracted to him was ridiculous. Still, such things did happen. It was a matter of public record. Johns was honest with himself. It had been a number of years since any woman, Lou included, had affected him the way that Miss Chambers had. All he'd had to do was look at her to desire her. And bio-chemical reaction was a two-way road.

Then Kelly had mentioned her breasts, the original apples in the

Garden of Eden, the fundamental means of sustaining, if not conceiving life.

Just grow a pair of whatcha-ma-call-ems like she has. Geez. I'd give a week's pay just to look at them. You know how I mean.

Despite the warmth of the day, small beads of cold sweat formed on Johns' forehead and cheeks. He realized his mouth was dry and he was swallowing with difficulty. He was a fool, an old fool, to even think of such a thing. His virility asserted itself. Or was he? He was, after all, only forty and—he sought for a description of himself and came up with—reasonably distinguished looking. If there was anything to what the reporter had said about the way Miss Chambers had looked at him, looking her up might prove interesting. So he was a circuit court judge. A judge had the same passions and appetites and failings all men have.

On impulse he walked past the plate glass door of the stodgy private club in which he usually took his midday meal, and turned down the south side of the courthouse square, telling himself he intended to look at his new chambers before he ate—and knowing he was lying to himself.

It was the first time he'd been in the Elite Cafe. The restaurant was a combination bar and grill, comparatively new and air conditioned. At this hour of day there were few customers in it. A swart man of obvious Greek-American ancestry came out from behind the chrome and red leather bar and insisted on shaking his hand.

"This is an honor, Your Honor."

Johns said the first thing that came to his mind. "As you undoubtedly know, I'm assuming my new duties in the courthouse next week so I thought I'd sample your food."

"An honor," the swart man repeated. "I hope you find us satisfactory, Judge Johns. I would be very pleased to number you among my customers."

Johns followed the swart man down a carpeted aisle and allowed himself to be seated in an unoccupied booth. He tried to tell himself he was being very foolish in doing what he was doing. Jim Kelly had exaggerated. Reporters were notorious for making something out of nothing. To the blond girl who had stood in front of his bench a few hours before he was merely a graying jurist. Still, thinking back, there had been a certain something in her smile when she had turned in the doorway, in the way she had closed her fingers against her palm, more in invitation than farewell.

Johns studied the menu the Greek had given him. In his state of mind the fine print on the menu blurred. He could sense the blond girl standing in front of the table before she spoke, and he raised his eyes with an effort.

Changed into a sheer pastel green nylon uniform that revealed her bare shoulders and soft white concave bare mid-riff under her peaked satin brassiere, Miss Chambers was even more physically attractive than she had been in her street clothes.

"Well. Hello," she smiled.

There was a slightly breathless quality to her voice. Her drawl was more pronounced than Johns remembered it. The natural perfume of her body, fresh and clean and young and vital, made Johns perspire even harder. It was an effort for his lips to form the word. "Hello."

"I hoped you might come."

"It would seem I'm here."

"So I see," she said simply. "I'm glad."

The way she said it, the way she was looking at him, the slight rise and fall of her breasts as she spoke, the pressure of the muscular young thigh pressed hard against his arm, left no doubt in Johns' mind. Jim Kelly had been right. The blond girl was as attracted to him as he was to her—and with the same purpose in mind. There was no need for preliminary maneuvering or argument or citing legal precedent. All that needed to be done was to name the place and time.

He would, of course, have to be very discreet, but there was always the lake cottage. Johns was glad now Sam Langley had died. With Lou in Atlanta there was no one to whom he had to account for his time. It should prove to be a very interesting week-end.

CHAPTER FOUR

The wind died shortly after six o'clock but early evening continued pleasant. Johns had never realized that hours could pass so slowly. He bathed and shaved again and put on another fresh suit, then built himself a drink before sitting down to the over-done roast and not quite boiled potatoes that Hattie Belle set in front of him.

She complained, "You're jist pickin' at your food."

Another time Johns would have been tempted to tell her why.

Tonight he merely shrugged, glad that Hattie Belle didn't sleep in. "It's the heat, I guess," he lied. "You may go as soon as you finish the dishes."

"Yes, sir."

"And, Hattie Belle."

"Yes, sir—?"

"For the few days Mrs. Johns is in Atlanta it won't be necessary for you to prepare any meals. In fact you might as well take the week-end off."

"Where you goin' t' eat?"

"In one of the restaurants downtown. Then, again, I may spend the week-end fishing."

"Fishin'," the colored girl sniffed. "That's all men think about. That man of man has lost more jobs—" She realized her personal affairs were of no interest to Johns and failed to complete the sentence. "But hit's for you t' say. I'll be glad t' git the time off."

Johns waited until she was gone and he was alone in the house before mixing another drink. It was the last of the liquor in the cabinet. He would have to pick up a bottle or two before he met Dale. It was still difficult for him to believe the almost incredible simplicity with which their rendezvous had been arranged.

"What are you doing tonight?" he'd asked her.

"Going out with you," she'd told him. "But I know how it is with a man like you. You can't be seen with a girl like me."

"So?"

"So park off the lake road, in that clump of chinaberry trees just beyond the school house."

"And?"

"I'll be there at five after ten. Just as soon as I get off work. You know some place we can go? An' I don't mean a night club or a juke."

"I do."

"Then park where I told you an' I'll be there."

That was all there had been to it. A thought amused Johns. If Kelly knew how right he had been he could write a story for the *Courier* that would compete with Sam Langley's mysterious disappearance.

The possible danger involved, the possibility that someone might see him with the girl, sobered Johns. Even a breath of scandal would end his career on the circuit court bench before it started. Perspiration beaded on his face as he sipped his drink thinking of Dale, remembering the pressure of her young thigh, the sight and feel and perfume of her, the frank, almost primitive, desire in her wide-set gray eyes.

All things considered, the goal was worth the risk. Or was it? Perhaps he was entering his dangerous years. His dangerous years.

The phrase recalled an admonition he'd heard as a young lawyer, an admonition delivered by an aged circuit court judge to a middle-aged defendant charged with attempting to have relations, against her will, with a fifteen year old girl with whom he claimed to be in love.

"There are some," the aged judge had lectured, "who hold that a man's most dangerous years are in the time of his youth. I have never subscribed to this theory. The young lions are less crafty than the old, therefore less to be feared. A young man shrugs off a rejection and looks for another pretty face. But for the aging would-be-lover there is no such simple solution. His remaining street cars are few and far between and when refused permission to board one, in his ire and frustration, he is frequently tempted to use force. And the prisoner is admonished that at his time of life the breach of the peace with which he is charged is inimical to his gray hairs. Fortunately, for the prisoner, in this instance he did not succeed in his desire. I am therefore, reluctantly, forced to release you. But let the prisoner keep in mind if he is not to be brought before this court again on perhaps an even more serious charge he will have to learn how to grow old gracefully. He will have to be constantly aware it is during the twilight of his life that a man lives through his most dangerous years."

Johns finished his drink and washed the glass in the kitchen sink. The admonition, sound as it was, didn't apply to him. He wasn't old. He was only forty. No force was implied or necessary. Dale wanted him as badly as he wanted her. Nor had he any intention of falling in love with or making a habit of her.

He walked out to the garage and got a glass rod and spinning reel, a new outfit he'd never used, and put it and his dusty tackle box in the back seat of the car. Telling Hattie Belle he might go fishing had been an inspiration. The lake cottage was in an isolated cove. Few of the cottages on the lake were occupied this early in the year. But if someone should chance to see a light and drop by, the rod and tackle box would give credence to his story.

He felt younger, freer, less-married, than he had in years. "No. I wasn't particularly lonely," he'd tell Lou on her return. "In fact I drove out to the lake and got in a few days fishing." More, if Lou should chance to phone him from Atlanta his driving out to the lake would explain his not being home.

Re-entering the house he closed all the windows on the off chance it might rain, then locked both the front and back doors and drove the five blocks to the package store across the street from Clay City's combination city hall and police station.

Pop Emery was amused as he sacked the bottles and gave him his change. "Kinda celebrating a little, eh, Your Honor?"

"In a manner of speaking," Johns admitted.

"I don't blame you, Evan," the package store clerk confided. "I've seen 'em come. I've seen 'em go. I saw you hang out your shingle. I voted for you the first time you ran for the city bench. And it isn't every young lawyer who gets to be a circuit court judge."

"No. That's true."

"It's quite a responsibility."

"Yes. It is."

Johns put the sacked liquor in the front seat of his car and checked his watch against the clock in the court house tower. He still had two hours and fifteen minutes to kill.

For want of something better to do, he crossed the street and climbed the worn stone stairs of the station. Another meeting of minds was taking place in Jack Eagan's office. Plainclothes and uniformed officers were trekking in and out like so many busy ants.

"What now?" Johns asked the night desk sergeant.

Phinny put down the cardboard container of coffee out of which he was drinking. "Well, look who's here. I thought we'd got rid of you."

Johns lit a cigarette. "I just happened to be in the neighborhood. What goes on in Eagan's office?"

"A new twist in the Langley case."

"The boys have found his body?"

"No. Sam is still missing." Phinny drank from the container again and wiped his mouth with the back of his hand. "But the way I get it, late this afternoon, some big shot from Ohio, in the same business Sam was in, showed up at the ceramic plant."

"What's so odd about that?"

"He claims Sam sold him the plant last week for two hundred thousand dollars—cash."

"He what?"

"That's what the man claims. What's more, he has papers to prove it."

Johns crossed the oiled station house floor to the open door of Eagan's office. A well-dressed, florid-faced man was sitting in one of the chairs beside Eagan's desk. As Johns stood in the doorway, he said, "Now, just a minute, Lieutenant. I can't see what all this fuss is about. Langley and I have been negotiating the sale for some months. There was no secret about it."

Eagan asked, "And on what date was the sale of the ceramic plant consummated, Mr. Squires?"

"On Tuesday of last week."

"Where?"

"In the office of my attorney in Canton, Ohio."

Coy White of Eagan's squad offered, "That checks with what Mrs. Langley told me, Jack. She says Sam was out of town Monday, Tuesday, and Wednesday of last week. On a business deal."

"He told her he'd sold the plant when he got back?"

"No, he didn't."

Eagan picked a shred of cigar tobacco from his lip. "Damn and double damn. This thing gets more and more screwball."

Mr. Squires leaned forward in his chair. "May I ask what is so strange about one manufacturer selling his plant to another business man in the same line of business?"

"You say Langley insisted on being paid in cash?"

"He did."

"Didn't that strike either you or your attorney as rather strange?"

"Frankly, it did. But at the time we assumed that Mr. Langley wanted the payment in specie for tax purposes."

"In other words you and your attorney assumed he intended to defraud the government."

"In other words. Especially as he insisted that payment be made in bills of ten, twenty, and fifty dollar denominations and no record be kept of their serial numbers. But I still can't see why you should be so interested in the deal."

Lieutenant Eagan told him. "Mr. Langley is missing, has been since last night when he laid down an almost perfect bridge hand and got up from the table in the game room of his home with the avowed intention of shooting a howling dog."

"Make sense, Lieutenant."

"I'm trying to," Eagan said wearily. "You see, up until now, at least until you drove into town this afternoon, because of certain physical factors we have assumed Mr. Langley was murdered. Now I'm not so certain."

"You say his wife knew nothing of the deal with me?"

"So she says."

"And the two hundred thousand dollars I paid him for his plant?"

"Is missing along with Langley." Eagan pushed back beside the door. "Nice, eh, Evan?"

"A headache."

Eagan filled a paper cup with water. "Look. As young men you and Sam were fairly close. How was he about women?"

"Just what do you mean?"

"Was he a chaser?"

Johns thought back down the years. "N-no. Not particularly. I can remember a couple of times when he went down the line with the boys, but he never seemed over-rabid on the subject."

"That's the way I had him pegged."

"He's clean as a whistle on that score," Coy White said. "Oscar and I have been asking all around town, since eight o'clock this morning. You know, in the jukes and bottle clubs and by-the-hour motels, everywhere a guy might take a babe. And none of them even know Langley except by name."

Eagan crumpled the paper cup in his hand. "I don't get it. If Sam wanted to walk out on Ella, why bother to come back from Canton after he closed his deal with Mr. Squires? And why three shots and the blood? And why didn't someone see him go wherever he went? And how did he go? Both of his cars are still in the garage. Now I don't know whether to look for a body or a missing man."

Johns asked Eagan if his office had checked into the financial status of Tom Harper's estate.

"No," the homicide man admitted. "But it's a good idea. Get the cashier of the First National on the phone, Coy."

Johns edged his way out of the office. There was nothing he could do. He didn't want to become involved in anything that might make him miss his date with Dale. It could be that Sam Langley, fed up with the life he was leading, with two hundred thousand dollars in cash, had just walked out on Clay City and Ella.

Johns put the matter out of his mind as he drove slowly out of the town and explored the network of secondary and farm roads surrounding Clay City, enjoying the Spring night, killing time, anticipating his rendezvous with Dale. It had been a long time since he'd been unfaithful to Lou, once at a bar association meeting in Mobile when some of the boys had insisted on bringing in some pretty girls just to see how the other half lived. And once when an unhappily married college chum of Lou's had been their house guest and had insisted on adding him to the collection of horns she was growing on her elderly husband's brow.

Johns attempted to justify what he intended doing. He loved Lou. To the best of his knowledge Lou loved him. For a long period of time, up until a few years ago, he'd had no need of any other woman. But with the fragile something they'd once had, lost, seemingly beyond recovery, their relationship, both physical and social, had become a dreary affair, with Lou as discontented and as unsatisfied as he.

It was exactly ten o'clock when he parked in the clump of chinaberry trees on the road leading out to the lake. With the lights and the motor of his car turned off, it was dark and still in the grove. The only sounds he could hear were the chirp of the cicadas, the booming of the frogs in the sloughs, the far-off howl of a dog and the thumping of his heart.

Despite all his arguments to the contrary, he was acting foolishly. A circuit court judge didn't make and keep a rendezvous with a little blond waitress whom he'd only known a few hours. Still, Dale was very lovely. What was more, she realized their need of being discreet.

"I know how it is with a man like you," she'd told him. "You cain't be seen with a girl like me."

His masculinity asserted itself. He wasn't doing a thing that wasn't done every night in the week, three hundred and sixty-five nights a year by doctors, lawyers, merchants, chiefs, rich men, poor men, beggar men, thieves. And judges for that matter. All men were endowed with certain inalienable rights. He had every human if not moral right to wring what he could out of life before life entirely escaped him.

It was five minutes after ten when a pair of car headlights bobbed down the road and a black car turned into the grove and parked under a tree a few yards from where he was waiting. A moment later Dale opened the door of his car. There was the same slightly breathless quality to her voice he had noticed in the cafe.

"Am I on time?"

It was difficult for Johns to force the words past the constriction in his throat. "To the minute."

"An' you don't think I'm bein' cheap?"

"Of course not."

The scent of her filled the car. It was too dark for Johns to see her face but she seemed to be searching for words. "I don't usually do things like this, Mr. Johns. Believe me."

"Call me Evan."

"Evan, then," Dale said. "In fact, it's the first time I eveh have." She was breathing as hard as he was. "But when I saw you this mornin', sittin' there back of your desk in the courtroom, well, I cain't explain it, but somethin' happened."

"I felt the same way," Johns admitted.

Dale moved closer to him. "Why don't you kiss me then? I've been wantin' you to for hours."

They kissed for a long time, her fevered lips sweet and soft under his. Then they were touching, fondling, exploring each other, filled with the wonder of each other's body, almost as if they were the first man and woman in the world.

Then Dale squirmed uncomfortably and moved out of Johns' arms. "What in the name of time am I sittin' on?"

"I bought a couple of bottles of whiskey."

There was mild reproach in the blond girl's voice. "You don't need to get me drunk."

"I know," Johns said thickly. "I know."

CHAPTER FIVE

The hour before dawn lay dark and heavy on the clearing. Through the open window Johns could hear the faint lap of the lake on the beach. He lay looking at Dale, content just to hold her, the yellow glow of the oil lamp on the dresser giving an added feeling of intimacy to the small bedroom.

The night had been as beautiful as he had hoped it would be, something to treasure and remember. The two bottles of whiskey were unopened. They'd had no need for outside stimulant. He lit two cigarettes and gave one of them to Dale.

"Are you sorry?" she asked him.

Johns was truthful. "No."

"Neither am I." She lay a moment puffing on the cigarette he'd given her, then turned her head on the pillow. "You won't be angry if I tell you something?"

"Of course not."

"This is the first time in three years that, well, anything like this has happened."

Johns wished Dale hadn't brought up the subject. The knowledge that any other man had been privileged to know and enjoy the perfection of her body saddened him.

Dale blew a small puff of smoke at the ceiling. "He was my husband."

"You left him?"

"No. He was shot down over Korea. In the last days of the war, while there was supposed to be a truce."

The knowledge that her husband had been a fellow flyer imbued Johns with a fierce desire to protect her. "You poor kid."

"That's the way it goes, I guess, sometimes. But for a few months I was a lieutenant's wife. Little old cotton-pickin' me. An' once a girl gets used to bein' married, well, sometimes I've thought I would go out of my mind."

"You poor kid," Johns repeated.

Dale moved her head on the pillow. "But I just couldn't bring myself to be cheap with any man."

"Of course not."

She smiled her slow smile. "I just kept hopin' Mr. Right would come along. An' sure enough, you did."

Johns was flattered. "Thank you."

Dale added earnestly, "Not that I want or intend t' make any trouble for you. I know there is a Mrs. Johns an' all I can ever hope to be is just your sometime girl. But if you can figure a way so t'night won't be the only time, I'd like that."

Johns forgot his good intentions of not making a habit of Dale. "I think that can be arranged."

She fondled his face with her free hand. "I'm glad."

"What time do you have to go to work?"

"Not until Monday morning."

"How come?"

Dale continued to be frank. "Because I knew if t'night turned out like I hoped it would, like it did turn out, I wouldn't feel much like carryin' a tray this mornin'. So I told Mr. Poulous, he's the man who owns the Elite, that I had t' drive to Natchez to see a man in the V.A. office there about somethin' concernin' Tom."

"Tom?"

"That was my husband's name."

"You get a widow's pension?"

"No."

"Why not?"

"Because I signed it and his insurance over to Tom's folks. He got t' be a lieutenant but his folks are just share croppers an' both of them sort of old an' we'd only been married a few months an' I didn't even have a baby for him so I didn't feel that rightfully I had anything coming."

Johns' respect for the blond girl rose immeasurably. "What a nice thing for you to do."

Dale snuffed her cigarette and lay with her hands clasped under her head. "It seemed only right. What time do you have to be in court?"

"Not until Monday morning."

"How about Mrs. Johns?"

"She's in Atlanta. She left this afternoon, as a delegate to the tri-state convention of the local woman's club."

Dale was little girl pleased. "You mean we have all t'day an' t'night an' t'morrow an' t'morrow night?"

"That's what I mean."

Dale took her hands from under her head and turned on her side, the peaked tips of her firm young body brushing Johns' chest like twin butterflies. "Then maybe we'd best get some sleep." Flecks of green specked her gray eyes. "Unless you have a better idea."

Johns took her in his arms. "It might be I can think of something."

It was long minutes later and the green flecks were gone from her eyes when Dale sat up on the edge of the bed. "Know somethin', Mister?"

"What?"

She continued an odd mixture of practibility and naiveté. "I like your ideas. An' I like you. You're nice an' you're sweet. An' you make me feel like a lady even when I don't belong t' feel that way." She bent and kissed Johns without passion. "Is there a beach in front of this place?"

"A good beach."

"Then why cain't we go swimmin' before we go t' sleep?"

"No reason."

"No one will see us?"

"Not if we're back in the cottage before it gets light." Dale put on her high heeled shoes and nothing else and stretched like a tawny young cat. "Come on. I'll race you down t' the beach. An' the last one in is a dirty name." The morning mist was rising from the lake. The water was clear and cool, but not too cold to be enjoyable. They played near the shore for a moment, then Dale spotted the diving raft in the first red feelers of dawn and treading water, suggested, "Let's swim out to the raft an' back. Then we'd best get inside before some nosey-minded body sees us. It's a going to come day dawn in a few minutes an' I meant what I told you in baid. I don't ever want to cause you any trouble. An' if I thought I would, I'd never see you again."

It was an effort for Johns to swim out to the raft. He was more tired than he realized. It had been a long, strenuous, night. Dale had been very demanding. And he wasn't as young as he had been. Forty wasn't twenty, even thirty. He would be glad to get some sleep.

Dale reached the raft easily but couldn't climb up on it. "Push me up, Evan, please. We'll rest a minute, then swim back."

Johns pushed her up on the raft and was no longer either tired or sleepy. It was an odd sensation. His flesh seemed to feed on hers. Just touching Dale's young body refreshed and strengthened him. He lay beside her on the raft watching the morning awaken, thinking how wonderful it would be to be married to a girl like Dale. He knew she wasn't socially minded. He doubted if she would care what her man did for a living. If he were married to Dale he could resign from the bench and hang out his shingle again and spend all his spare time hunting and fishing and making love to her.

Johns put the thought from his mind. It was an absurd impossibility. He had assumed certain obligations. He was married to Lou. He intended to stay married to her. All Dale could ever be to him, or he to her, was a source of mutual physical gratification, a hide-away corner of his life in which he could forget his judicial duties and dream of things as they might have been.

Dale rested her wet hair on his shoulder. "Know somethin' else, sugar?"

"What?"

"If I had a cottage like you have, I purely wouldn't live in Clay City."

Johns patted her lightly. "You're talking like a little Cracker."

Dale snuggled even closer. "That's what I am. Remember? I wait table in the Elite Cafe." She giggled. "I'm the lil' ol' girl who went seventy-five miles an hour in an old beat-up Plymouth." Her voice filled with awe. "I'm glad now I did, but I still don't know how I did it. Maybe I ought to go back and give that used car dealer another fifty dollars for introducin' me to you."

"Out of your two dollars a day?"

"Countin' tips, I don't do so bad. And that's another thing. I want you to promise me something."

"Anything." At the moment Johns meant exactly that.

"I don't want you to ever offer me money or think you have to buy me expensive presents."

"Why not?"

"Because it would make me feel I was being bad for pay. An' if there's one thing I'm not it's a—well, you know what I mean."

Johns kissed her wet hair, then her eyes. "I know what you mean."

"Not that men haven't offered me money. That dirty talkin' reporter for one. What's his name?"

"Jim Kelly?"

"That's him. And Mr. Poulous for another. You know I purely believe if I was so minded I could wind up with the Elite Cafe."

"Instead, you picked me."

"That's because I like you."

Johns started to kiss the lips under his, but looked over the lake instead as the high-pitched whine of a not too distant outboard motor shattered the stillness of morning.

Dale turned on her stomach and looked where he was looking. "Must be some early risin' fisherman trying to get himself a mess of bream."

"More likely someone after bass," Johns said. "They strike best just at daybreak." As the whine of the motor came closer he slipped over the side of the raft and helped Dale down into the water. "And we'd better get back to the cottage."

"It's for you to say."

When they reached the beach Dale picked up her shoes and crossed the packed sand to the screen door of the cottage. Johns started to follow her inside and stopped as the whine of the outboard motor cut out and a man's voice carried clearly over the placid surface of the lake.

"There's a light in Judge Johns' cottage," the man said. "Let's ask if we can use his phone."

"Okay," a second male voice answered him. "Twist her tail and I'll head for the cove."

The motor misfired then caught and the high-pitched whine resumed. Johns followed Dale into the bedroom and snatched a pair of old fishing pants off a nail. "You stay in here and keep quiet. I'll get rid of them as soon as I can." He realized Dale was trembling and took her in his arms. "And don't be so frightened."

"I cain't help it. What if they saw me?"

"They didn't." Johns kissed her lightly. "You towel and get into bed. And pull something over you. You're not only frightened, you're cold."

Dale continued to cling to him. "You won't be long?"

"Not a minute longer than I can help."

Johns had difficulty pulling the trousers over his wet legs. A wool shirt and a pair of old sneakers gave him even more trouble. Finally dressed, he strode out onto the porch, snatched up his now spinning outfit and walked down to the shore of the lake, reaching it just as the motor cut out a second time, and a flat bottom skiff beached on the sand. There were two men in the boat, neither of them known to him.

Johns forced a calmness he didn't feel. "Hi. You fellows are out rather early, aren't you?"

"That's for sure," one of the men said. He spat tobacco juice over the side of the skiff, then introduced himself. "I'm Sam Ogden, Judge Johns. From over Mud River way. And this is Al Pearson, my neighbor. You don't know us but we know you and when we saw your light Al and I thought it might be best if instead of heading back to the bait camp we asked if we could use your phone."

"I'm sorry," Johns began. "But—"

Pearson got out of the boat and stood ankle deep in water staring at a bulky object on the duck boards of the skiff. "Damnedest thing that ever happened to me, Your Honor. On my first cast, too. You're a bass fisherman. You know. It being kind of warm these last few days and knowing bass head for deep water when it's warm I was trying a deep-running spoon and for a few minutes I thought I was snagged until I reeled in and it bobbled to the surface."

Johns waded out to the back of the skiff. "Until what bobbled to the surface?"

Pearson pointed to the object on the duck boards. "Him. And being weighted down the way he is with all that old iron we had one hell of a time getting him into the boat."

The lake water cold on his feet and the morning wind cool on his wet flesh, Johns stared at the iron-weighted body of the man lying face up in the now rapidly brightening dawn. Sam Langley hadn't walked out on Ella Langley intentionally. He was dead, shot three times through the head.

"You searched the body?" he asked.

"Not us," Ogden told him. "We know enough law for that, Your Honor. We didn't handle him anymore than need be to get him out of the lake and the hooks of Al's spoon out of his coat. You don't mind if we use your phone to call the sheriff?"

There was nothing else Johns could say. "Of course not."

The night just past, so beautiful a moment before, was sour in his mouth. God knew what would happen now. He was glad for one small break. Neither Ogden nor Pearson had seen Dale. The phone was in the living room. There was no reason for either man to enter the bedroom.

Once they had phoned Sheriff Bodin he could send them out to stand guard over the body. Then if Dale kept her head and didn't panic, it being as early in the morning as it was, with a little luck, it might just be he could sneak her out the side door of the cottage and back to her own car and Clay City before the isolated clearing on the lake filled with police and reporters.

CHAPTER SIX

The walk back across the hard-packed sand of the beach to the cottage seemed interminable. The sun was higher now and objects were brighter. The spring on the screen door rasped in protest, as Johns entered. He pointed out the phone with a nonchalance he didn't feel. "Help yourself. I'll be with you in a minute."

He opened the door of the bedroom and closed it behind him. Dale was standing, terrified, holding an oversize bath towel in front of her. When she would have spoken, Johns motioned for her to be silent and a moment later Al Pearson's drawling voice penetrated the thin wood partition.

"Operator? Get me Sheriff Bodin's office, will you? I want t' report findin' a body." The connection was bad and he had to raise his voice. "That's right. A body. In Loon Lake."

Dale's lips moved in silent question and Johns answered her as silently. "Sam Langley. Get dressed."

Her eyes wide and frightened, Dale sat on the edge of the bed as her knees refused to hold her. Johns gathered her lingerie and stockings and dress and laid them on the bed beside her. Things had gone well so far. At least, Dale hadn't panicked and screamed. Now if he could only get her out of the cottage without either of the two fishermen seeing her.

He pressed his lips to one wet ear and whispered tersely, "Get dressed. Fast. I'll be back in just a minute." He kissed her to give her confidence, then picking up one of the unopened bottles of whiskey from the dresser, he returned to the living room.

Ogden was looking out the screen door, Pearson was still holding the phone, talking to one of Sheriff Bodin's deputies. "No. I don't know who he is," he told the deputy. "Like I told you I was fishing a deep-running spoon an' for a time I thought I was snagged."

Johns cut the seal of the whiskey bottle with his thumb nail. "Tell him it's Sam Langley's body."

The connection continued poor and Pearson had to shout into the mouthpiece. "Judge Johns says to tell you it's Sam Langley. That's right. I'm callin' from the Judge's cottage. He was just getting ready to put out when we pulled in with the body. Yes, sir. We'll stay right here."

Despite the cool of the morning, when Pearson hung up, he was perspiring profusely.

Ogden turned from the screen door. "Langley? That's the fellow who owns the ceramics factory, ain't it?" He corrected himself. "Owned it, rather."

Johns got three tumblers from the kitchen and poured a generous portion of whiskey into each glass. "That's right. He disappeared mysteriously last night and the Clay City police have been looking for him ever since."

"Well, I'll be damned," Pearson said. He accepted the whiskey gratefully. "I didn't get to read the *Courier* last night but I can sure use this. You've no idea what a shock it was to see him bob to the surface."

Ogden gulped his drink and set the glass on the table. "Never see nothing like it. Someone sure didn't like the guy, him all weighted down like that. The police any idea who done it?"

"No idea," Johns said.

Pearson asked. "So what do we do now?"

Johns led the way back to the porch. "I'd suggest you men wait with the body. Meanwhile I'll drive to Clay City and contact Lieutenant Eagan and the dead man's widow."

"That's right," Pearson agreed. "Someone ought to let her know."

To get them as far away as possible, Johns walked back to the skiff with them. Ogden had been right about the weights. Whoever had killed Langley hadn't meant for his body to be found. It was only by chance that it had been.

"You wait with him," Johns said. "I'll be back. As fast as I can make it. But the sheriff's men will probably be here before then."

Ogden sat on a thwart of the skiff. "I hope so. The one day we get to go fishing and what do we catch? A body."

Johns returned to the porch. His car was in the rear of the cottage. There was no danger of either Pearson or Ogden seeing Dale from the skiff. His problem now was to get her to her own car in the clump of trees near the school house before the lake road was filled with police cars.

He opened the door of the bedroom. Dale had pulled on her dress and put on her shoes without bothering to stop for stockings or lingerie but, womanlike, she'd taken time to run a comb through her wet hair and apply lipstick. Even frightened as she was, she was still pretty.

As Johns watched, she stuffed her sheer bra and panties and stockings into her purse. "What did you do with the fishermen?" she asked him.

He told her. "They're guarding the boat."

"They can see us from the water?"

"No."

Some of her fright seemed to leave her. "Good. Now if we can just get back to my car before someone sees us together. Darn. Somethin' like this would have t' happen."

Johns led the way out the side door of the cottage and opened the door of his car for her.

"It was Mr. Langley's body?" she asked.

"Yes."

"But it said in the *Courier* last night that he walked out in his own yard to shoot a dog."

Johns put his car into gear and drove down the narrow road as rapidly as he dared. Everything depended on speed. "There's a lot more to it than that," he told Dale. Johns remembered that Langley was reputed to be carrying two hundred thousand dollars when he disappeared and that as an officer of the court he should have searched the body. Either Jack Eagan or Sheriff Bodin would be certain to call him on that, but it was too late to do anything about it now.

"How did they happen to find him?" Dale asked.

"They were fishing, deep, and one of their spoons caught in his clothes."

Dale used her compact to powder her nose. "Darn," she repeated. "This would have to happen to us."

Johns was gaining confidence with every passing mile. It would take some time for the deputy on duty to contact Sheriff Bodin and more time for the sheriff to dispatch the men he wanted to the lake.

Man, he thought, was an odd creature. Worried as he was about being seen with Dale, the question of jurisdiction intrigued him. If Langley had been killed at the lake it was Sheriff Bodin's baby. On the other hand, if Langley had been killed in Clay City and his body carried to the lake, it was Jack Eagan's headache.

The road here was deeply rutted. Dale clung to the door of the wildly careening car. "What are you thinking about?"

"Jurisdiction."

"What does that mean?"

"Who has charge of the investigation. Sheriff Bodin or the Clay City police."

"Who has?"

"I don't know," Johns admitted. "It will be up to the technicians to determine where he was killed."

"They can do that?"

"They can."

As they neared Clay City and the road grew smoother, Dale resumed powdering her nose. "What did you mean back there at the cottage when I talked about the story in the *Courier* and you said there was a lot more to it than that?"

Johns increased the speed of his car. "Just that. Just before I met you I stopped in at the station house and there was a ceramics manufacturer in Lieutenant Eagan's office who claimed he bought Langley's factory last week. For two hundred thousand dollars. In cash."

There was respect in Dale's voice. "That's a lot of money. Did Mr. Langley have it with him?"

"No one knows."

They rode in silence for a moment. Then on the chance that they might pass or meet a car, Johns said, "If we should pass a car or see one coming toward us, scrunch down."

"Please give me credit for having some good sense," Dale said hotly. "If we're seen together you may not get t' be a judge of the circuit court but with some of the men pesterin' me as they have been, it wouldn't do me any good either. I tol' you last night I wasn't cheap."

Johns was contrite. "I'm sorry."

Dale ran a comb through her wet hair. "You should be, t' get me in such a mess. Why, if it'd been a little lighter, those two fishermen might have seen us lyin' mother-nekkid on that raft."

Her remark broke the tension. Johns laughed. He could see the clump of trees by the school house now. "Don't worry your pretty head. No one is going to see us together."

It was Dale's turn to be contrite. "An' I suppose I won't eveh see you again?"

Johns slowed for the clump of trees and turned in. "Why not?" he said as he parked beside Dale's 1948 Plymouth. "It was just a bad break that things happened as they did. Of course you'll see me."

"Where?"

"I'll drop by the restaurant and we'll figure some place to meet."

Dale kissed him, lightly at first, then with increasing passion. "I hope you mean that, because, even after what all's happened, I like you. I like you very much."

Johns forgot the element of time and kissed her as she wanted to be kissed. Even after the use he'd made of them last night, her lips were sweet and fresh, almost virginal. "I like you, too," he assured her. "Most girls would have lost their heads and panicked. But you've been a little soldier."

Dale's lips continued to feed on his. "An' you'll come by the restaurant t'night and tell me everything that happens when you get back to the cottage?"

"I thought you told Mr. Poulous you were going to drive to Natchez."

"I can tell him I changed my mind."

"I'll be by," Johns promised. He kissed her lightly. "Now you get in your own car and get. In just about three minutes, a car from the sheriff's office is going to come roaring down the road."

Dale kissed him a last time. "Until tonight."

"Until tonight."

Johns watched her start her car and disappear into the maze of streets leading to the heart of Clay City. They were safe from discovery now. She was just another waitress on her way to work. He backed his own car onto the road. And he was a graying circuit court judge on his way to report the finding of a body.

He was passing Chuck's Hamburger Place when he heard the first siren and a quarter of a mile farther on when the first sheriff's car appeared and braked in a squeal of tires beside him.

Deputies Phil Hanson and Tony Terrill were in the front seat of the car. "I thought we might pass you," Hanson said. "A hell of a mess, eh, Judge?"

"A hell of a mess," Johns agreed.

"He was murdered?"

"I'd say shot three times through the head."

"You know the guys who found him?"

"No. But they're waiting with the body."

Hanson raced the motor of his car. "Good. We'll see you back at the cottage. The sheriff is right behind us."

The car drove on down the lake road, and Johns drove into Clay City and down the semi-deserted streets to the square. There were cars waiting in front of the station. Men boiled in and out of the building, a combination of city hall, police station and magistrate's court. The sheriff's office had notified Eagan. There was really no reason for his drive into town but in the excitement he doubted that anyone would stop to think of that.

He braked his car behind the last police car in line and sat a moment before getting out, attempting to analyze his emotions. One of his boyhood friends was dead, obviously murdered. He should feel sorrow or anger, or at least compassion. He didn't. All he felt was cheated. All he could think of was Dale. When he'd told her they could spend the entire week-end together she'd been little-girl pleased. She'd said, *You mean we have all t'day an' t'night an' t'morrow an' t'morrow night?*

Now this.

Perhaps he was wrong about himself. He would see Dale again. Nothing could stop him from seeing her. He could close his eyes and feel the young vitality of her body pressed to his, taste her lips, see her big eyes fleck with green as he caressed her. Perhaps the admonition he'd heard the old judge deliver applied to him, after all.

Perhaps he was entering his dangerous years.

CHAPTER SEVEN

Johns used the phone on the booking desk to call Ella Langley. He told her that Sam's body had been found and offered his condolences. She cried so hard he couldn't hear what she said. By the time he'd finished the conversation most of the officers in reserve were already on their way to the lake.

Sergeant Mercer had just taken over the desk from Phinny, the night man. "Tough," he said. "Tough. No chance of it being suicide, eh?"

"Not with all that iron on him," Johns said. "He was weighted to stay put. Besides, a suicide doesn't shoot himself three times."

Johns walked out of the station and back down the street to his car. As he started the motor, Jim Kelly hurried up the street and stopped beside the car. The reporter's eyes were blood shot and his breath was heavy with whiskey. "The one night I tie one on," he complained, "and something really big breaks. Now, to make matters worse, my damn car won't start. Mind if I ride with you?"

Johns opened the door for him. "Of course not." He was secretly amused. His thoughts of the night before were still true. If Kelly knew what had really happened at the lake, the reporter could write a story that would compete with Sam Langley's murder.

Kelly took a pint bottle from the pocket of his coat. "Care for a drink?"

"No, thank you."

"Mind if I do?"

"You're twenty-one."

Kelly drank deeply from the bottle. "Just to put some hair back on the dog." He found a wad of crumpled copy paper and a pencil. Hungover or not, he was still a good reporter. "Now, if you'll just fill me in, so I can phone back something from the cottage. Judging from your clothes, you were out at the cottage fishing."

"That's right."

"With Mrs. Johns?"

"No. She's in Atlanta."

Kelly shook his head. "That's right. We ran that in the last edition. She replaced Ella Langley as the Clay City Woman's Club delegate. All right. You were out at the cottage."

Johns told the story the two fishermen had assumed. "And I was just about to put out on the lake when two fishermen hailed the shore and asked if they could use my phone."

"This was what time?"

"Shortly before six. It was just beginning to get light."

"You get their names?"

"Sam Ogden and Al Pearson. They said from over Mud River way."

"How'd they happen to tie into Sam?"

Johns told Kelly what Pearson had told him. "One of them, Pearson, I believe, said because it had been running so warm the last few days, he was fishing a deep-running spoon and the hook caught in Langley's coat."

"I'll be damned. I will be damned," Kelly said. "The one chance in a thousand, eh, that the body would ever be found?"

"At least until summer."

"Sam was weighted?"

"With at least a hundred pounds of iron."

Kelly returned the copy paper to his pocket and drank the whiskey left in the pint bottle. "That gives me enough for a lead. God knows what happens from here in."

"God knows," Johns agreed. His feeling of having been cheated deepened. Instead of sleeping all day, with Dale snuggled in his arms, it would be a hard day and a long one.

Kelly asked, "He was shot?"

"I'd say three times through the head."

"You'd say?"

"It was still pretty dark when I looked at the body."

"You searched him?"

"No," Johns admitted. "I didn't. I slipped up there. But if he was killed for the two hundred thousand dollars he got for his factory it isn't likely his killer put the money in the water with him."

"No," Kelly answered, "not likely."

The reporter irritated Johns. Still, it was his job to ask questions. And a smart jurist, with an eye toward the future, always maintained pleasant relations with the press.

Kelly was smug. "Anyway, it checks with my lead last night. I went out on a limb by insisting that Langley was dead, strictly on the coroner's estimation of the amount of blood on the apron of the garage."

"So it looks like you're right," Johns said.

There were about two dozen cars in the clearing. Sheriff Bodin and Jack Eagan were using the living room of the cottage to question Sam Ogden and Al Pearson. Down on the shore of the lake, standing near the skiff, Doctor Avers was wiping his hands on a towel he'd taken from his bag. A combined group of technicians had taken over the body in the skiff.

Johns retrieved his glass rod and spinning reel from the beach. The coroner nodded cordially. "I was right, eh, Evan? I said no man could lose five litres of blood and live. More, according to the condition of the body, they must have brought him right from where he was shot to the lake."

Johns blew sand from his reel. "How?"

The coroner folded the towel neatly and returned it to his bag. "That's not in my department. Bodin and Jack Eagan can figure that out."

Johns crossed the sand of the beach to the cottage. Pearson and Ogden seemed glad to see him. Sheriff Bodin looked old and tired. Eagan glanced up from the chair he'd preempted. "You don't mind, do you, Evan?"

Johns stood the glass rod in a corner of the room. "Of course not."

"You called Ella?"

"From the station."

"She took it hard, I imagine."

"Very hard."

Johns glanced at the door of the bedroom. He'd closed it when he and Dale left. He hoped it had stayed closed. Anyone could tell just by glancing at the bed the purpose for which it had been recently used.

Kelly squatted down beside Pearson. "What part of Mud River are you from, Mr. Pearson?"

"Rural Route One," the man told him. "The same with Sam. We're both of us farmers."

"You fish Loon Lake often?"

"Four or five times a year."

Sam Ogden had had enough. Sam stood up and ran his fingers through his grizzled hair. "How much longer does this go on?" he demanded. "We've told you all we know. Judge Johns can tell you that. All we know is that we snagged a body and like you're supposed to do, we called the law right away."

Eagan looked up at Johns. "How about that Evan?"

"I'd say that was correct," Johns said. "I heard them out on the lake before I saw them. I heard the whine of their outboard motor. Then one of them, Mr. Ogden I believe it was, said, 'There's a light in Judge Johns' cottage. Let's ask if we can use his phone.'"

Ogden bobbed his head. "That's right!"

"Then Mr. Pearson said, 'Okay. Twist her tail and I'll head for the cove!' And they put in with the skiff and the body just as I was about to put out. They explained how they happened to snag it."

Sheriff Bodin said, "The little things. Only in this case it doesn't tell us a goddamn thing. The men didn't know it was Sam?"

"I'm positive of that," Johns said. "When Mr. Pearson was calling your office I had to tell him to tell your deputy it was Sam Langley's body they'd found. Later, when I offered them a drink, Mr. Pearson said he hadn't read last night's *Courier*."

Pearson asked, "What's so important about us knowing or not knowing who he was?"

Jim Kelly got to his feet with obvious effort. "Two hundred grand," he said wryly.

Lieutenant Eagan explained. "Mr. Langley sold his factory for that much last week—in cash. And seeing as the money hasn't been found, the assumption is he had it on or with him when he disappeared."

Pearson mopped his face with a grimy handkerchief. "That's a powerful lot of money but we never saw it. Like we told the judge when he asked us, both of us know enough about the law so we didn't handle the body any more than it took to get the spoons of my hook out of his coat."

There was no doubting his sincerity.

"Well, that's all for now," Lieutenant Eagan said. "But before you go, I would appreciate it if you'd run a couple of my men out and show them about where you snagged the body."

"We'll be glad to," Pearson said.

Eagan detailed two men to go with them, then got up and walked around the room. "I've seen some cuties in my day but this one is a lulu. A man lays down a perfect bridge hand to go out and shoot a howling dog and winds up on the bottom of Loon Lake."

Kelly made a few notes on his pad. "How about jurisdiction?"

Sheriff Bodin seemed relieved. "We've agreed to share it. Doc Avers says Sam has been dead since shortly after he disappeared night before last. But there bein' blood on the apron of his garage don't tell us for sure if he died right there or on his way out here."

Kelly asked, "How about that business of none of the neighbors hearing a car?"

"That sticks me," Lieutenant Eagan admitted. "To be frank, all I know is Sam is dead and, at least to date, two hundred thousand dollars in bills of ten, twenty and fifty dollar denominations are missing." He turned on his heel and looked at Johns. "And there's a topper to that one, Evan."

"What?" Johns asked him.

"You remember suggesting that I check into Tom Harper's financial status?"

"I do."

"Well, I did. And that one is as screwball as this one. Tom left Mrs. Harper the house, twenty-thousand dollars in insurance and a business worth maybe thirty thousand more. But the day before he disappeared, he closed out his business account for sixty thousand and cleared out his safety deposit box. There isn't a thing left in it but his insurance policies and the deed to the house."

Johns whistled softly. "Murder for profit."

"And a big one. If these two jobs were done by the same man they've netted him close to three hundred thousand dollars."

"But how—?"

Eagan cut Johns short. "You tell me that. Both Tom and Sam were good business men. And even if they weren't, even if it was a swindle of some kind, just how did the killer get Tom to drive his car into the river and Sam to wind up at the bottom of the lake, neither one with a dime in his pocket?"

"I'm glad I'm a judge," Johns said.

"You should be. The sheriff and I are in a spot. We haven't a thing to go on but if we don't figure out both murders it will probably cost us our jobs and our pensions."

Coy White said, "I read a story once where a smart hypnotist—"

Lieutenant Eagan was in a black mood. "Stuff. No hypnotist, no matter how good he was, would be able to hypnotize two men as smart as Tom Harper and Sam Langley into liquidating their assets and going willingly to their deaths. We've got to come up with a lot better solution than that."

An idea tugged at Johns' mind but he couldn't make it come clear. He asked, "Have you found any connection between the two men?"

"None."

"How about Ella having a lover?"

Lieutenant Eagan ran his fingers through his hair. "That's an even bigger laugh. I had the Langley maid on the fire for two hours after you left last night. And from what she tells me, Ella Langley lost her interest in sex so many years ago it isn't even funny. She gave Sam what he wanted when he wanted it. But strictly as a favor. And for almost a year, if I can believe what the maid tells me, there hasn't even been much of that." Eagan looked thoughtfully at the bottle of whiskey Johns had opened for Ogden and Pearson, and Johns remembered his duty as a host.

"How about a drink?" he asked.

Eagan was honest. "I'd like one. A big one. So we're on duty. I'd just as soon lose my job for having whiskey on my breath as I would for not being able to solve a Chinese puzzle."

Johns washed the three glasses he'd used and got more from the kitchen. "Drink up. I have another bottle in the bedroom." He was partially truthful. "I was going to celebrate changing jobs last night but didn't get around to it."

Eagan slopped whiskey into his glass. "I sure can use this."

Sheriff Bodin followed his example. "Amen."

Johns pushed the bottle to Coy White and Oscar Fell and opened the bedroom door to get the unopened bottle. It was standing where he'd left it, beside the bottle of mixes. He reached for the whiskey bottle and as he did he saw the bed reflected in the mirror of the dresser. Both pillows were indented and the sheet was rumpled. More, in stuffing her hose and lingerie into her purse, in her haste, Dale had allowed one of her sheer hose to fall to the floor and neither of them had noticed it.

Sweat beading on his forehead, Johns fluffed the pillows, then drew the top sheet up and hastily stuffed the stocking into the pocket of his fishing pants, as he realized that someone was standing in the doorway of the bedroom.

He straightened with an effort to find Kelly looking at him. Johns glanced at the bed. It looked all right now. At least it would pass casual inspection. But he'd been so engrossed in his tidying that it was impossible for him to tell just how much the reporter might have seen.

"What do you want?" Johns asked.

Kelly wet his lips with his tongue. "A drink. That's all. Just a drink.

I thought you said you had another bottle in here. Or wasn't I included in the invitation?"

Judge Johns realized that he was holding his breath and exhaled. Kelly was smart. It was Kelly who had first pointed out that Dale was attracted to him. It was Kelly who had said:

Every male in town except you has been eating the Elite Cafe out of supplies, hoping the big-chested little blonde will give him a tumble and all she's put out is checks. But she takes one look at you and those big gray eyes of hers light up like she is Mrs. Thomas Edison the night he discovered the first incandescent bulb.

It could well be that Kelly realized he'd been equally attracted to Dale. A lump formed in Johns' stomach, then dissolved as reason asserted itself. Kelly might or might not know that he'd gone to the Elite Cafe. Kelly might even suspect he'd dated Dale. One thing, however, was certain. Kelly might be smart but as long as he'd gotten Dale out of the cottage without anyone seeing her, the reporter couldn't prove a thing.

"Of course," Johns said evenly. "Of course." He picked the whiskey from the dresser. "Come along. I was just straightening up a bit before I got the bottle. You know how things get when a man is batching it."

The reporter's voice was as expressionless as his face. "Yeah. Sure. Of course. I'm a bachelor."

CHAPTER EIGHT

The day was as hot and long as Johns had expected it to be. There was only one nice thing about it. It was good to be back in the woods again, if only as a member of a posse of men trying to find the point along the shore line at which Sam Langley's body had been put into a boat and rowed out to the spot where it had snagged.

Along with the other members of the posse he'd beaten the underbrush all morning without any of them finding any clue that could possibly be back-tracked. At noon they had gathered at the several bait camps and one resort open on the far side of the lake for a sandwich and a beer or a soft drink. Then they had begun to search again. Now with night less than an hour away, it would seem that the day had been wasted.

Neither of the two bait camp men or the proprietor of the resort had seen or heard anyone on the night that Langley had disappeared. Nor had any of the posse found anything for either Lieutenant Eagan or Sheriff Bodin to work on.

Judge Johns sat on a fallen log and fanned himself with the battered fishing hat he'd snatched from a peg in the cottage. It could be they'd overlooked the spot. It could be the killer had left no trace of his arrival at the lake. Still, the fact remained that either Langley or his body had been transported from the apron of the Langley garage to the deepest part of Loon Lake.

Johns attempted to substitute reason for physical activity. Only one road led out to and past the lake. Another road partially encircled it. The shore line was dotted with cottages similar to his own, most of them still closed for the winter. The man who'd murdered Sam Langley knew the lake. The fact that the body was sunk in the deepest part of the lake proved that. Most of the cottages had boats, some bobbing at piers, some pulled up on the beach and overturned, some merely left upright. During the day just past he'd examined at least thirty boats for signs of recent use, or blood, or any tangible clue that one of them might reveal. The other members of the searching party had done the same. They were still where they had been when they'd started that morning.

On the surface, Sam Langley had laid down an almost perfect bridge hand and gone out to shoot at a howling dog who'd annoyed him, and somehow had bridged the five miles between the Langley house and the spot in the lake where his body had snagged. Miraculously none of his neighbors heard or saw him or a car. The situation didn't make sense. If Langley had been killed in his yard his killer couldn't have carried him off in his arms or on his back without someone seeing him. If Langley had left the yard of his own volition why had he done so and where had the blood on the concrete come from?

The mosquitoes grew more vicious with approaching night. Johns sat slapping at them, trying to think of some spot, some cottage he might have overlooked. Time was, when he and Lou had spent almost every week-end at the lake, that he'd known the shore line as well as he knew the four sides of the courthouse square in Clay City. But that had been years ago.

He got up and fought on through the underbrush. As far as he was concerned, only three things were certain. The killer was familiar with the lake. Dead or alive, Sam Langley had been brought to the lake in a car. And once the lake had been reached, a boat had been used to transport Sam's body to the spot where it had sunk.

Johns stopped suddenly and looked back the way he'd come. Two hundred yards back down the shore, just beyond the fallen log where he'd stopped to rest, he'd been forced to wade knee-deep in the lake to get around a clump of underbrush growing out into the water. A vague memory stirred in his mind. If he remembered correctly and he thought he did, the out-jutting underbrush hid the mouth of one of the shallow creeks that, with its natural springs, fed Loon Lake. Just how far back the stream went or whether it ran under the road which partially encircled the lake, he couldn't remember. But if it was the stream he thought it was, he and Lou had once explored it.

Johns fought his way back the way he had come and forced a path under and through the out-jutting brush. He found himself in a narrow green tunnel, roofed with interlaced tree branches. He had remembered correctly. It was the stream he and Lou had explored. He took a few steps into the tunnel. The branch-covered brook was narrow but knee deep and wide enough for a determined man to force a boat down it and through the brush into the lake, even if he boat contained another man's body.

Johns considered calling for someone to help him search the creek and decided against it. The lake was three miles long and two miles wide, with perhaps twice that much shore line. The searchers were widely scattered. It would be time enough to shout for help if he found anything.

He walked upstream slowly, sometimes in water only to his knees, at other times waist deep. The bottom was muddy and slippery. Twice he slipped and fell, but persisted. The creek was longer than he remembered it. A second memory stirred in his mind. This was the spot on the lake where the encircling road was broken. The stream had no real head. It began in a slough over which it had been impossible to build a road. At this point there was a gap of about three hundred yards between one dead end of the road and the other.

He waded on, searching the darkening green on either side of the creek for a boat. Night wasn't far away and he was about to turn back when he found what he was looking for. The boat, a flat-bottomed ten foot skiff, had been pulled up a few feet into the trees and underbrush bordering the creek. Johns pulled it back into the water. It had been used recently. Water, not rain water, sloshed on the duck boards. Here, while it was too dark for him to see them clearly, there seemed to be dark stains on the thwarts, dark stains that could be blood. He returned the boat to the bank and leaving the stream, he fought his way through the thick tangle of vegetation in the general direction of the road.

There were no cottages here, not for at least a mile. The nearest fellow searcher was at least the same distance away. Judge Johns took a bearing in the last of the fading daylight and fought on through the woods. Once he found the road, he could walk around the lake to the cottage or until he encountered a car and return with Lieutenant Eagan and Sheriff Bodin. They had something to work on now. If the stains on the thwarts of the skiff should prove to be blood, they would know how the killer had gotten Sam into the lake without anyone seeing him. The boat itself could be traced. There might even be tire tracks on the soft shoulder of the road.

It was completely dark now. He came on the road unexpectedly. If his estimation of the distance was correct, it was less than two hundred yards from the spot on the bank of the creek in which the boat had been hidden. It might be even less. At night a man had a tendency to circle.

It felt good to be out of the brush. Johns stood a moment slapping at the mosquitoes hovering around him in swarms. When he was rested he started on and stopped to study what looked like a large boulder or a small construction shack looming out of the darkness where the road dead-ended. Then he realized what it was—an unlighted car.

It was much too dark for him to see its shape or outline. He sensed more than saw what it was. He took a step toward it, then another. It could be that after transporting Sam Langley's body to the lake, the killer had mired his car and been afraid to call a tow truck.

Johns took a third step toward the object, then flung himself sideways. He was not quite quick enough, however, as a dry branch snapped behind him and a viciously swung club swished through the dark. Because he was falling at the time, the blow caught the side of his head and stunned him but failed to knock him out. Johns rested his weight on his knees and the palms of his hands, shaking his head from side to side in an attempt to clear it. But before he could regain his senses, there was a bright flash, as of lightning, and he felt the soft muck of the road rise and fill his mouth and nose. He made a feeble attempt to push his face out of the mud. Then his body twitched and lay still....

Outside of the fuzzy feeling in his head, Johns had never been more comfortable. He was lying on something soft with someone holding him. Rain was pattering on the roof over his head.

He lay with his eyes closed, trying to remember where he was. Of course. He was at the cottage. He'd spent the night making love to Dale. Then they'd slept all day and now it was night again. It was time to get up and eat. He started to speak Dale's name and was glad he hadn't when the fuzzy feeling in his head became intense pain and a bright light shone in his eyes.

Doctor Avers said, "He's coming around now. He'll be all right. Evan is slight but tough. I know. I've seen the scars left by the flak he picked up over El Alamein."

Johns swallowed the mud in his mouth and opened his eyes. He was sitting in the back seat of a police cruiser. Jack Eagan was holding him and rain was pattering on the metal roof. Doctor Avers was swabbing a stinging liquid on his lacerations on the side and back of his head. Other faces were peering at him through the rain-streaked windows and over the back of the front seat.

"Easy makes it, fellow," Eagan said. "Don't try to talk until Doc gives the word."

"He can talk," Avers said. "There's nothing the matter with him but a couple of nasty lacerations on the back and the side of his head. I'd say someone hit him with a club."

Johns forced himself to sit erect. "They did." Eagan put a cigarette in his mouth and lit it. It tasted good. Johns sucked smoke into his lungs before continuing. "How did you happen to find me?"

Eagan said, "We almost didn't. We were ready to start back to town when we noticed your car was still at the cottage and fanned out again." He nodded at one of the men in the front seat. "It was Coy who found you. On the chance that you'd gotten lost and tried to make your way to the road, he and Oscar drove around the lake and here you were, lying at the dead end."

"There was a car?" Johns asked White.

The plainclothesman shook his head. "Not when me and Oscar got here. You were on your back on the shoulder of the road and the rain beginning to come down pretty hard by then."

Johns sucked more smoke into his lungs. "What time is it?"

"Almost ten o'clock."

Johns considered the information. Whoever had clubbed him had done a good job. He'd been unconscious for over three hours.

"What's this about a car?" Eagan asked.

"There was a car," Johns told him. "Don't ask me the year or the make. I don't know. It was just a deeper blob of black against the night. There's also a boat, somewhere down there on the bank of the creek."

Outside in the wet night, a powerful police trouble light winked on and Sheriff Bodin said, "All right. Let's see if we can find it, boys. Judge Johns says there's a boat in the creek."

Eagan lit a second cigarette and put it between his own lips. "The creek empties into the lake?"

Johns' head continued to ache. "It does. The mouth is just back of a clump of jutting underbrush."

"We should have thought of this spot," Eagan said. "How come you happened to?"

"I don't know," Johns said. "But Lou and I explored it once, and I was trying to think of some spot that we might have missed."

There was shouting outside the car and a crashing in the underbrush, as a dozen men bulled the skiff that Judge Johns had found through the thickets up to the road.

"Here she is," Hal Terrill said. "Tucked away as neat as can be, less than two hundred feet from the road. No wonder none of the bait camp men heard anyone on the lake that night."

Another of the posse said, "Whoever the guy is, he sure knows the lake."

Lieutenant Eagan got out of the car. "Don't handle the boat any more than you have to."

Hal Terrill was pessimistic. "I doubt if it's going to tell us much. There's thirty more like it on the lake and it's been raining for three hours."

Doctor Avers finished working on Judge Johns' head and joined the men standing in the rain around the boat. Johns looked at it through the open door of the cruiser. In the bright glow of the trouble lights the dark stains on the thwarts and floorboards were even more pronounced than he remembered them.

Terrill dug into one of the thwarts with the point of his knife. "Blood, and plenty of it. Whoever killed Sam drove him directly here, then poled and rowed the body out where it was snagged."

"Looks like it," Coy White agreed. "But if Sam lost so much blood back there by his garage, how could he bleed so much here? And why didn't someone hear them drive away?"

The identification man shook his head. "There you have me."

Lieutenant Eagan returned to the car and stood just outside the open door of the cruiser. "Now about this car you mentioned, Evan."

Judge Johns shook his head. "All I know is that there was a car. I'd started to walk down the road when I realized what it was and turned back to investigate."

"And someone clubbed you?"

"And someone clubbed me."

Johns got out and stood in the rain. It felt good on his flushed face and injured head.

Coy White broke the silence that followed. "That means someone saw the judge find the mouth of the creek and beat it back here to wait for him."

Sheriff Bodin wiped the rain from his mustache. "And that means he's one of us."

Judge Johns tried to think of something to say. There didn't seem to be anything.

CHAPTER NINE

It was eleven o'clock by the time Judge Johns returned to the cottage and bathed and changed his clothes, ready to leave again. The rest of the posse men, carrying the boat with them, had already returned to Clay City. Only Eagan had waited to ride in with him.

"Just in case," Jack had put it.

Johns studied the disordered bedroom as he tied the knot in his tie. It certainly hadn't proved to be the type of week-end he'd planned. Judging from the way his head felt and from what Doctor Avers had told him, he was lucky to be alive. All because he'd located a boat.

The vicious attempt on his life didn't make any more sense than anything that had preceded it. Whoever had clubbed him in the dark dead end road had had plenty of time to do whatever he wanted to do. And if he'd meant to kill him, why had he left him alive?

From the living room, Lieutenant Eagan asked, "Can you estimate the size of the guy, if he was big or a little man?"

"I haven't the least idea," Johns told him. "I just heard a branch snap in back of me—and that was it."

"I suppose the same holds true of the car?"

"The same. The boys didn't find any tire prints or anything like that?"

"None," Eagan said. "The rain took care of that."

Johns tried to put on his hat and couldn't. He turned out the light in the bedroom and walked into the living room carrying his hat in his hand. "Well, I guess I'm ready."

Lieutenant Eagan got up from the chair. "You coming back here after you eat?"

"I haven't made up my mind," Johns admitted. "Why?"

"If you do, I'd advise you to bring a gun back with you."

"But why should anyone want to kill me?"

Eagan opened the door of the cottage. "You tell me that. You can drive all right?"

"I'm fine. I feel fine," Johns lied.

He drove slowly down the road toward Clay City. Eagan had a one track mind. "You don't remember which of the boys was closest to you?"

Johns thought back. "No. You know how it was all day. You were constantly passing or bumping into one of the boys."

"I know."

Johns took exception to Sheriff Bodin's snap conclusion. "What's more, I've been thinking it over and I doubt that it was one of the boys."

"Why?"

"Because I think it's a safe assumption that whoever clubbed me is the same man who killed Sam and, undoubtedly, Tom Harper. And I can't think of one of the boys who could possibly talk either Sam or Tom into liquidating their assets, turning the money over to them and then walk willingly to their deaths."

Eagan sighed. "And me with only three years to go for my pension."

"You'll get him."

"When?"

Johns shook his head and wished he hadn't. "It may take time but you will. Every killer slips up one way or another. How about the boat?"

"No help so far." Eagan mentioned a local boat building firm. "Dennis has put out hundreds like it in the past ten years. All we know is it's four or five years old and probably stolen from one of the cottages on the lake. I doubt if we can even trace it."

"Then why was the killer concerned?"

"That's another thing I don't know. It may be he just panicked. It may be he thought if he killed you the boat would never be found. Then, of course, there's the blood."

"The rain left enough for the lab boys to work on?"

"Plenty. They're working on it now. And if it comes out the same type as Sam Langley's, we'll know without a doubt that it was the boat the killer used, that he had it pulled up in the creek waiting. But that's another thing."

"What?"

"Doc Avers swears no one man could bleed that much."

"It's a sticker."

"It's all of that."

As he passed the clump of trees near the school house, Johns felt momentary guilt in withholding from Eagan the fact that he'd not been alone when Ogden and Pearson had beached the skiff containing Langley's body. He knew Eagan well enough to know the other man would be discreet. Still, bringing Dale into the matter wouldn't help anything. Dale hadn't killed Harper or Langley. All she knew about either man was what she'd read in the *Courier*.

"When will Lou be back?" Eagan asked.

Johns looked sideways at him. "Monday or Tuesday. Why?"

"I just wondered," Eagan said. "If this thing gets much more screwball I may try to pin it on her. You know, local socialite kills wealthy ceramics manufacturer so she can replace his wife as delegate from Clay City's Woman's Club."

Johns laughed shortly. "It's not that bad."

Lieutenant Eagan grunted. "You haven't read the *Evening Courier*. What I mean, Kelly really took us apart."

"It's his job, I suppose."

"I suppose. And he did a good job of it."

Judge Johns rounded the courthouse square and parked in front of the station house. "You coming in?" Eagan asked him.

"For a minute," Johns said. "I'd like to see if that lab report is in."

They climbed the stairs of the station together. "A shame," Eagan said. "A dirty shame."

"What's a shame?" Johns asked.

"That all of this had to come up on the one week-end you had a chance to get away. I know how you like to fish."

"At least I used to."

"Yeah," Eagan said. "Yeah. I know what you mean. But I meant what I said out at the cottage. If you do go back out there, you take a gun with you."

"I'll do that."

The atmosphere inside the station was like a funeral house. Even Phinny had a long face. Johns walked on into Eagan's office with him. Coy White was sitting in one straight chair with his feet up on another. "How you feel?" he asked Johns.

Johns shrugged. "All right. I've been hit on the head before. Anything new on the boat?"

White inclined his head toward Eagan's desk. "It's all there on the clipboard. Dennis says it's one of his boats but he hasn't the least idea who he sold it to or when. And the blood is AB Rh positive."

"The same type as Sam's?"

"According to the lab. And also according to the lab, even with what the rain washed away, no one guy could bleed so much."

Lieutenant Eagan sat back of his desk. "If just once something would make sense."

Judge Johns attempted to put on his hat again and winced. "Well, that's all I wanted to know. See you in the morning. And if not then Monday morning." He corrected himself. "No. That's right. Monday I start the new court."

Lieutenant Eagan said wryly, "At least we have one consolation."

Johns turned in the doorway. "What's that?"

Eagan repeated what Johns had said on the morning he'd first learned of Sam Langley's disappearance. "Now you're on the circuit bench, when we do find the killer, you can throw the book at him."

"That's a promise."

Johns walked back to his car. It was his nerves, nothing more. But, somehow, Clay City felt different, as if the knowledge of an uncaught killer on the loose had permeated the very air. It was an unwholesome sensation.

There was one last *Courier* left in the wire stand beside the station doorway. Johns dropped a nickel into the metal container, folded the paper under his arm and drove on around the square to the Elite Cafe.

It was one of four cafes lighted. He debated going to one of the other cafes but he'd promised Dale he would drop by and tell her all that had gone on at the cottage. They could figure out some place where they could meet, if she was still on duty.

He opened the door of the Elite and was disappointed to find Jim

Kelly sitting at the counter drinking coffee. "You would," the reporter grinned.

Johns sat in the booth he'd sat in before. "I would what?"

Kelly told him, "Get yourself almost killed, way past my deadline." Kelly sobered. "Seriously, how do you feel?"

Johns picked the menu from the table of the booth. "All right." He almost hoped Dale wasn't on duty. She was. She came from the back of the cafe, carrying a glass of ice water. "Good evening, sir," she said, discreetly.

Johns changed his mind and was glad he'd come. It made him feel better just to look at Dale. He hoped she continued to be discreet in front of Kelly. "Good evening," he said, "I'm not too late to get a steak, am I?"

Dale poised her pencil over her pad. "No, sir."

Johns put the menu back on the table. "Then I'll have the T-bone and French fries. And a cup of coffee, while I'm waiting, please."

Dale wrote the order on her pad. "Yes, sir."

Kelly swung around on his stool and sat facing the booth with his elbows on the counter behind him. "They tell me all hell broke loose after I left to write my story."

Johns unfolded the *Courier*. "And Eagan tells me you gave him hell."

The reporter shrugged. "Not him, particularly. Nor Bodin, for that matter. It's just a lousy break as far as they're concerned. But it gave me one sweet story. I could have written the Great American novel in the length of time it took me to cover all the points."

Johns looked at the scare headline. It read—

WHERE WILL KILLER STRIKE NEXT?

It was small wonder he'd sensed a change in the atmosphere of Clay City. The story itself was as bad. Starting with the lead he'd given Kelly that morning on the way back to the lake, the reporter, from a newspaper angle, had done a good job. He leaned heavily on the fact that both Harper and Langley had been wealthy men and that, between them, nearly three hundred dollars in cash was missing.

There were pictures of both men and of Mary Harper and Ella Langley. Judge Johns turned to the second page and realized that Dale was standing beside the booth, holding a cup of coffee. "Excuse me, please," she said.

Johns picked his napkin from under his silverware. "Of course." Unless Kelly left before he did, and it might prove difficult to out sit him, he would get no chance to talk to Dale tonight.

Johns read the story to the end and re-folded his paper.

"What do you think of it?" Kelly asked him.

"You don't seem to have left out a thing."

"Just one thing," Kelly said.

"What's that?"

"The same thing that's sticking Lieutenant Eagan and Sheriff Bodin. Why? It's easy for me to make chumps of the police but I'm as much in the dark as they are. No two mature men in their right minds are going to act like Harper and Langley did." Kelly warmed to his subject. "Now, if they were chasers, I could figure out something. When a dame is involved, a man will do strange things, but I was checking with Coy White this afternoon and he claims he and Oscar have combed the town without finding anyone who ever saw either man with a dame. And after that, I did some checking on my own. Harper and Langley were just what they appeared to be, good family men."

"That's the way matters seem to stand." Judge Johns made room for the steak Dale brought. It looked good. He took a bite. It was.

"Will there be anything else, sir?" she asked.

Johns shook his head. "Not tonight."

She wrote a figure on his check and tore it from her pad. Putting the check beside the sugar bowl, she said, "Thank you very much."

Apparently she was the only waitress on duty. She filled a tray with dirty dishes from the next booth, carried the tray back to the kitchen and went back of the counter to examine the level of the coffee in the steamer.

Kelly swung around to face her. "Hi, beautiful. How's for you and me going out on the town when you get off?" The reporter looked at his wrist watch. "In exactly twelve and a half minutes."

"Please," Dale said, wearily. "How many times do I have to tell you I don't date?"

"Well, you can't blame a guy for trying."

Dale poured more water in the steamer. "I can."

Johns ate his steak as he watched her. He felt like he had that morning when he'd pushed her up on the raft. Just looking at her youth and vitality refreshed him. He wished Kelly would drop dead or go home and go to bed, so he could arrange for some place to meet

Dale. It was easy for a married man to talk of getting away from the house. He usually could for a few hours. But once Lou came home again, there would be no more all night parties with Dale or anyone else. He was, after all, a respectable married man, a judge of the circuit court.

At the counter, Kelly continued to plague the blonde girl. "Now, don't be like that, baby."

The door of the cafe opened and a black-haired girl came in. Dale greeted her with easy familiarity. Johns judged from their conversation the Elite stayed open all night and the dark girl was the night waitress.

Kelly kept up his banter. "All right. You keep on treating me like you do and I'll ask Amy for a date."

"You do that," Dale said.

The black-haired girl put her purse under the counter. "My husband may have something to say about that."

Johns had long since finished his steak. It was obvious that Kelly had no intention of leaving. Perhaps if he waited a few doors down the street he might get a chance to have a few words with Dale. He reached for his check and discovered there were two of them. On the top check Dale had totaled his meal. On the one under it she had written:

> In the same clump of trees. Please. As soon as I get off at midnight. I have to talk to you.

The word *have* was underscored. Judge Johns crumpled the second check and put it in his pocket. He walked up to the front of the restaurant where Dale was totaling her cash against the register before turning the Elite over to the night girl, and laid a five dollar bill on the counter.

"You going back to the cottage?" Kelly asked him.

"I haven't made up my mind," Johns told him. "Why?"

"I just wondered. What with a killer loose, none of that lake stuff for me. I'm glad I live right in town. After the beating they tell me you took I should think you'd feel the same way."

Johns lit a cigarette. "If I do go back I'll take a revolver with me."

Kelly shook his head. "You outdoor guys are all alike. I'm glad I collect stamps. Now me, I wouldn't go out there tonight if they gave me two machine guns and a platoon of marines. Well, maybe, if they gave me a platoon of marines."

"Your change, sir," Dale said.

As Judge Johns held out his hand he inclined his head slightly. After their narrow escape that morning he knew he was being foolish in meeting Dale. But Lou would be gone only for the one week-end. And Dale was very lovely and wanted to talk to him. He was honest with himself. Tired and sore as he was, as badly as his head still ached, he wanted to talk to Dale, especially now that he'd had a sample of her conversation.

CHAPTER TEN

As he waited in the clump of trees near the school house, Johns refrained from smoking, in case a police car should pass the grove and the driver should spot the glow of his cigarette. Tonight every man on the force would be especially edgy.

He wished he knew where he could take Dale. He didn't dare to take her back to the cottage. It wasn't fair to Lou to take Dale to the house. He was damned if he'd get into the back seat with her. He might be an old lion but he wasn't that old. Besides, Dale had made it clear that she wasn't cheap.

He waited five minutes, then ten. At twenty-five minutes after twelve, a car he thought was Dale's passed by, then turned around a few hundred yards up the road and came back. Its headlights dark, it turned into the grove.

Johns wished he'd stopped by the house for his revolver. He got out of his car and stood behind a tree until he was sure the driver of the car was Dale. Then he opened the door of her car and slid in beside her. "What's the idea of going past, then coming back?"

"Kelly," she said, dryly. "I wanted to be sure he wasn't following me." She was still agitated and her firm young breasts rose and fell with her labored breathing. "One of these nights I'm going to break a steak platter over his head."

"He gave you trouble?"

"He tried to. He was waiting outside when I left and tried to wrestle a kiss, but I got away from him before he could." Dale's voice was plaintive. "He was so damned determined, though, I was afraid he might follow me. But maybe he didn't have his car."

Johns put his arm around Dale's waist and pulled her over to him.

"He said something this morning about not being able to get his car started. Now what's this about you're having to see me?"

"Kiss me first," Dale demanded.

Dale's lips hadn't changed. Johns kissed her and didn't want to stop. Dale stopped him. "Not now or here. I thought you wanted to know why I wanted to see you."

It was an effort for Johns to keep from acting juvenile. He managed and said, "I do."

"I should think you'd know," Dale said. "I kept waiting all afternoon for you to show up and you didn't and I didn't know what had happened to you. Then around ten o'clock tonight, one of the detectives from the station, White, I think his name was, stopped by for coffee and was telling everyone at the counter something about you finding a boat and someone trying to kill you. Then you walked in when you did and Kelly was there and I couldn't even let on I knew you, you know how I mean, let alone ask you how you were."

Johns was pleased that Dale had been worried about him. "You sound like you might be rather fond of me."

"I think I gave you proof of that last night."

Johns kissed her again. "You did."

Dale allowed him to caress her this time. "I damn near died, standing there taking orders from slobs I didn't care anything about and not even knowing if you were dead or alive. You are all right?"

"Just a couple of knocks on the head."

"And you still love me?"

"Very much."

Dale slid lower in the seat. "You're sweet."

"Don't tell me you've been working since I drove you into town this morning?"

Dale rolled her head from side to side. "No. Just since four o'clock. I slept until almost three. Then I took over the four to midnight for a girl who had to drive to Mobile with her husband." Dale added, "And don't get too interested in what you're doing. That's one of the things I want to talk to you about."

"What?" Johns asked, thickly.

"Us," Dale said. "Now stop. You're wrinkling my skirt. Sit up and give me a cigarette and listen to me."

Johns sat up, lit two cigarettes and gave one of them to her. "I'm listening."

Dale sucked smoke into her lungs. "Well, I got to thinking how wonderful last night was and how we'd hoped t' be t'gether all t'day and t'night and t'morrow and t'morrow night. And then just because some fool got himself killed we had to run like a pair of scared cats. So when I agreed to take over for Mable, she's the girl who had to go to Mobile, I made a deal with her."

"What sort of a deal?" Johns asked.

Dale took a house key from her purse. "The use of her house until Monday morning. It isn't much of a place. I've been there. But it's about two miles out of town, set off by itself with no neighbors. And I could leave my car in front of my rooming house and you could drive us out there. Once you put your car in the garage and closed the door no one would even know we were there. And we could have our week-end after all."

"You tempt me," Johns admitted.

Dale nibbled the lobe of his ear. "I meant to." She was disappointed. "Of course, if you don't want to."

Johns pulled her to him roughly. "Stop talking like a pretty idiot. I was just wondering what might happen if Lieutenant Eagan and Sheriff Bodin should try to get in touch with me."

"You're a judge, not a policeman."

"True."

Dale added, "Besides, there's a phone. You could call into town any time you wanted to. They wouldn't need to know *where* you were calling from."

If this was being a fool, Judge Johns liked being a fool. "Then what are we waiting for?" He opened the door of Dale's car. "You go on ahead. I'll follow you into town and pick you up as soon as you park."

Dale stopped him. "There's just one other thing."

"What's that?"

Dale unlocked the glove compartment of her car and took a .45 caliber Officer's Model Colt Automatic Pistol out of it and handed it to Johns. "I want you to have this," she said, simply. "It was Tom's. One of his buddies brought it back from Korea with the rest of his things. And as soon as I heard that detective say that someone had tried to kill you, I knew right then I wanted you t' have it."

It had been a long time since Johns had been so touched. "You're a sweet child," he said tenderly. "I'll see that you're amply thanked."

Dale lifted her face to be kissed. "That's a promise?"

"A promise."

The house was white and small, set off by itself, as Dale had said, with no immediate neighbors. Johns unlocked the garage and drove his car inside, then closed and locked the door. As he did, a wave of fatigue swept over him. He hadn't slept at all the night before. He'd spent the day beating the brush. Then someone had beaten him. Dale pressed close to him. "Tired, honey?"

"A little," Johns admitted.

Dale hooted. "Listen to the man. A little. You must be almost dead. You've had a nasty experience." She opened the door leading from the garage into the house. "And I want to hear all about it as soon as we're inside."

The interior of the house was in keeping with the outside. It was plain but clean, the type of house a working man married to a waitress would have. The furniture was serviceable but inexpensive.

"What happened to your friend?" Johns asked. "I mean, why did she have to drive to Mobile?"

Dale fluffed her hair. "It wasn't Mable. It was her husband. Anyway, his father. They don't think he's going t' live and they thought he ought to be there."

"Oh."

"I don't suppose you're hungry, not after that steak you ate?"

"No," Johns laughed, "I'm not."

The bedroom opened off the kitchen. Dale switched on the lamp beside the double bed and turned off the kitchen light and closed the door. "Then you sit right down there on that bed and get some rest, and we can talk while you're resting. I want to hear all about it, what happened every minute after you went back to the cottage this morning."

Johns took off his coat and hung it over a chair, while Dale unknotted the knot in his tie.

"Now off with your shirt and the rest of your things," she insisted. "And remember we have all night and all t'morrow and all t'morrow night."

"I'll try to remember," Johns promised.

Dale insisted on unlacing his shoes and Johns permitted her to do so. It was nice to be waited on, to have things done for him that Lou had once done, how many years ago he couldn't remember. Dale was an odd combination of wanton, Puritan and practicability. He almost wished they hadn't met. It was going to be hard to forget her. She was so completely everything a man needed.

Dale turned down the bedspread and the top sheet. "Now you lie down and tell me everything that happened while I brush my hair."

It felt good to lie on his back. Johns lay a moment, blowing smoke at the ceiling, watching Dale brush her golden hair up and away from her scalp, then down in long brush strokes that returned the natural curl. It seemed incredible that they could have become so intimate, so much a part of each other in a few short hours.

"Well, for one thing," he began, "when you stuffed your things into your bag, one of your stockings fell to the floor and Kelly damn near saw it."

Dale turned to face him. "No!"

"But yes. I just got it into my pocket in time."

"What was he doing in the bedroom?"

"Looking for whiskey," he said. Johns wished Dale would take off her dress so he could admire the youthful perfection of her body.

She brushed her hair a few more strokes. Then, as if she'd read his mind, she laid down the brush and stood up and pulled her dress over her head. Opening the window wider, she said, "Whew, it's hot in here." She took off her filmy underthings, laid them on the same chair with her dress, then resumed brushing her hair. "Go on. What happened then?"

Johns lit a cigarette from the butts of the one he was smoking. "Well, Lieutenant Eagan and Sheriff Bodin questioned Ogden and Pearson, the two fishermen who found the body, until they were satisfied the men had nothing to do with Langley's murder. Then one of the boys, I forget who, suggested that we search the shore line to see if we could find the boat that the killer had used to get Langley into the lake. They figured Lieutenant Eagan and the Sheriff could backtrack from there. So we did. All day."

Dale stopped brushing her hair and sat facing Johns. "And you found it?"

"Not until almost dark. Then I made a botch of it."

"How?"

"Well, it was back up a little creek, perhaps a half mile in from the lake, right where the road that runs around the lake dead ends. And it seems that the killer was smarter than I was. He was waiting for me."

Dale stood up and stretched her arms over her head in the same lithe, tawny cat manner that Johns had admired that morning. "But you saw him?"

Johns shook his head. "I didn't even get a glimpse of him. I heard a branch crack in the dark. The next thing I knew someone had clubbed me and I was lying face down in the mud. The next thing I knew after that it was three hours later and I was in a police cruiser with rain outside and Jack Eagan holding me while Doctor Avers worked on my head."

Johns grinned at the recollection and Dale sat on the bed beside him. "What's so funny?" she asked.

Johns told her. "For a moment, when I first came to, I thought I was back in the cottage and that we'd slept all day and that Jack was you. In fact, I nearly called him Dale."

Dale's eyes widened. "Did you?"

"No," Johns said. "I wasn't quite that groggy. There is, after all, quite a difference between you and Lieutenant. Eagan."

"I should hope so," Dale said, primly. "Now I'm going to turn off the light and you're going to get some sleep."

"With you lying next to me?"

Dale turned off the light and stretched out on the bed. "With me lying next to you."

"How?"

"You can pretend I'm Lieutenant Eagan."

Johns took her in his arms and pulled her close to him. "Uh uh. The few stolen hours we have together are apt to be too short for us to waste them. Besides, I'm not that sleepy."

Dale's lips found his in the darkness. "No," she admitted. "It would seem you're not."

CHAPTER ELEVEN

Monday morning dawned clear and slightly cooler. Judge Johns awakened, as usual, at exactly seven-thirty. His mind still fogged with sleep, he attempted to take Dale in his arms. Then he remembered. He was in his own bed, in his own house, alone. He'd kissed Dale good-bye for the time being, shortly after driving her back to the rooming house in which she lived.

Every object in the room reminded him of Lou. He tried to feel a sense of guilt for the manner in which he'd spent the week-end but couldn't. It seemed so right, so natural, so normal for him to spend the week-end with Dale. He wished he could spend the balance of his life with her.

It was eight o'clock by the time he'd showered and shaved and put on a clean white suit. His normal routine had resumed. Hattie Belle had breakfast, lukewarm and poorly cooked, waiting on the dining room table. If Hattie Belle had bothered to read the *Courier* she didn't mention Sam Langley.

"You have a good time fishin'?" she asked him.

Johns ate a bite of burned toast. "So so."

It was incredible, looking back, the number of things that Dale could do so well. Along with her other capabilities, she was a good cook. The Sunday dinner she'd concocted from the odds and ends in her friend's refrigerator had been one of the best meals he'd ever eaten.

Hattie Belle paused in the kitchen doorway. "Mrs. Johns will be back today?"

"Either today or tomorrow," Johns told her.

He wished the convention in Atlanta would last for ten years. Once Lou returned, it was going to be difficult to figure out how to continue seeing Dale. But, somehow, he meant to manage. After the week-end he'd just spent, he should feel physically and emotionally drained. Surprisingly, he didn't. Dale renewed his youth. He'd never felt more fit.

"How about dinner tonight?" Hattie Belle asked. "You want I should cook one?"

"I'll phone from the courthouse," Johns said. "If Mrs. Johns is coming home today, she will probably wire me from the airport."

"Yes, sir," Hattie Belle said and closed the kitchen door behind her.

Judge Johns finished his coffee but didn't even try to eat his overdone eggs and underdone ham. The big house depressed him. It reminded him that he was back on the same old treadmill that apparently had no end.

He thought of something pleasant and smiled. While they'd been lying on the raft, watching the day dawn on the morning that Langley's body had been found, Dale had rested her wet hair on his shoulder and asked:

"Know somethin' else, sugar?"

He'd asked her what. Then she'd said:

"If I had a cottage like you have, I purely wouldn't live in Clay City."

Then he'd called her a little Cracker and swatted her. Johns looked at his hand. It still tingled. If a man had a wife like Dale, he could really live.

The swellings on his head subsided, and although his hat fit tightly, at least he could get it on. He wouldn't have to show up for his first morning in circuit court like some bare-headed high school senior.

He backed his car out of the drive and was half way to the square before he remembered that he'd left home an hour earlier than need be. He was on the higher bench now and his court didn't convene until ten. On impulse, he drove to the station house to see how the investigation was proceeding.

The atmosphere was somewhat brighter than it had been, possibly because the *Courier* had had nothing new to print in its Sunday edition. Even the headlines had been considerably milder. Instead of the scare head—WHERE WILL KILLER STRIKE NEXT?—the best Kelly had been able to come up with was—LANGLEY INVESTIGATION BOGS DOWN.

The reporter hadn't even bothered to play up the attack on himself, possibly because there was little to write about. He'd discovered the boat the killer had used to transport Langley. The killer had been waiting for him and had clubbed him unconscious. And that was all any of them knew. They were still as much in the dark as they had been when the phoned information had first come in that Sam had laid down his almost perfect bridge hand to shoot at a howling dog and had mysteriously disappeared.

Mercer, the desk sergeant, greeted Judge Johns cheerfully. "You're in the wrong court, aren't you? I thought we'd gotten rid of you."

"You will in a few minutes," Johns promised him. "I just dropped by to see if there was anything new. Jack in his office?"

"I doubt it," Mercer said. "He and the rest of the boys spent all day yesterday out at the lake. And now I think Lieutenant Eagan is talking to Mrs. Harper, you know, to try and find out if she remembers anything unusual happening during the few days before Tom disappeared." The desk sergeant added, "But I think Hal's in Jack's office. It seems that yesterday wasn't entirely wasted."

"Oh," Johns said. He opened the door of Eagan's office and walked in. The old station was pressed for space. Terrill was using Eagan's desk to compare, under a microscope, a stack of photographs with a picture he'd laid to one side.

"Good morning, Judge Johns," Terrill said.

Johns started to remove his hat and thought better of it. "I just thought I'd stop by," he said, "to see if there's anything new."

The combined identification and ballistics man shrugged. "Yes and no. We spent most of yesterday out there at the end of that dead end road, screening the mud and leaves to see if we could come up with something."

"And did you?"

Terrill handed Johns a small, battered piece of lead. "Only this. We don't know for certain but we think this may be one of the slugs that killed Langley."

"But I thought he was killed at the house."

Terrill shrugged again. "Your guess is as good as mine. We screened the Langley grounds, too, without coming up with a thing. But we did find this out at the lake, in the mud, just about where the car you saw must have stood."

Johns weighed the slug in his hand. "What caliber?"

Terrill's smile was wry. "It seems what few breaks we've gotten so far have been bad. I can't even tell you that. If it is one of the slugs that killed Sam, it hit metal shortly thereafter, and part of it was sheared off, the part we couldn't find." He picked the piece of lead from Johns' palm. "It could be a thirty-two or a thirty-eight, possibly even a forty-five. But as it weighs right now, it's a little over a twenty-five."

"A shame."

The ballistics man was philosophical about it. "We did get one break." He traced a minute scratch on the slug with the point of his pencil. "This one side is undamaged and if we should happen to pick up the gun or I find a slug to match it in the files, I can tell which gun it came out of."

"Good," Johns said. He added, "But the amount of blood found at the Langley place and in the boat—?"

Terrill cut him short with a laugh. "Let's not get off on that. Doc Avers still insists that Sam must have been two men to bleed so much. How are you feeling this morning?"

"Fine."

"Good," Terrill said and returned to his microscopic inspection of the stack of photographs. "When I first saw you out there at the lake Saturday night I was afraid we were going to need a special election to choose a new circuit court judge."

Johns started to point out that in such instances the governor usually appointed some judge from a lower court bench to fill in the unexpired term and didn't bother. It was immaterial. After all, he hadn't been killed. He stood a moment, impressed by Terrill's thoroughness. What he'd told Eagan in the cottage held true. Sooner or later they would get the man who'd killed Tom Harper and Sam Langley. It didn't matter whether a town was small or large. A criminal could outsmart one policeman. He could outsmart fifty. But he couldn't beat the system. The slowly closing net of law enforcement was as inexorable as death and taxes.

Judge Johns watched a moment longer, then walked out to his car and drove to the courthouse. There was a freshly painted sign behind one of the slots in the parking lot reading—Judge Evan Johns.

It was a small thing but it pleased Johns. It could be that Hal Cass and Lou had been right, that he would go on to hold even higher office. Johns thought, wryly, of Dale. Not that he wanted to. The way he felt right now he would trade the attorney-generalship of the United States for the privilege of spending the few years left him in a rustic lake cottage with Dale.

The elevator operator was properly obsequious. "Good mornin', Your Honor. Welcome t' the courthouse." Johns acknowledged the recognition. It pleased him even more than the sign in the parking lot. So did the fresh gold leaf on the door of his new private chambers. He opened the door and walked in.

With her hair hastily done and eyes swollen with crying, Lou, surrounded by dress boxes and luggage, was sitting in one of the leather chairs.

"Well, where did you come from?" Johns asked her. Lou got to her feet, trying hard not to cry. "The airport. I phoned the house as soon as my plane landed and Hattie Belle said you'd started for the office. And I've been waiting, it seems, for hours." She touched his cheek with the tips of her fingers. "You're all right, Evan?"

Johns took off his hat. "Of course."

Lou kissed him hard. "Thank God. It wasn't in yesterday's paper. I guess the big shots up in Atlanta don't think what happens to us little folk here in Clay City is important. But I happened to wake up early this morning and sent down for coffee. There was a paper on the tray with a little squib about that big, saying you'd been nearly killed, while assisting the posse in its search for Langley's killer." Lou lost her battle and burst into tears. "You can imagine. I just threw my clothes on any which way and started for home on the first plane

I could get."

Johns was pleased that Lou should have been worried about him. It proved that what they once had wasn't entirely dead. "Now, now," he consoled her. "All I got was a couple of whacks on the head."

Lou examined the lacerations on his head with the tips of her fingers. "There's no permanent damage?"

"Absolutely not."

Lou kissed him again. "Thank God. But what if whoever it was should make another attack on your life?"

"He won't," Johns assured her. "But if he should, I'm prepared." Johns noticed that the door leading from his chambers to the courtroom had opened and that his new clerk was standing in the doorway. The man cleared his throat. "Yes?" Johns asked.

"Good morning, Judge Johns," the clerk said. "It is exactly ten o'clock. Whenever you're ready."

"Any time."

The clerk nodded to the bailiff and the familiar mumbo jumbo began. As usual, all Johns could catch of it was—".... is now in session, the Honorable Judge Evan Johns now presiding."

Lou kissed him a last time. "I'll have a nice supper tonight."

"You do that," Johns smiled. He patted Lou's most convenient curve and was mildly surprised to find that even after the week-end with Dale, Lou still had the power to excite him.

The clerk of court opened the door into the courtroom a little wider. "If you are ready, Judge Johns."

Johns walked past him into the courtroom and took his seat behind the new bench. He squirmed uncomfortably as he felt something hard beneath him. Then he realized what it was and barely repressed a smile. He'd transferred the pistol that Dale had given him to the right hip pocket of his fresh suit when he'd dressed. He was, probably, since reconstruction days, the first circuit court judge of Hess and Clay and Calhoun counties to hold his first session with a .45 caliber pistol in his hip pocket.

CHAPTER TWELVE

It had been a good session. Johns was pleased by the manner in which he'd conducted it. He was going to like this higher court. It gave a man a chance to display some mental agility instead of sitting like a dolt while the lesser offenders against the law filed past him, most of them eager to pay their small fines and get done with it.

Here men and women faced long prison terms or unwanted separations. Even one true bill alleging murder had been filed. Judge Johns put the briefs concerning it in his brief case to study at his leisure. He hoped that before long Jack Eagan could bring Sam Langley's killer to his court. He hoped the case didn't drag on long enough for Ella Langley to raise so much hell that both Jack Eagan and Sheriff Bodin lost their jobs. They were doing the best they could.

The cool of the morning had dissipated. After the carefully controlled temperature in his new courtroom and chambers, the heat in the parking lot was almost unbearable. Judge Johns put his brief case in his car and debated where he should eat lunch.

He never went home at noon. And there was no use going to the Elite, if only to look at Dale. She claimed that sex made her sleepy. God knew she had reason to be tired right now. Late Sunday afternoon she'd called the cafe and arranged to keep Mable's shift. Johns looked at his watch. It was shortly after one thirty. Right now Dale was sleeping the sleep of the lusty innocent, dreaming, he hoped, of him. That left only one place to get a meal, the club in which he usually dined before he'd met Dale.

Johns left his car in the parking lot and walked around the courthouse and across the square. After his hours with Dale, his reaction to Lou puzzled and embarrassed him. To his knowledge, there was nothing abnormal about him. He wasn't a satyr. He was just an average man. Perhaps his feeling had been caused by the fact that both women had something to offer him; Lou, emotional stability and the solid, if dull, security known only in marriage, while Dale offered a semblance of youth and reasonable facsimile of the dreams that he had once dreamed. There was something to be said for polygamy. At least a man would never be bored.

The club, as always, was crowded with successful professional and business men. Johns had a drink at the bar, then assured the white-polled colored head waiter, Henry, that he didn't mind sharing a table and found himself at a table for two with Otto Shribe who owned the Shribe Machinery Company.

Johns knew the other man casually. They belonged to the same country and service clubs and had served on several civic committees together.

Shribe greeted him cordially. "Congratulations, Your Honor. Your first day in your new court, eh?"

"That's right."

"It's quite a step up."

"A small one."

Shribe seemed amused about something. "But still in Clay City."

"I'm afraid so," the statement intrigued Johns. "But just what do you mean by that?"

The machine manufacturer shrugged. "Nothing in particular. I was just thinking of Samoa. Ever been there?"

Johns ate his appetizer. "No, I haven't. I ended my tour in North Africa."

It was almost as if Shribe hadn't heard him. "Lovely country. I was there as an exec of a destroyer during the last unpleasantness. In fact, I spent eighteen months in the islands. A wonderful place. Palm trees and blue sea and white beaches as far as you can see. And peace and quiet. None of this cutthroat business of trying to cut the other guy's price a dollar so you can pay your own income tax. The people there believe in living and let live." A little ashamed of having enthused so much over any place but the one in which he made his living, Shribe added quickly, "Of course, Clay City is very nice, too. You and Mrs. Johns will be at the Junior League dance, I presume?"

"We never miss it," Johns said grimly.

Shribe's smile was wry. "Yeah. That's what I mean. The same damn thing, day in and day out, month after month. If you ask me, Sam Langley rowed out on Loon Lake, tied those weights around his middle and shot himself through the head."

"Three times."

Shribe's smile turned thoughtful. "I hadn't thought of that."

"And what about the two hundred thousand in cash he received for his factory? And where did the sixty thousand Tom Harper drew out of the bank, plus whatever he had in his safety deposit box go?"

"You've a point there," Shribe admitted. "Several points, in fact." A few minutes later he finished his meal and stood up. "Well, see you around."

"Around."

Johns ate a substantial meal, then considered checking with Lieutenant Eagan to see if there were any developments in the Langley case and decided, he would only be making a nuisance of himself. Eagan had enough to contend with. Besides, if and when the case did come before him, Johns didn't want any defense attorney to be able to claim that he'd shown unusual interest in the apprehension or conviction of the defendant. In the upper courts a man had to walk lightly.

He decided to return to the parking lot, reclaim his brief case from his car and spend the afternoon working in his new chambers. He seldom went directly home after court. Lou wouldn't expect him before five, at the earliest. After her emotional upset and the hasty plane trip from Atlanta, she would probably spend the rest of the afternoon sleeping. His new chambers would be cool and quiet, the best possible place for him to work. A thought brightened the heat of the day, as Johns walked back to the courthouse. And when he'd finished checking the briefs that had been filed that morning for possible legal flaws, Dale would have come on duty. Before going home he could drop into the Elite Cafe for a cup of coffee. Even if he couldn't talk to her and take her in his arms, he could admire her.

Johns shook his head at his own involvement. And he was involved. After fourteen years of being the average husband, in a little more than sixty hours, he'd really gotten himself into something. Heaven only knew where it would end. The hell of it was, even considering the possible risk of discovery and disgrace, he felt that Dale was worth it. The late summer she'd brought into his life with her youth and vitality and naiveté was worth anything it might cost. If worst came to worst, he could let Lou divorce him and resign from the bench. He could always make a living for himself and Dale as a small town lawyer.

It was fifteen minutes after five when he finished with the briefs. Johns washed his hands and face and adjusted his broad-brimmed hat at a jaunty angle. When he arrived at the Elite he was disappointed to find that, apparently, Dale hadn't as yet come on duty.

He ordered a cup of coffee he didn't want from one of the waitresses behind the counter, wondering how to inquire about Dale without making the question sound too personal and found what he thought was a solution.

"I'm Judge Johns," he introduced himself.

"Yeah, I know," the girl said. She was not impressed.

"One of the girls who works here, a Miss Chambers, I think her name is, was in my court the other day, charged with a minor traffic offense."

"Yeah, I know," the waitress repeated.

"Does she happen to be on duty?"

"Naw. She called in and said she would be two hours late."

Johns attempted to be bright. "And that was all right with the proprietor?"

"Look, mister," the waitress said. "Who are you tryin' to fool? If you want to see Dale she'll be on around six o'clock. As far as men are concerned, anything Dale does is all right. That's why Mr. Poulous practically lets her set her own hours. That's why you let her off scot free when she was caught doing seventy-five miles an hour in a thirty-five mile zone. That's why she makes more tips than all the rest of us girls put together. I only wish I had her baby smile," the waitress outlined the improvement with her hands and was as descriptive as Kelly had been, "and a pair of headlights like she has. You wouldn't catch me waiting table in no restaurant in Clay City. I'd beat it to Atlanta or New York on the first train out of here and catch me a rich sucker."

The girl moved on down the counter to take an order and Judge Johns considered himself told off. The waitress had certainly told him. Still, he felt a certain smug glow. It was nice to know that even with the body and looks to do so, instead of going to Atlanta or New York and marrying some rich man she didn't love, Dale had preferred to wait table for three years after her hero husband had died ... She'd waited to give herself to any man until the right man had come along. It was equally comforting to know he'd been the right man.

Johns finished and paid for his coffee and got his car and drove home. The house hadn't changed during the day. It was just a house. It still depressed him. Lou was glad to see him. She'd changed into one of her prettier dresses, but her first shock over and knowing he was all right, she kissed him with less warmth than she had in his chambers. After all, they'd been married fourteen years.

The 'good' dinner Hattie Belle had cooked wasn't much of an improvement on the breakfast she'd ruined. The roast, a choice cut of meat, and the rest of the dinner, although well-planned, was ruined in the preparation. Still, when Judge Johns would have reproved her, Lou refused to allow him to say anything to the girl.

"Please, Evan," she pleaded. "Be patient. She'll learn, in time. And maids are hard to get."

After dinner they sat in the living room and Lou talked on and on and on about her brief trip to Atlanta. When they ran out of small talk they watched television. It wasn't one of the good nights and at a quarter of eleven, when Lou suggested that they go up to bed, Johns was glad to second the suggestion until he realized that this might be one of Lou's rare amorous nights, and she would probably expect him to have relations with her.

Johns doubted if he was capable. Now he'd begun to let down, the physical strain of the week-end just past was beginning to tell. Taking Lou after having Dale for two nights and two days would be like asking a man to enthuse over a stale crust of bread when he had just gorged himself on frosted angel food cake.

Lou preceded him up the stairs. "Make sure the doors are locked, will you, sweetheart?"

Johns walked down the hall to the kitchen. Hattie Belle, as usual, had forgotten to lock the back door. Johns locked the door and pushed sharply at a dripping faucet in the sink, remembering something Otto Shribe had said during lunch.

The same damn thing day in and day out, month after month.

And year in and year out, Johns thought.

He climbed the stairs to the bedroom that he and Lou shared. There was no doubt of Lou's intentions. Instead of creaming her face and filling her head with metal curlers, she'd left her make-up on and turned down the top spread of only one of the beds.

It was an odd sensation. Johns felt trapped. He sat on the other bed and unlaced his shoes, watching Lou as she undressed, comparing her to Dale and realizing he wasn't being fair as he did so. Time was when Lou was every bit as pretty and possessed just as beautiful a body. But that had been years ago, when Lou had been Dale's age. Then, too, he'd been to the same well so many times.

Lou took a sheer nightgown from a drawer and unhooked her brassiere. "Miss me while I was gone, sweetheart?"

Johns lied dutifully. "Of course."

Lou stooped and kissed him lightly. "It looks like I shouldn't have gone to Atlanta. Every time you go out to that dirty old cottage at the lake you get into trouble of some kind. I wonder what we ever saw in it."

It was a statement, not a question. Johns wished he could make Lou understand just what the cottage meant to him.

Lou stretched out on her bed and smiled invitingly. "Anyway, it's nice to be home."

Johns had stalled as long as he could. He stepped out of his shoes and took off his coat. He was reaching for the buckle of his belt when the bell of the extension in the bedroom rang. Johns' relief was out of all proportion. The ringing bell was like a last minute stay from the governor. He uncradled the phone, "Judge Johns speaking."

"Jack Eagan here," the voice on the other end said. "Look, Evan. I know it's late but I wonder if you can come down to the station?"

"Of course," Johns said. "What's up?"

"We've another one, I'm afraid," Eagan told him. "Look. You had lunch with Otto Shribe at the club today, didn't you?"

"Yes, I did."

"Well, he hasn't been seen since he left the club. He didn't go back to his office, and he didn't go home. Mrs. Shribe is in my office now, almost hysterical. She claims it's the first time in sixteen years that he hasn't come home unless he phoned her where he was going."

CHAPTER THIRTEEN

The faces in Eagan's office were the same faces that Johns had seen on his last morning in the lower court but they looked old and tired and lined with fatigue. They had reason to look tired. Most of the plainclothes and uniformed men and deputies from Sheriff Bodin's force had worked straight through for seventy-two hours with little or no sleep.

Only one face was new. Mrs. Shribe was a pretty, brown-haired woman about the same age as Lou, or perhaps a few years older. She had, obviously, been crying but for the time being had her emotions under control.

As Johns entered the office, Lieutenant Eagan stood up back of his desk. "I believe you know Judge Johns."

Mrs. Shribe offered Johns her hand. "Yes. We've met quite

frequently. It was very kind of you to come, Judge Johns."

Johns drew up a chair and sat facing her. "Not at all. I'm only glad to be of any help I can. Now what's all this about?"

Kelly answered before either Mrs. Shribe or Lieutenant Eagan could. "I'd say another scare headline for the *Courier*," he said, grimly. The reporter looked around the circle of officers and deputies ringing the lieutenant's desk. "Not that I'm knocking you guys, understand. I know you're doing all you can. But if this keeps up, if prominent business men keep disappearing and wind up being found at the bottom of a river or lake, I know what the editorial copy of the *Courier* is going to be. We're going to demand that the governor send in the state militia."

Eagan said, without heat, "Oh, keep quiet, Kelly. Please. There may be a logical answer to why Otto has dropped out of sight."

"Yeah. Sure," the reporter said. "That's what we thought about Tom Harper and Sam Langley."

Mrs. Shribe began to cry softly.

Eagan addressed himself to Johns. "You did have lunch with Otto?"

Johns nodded. "Yes. Not intentionally. I mean we didn't have an appointment. But we shared a table."

"How did he act?"

"I'd say, very normal. He congratulated me on my first day in Circuit Court. He said it was quite a step up, but—" Johns ran down like an unwound clock.

But what?" Lieutenant Eagan asked.

A vague picture began to take form in Judge Johns' mind but it was still too nebulous to put into words. "But still in Clay City," he said, quietly.

"What did he mean by that?"

"I'm beginning to wonder," Johns said. He turned to Mrs. Shribe. "Did Otto talk much about the islands, Mrs. Shribe? I mean those in the Samoan group in which he spent so much time during the war?"

She wiped her eyes with a handkerchief that one of the officers had given her. "Yes, he did. He talked about them constantly. In fact, at one time, a few years ago, he talked about selling the plant for what we could get for it and moving to Samoa."

"But you wouldn't agree to that?"

Mrs. Shribe was mildly indignant. "Of course not. He was just getting a good start in business. Besides, all our friends are here."

"Of course," Johns said.

"What are you getting at, Evan?" Eagan asked him.

Johns tried to put the vague picture forming in his mind into words. "I'm not quite certain. I don't know what Tom Harper's secret desire might have been. I do know that, despite the fact that his factory was making him a lot of money, Sam Langley would have traded his executive's desk for a bait camp or any other form of outdoor life. And while I was having lunch with Otto, he talked about the islands, how beautiful they are, the quiet and the peace, the friendliness of the people. More, if Mrs. Shribe can pardon me for saying it, Otto seemed quite fed up with the daily routine of Clay City. In fact, and these are his exact words, he said, 'The same damn thing day in and day out, month after month. If you ask me, Sam Langley rowed out on Loon Lake, tied those weights around his middle and shot himself through the head.'"

Kelly scoffed, "Are you trying to make us believe that Shribe committed suicide?"

Johns' eyed the reporter thoughtfully. "No," he said and left it there.

Sheriff Bodin said, "No suicide shoots himself three times."

"I pointed that out to him," Johns said. "I also asked him what he thought had happened to the almost three hundred thousand dollars in cash that Harper and Langley were known to have had. It made Otto very thoughtful. He said I had a point, several points, in fact. Then he finished his lunch and left and, as you tell me, hasn't been seen since."

Lieutenant Eagan nodded. "That's the way it stacks up. Oh, he was seen on the street. But in spite of the fact that he had several urgent business appointments, he didn't go back to his office and he didn't go home." Eagan glanced at his clipboard. "Of course, we haven't had much time in which to work since Mrs. Shribe notified us that he hadn't come home but from the back-tracking we've been able to do, after leaving the club, he made a phone call from one of the booths in the lobby of the Commercial Hotel, then got his car from the lot where he'd parked it and drove out of town."

"In which direction?"

"No one seems to know."

"How about money?"

"No one knows that, either. I've talked to the tellers of all the banks in town and while Otto had business accounts in several and a joint checking account with Mrs. Shribe, he seems to have done the bulk of his business in cash."

Mrs. Shribe wiped her eyes. "I could have told you that. In addition to the machinery he manufactured, Otto bought and sold used machinery and he always carried large sums for that purpose. In fact, one of his favorite mottoes was, 'Cash talks.'"

Kelly put his wad of copy paper in the pocket of his coat. "There's my headline. So what do we do now, drag the lake or the river?"

Eagan lost all patience with him. "For God's sake, get out of here and stay out."

The reporter shrugged and left the office.

Mrs. Shribe lost what control she had and broke down. "He's dead. I know he's dead," she sobbed.

Johns stood up and swung his chair back to the wall. "I don't like what I'm thinking," he admitted. "It could be that my little talk with Otto put a bug in his ear, and when he was seen driving out of town, he was on his way to have a talk with someone."

Lieutenant Eagan crumpled a cigarette between his fingers. "Now all we have to figure out is who. And according to the last census, it could be anyone of twenty-six thousand people."

Sheriff Bodin rested one hip on Eagan's desk. "I'm beginning to get the picture. Arranged disappearances, eh? In both Tom and Sam's case, they left their wives well provided for but still had enough cash in their own pockets to take them any place in the world and live well for the balance of their lives. Only neither of them got very far."

Mrs. Shribe lost complete control of herself and began to scream. "Otto's dead. I know he is."

Doctor Avers said, "I'd better take her home and give her a sedative. Give me a hand, will you, Coy?"

"Sure thing," the detective said.

Between them, half carrying her, they led the hysterical woman from Eagan's office. It was unnaturally quiet when she was gone. The only sounds were the purr of the motors passing on the street in front and the far-off whistle of a train, as it signaled for some lonely rural crossing.

Eagan broke the silence. "So we start all over from scratch. In all three cases, the men were dissatisfied with what they had and someone sold them a bill of goods he had no intention of delivering. The question now is who is the super salesman?" He nodded. "Get me our con files, will you, Hal? And get a wire off to Natchez, Mobile and Atlanta for a make on any con man who might have promised Paradise to tired business men."

Johns doubted if access to the files of the nation would do Eagan any good. The racket was too new, too distinctive, too good, to be worked more than once in one town or in the present instance, three times. His talk with Shribe had made the other man suspicious and Otto had driven off to check on the possibility of a cross and had failed to return. His body could be any place within a radius of a hundred miles. Hess and Clay and Calhoun were all large counties.

He walked to the door of the office and Eagan asked him, "Where are you going?"

"To take a walk," Johns told him. "I want to think. I'll be back."

Once outside the station, he walked down the semi-deserted streets of the main business section of Clay City, past the unlighted plate glass windows of the stores. No one was perfect. The killer must have made one mistake. It was axiomatic.

Judge Johns knew the Sam Langley case best. He turned it over in his mind. Sam and Mrs. Langley had been playing bridge with the Hammonds. According to Hammond, Sam had seemed preoccupied all evening. Shortly after being dealt an almost perfect bridge hand, the howling of a stray dog, the easiest of all animals to imitate, had so annoyed Sam that he'd taken a pistol from a drawer and announced he was going to shoot the dog. The howling could well have been part of a prearranged signal. Sam could have thought that, with two hundred thousand dollars in cash in his pocket or cached away, he was walking out of the house that bored him, away from a life he despised, to spend the few years he had left in one of the outdoor Paradises that had always been his dream, leaving behind him an unsolvable murder. Such would have been the case, at least on the surface, if Al Pearson hadn't chosen to fish with a deep running spoon.

On impulse, Judge Johns turned down the next cross street and walked two blocks to the emergency entrance of the Clay City General Hospital. A tired and overheated intern was smoking a cigarette under the AMBULANCE sign.

Johns didn't know him. The intern didn't know Johns. "Well, for a change," the intern said, "a walking case. What's the matter, Mister? Did you take sleeping pills and change your mind and want your stomach pumped?"

"No. Not exactly," the judge said. He introduced himself and the intern apologized.

"Glad to meet you, Judge. Up to now you were just a name to me. But I voted for you at the last election because the resident and some of the other fellows said you were a good guy."

"Thank you," Johns said, soberly. "I won't take much of your time. I just want to ask a question."

"Glad to be of any help I can."

"There is a local blood bank?"

"There is."

"Blood or plasma?"

"Both."

"Of all types?"

"It wouldn't be any good otherwise."

"Could I buy some, say five litres?"

"You mean, just like that?"

"Just like that, to take out."

The intern shook his head. "Uh uh. In the first place, most of it is credited to individuals or organizations. In the second place, it's not a commercial bank."

"But such blood banks do exist?"

"In most of the large cities. I think, but I'm not sure, that there is one in Atlanta." The intern dropped his cigarette on the concrete and snuffed it with his heel. "There's been quite a lot of talk about them. I mean commercial blood banks in general. You know that there ought to be more supervision of them than there is. For example, out in Los Angeles, where I went to school, we have a couple that buy blood from winos just getting out of jail for five dollars a pint, then sell it on the open market for all the traffic will bear."

"They'll sell to anyone?"

"Anyone with a real or, I imagine, forged authorization to buy it."

"Thank you," Judge Johns said. "Thank you very much." He turned to walk back down the driveway, then stopped and looked over his shoulder. "I don't imagine anyone else in Clay City has asked you the same question?"

The intern shook his head. "I'm sorry."

Johns had almost reached the street when he heard footsteps behind him and turned to see the intern hurrying after him.

"Just a minute, Judge Johns," he said. "I don't know what this is all about but being of normal intelligence, I assume it has something to do with that guy who was found in the lake the other day."

"That's right."

The intern lighted a fresh cigarette. "Well, this may or may not help you. You know how it is when a man is interning. We don't have much money to spend and we pass what spare time we do have in bull sessions. You know, talking about what hot shot doctors we're going to be and how nice it would be to lay the little nurse in Ward A and who's going to win the series and maybe it might be best to take a commission and go right into the Army and get our tour of duty over with."

"I know," Johns said. "It's much the same with young lawyers."

The intern sucked hard at his cigarette. "Well, I just happened to think, about six months ago, I think it was, during one of our bull sessions, one of the boys did mention that some local reporter had asked him a lot of questions about the local bank and the commercial banks in the larger cities. As I recall, he said he wanted to write an article about them."

Johns was almost afraid to ask. "You don't happen to remember the reporter's name, do you?"

The intern snapped his fingers. "It slips me at the moment, but I saw it just the other day. He has a by-line in the *Courier*." He thought a moment. "Kelly. Yeah, that's the name. Jim Kelly."

"Thank you. Thank you very much," Judge Johns said.

CHAPTER FOURTEEN

The phone in the *Courier* office rang for a long time without any one answering it. Judge Johns hung up and dialed the number again on the chance that he'd rung the wrong number. He hadn't. The *Courier* was an evening paper. There was no one in the office, not even a porter or a cleaning woman.

Johns cradled the phone and sat a moment looking through the glass door of the booth into the lobby of the Commercial Hotel. Otto Shribe had made a phone call from the Commercial, possibly from this booth, then had disappeared into the same limbo that had swallowed Tom Harper and Sam Langley until their bodies had been found. He considered calling Lieutenant Eagan and decided against it. He wanted to talk to Kelly first. The reporter could have written a story on blood banks. Johns moved on the narrow bench and the .45 caliber pistol Dale had insisted he carry was comfortably uncomfortable. Besides, he had no need of Eagan until he'd determined and evaluated just how much the information from the intern was worth.

Johns opened the door of the booth and walked out into the lobby. The night bellman recognized and greeted him cordially. "Well, out rather late, aren't you, Judge Johns?" Johns looked at his watch. It was five minutes of one. "Late for me," he admitted.

He walked through the door and down the street to the courthouse square. Dale got off duty at midnight. But it was possible, just possible, that the night girl at the Elite might know where Jim Kelly lived.

The thud of his heels sounded hollow on the deserted walk. With the street lamps shining in the windows of the closed stores on the square and the glass reflecting his image, it was almost as if someone were walking beside him.

When he reached the Elite Cafe he turned in. He'd expected to see the black-haired girl whom Kelly had called Amy and was pleased to find that Dale was still behind the counter.

He sat on a stool and ordered. "A cup of coffee, black."

Dale drew it from the steamer and set it in front of him. "Speak of pleasant surprises," she smiled. She added, *sotto voce*, "But don't talk too loud. The cook is a nosey snoop. I think he cooks with one ear at the slot."

Judge Johns glanced at the rear of the restaurant. "Otherwise we're alone?"

Dale kept her voice down. "The two of us. What are you doing out so late? I heard your wife is back in town."

"She is."

Dale looked puzzled.

"Another man has disappeared," Johns told her. "A machine manufacturer by the name of Otto Shribe. But speaking of being out so late, what are you doing here? I thought your shift ended at midnight."

Dale wrinkled her nose at him. "It's all your fault."

"My fault?"

"Mm hmm. You got me so darn tired that I overslept this afternoon. And what with coming and going as I have ever since Friday night, Mr. Poulous is disciplining me." Dale glanced at the clock on the wall. "He said I had to make up the time and that means I'm stuck here until two o'clock." She added, "But Mable is still out of town. And after two o'clock, when Amy comes on to relieve me—" She wet her lips with her tongue.

Johns shook his head. "Not tonight. As much as I might like to." He made a pretense of drinking his coffee, in case the cook was watching them. "As I said before, another man has disappeared. And I'm trying to locate Jim Kelly."

Dale's forehead creased in a frown. "What do you want with that rat?"

"To talk to him," Johns told her. "You remember when I was reading the Sunday paper?"

"How could I forget Sunday?"

"I'm talking about reading the paper. Remember I pointed out Doctor Avers' statement to the effect that between the amount of blood found on the apron of his garage and the same type of blood found in the boat, Mr. Langley had bled enough for two men."

"Vaguely," Dale said. "Very vaguely. But what has that to do with Kelly?"

Judge Johns told her. "I just came from talking with an intern at the hospital and he said that about six months ago, Kelly made some pointed inquiries about commercial blood banks."

Dale shook her head. "Maybe I'm dumb. But I still don't get it."

Johns took a chance on patting one of her hands. "Forget it. It's just a theory I'm kicking around, rather a possible solution as to why there was so much blood."

"Oh," Dale said.

Johns lit a cigarette. "I phoned the *Courier* but there was no one in the office. You don't happen to know where Kelly lives, do you?"

Dale thought a moment. "As a matter of fact, I do. God knows he's asked me out there enough times." She confided, "One of the girls went. And she says nothing happened, but I don't believe her. It's tough enough trying to wrestle that guy right out on the street. And there's another funny thing, if it means anything to you. I thought it was funny Saturday night, you know, when you were in here, just before we went out to Mable's."

"What is funny?" Johns asked.

Dale said, "That big act that Kelly put on when you said you might go back out to the lake. Remember? And he said he wouldn't go if he had two machine guns and a platoon of marines?"

"I remember."

Dale said, "Well, he lives out at the lake."

Johns' pulse quickened. "You're kidding?"

Dale shook her head. "No. He used to live in some flea bag up the street. Then about three or four months ago, he came in here one night boasting about what a wonderful cottage he'd rented on Loon Lake for forty dollars a month and invited all of the girls to come out for a swim, or whatever. And, like I said, one of them went."

"Do you know where this cottage is?"

"No," Dale said. "I don't. But you may. He said he had rented the Martin cottage. Do you know where it is?"

"Very well. It's almost directly across the lake from mine in the same kind of a cove."

"Maybe I should have told you Saturday night. But I thought he was just kidding. An' I'd been so worried about you an' I was tryin' t' scheme how we could meet an' spend the week-end t'gether—"

Johns wanted to kiss her so badly the desire was a physical pain. "Stop blaming yourself," he said. "There was no reason then why you should have told me." He laid a half dollar on the counter to pay for his cup of coffee.

Dale put her hand on his. "You're goin' out there now?"

"I am."

"Alone?"

"Alone." Johns was a trifle pedantic. "You see, according to our system of legal jurisprudence, a man is assumed innocent until he has been proven guilty."

Dale was more puzzled than she'd been at the mention of blood banks. "If you say so. Whatever all those big words mean."

Johns stood up. "They just mean I want to have a talk with Kelly before I do anything."

Dale walked to the front of the restaurant with him. "You will be careful? Promise?"

"I promise," Judge Johns promised.

Outside on the walk in front of the cafe, he looked back. Dale opened and closed her fingers on the palm of her hand in the same gesture she'd made when she'd left his courtroom on the first morning he'd met her. Johns blew her a kiss and walked back to the station house to get his car. He drove out of the heart of town and down the maze of side streets leading to the lake road.

He was no longer tired. His brief talk with Dale had rejuvenated him. Man, he thought, was an odd creature. He hadn't wanted to stay with Lou. But if the two women had been transposed, if it had been Dale smiling at him from the bed, he wouldn't have been able to undress quickly enough.

Johns forced his mind back to the subject of his early morning drive. It could be he was entirely wrong about Kelly, that, mentally baffled by the two murders, and Otto Shribe's disappearance, he was snatching at straws. Still, of all men in town, the reporter was in as good a position to know the social status of Clay City's leading citizens, as anyone except their doctors, ministers and bankers. Kelly would know who went where and when and with whom, who had money and who didn't, who had reason to be discontented with the life he or she was leading. Kelly liked to live well. It could just be the reporter had dreamed up a get-rich-quick scheme of selling the promised land to bored and tired business men and had then double-crossed them. Harper could leave Mrs. Harper well-provided for and still have the new life of which he dreamed. The same held true for Langley and Shribe. Only, instead of winding up in paradise, Tom Harper had begun his new life on the bottom of the river, Sam Langley in Loon Lake and Otto Shribe wherever he was.

After his talk with Shribe, while they'd been having lunch, Otto could well have gotten suspicious and called Kelly's hand. Then what?

The more Johns thought on the subject the less he thought of the solution he'd evolved. If Harper or Langley or Shribe had wanted to leave Clay City and their wives, they had no need of Kelly's help or advice. All three men had been mature, intelligent. If they wanted out of Clay City, all any of them would have had to do was to put on their hats and phone the local airport.

Johns slowed his car, tempted to turn around and drive back to Clay City. Either the picture he'd formed in his mind was forced or there was still part of it missing. It could be that in going out to see Kelly, he was making a complete ass of himself, and the reporter would be certain to return the compliment in the next edition of the *Courier*. Still, there was the matter of excess blood. If Kelly had nothing to hide, why had he talked the way he had when he, himself, was living in one of the cottages?

Johns drove on. He reached the near end of the lake and drove past the lane leading to his own cottage, then turned left on the road partially encircling the lake, glancing at a name on a mail box from time to time to make sure he didn't pass the lane belonging to the Martin cottage.

It was quiet on the lake and dark. There was no moon but the night sky was filled with stars. From time to time, when the road wound close to the shore of the lake, he could see a phosphorescent streak in the water, as some night feeding fish sought out its prey. Johns subconsciously relaxed, as he always did when he was on or near the lake. What was it Lou had said:

"It looks like I shouldn't have gone to Atlanta. Every time you go out to that dirty old cottage on the lake you get into trouble of some kind. I wonder what we ever saw in it."

He reached what should be the Martin mail box but was unable to distinguish the weathered printing. Johns parked his car on the shoulder of the road and walked back. He'd come to the right place. The name was still Martin. Either Kelly wasn't having his mail delivered to the lake or he wasn't over-eager to let the general public know that he'd rented the cottage.

On the off chance that he was right about Kelly being involved in the two murders and one disappearance, Johns took the pistol Dale had given him from his hip pocket. He made sure the clip was full, then slipped the slide and ejected a shell so that there was a live shell in the firing chamber. Satisfied that he was prepared to defend himself, he dropped the gun into his side pocket and walked down the rutted lane to the cottage built on the shore of the lake.

It was very dark. The stars hung low and big but gave little light. He had to feel his way.

The crude mullioned windows in the living room of the cottage were lighted. Walking as quietly as he could, Johns felt his way across the weed grown yard and looked through one of the small panes of glass.

The Martin house had changed since he'd last seen it. Kelly was probably renting it furnished but he'd made certain improvements. Instead of the cheap furniture and cast-offs with which most of the cottages, his own included, were furnished, everything here was new and expensive. The chairs were huge affairs, overstuffed and upholstered in red and green leather. There was an immense Navajo rug on the floor and smaller throw rugs scattered about. A substantial liquor cabinet was open and well-stocked. It looked more like a wealthy sportsman's lodge, as pictured in "Esquire" or "True" than it did like a week-end cottage on Loon Lake.

More, Pete Martin hadn't refurnished it. Because of his arthritis, Pete and Mrs. Martin had been living in Florida for a year.

Johns thought, for a moment, there was no one in the living room.

Three smart traveling bags were standing near the door but he could see no life or movement. Then a hand reached out from one of the chairs to get a half-filled high ball glass, and Kelly sat erect in the chair. Running his free hand over his face in a gesture that could mean anything, he continued to sit up straight. Johns wished he could see Kelly's face, and obligingly, Kelly turned to look at the window through which Johns was staring.

The expression on his face was as broad as the gesture with his hand had been. He looked impatient and frightened, worried and a little drunk. As Johns watched him, the reporter glanced at the watch on his wrist, then leaned back in the chair again, with only a few hairs on the top of his head showing.

Johns walked around the house and up on the porch. He rapped lightly on the door.

From the chair, the reporter said, "It's about time you got here. I've been sitting here, going nuts."

There was the creak of leather as he got up. Muffled footsteps crossed the floor. A bolt snicked in its slot and the door opened.

Their faces only inches apart, Kelly breathed heavily as he looked at Johns, out into the night behind him, then back at Johns. "What the hell are you doing here?" he asked.

Johns slipped his hand into the pocket of his coat and around the comforting butt of the pistol. "I don't seem to be the party you expected."

Kelly took a deep breath and exhaled. "No," he admitted. "As a matter of fact, you aren't."

CHAPTER FIFTEEN

Judge Johns took a step forward. There were only two things Kelly could do. One was to refuse him entrance to the cottage. The other was to step back. The reporter chose to step back.

Johns stood in the open doorway, looking at the three bags. All of them were new, of the type known as airplane luggage. "Going somewhere?" he asked.

Kelly had recovered his composure. "That may or may not be, but it happens to be my business."

"True," Johns admitted. He admired the living room. "You do yourself well, Kelly."

"Thank you," Kelly said, wryly.

"But I thought you didn't like the lake. I thought you wouldn't live out here if they gave you two machine guns and a platoon of marines."

Kelly got his drink from the end table on which he'd set it. "I was just kidding you. All right. Let's have it, Your Honor." He over-stressed the two words. "What are you doing out here at one-thirty in the morning and who told you where I lived?"

"I want to talk to you," Johns said. "And Dale told me you were living here."

"How cosy," Kelly grinned. "Now, if only you were Dale and she wanted to talk to me—" He left the sentence unfinished.

Johns had all he could do to keep from slapping the smug smile off the reporter's face. "Let's leave Miss Chambers out of this."

Kelly sat on the arm of the chair in which he'd been sitting. "How formal. Did you call her Miss Chambers at your cottage when you helped her take off that stocking I saw you stuff into your pocket the other morning? Break down. Be human. How is she? Pretty nice stuff, eh?"

This was an angle Johns hadn't thought of. Kelly knew or guessed that Dale had spent a night in his cottage. He would undoubtedly attempt to use the knowledge to his own advantage. And the least suspicion of scandal could cost him his new bench.

Kelly continued to needle him. He made a descriptive gesture with his hands. "How are they, bare and pointing up at you? Something to look at, I'll bet."

Johns began to sweat. He almost wished he hadn't come to the lake, that he'd gone directly home after he'd given Jack Eagan what information he could. He was, after all, a judge, not a policeman. He forced himself to speak. "I don't know what you're talking about."

Kelly was enjoying himself now. "I'll bet. I was in court that morning. Remember? And she hit you as hard as you hit her. In fact, if it had been Christmas and you had been Santa Claus you couldn't have gotten up the chimney. And directly after court, where did you eat? The club where you've eaten for years? No. Just by the merest chance you happened to drop into the Elite."

Johns recovered some of his self control. This was an old military strategy. When attacked, counter attack. "You don't know a thing," he said.

Kelly shrugged. "When you're a reporter with your own by-line you don't have to know. All you have to do is suspect. Words are funny things. And the public is naturally dirty-minded. You'd be surprised what you can do by inference. I can write a stick and tuck it away in my classified section of the *Courier* that would fix it so you couldn't ever be re-elected dog catcher in this section of the country."

It was the wrong tack to take with Johns. It only made him more bull-headed. "All right. You write what you please. I still want to ask you some questions."

Kelly mixed himself a fresh drink, a high ball glass half-filled with whiskey topped by a splash of ginger ale. "Okay. As Dewey said to his executive officer on the morning of May 1st, 1898, 'You may fire when ready, Gridley.' What do you want to know?"

"About six months ago you made some inquiries at the local hospital concerning commercial blood banks."

"I may have. A reporter is always asking questions. As a matter of fact, I think I did. It was something in connection with the drive to build up the local bank." Kelly laughed. "But have a heart, Your Honor. God knows how many thousands of words I've ground out on my mill since then. Don't tell me you came out here to ask me about a story I wrote six months ago."

"I did."

"May I ask why?"

"Doctor Avers thinks that Sam Langley lost too much blood."

"Yeah. I know. As I remember, I ran the statement in italics in the Sunday paper. What about it?"

Johns was beginning to feel more and more like a fool. "Well, I've evolved a possible solution to Sam Langley's murder."

"I'm all ears."

"Sam was discontented with the life he was leading."

Kelly shrugged. "How many of us aren't? You should work for a small town newspaper for seventy-two fifty a week with a fifteen dollar a gallon tax on whiskey and every babe you take out thinking she's Zsa Zsa Gabor and you holding as heavy as Rubirosa. Get to the point."

"I don't think Sam knew he was to die. I think he laid down that bridge hand and walked out to shoot that dog, thinking he was merely taking part in the first act of a staged drama that would end with him allegedly dead but in reality beginning a new life with two hundred thousand dollars in cash in his pockets."

"An interesting deduction. May I ask you to define your reasoning?"

"Let's say someone, as yet unnamed, was helping him stage his disappearance and when Sam walked out to shoot the dog, this someone was waiting with five litres of blood, purchased from a commercial blood bank, to pour on the concrete apron of Sam's garage to mystify the police. And that after this person fired three shots into the air to substantiate Sam's story, they walked a block or two to a waiting car and drove away, Sam thinking he was beginning a new life when, in reality, Loon Lake was as far as he got. And when he reached Loon Lake, this party supposed to be helping him, shot and killed him and put his body in that boat I found and rowed it out and sank it where Al Pearson accidentally snagged it."

Kelly thought a moment and shook his head. "My city editor wouldn't print it. We print news, not fiction." He got up from the arm of the chair. "Sorry, but if that's all you wanted to talk to me about, I think you'd better get back in your canoe or on your hobby horse or whatever you came on and blow. I'm on my two weeks vacation, starting tomorrow morning, and as soon as the little babe I'm expecting can get away from her husband, we're driving down to Panama City and just lie on the sand for two weeks." He grinned. "And do whatever else comes naturally. And I don't want her to be embarrassed by having Clay City's leading legal light witness our departure."

Johns began to sweat harder. His bluff had been called. He didn't have an iota of proof connecting the reporter with Tom Harper or Sam Langley's murder or Otto Shribe's disappearance. "What if I try to stop you from leaving town?"

"How?"

"By phoning the police and telling Lieutenant Eagan that I want him to arrest you on suspicion, that I think, in some manner, you are connected with the recent crimes."

Kelly thought a moment. "He'd do it, too. Right now his tongue is hanging out so far, he'd try to pin what has been happening on his mother if he thought it would get we the people off his neck." He picked up two of the three bags standing near the door and set them out on the porch and returned to the living room. "There's the phone. Go ahead." His voice turned ugly. "But remember this, Johns. You have me pulled in on some bum rap and I'll crucify you. I'll do some leg work to prove your recent bed work. And I'll see to it that it's printed on the front page of the *Courier*. And won't the good people of Hess and Clay and Calhoun counties, the good Bible reading electorate be pleased to learn you spent last Friday night laying a little blond waitress and then, after being a hero by snooping into something that was none of your concern, you crawled right back into the sack for more of the same Saturday night and all day Sunday and Sunday night up until four o'clock in the morning."

The sweat on Judge Johns' face turned cold. It was an effort for him to speak. "Now, wait a minute."

Kelly picked up the remaining bag. "I intend to. But you aren't. You're leaving as of now." He carried the bag through the doorway and disappeared into the darkness of the porch. From there, his voice slightly muffled, he added, "Now put up or shut up. Either make your call to Eagan or—" He stopped in the middle of his sentence and his voice turned agonized. "No," he pleaded. "No. For God's Sake—"

A shot cut him short this time. Two more shots followed in rapid succession and there was a thud as of a body falling to the porch.

The silence that followed was deafening. Johns drew the pistol Dale had given him from his pocket and strode to the open doorway and stood, illuminated by the brightly lighted room.

"Kelly—" he began and the flash of a fourth shot brightened the night and a lead wasp buzzed angrily past his head and embedded itself in the door jamb.

Johns' reaction was instinctive. He raised the pistol in his hand and fired at the vague form behind the gun flash.

The sear of the pistol had been filed and the five shells remaining in it were expelled with the one pressure on the trigger. At the distance he couldn't miss. The sweat on Johns' forehead turned colder. At the distance he couldn't miss but somehow he had.

The vague shadow on the end of the porch, a blur of movement against the night, slipped around the corner of the cabin and as instinctively as he'd triggered his gun, Johns followed it into the dark. As at the dead end road, there was a blinding flash of light as he turned the corner of the cabin in pursuit and a great weight crashed down on his head.

Johns' voice was that of a hurt child. "No," he said. "No." Then his knees buckled under him and he pitched forward into the weeds.

His period of unconsciousness was brief but long enough. He lay, face down, in the grass, wishing he didn't have to get up, that he never would have to get up again. The blow had induced nausea. He turned his face to one side and was sick on the back of his hand. Kelly was dead. Johns knew. He almost envied him. What happened from here on in wasn't going to be pleasant.

He rose to his feet with a tremendous effort of will and searched the ground where he'd been lying. The automatic pistol was gone. That was logical. He hadn't expected to find it.

In the gleam of the stars a flash of white caught on a bush near where he'd been lying attracted Johns' eyes. He picked up the bit of fabric and put it into the pocket of his coat. Arriving at the porch, he found that the three bags Kelly had set out were gone. But the reporter wasn't going any place. He was lying on his back, one leg twisted under him, looking at the night sky he could no longer see.

Johns fought another desire to be sick. Everything had been so beautiful. Now this. Of course. He should have known. He was an adult male. And after a man had passed a certain age, there was no never never land nor any sugar plum tree on the shore of the Lollipop sea. What a man got he paid for, one way or another.

He walked into the cabin and poured himself a stiff drink. This whiskey tasted good. He would need it. Finished with the drink, he lit a cigarette and sucked smoke into his lungs and stood tempted, briefly, to just walk out the door again and down the lane to his car and drive back to Clay City and let whoever would, discover Kelly's body. That was the way it was planned. That was why he was still alive.

Then the habits of a lifetime overcame his temptation. He had no choice. No matter what happened to him, there was only one course he could take.

He located the phone and waited for the operator to come to life. When she did he gave her the number of Jack Eagan's office.

Eagan was annoyed with him. "What the hell happened to you? You said you were going to take a walk around the block and think. That was two hours ago."

Johns had never been so tired. He said, "Never mind about me. Jim Kelly is dead on the porch of the Martin cottage at Loon Lake. But don't send all your men out here. Have them waiting in front of the station. I'll be there as fast as I can drive. If we hurry, I think we can pick up the party responsible for Tom Harper and Sam Langley and Otto Shribe's deaths. If we are in time, you might even recover the money they had on their persons."

Lieutenant Eagan was incredulous. "Are you crazy?"

Judge Johns considered the question. "No, not now," said, soberly. "But I have been."

CHAPTER SIXTEEN

Johns could see the revolving red lights of the waiting police cars blocks before he reached them. He parked across the street from the station house and walked to the other side. The walk was black with men. Jack Eagan was waiting beside a squad car.

When Johns would have entered the station, Eagan caught at his arm. "I thought you said we had to hurry."

Johns shook his head as if to clear it. "Yes," he said, "we do. But there is a phone call I have to make first. I tried to make it from the Martin cottage, but the number is on a party wire and the line was busy."

Johns walked on into the station and picked up the receiver of the phone on the booking desk. "I want to call a Mr. Poulous," he told the operator. "I don't know his first name. I tried to phone him a few minutes ago and the line was busy. I do remember the operator saying that he lived at 1011 Jackson Street."

"Just one moment, sir."

"For God's Sake," a voice said and Johns realized that Lieutenant Eagan had followed him into the office. "Don't tell me the Greek that runs the Elite Cafe has been behind these killings."

"No," Johns said. "It wasn't Poulous."

The line was clear this time. He could hear the restaurant man's phone ringing. Johns waited, hoping against hope that he was wrong and knowing in his heart that he wasn't.

When Poulous came on the wire, his voice was fogged with sleep. "Yes—?"

Judge Johns introduced himself and apologized for disturbing him. "But it's important that I ask you a question."

"Yes—?"

Johns took a deep breath and exhaled slowly. "Do or did you, until this Saturday just past, have a girl working the four to midnight shift in your cafe? A girl by the name of Mable who asked for a few days off because her husband's father was dying and she and her husband had to drive to Mobile."

"N-no," Poulous said. "I haven't any girl by the name of Mable working for me. And none of them asked for time off so they could drive to Mobile with their husbands."

"Thank you," Johns said and hung up.

He fought off another attack of vertigo and would have fallen if Eagan hadn't steadied him. "You've been slugged again," Eagan said.

Judge Johns nodded. "Yes."

"So where do we go from here?"

Johns' tongue felt too big for his mouth. "I don't know the exact address," he admitted, "but I know how to get there. It's a small, square white house, set off by itself, about two miles out of town."

Johns rode in the first car with Eagan. Coy White drove while Johns told him when and where to turn. The two-way radio was crackling now and the officers that Lieutenant Eagan had dispatched to Loon Lake had found Kelly's body. The dispatcher relayed their report to Eagan.

"They say he was shot in the back by a gun held so close it set his coat on fire. Low down, like a short person would do it."

Eagan flipped the two-way over. "Tell them to stand by. Then notify Doc Avers."

"Yes, sir," the dispatcher acknowledged the instructions. "Over and out."

Johns felt like he was riding through a nightmare in a car propelled by jet power, so fast they had pierced the sonic barrier and all he could feel was pressure, all he could hear was the beating of his own heart.

"Whenever you're ready, Evan," Eagan said.

Johns forced himself back to reality. "Of course."

"Jim Kelly in this thing?"

"Yes."

"How deeply?"

"Up to his neck. I doubt, now that he's dead, if you'll ever be able to prove it but the way I see it, he was the trigger man, the man who committed the actual murders."

"You know this?"

"I know."

"Where did he kill Sam Langley?"

"Out at the lake."

"But how in the name of time did he get Sam out there?"

Johns took a deep breath and wished he could hold it forever. Unfortunately, he couldn't. He said, "Sam went willingly. I don't know just where he expected to go when he laid down that bridge hand and walked out to shoot at the dog. I do know he didn't expect to die."

"What was he thinking about?"

"Starting life all over."

"He walked away from the house by himself?"

"I doubt that very much. I think he was met by somebody."

"By Kelly?"

"No."

"But the blood? If he wasn't killed at the house, where did all that blood come from?"

"A commercial blood bank. That was part of the plan connected with his disappearance and Sam went along with it willingly. He wanted you and Ella and everyone in Clay City to think that he was dead so that no nationwide search would be made for him. He wanted you to assume he'd been killed for the money he'd received for his factory."

"And Tom Harper?"

Johns shook his head. "I don't know anything about Tom but I imagine when he went into the river, or shortly before, he was in much the same frame of mind as Sam. Turn left at the next crossroad," Johns told White. "Then straight ahead for a mile and a half. The house is on the right hand side of the road."

"Yes, sir, Judge Johns," Coy White said. "But it's kind of funny, huh?"

Johns wondered what possibly could be funny. He asked White and was told.

"I just meant us being cops and you a judge and you having to figure out the score."

Johns repressed a shudder. "I was helped."

"How about Shribe?" Eagan asked.

"I don't know a thing about Otto," Johns answered. "We may find his body where we're going but I doubt it." He amended his previous statement. "I do know this much. What I said while we were having lunch together did make Otto suspicious and he drove to one of two places, either the Martin cottage or to the house where we're going. He was seeking assurance that his own plan to disappear wasn't a plot to get the money he was carrying, instead of joining him in the new life he hoped to begin. His going wherever he did go, in the frame of mind he was in, threw off the time schedule planned by the others in the plot. They were forced to kill him to close his mouth and dispose of his body as best they could. That's why Kelly was packed and ready to leave when I reached the Martin place."

"They?" Eagan asked. "Join him in the new life he hoped to begin?

All right. Let's have it, Evan."

Johns' tongue still felt thick. He doubted if it would ever feel normal again. "There's a girl in this, of course," he said. "We should have realized that from the start. A girl young and pretty enough to make any man make a fool of himself over her." He rested his head in his hands a moment. "This is the way I see the story. This girl and Kelly knew each other in whatever town they lived in before they came to Clay City and between them they schemed this thing, although I imagine the idea was originally hers. In a way, Kelly was just as much a chump and a tool as the other men involved. In the end it cost him his life."

"This girl we're on our way to pick up killed Kelly?"

"Yes." Johns remembered something and felt in his coat pocket for the scrap of fabric he'd taken from the bush near the Martin cottage. He found it and gave it to Lieutenant Eagan, feeling like Judas, even knowing what he now knew. "Here. You'd better keep this."

Eagan examined it in the light from the dash board of the squad car. "What is it?"

"A piece of her skirt," Judge Johns told him. "She snagged it on a bush out at the Martin place, just after she'd killed Kelly and I'd shot at her five times with an automatic pistol loaded with blanks."

Eagan and White waited for him to continue.

It took a moment for Johns to force the words past the constriction in his throat. "I doubt, I doubt very much if you'll be able to convict her of the deaths, even of complicity, in the cases of Harper, Langley and Shribe. But I do think she can be convicted of the murder of her partner."

"Once is enough," Eagan said quietly.

Johns felt for his cigarettes and found them, then returned the package to his pocket, afraid to try lighting one with his hands trembling the way they were. "As I said before, the way I see the story, this girl, a very smart girl, along with being very beautiful, realized a fundamental human weakness and attempted to parlay several such weaknesses into a fortune. All men, when they reach a certain age, are discontented, tired of the humdrum existence of a life that didn't turn out as they had hoped it would. Very well. She would be all things to a few carefully chosen men. Whatever Tom Harper wanted to do she would do it with him. We know Sam loved the woods and outdoor life. All right. She would go to the north woods or wherever with Sam and renew and rejuvenate his waning vitality and sexual prowess with her own youth and beauty. Meanwhile, mind you, she gave out generous samples to prove she could do just that."

Eagan looked sharply at Judge Johns but said nothing.

Johns continued, "You heard Mrs. Shribe tell us the way Otto felt about the Samoan Islands. But would Mrs. Shribe go with him? No. She thought the idea was foolish. She was content with the rut they were in. All her friends lived in Clay City. Otto was just getting a good start in business. She would miss the annual Junior League dance and Women's Chamber of Commerce banquet. She couldn't get along without her bridge club. No. Mrs. Shribe wouldn't go with Otto. This younger woman would, however. At least, she promised she would. But it's obvious she couldn't disappear and start life all over again with more than one man. And none of her lovers had enough money to satisfy her. I haven't the slightest idea what total she'd set in her mind. But it was high, possibly half a million dollars. So this girl did the only thing she could do. She carried on affairs with God knows how many prominent men, each one of whom was convinced she loved him and him alone, and waltzed them out one by one into Jim Kelly's butcher shop, where they went willingly as part of their 'planned' deaths or disappearances, under the illusion that they were going to start a new life with her. Instead, they got death."

Johns took a chance and lit a cigarette. If Eagan noticed his trembling hands he made no comment. The smoke tasted raw and hot in his mouth. When Johns could, he continued.

"In a way, she and Kelly got some bad breaks. If the line man for the power company hadn't happened to climb that pole, Tom Harper would still be sitting in his car at the bottom of the river. If the weather hadn't turned warm and Al Pearson hadn't happened to be a good fisherman and fished a deep-running lure, and if I hadn't happened to lunch with Otto he wouldn't have called for a showdown and—"

As Judge Johns hesitated, Lieutenant Eagan said, "And there is no telling how many other prominent Clay City business men might have disappeared."

Unable to speak, Johns nodded.

"I think I see the house," Coy White said. "Shall I kick on the siren?"

Johns moved his head from side to side. "No. I think it is best if we do this quietly. I have reason to believe this girl thinks she has more time than she has."

Again, Eagan looked at him sharply but said nothing. He ordered White to stop the squad car a hundred yards down the road from the house and as the other cars, city and county, stopped behind them, Eagan deployed the men in them so that the small, square white frame house would be surrounded.

"She's here, all right," White said. "The windows are lighted."

Judge Johns' feeling of moving through a fantastic nightmare deepened, as he walked through the dark with White, Eagan and Bodin. The door of the attached garage was open and a battered 1948 model Plymouth was standing on the drive. Johns looked through the rear windows of the car. The three traveling bags he'd seen in the Martin cottage, plus two more, were lying on the rear seat.

"From the amount of luggage," Coy White said, "she's really all set to take off and never come back again."

Judge Johns drew a deep breath. "All right. Let's get it over with." He motioned for Eagan to precede him. "You're in charge. You should find a dress or a uniform with a tear in it that matches that piece of goods I gave you. Also a recently fired pistol or revolver that Terrill can match up with the slugs Doctor Avers takes out of Kelly's body. Also a .45 caliber Colt Automatic pistol I believe can be identified with the fragment of a slug you found out at that dead end road."

The two men had known each other for a long time. Lieutenant Eagan phrased the question as delicately as he could. "You've told us all you care to tell us, Evan?"

"At this time," Johns said.

He mounted the stairs of the unlighted back porch with Eagan and the sheriff and looked into the lighted window. The linoleum in the kitchen had been freshly scrubbed. A smart, light-weight traveling suit was hanging over the back of a chair with a hastily taken off pastel nylon green uniform lying under the skirt of the suit. A new and expensive director's case was propped against one of the legs of the chair. On the table beside it were two guns, one the Colt Automatic Dale had insisted on giving him to 'protect' himself, the other a business-like-looking .38 caliber revolver.

As the three men and the men behind them watched, the blond girl in the kitchen, stripped to her filmy scanties and brassiere for comfort while she worked, scrubbed industriously with a rag in an attempt to remove any of her own fingerprints.

Eagan watched her for a long time. "I can't say I blame Tom and Otto," he said finally. "Or any of the other men to whom she gave herself. She could have sold me a bill of goods and I wouldn't have asked any questions. Well, let's get it over with."

On the chance that the door might be locked, he gripped the knob and burst the door open with a powerful thud of his body and Dale turned, more in surprise than fright, as plainclothesmen and uniformed officers filled the kitchen.

Sheriff Bodin walked directly to the table and sniffed the barrels of the guns. "Fired recently," he announced. "I'd say, within the last hour."

Eagan opened the director's case. It was packed neatly with bills, more money than Johns had ever seen in his life. Most of the bills were still in sheaves as they'd come from the bank of their origin. Eagan turned his attention from the money to the nylon uniform on the chair. Spreading it on the table, he looked for and found a torn spot. The piece of fabric which Johns had given him matched the tear exactly.

Lieutenant Eagan turned and looked at the blond girl. "I'm sorry, Miss," he said quietly, "but I am forced to arrest you for the murder of Jim Kelly and complicity in the deaths of Tom Harper and Sam Langley."

"Oh?" Dale said. "I wonder if one of you gentlemen has a cigarette."

One of Bodin's deputies offered her his package, and her barely concealed young breasts rose and firmed with the movement of her chest. They remained high and haughty even when she exhaled the smoke in a thin, acrid film. She looked directly at Judge Johns, then away from him. "In that case, I'd better get dressed. But, may I say at this point that you've made some very serious charges and I doubt, in fact I doubt very much, that you can prove them in court."

As unconcerned as if she were alone in the kitchen, she put on a modest blouse, then her hose and shoes, then the skirt of the suit.

Johns stood watching her, sweating as he'd never sweat before. Still, a vague hope glimmered in his mind. Dale didn't dare to talk about their brief affair. It was all so clear now. She'd called herself to his attention with a minor traffic violation, then deliberately seduced him—because she wanted a pipe line into Jack Eagan's office, some fool who would tell her the things that even Jim Kelly couldn't find out. She also wanted a highly placed friend in court in case such an emergency as this one should happen, a man who would work in her behalf in order to save his own skin.

Johns wiped his face with his handkerchief. Jack Eagan and

Sheriff Bodin were wondering, in fact, they probably knew, how he knew as much as he did about the three murders, how he'd known where to lead them. But, possibly, just possibly, if he kept his mouth shut and sat, impartial, on his bench while a jury debated Dale's guilt or innocence, he could still get out of this without losing everything he'd spent fourteen years in building.

His mind raced on. Of course. All he had to do was keep his mouth shut. Dale wouldn't talk. She wanted him to preside over her trial. And neither Jack Eagan nor Sheriff Bodin would push him. Both men would be content to protect their jobs and their pensions by taking credit for the solution of the murders.

After all, he was one of the boys.

CHAPTER SEVENTEEN

Despite the fact it was only a preliminary hearing, every seat in the air-conditioned courtroom was occupied. Angry men and women, unable to get seats, filled the halls and corridors and jammed the stairs. They even stood on the parched lawn outside, looking up at the courtroom windows with hot eyes.

Judge Johns felt as if he hadn't slept in two weeks. He hadn't. There were deep lines in his face and purple pouches under his eyes. Conversely, the two weeks she'd spent in jail had left Dale looking rested, virginal and starry-eyed. If she were worried, it didn't show in her face. She sat at the defendant's table, turning from time to time to talk earnestly to the high-priced lawyer whom she'd imported from Atlanta to defend her. They seemed to be arguing about something.

Johns permitted his eyes to rove over the room, as the state's attorney read the charge which he hoped to prove. After a meeting of minds, it had been decided to try Dale for Kelly's murder only. With the reporter dead, the state doubted that it could convict her of the crimes against Tom Harper and Sam Langley. To date, the state had been unable to find one witness who had ever seen Dale with either man. The state was unable to prove that the almost three hundred thousand dollars found in the director's case was the same money Tom Harper had drawn from his bank, for which Sam Langley had sold his factory and which Otto Shribe had been carrying. If the verdict should be 'not guilty', reluctant as it would be to do so, the state would have to return the money to Dale.

Johns thought, she was clever with Tom and Sam and Otto, as clever as she was with me. Between the rented Martin cottage, the white frame house, allegedly belonging to a friend and such hideaway places, similar to his own cottage, that Harper and Langley and Shribe might have had, Dale had plenty of places in which to entertain her lovers without any of them meeting or appearing in public with her. Dale had been a busy young woman. The thought sickened Johns. The blond girl had told him:

"This is the first time in three years, that, well, anything like this has happened ... Sometimes I've thought that I would go out of my mind ... But I just couldn't bring myself to be cheap with any man."

And male fool that he was, in his ego, he'd believed her, when, in reality, he'd only been one in a parade of men. Johns saw Lou sitting on the aisle in the last row of seats in the courthouse and was displeased with her. He wished Lou hadn't come to the hearing. Lou knew he hadn't slept. Lou knew something was troubling him. With her woman's intuition, she probably guessed what it was.

Johns forced himself to listen to the state's attorney. Phil Lester was a capable prosecutor. But Dale had been fantastically clever. There was so much that wouldn't come out, couldn't come out, under the legal procedure that governed a criminal trial. In trying her for Kelly's death, Lester wouldn't be able to mention the money or her complicity in the other two deaths or the fact that Shribe's body had not been found. A jury, composed mostly of men would spend more time admiring and coveting Dale than they would listening to the arguments of the prosecution.

The state's attorney finished outlining the charge and the clerk of the court cleared his throat. "Will the defendant approach the bench?"

Dale got slowly to her feet and, accompanied by her attorney, stood in front of Johns' bench, looking up at him, calm, unafraid, very lovely.

"How do you plead?" Johns asked her.

A faint smile brightened Dale's lips. Her voice was clear. "I plead not guilty, Your Honor." She took a deep breath and continued. "And after due conference with my attorney I waive my constitutional rights to a jury trial and ask that Your Honor determine my guilt or innocence."

Johns could feel the walls of the courtroom closing in on him. His collar was too tight. Just breathing was an effort. This was one possible eventuality he hadn't thought of. Dale was taking one last big gamble. She was afraid a jury *might* convict her, might even bring in a verdict that would make it mandatory for him to sentence her to die in the electric chair. And Dale was gambling that he couldn't do that to her, that he would find her not guilty, that he couldn't and wouldn't destroy the warm, pulsing flesh that had throbbed in his arms.

Johns poured water into the glass on his bench and drank it. There were three things he could do. He could try her and find her guilty, as he knew she was. He could try her and find her innocent because, despite her evil core, Dale was very lovely and desirable. He hoped God would have mercy on both of them, but he was still in love with her. Dale was his lost youth, his dreams. She was all the things he would never have again.

Johns studied the girl's face carefully. Her full lips were slightly parted. There was open promise in her eyes. Her eyes were saying:

The other men don't matter. They were merely means to an end. Try me and find me innocent and we'll go away together, anywhere you want to go. Just you and I and all that money. And you won't be sorry. I promise.

Johns was tempted. He would never forget one minute of the time he'd spent with Dale. The easy way out was to try her and find her innocent and Dale would never dare leave him. They would be pariahs to the rest of the world but inexorably bound to each other.

Or there was a third alternative.

The silence in the courtroom deepened. Johns sat a moment longer thinking, then took his pen from its stand and wrote for what seemed a long time. When he'd finished, he said, quietly, "I'm sorry. But for a judge to sit in judgment in a murder trial, he must be absolutely impartial. And I'm afraid in the present instance that is impossible."

Johns raised his head and looked at the spectators in the courtroom. "And I make this public confession. It is impossible for me to be impartial in the present instance because, forgetting my marital vows and the woman I promised to cherish until death did the two of us part, I have had carnal knowledge of the defendant, not once but innumerable times, in my cottage at Loon Lake and in the house in which she was arrested. Which leaves me with the choice of making this public announcement and bringing to an end a career I now realize has meant very much to me, or permitting the defendant in this case to literally get away with murder. This I cannot bring myself to do."

Johns folded the piece of paper on which he'd written and handed it to the state's attorney. "To that effect I not only disqualify myself as a fit judge to hear this case, I hereby tender my resignation to the attorney general and ask that the state's attorney petition the proper source to appoint a truly impartial judge to try the case of the State versus Miss Dale Chambers."

Johns got up from his chair and walked around his bench. In the deep silence that followed his pronouncement, he stood a moment, looking at Dale. The blond girl had gambled and lost. Her shoulders drooped. Her firm flesh seemed to shrink like a balloon pricked with a pin. Her eyes were no longer inviting. They were haunted.

"I'm sorry, Dale," Johns said. "It seems you seduced the wrong judge. I may be a heel. I undoubtedly am a heel, but not quite that big a one."

Johns had never wanted anything as badly as he now wanted to be alone, behind a closed and locked door. But he had to face reality sometime. It might as well be now.

He opened the gate in the rail separating the first row of spectators from the counsel tables and walked slowly up the aisle. Men who had respected and voted for him for years looked at him with open contempt. Women turned their faces away as he passed. He didn't need a closed door. He'd closed one. Johns had never felt so alone. Then, as he reached the last row of seats in the courtroom, Lou stood up and slipped her hand in his. She was crying, but she held her head high.

"I'm still with you, Evan."

Johns looked at her, dull-eyed. "Why?"

Lou met his eyes. "Perhaps because I'm proud of you. Then, too, I happen to be your wife."

Johns squeezed the hand in his and together they went out into the hall. He would never again hold public office. His future lay behind him. After all the facts in the case came out he might even be disbarred. He had only one consolation—Lou. Johns felt a wave of tenderness toward her. Somehow, someway, together, they'd work this out. He'd been a fool. True, Lou was no longer as young and as pretty as Dale. She'd already given him her girlhood. But there was nothing that Dale or any other young woman could do for him that

Lou couldn't do because Lou loved him, because when the chips were down she, too, would gamble on her man. This could even mean the start of a new life together.

Johns squeezed her hand harder. "It's going to be rough," he told her.

"I know," Lou said. "I know." She was still quietly crying but back of her tears her eyes were shining.

THE END

The Big Kiss-Off

DAY KEENE

PART ONE
HORROR HARBOR

1
THE MUD LUMP

The six men, so much clay on the tide-swept mud lump, were dead. They had been dead some days, Cade imagined, dead of thirst and starvation.

Cade raised his eyes to a low-lying fringe of green, misty in the brightening dawn; the mainland, less than eighteen miles away. But so far as the men on the barren mud lump were concerned, it might have been eighteen hundred miles! Few boats ever came here. Now and then a fisherman taking a short cut to Grande Terre or Barataria Bay, or an occasional guided party of sports down from New Orleans after tarpon or ducks.

A small man, compactly built, barefooted, wearing only a pair of old dungarees, Cade lighted the pressure stove in the galley and put a pot of coffee to boil. Then, sucking at his first cigarette of the day, he returned to the open cockpit of the cruiser and resumed his study of the bodies. Morning was warm. Day was going to be hot. It was so still on the motionless water that the hollow silence subtly disturbed him. As closely as Cade could ascertain without breaking out the dinghy and rowing ashore, two of the dead had been Chinese. The other four could have been nationals of any country.

Cade spat on the glasslike surface of the water. Some of the boys, it would seem, were still in business. He wished he'd picked another anchorage last night, when it had been far too dark to make out the bodies. He wished he'd stood further out in the Gulf. If he had known, he wouldn't have come within forty miles of the south mud lump.

When the coffee had boiled, he forced himself to drain a cup of it black, smoking a second cigarette, sitting in one of the fancy fishing chairs bolted to the deck plates. He tried to concentrate on admiring the trim lines of his new thirty-eight-foot cruiser. He tried to think of how nice it was to sit in the sun, to feel the sea air on his face, how nice to be able to come and go as he pleased. Yalu, Pyongyang, Panmunjom were fast becoming just names, names of far places out of a bitter dream.

But his mind kept returning to windward. After two years of millet and rice and fish heads and dysentery, his stomach was queasy enough without this. It was surprising that the men caught in the tangle of grass and dead trees and driftwood had stayed on the flat as long as they had. The next flood tide would sweep them out to sea and there would be nothing on the green surface of the Gulf but mud and dead trees and silence.

Cade poured a second cup of coffee but before he could raise it to his lips he lost the first cup he'd drunk.

When the retching ceased, he swore softly under his breath. Always one bad oyster in a barrel. So a government cutter had gotten too close and some of the boys had almost been caught with a hot cargo. They'd been well paid to take that chance.

Depressed, he tinkered with the misfiring engine which had caused him to anchor the night before. The trouble proved to be minor. When the engine was running to suit him, he cut in its twin to make sure he wouldn't drift onto the flat, then up-anchored and felt his way back through the shallows. Out in the blue water again, he pushed the throttle wide open, holding for South Pass. Cade fingered his pencil-line mustache. He should have stayed in blue water.

He should have done a lot of things.

The day fulfilled its promise of heat, and he began to cheer up a bit. The hot sun felt good on his back. He liked the taste of the salt spray on his face. It felt natural—right. It was as if the past twelve years had never been.

Still, Cade was fair. He had to admit that five of the twelve years away from Bay Parish had been fun. He pushed his white captain's cap back on his crisp black hair, as he admired the wake the ship was leaving. He'd traveled fast. He'd flown a lot of wing. He'd drunk a lot of rum. He'd planted some very delightful oats in very beautiful, if unfertile, soil.

The hot deck plates burned his bare feet. Cade wished he hadn't thought of Janice. On the other hand, there'd be no real reason for her to wait. She was young. She was lovely. She had her own way to make. Who did he think he was? Washed-up Sabrejet pilots were a dime a dozen.

The day continued clear and hot. By noon he was back in the ship lanes, then he lost four hours when his port engine, stiff and new, cut out again. The Gulf had turned a deep purple by the time he entered South Pass. It was dusk when he cleared Pilottown and almost dark when he cut his engines and nosed into the hyacinth-choked slip beside the rotting wooden pier in front of the old frame house in which he had been born.

Neither the house nor Bay Parish had changed, at least on the surface. The old house back of the levee was merely more neglected and weathered than it had been. There'd been some improvements on the levees and the jetties. A few more canals had been dug. There was a new name over the poolroom. The shrimp cannery had changed hands. Sal had bought a big red neon sign that spelled out— *FOOD AND DRINKS*. But, on the whole, Bay Parish was as he had left it.

An aged Negro fishing in the canal laid down his cane pole and came over to where Cade was making fast his lines. The old man was troubled. "Excusin' I say it, captain, but that's Cade Cain's landin'."

"Yeah. Sure," Cade grinned. "I know. And I hit it right on the head—all the way from Tokyo."

The old man peered through the gathering dusk. "Why, glory be. Hit's you!" He touched the brim of his hat and, his wrinkled face wreathed in a toothless smile, he hobbled up the grass-grown road to town, eager to be the first to spread the news that Colonel Cade Cain was back from the war.

Cade finished making fast. From here on in, he had it made. He'd spent all his red-line and severance pay for the *Sea Bird*. He had just a five-dollar bill in his pocket. But there was food for the taking. The marshes and bayous and reefs were loaded with wild rice, ducks, shrimp, oysters. There was no better fishing anywhere. One party of sports a week would pay for his gas. All he had to do now was live.

The boat fast, Cade realized he was hungry. He lighted the pressure lantern in the galley and opened a can of beans and got out a loaf of bread. The first spoonful of cold beans gagged him. He didn't want beans and baker's bread. He wanted a drink of orange wine. He wanted some fresh fried roe and a tomato-and-onion omelette. With hot garlic bread, the way Nicolene Salvatore fixed it. And maybe a mess of frog legs to follow. Cade's mouth watered at the thought. He could worry about money in the morning. He wasn't going anywhere. He'd been.

He put on a clean shirt and sneakers and pants and walked up the grass-carpeted road. He could smell orange-blossoms and fish, oakum and fresh paint and the sweet-sour fragrance of the tide flats. Cade filled his lungs with air and held it. Jesus Christ, it was good to be home, he thought reverently.

He passed a group of giggling teen-aged girls. All of them looked after him, but none of them knew him. They'd been babies when he had left. Old man Dobraviche was standing in front of the poolroom. The retired river pilot insisted on shaking hands. "Welcome home, boy," he said warmly.

Cade smiled.

The news that he was back had spread. A dozen other men stopped him to say they were glad he was home. Miss Spence, the postmistress, kissed him.

Cade's glow continued to grow. It was nice to be liked, to be wanted. If Janice hadn't been such a greedy little bitch, she could have made his homecoming complete. Final divorce papers were a hell of a first-night bed partner when a man had been in a POW camp for two years. Still, Janice wouldn't have liked Bay Parish.

Salvatore's smelled familiar, of good food and orange wine and beer. Only the neon sign was new. The barroom was, as always, blue with smoke and crowded with fisher- and oyster-men and truck farmers and grove owners.

A chorus of shy "Hi Cade," and "Welcome home" greeted him. Cade, suddenly shy in turn, returned the greetings and sat in one of the booths against the wall. His throat felt strained. His lips ached from grinning. Being home was going to take some getting used to.

Sal was especially glad to see him. His teeth white against his swart face, the big Portuguese brought a quart of orange wine from the bar and set it and a glass in front of Cade. "It's nice to have you back. Tonight the eats and drinks are on the house. It's been some time."

"Twelve years."

"So Mamma and I were figuring. These last two, pretty bad, hey?"

"They weren't too good."

Salvatore was sympathetic. "Yeah. We figured that. And we were tickled, believe me, when we saw your name on the list of released prisoners. Now you're through with this flying business?"

"So the Air Force says."

Sal squeezed Cade's arm. "Good—good! Now let Mamma make you

some dinner. Say, fresh fried roe. A nice tomato-and-onion omelette. With garlic bread. And then a big plate of crisp fried saddles in batter."

Some of the strained feeling left Cade's throat. "You must be reading my mind."

Salvatore's booming laughter filled the bar. "I remember, hey? Once a good customer by Sal's, Sal always remembers."

He strode off to the kitchen to give the order to mamma. Cade sipped at the orange wine. It was as good as he'd remembered it. He drank the wine and refilled the glass. As he set the bottle back on the scarred table, something cut off most of the light in the booth and he looked up to see Joe Laval and the Squid standing in front of the table. Neither man had changed. They were just the same, only twelve years older. The gaunt Cajun sheriff still looked like a weasel. His deputy had been well named. The Squid was still mostly doughy white face and massive arms.

"Just come in from outside, huh?" Laval asked.

Cade sipped at the wine he'd poured. "That's right."

"By which pass?"

"South Pass."

"Come straight from where?"

"From Corpus."

"On compass all the way?"

The question irritated Cade. He considered telling Laval it was none of his business, but he didn't want any trouble on his first night home. It could be Laval had a good reason for asking. "I got a little off course," Cade admitted. "A spot of engine trouble."

"Near where?"

Cade took a cigarette from the package in his shirt pocket and palmed it into his mouth. He'd never liked Joe Laval. Twelve years of absence hadn't made him any fonder. He wondered if Joe was still bird-dogging for Tocko Kalavitch. It would be like Tocko to maroon six men rather than risk taking a fall. Cade ran a finger across his hairline mustache. "Why all the questions?"

"I've a reason," Laval said. "Where did you break down?"

Cade watched the other man's face as he answered, "Not far from the big south mud lump. In fact, I almost grounded on it in the dark."

Laval waited for him to continue. When he didn't, the thin-faced man exhaled slowly, almost as if he'd been holding his breath. "Oh," he said, "I see." He straightened the collar of his crumpled white linen suit. "Let's take a little walk, huh, Cade?"

"Why?" Cade asked, flatly.

"Tocko wants to welcome you home."

Cade thought of the suave Slavonian as he'd seen him last. If there was anyone in Bay Parish he liked less than Joe Laval, it was Tocko Kalavitch. There was nothing Tocko hadn't done, or wouldn't do, for money. His shrimp trawlers and his oyster fleet always showed a profit.

Cade shook his head. "The back of my hand to Tocko."

Laval smiled without mirth. "A big-shot colonel, huh? A hero. Or maybe not such a hero. While the other men you went over with were still dog-fighting all over Mig Alley, you were sitting it out on the ground, shot down over the Yalu."

Cade choked back a hot retort. He didn't want any trouble with Laval. He wished the other man would go away.

Laval stepped away from the table. "Okay. Bring him outside, Squid. And hurry up about it."

Cade tried to avoid the Squid's hand. It lifted him out of the booth like a drag-line and hurled him across the barroom and into the juke box so hard that the instrument stopped playing.

Salvatore came out of the kitchen. "Here. What the hell?" he asked.

"You keep out of this, Sal," Laval said.

The silence that followed reminded Cade of the silence over big south mud lump. None of the dark-complexioned men at the bar or in the booths, most of them of Montenegrin and Serbian and Dalmatian and Slavonian ancestry, attempted to interfere. In Bay Parish, a man fought his own battles and scrupulously minded his own business.

Moving fast for so large a man, the Squid followed up his advantage, smashing hard rights and lefts against Cade's face and body. "You come outside?"

Cade tried to fight back but pounding on the Squid was like beating on a brick wall. His breath rasped in his throat. Blood filled his mouth and choked him. Cade spat it out and backed away, feeling for a weapon. "You bastards," he panted. "If I had a gun I'd kill you both."

Laval continued to smile without mirth. "Why all the fuss? All we want is to talk to you."

Cade's groping hand encountered a chair. He smashed the chair on the floor, snatched up one of the legs and brought it down on the

Squid's head.

The Squid's scream was thin and haunting—like a woman screaming in ecstasy. One of his big hands moved forward, almost gently. Then all the lights in Sal's went out and Cade felt himself falling through space.

2
DARK MERMAID

From where he lay, his battered face pressed to the soft mud of the levee, Cade could hear familiar night noises; the thud of colliding driftwood logs, the troubled squeak of floating hyacinth bulbs rubbing together, the sigh of unseen grasses being fondled by the wind. Farther out, where the current surged toward the forking of the passes, the ceaseless din of the river.

Cade raised himself on one elbow. He'd wanted to come home. He had. He felt his face with muddy fingers. His nose was swollen. A flap of flesh hung down under one eye. His other eye was swollen almost shut. The Squid had done a good job on him.

He lay thinking back to the beating in Sal's. He remembered hitting the Squid with a chair leg. He remembered hearing the Squid scream. Then all the lights had gone out and when he'd come to again, he'd been standing in the ankle-deep mud of the levee with the Squid supporting him and Laval's thin face only inches from his. He could still hear Laval's tense voice.

"Cast off, Cade," Laval had warned him. "Get out of the Delta. Go on up the river to New Orleans or back to Corpus. But be gone by tomorrow noon. If you aren't, Tocko says to let Squid go all the way."

The thought made Cade sick. He lost the wine he'd drunk, then returned his torn cheek to the mud.

There ought to be a law. There was.

But why? What had he done to Joe Laval? What had he done to Tocko? Why should they be afraid of him?

The freshening wind was off the Gulf. There was the usual bustle on deck as a ship dropped anchor at Quarantine. Cade listened to the creaking of winches, the shouted orders which were carried to him by the wind. Farther out in the river, holding for South Pass, the running lights of a steamer were visible, a steamer bound outside for Martinique, Honduras, Rio, Buenos Aires. It could be bound anywhere.

Cade fought down a desire to be on her. He *liked* being where he was. Bay Parish had been home to eight generations of Cains, ever since a curious Kentucky flatboatman had wondered where the Mississippi went after it coiled past New Orleans. He had fallen in love with and bedded an olive-skinned Baratarian wench reputed to be kin to Jean LaFitte.

Cade, with an effort, turned on his back and fumbled his cigarettes from a shirt pocket. One thing was certain. Nobody was going to run him off the river—not after all the trouble he'd gone to getting home.

He put a cigarette into his mouth and lighted it. The beating didn't make sense. He hadn't done anything to Tocko or Laval. He hadn't even seen either man for twelve years. So six aliens had been marooned on south mud lump. It wasn't the first time. It wouldn't be the last.

Cade sat up in the mud. Most of his nausea was gone. The pain had lessened. He got to his feet and lurched down the levee toward the old frame house where he had been born. Weeds had taken the fence. The gate was hanging by one hinge. He tried the front door and found it locked. In the mood he was in, the old house depressed him. He'd open it up and air it out in the morning. He might even sell it. A single man had no need for a house.

He climbed the levee again. With the exception of the smear of yellow light spilling out of Sal's, the business section of the town was dark. The juke box had been repaired. It was playing *Jambalaya*. Cade stood sucking his sodden cigarette, debating going back and asking Salvatore if he knew what was eating Joe Laval and Tocko. But even if the Portuguese knew, Cade doubted that he would tell. Minding one's own business was a fetish in Bay Parish.

He'd see Tocko himself in the morning, Cade decided. He'd go directly to the brass. His fingers were bruised from beating on the Squid. His cigarette slipped from them into the mud. He ground it out with one heel and started out on the pier and stopped, every tensed muscle in his body aching as a darker blob of black moved out of the night to bar his way.

It wasn't easy for the Squid to talk. His voice sounded thin and unsuited to his bulk.

"You goin' to' leave like Joe tol' you?" he asked.

Cade tried to see the big deputy's face. "What's it all about, Squid? Why has Tocko got his knife in me?"

The Squid's smile was sly. "I ast you first. You goin' t' stay or shove off?"

Cade considered his answer. He was in no condition to take another beating. "I've until tomorrow to decide that."

The Squid's head, like his voice, was too small for his body. He bobbled it as he agreed. "Joe said until tomorrow noon." He sucked in his breath as he raised a big hand and ran it lightly over Cade's body. When he spoke, his thin voice was plaintive. "Don't go. Please."

Cade backed a step, embarrassed. The touch of the Squid's hand made his flesh creep. The Squid liked to know and give pain. Due to some flaw in his biochemistry, to the Squid pain was a woman. Cade sidestepped the big man and walked out on the rotting pier.

Light from the pressure lantern he'd forgotten to turn off flooded the cockpit. Cade jumped down into the boat, then turned and looked back down the pier. The Squid had blended with the night and the silence. In the thin moonlight mingling with the first of the fog rolling in off the river, the frame houses behind the levee and the unlighted business section of Bay Parish looked distorted and unreal, imbued with all the qualities of a nightmare.

Old man Dobraviche had shaken his hand. A dozen men had welcomed him home. Miss Spence, the postmistress, had kissed him. Sal had said the drinks and eats were on the house. The attack on him didn't make sense.

Inside the cabin aft, Cade studied his face in the mirror he used for shaving. It was bad but it would heal. He'd been hurt worse. He cleaned the wounds as best he could and painted them with merthiolate. Then reshaping his nose with his fingers, he bound it and the torn flap of flesh under his eyes with waterproof adhesive tape.

The mud had soaked through his clean shirt and pants. He stripped them and his sneakers off and lowered himself overside by the rope hanging over the transom.

The cold water felt good on his bruised body but the hyacinth bulbs clogging the slip were so many slimy little snakes with hands. Still clinging to the rope, Cade washed the mud from his body and pulled himself back into the cockpit and dried with a coarse towel.

There was a bottle half full of rum in the galley. He drank from it and put it back. Dumping the contents of one of his duffle bags on a bunk, he picked a .38-calibered Colt automatic from the mound of crumpled clothes and personal possessions and laid it aside before putting on clean dungarees and a skivy.

The uniform he had bought in Tokyo was in the bag. The silver maple leaves on the shoulders of the tunic looked strange and out of place in the cabin of a fishing cruiser. Cade made a mental note to get a mothproof bag in which to hang the uniform. It could be he had made a wrong guess on how to spend the rest of his life. It could be that in a few months he would be banging on doors back at Nellis, trying to get some flight surgeon to recertify him for duty. What the hell. He was only thirty-two. Once his nerves stopped jumping and he'd put on a few pounds, he could still fly a lot of jet. Maybe it had been a mistake—this business of coming home. Maybe he'd been airborne so long, he was out of place in any other element.

Cade turned down the pressure lantern and stuffed the pistol in the waistband of his dungarees. If Joe Laval and Tocko were as anxious to get him off the river as they seemed to be, perhaps the noon deadline was just a feint. A few slashes with a sharp knife and he wouldn't have any cruiser. He might as well be back in a POW camp, dreaming about the boat he was going to buy if he ever got out of where he was.

A wry smile twisted his lips. Sure. He had it made. From here on in, all he had to do was live.

He made certain the lines to the creosoted pilings were fast, and walked back down the pier and sat with his back against an upturned flat-bottomed skiff that had been pulled up on the levee.

The wind died but the night remained cool. Cade wished he'd brought the bottle of rum with him. He wished he'd brought the loaf of bread and the can of beans. He wished he knew where Janice had gone after she'd divorced him. The least she could have done was to have waited to say goodbye.

"Good luck, soldier. It was nice knowing you."

He wanted a drink. He wanted a smoke. He wanted a woman. He wanted to know why Laval was throwing off on him. The lean-faced Cajun had said:

"A big-shot colonel, huh? A hero. Or maybe not such a hero. While the other men you went over with were still dog-fighting all over Mig Alley, you were sitting it out on the ground, shot down over the Yalu."

The shaven hairs on the back of Cade's neck tingled. That louse

Laval.

On the far side of the river, in one of the oyster camps rising on poles out of the mounds of shells that had accumulated through the years, a hound pointed his muzzle at the waning moon and howled. His eyes troubled, Cade got to his feet and stretched, then swiveled his head stiffly as a faint splash in the slip attracted his attention.

A swimmer, attempting to be quiet, was pushing through the bulbs, stopping now and then to tread water, gasping for air, before moving on. Cade drew the pistol from his waistband and stood watching the phosphorescent ripple.

Now the swimmer was gone from sight. Cade could hear panting on the far side of the levee, a hoarse, almost animal gasping clearly audible in the still air.

A small head and a pair of slim shoulders showed over the levee, silhouetted vaguely against the dying moon. Cade started to call out and changed his mind. He wanted to know, he had to know, what the swimmer intended to do.

The small figure on the levee stood a moment listening to the music escaping with the yellow light from Sal's door, then looked at the dimly lighted cruiser surging at her ropes.

Now the figure was moving again, slowly, out on the pier, stooping low as if to keep from being seen by anyone aboard the boat. Now he was looking in through the ports, trying to ascertain if there was anyone in either the fore or aft cabin. Satisfied that no one was aboard, the newcomer jumped down into the cockpit and entered the after cabin. The door closed behind him.

Cade was grimly amused. The pistol ready in his hand, he walked out on the pier, glancing over his shoulder from time to time to make certain he wasn't being trapped between two fires.

At the transom of the cruiser he paused, then eased himself into the cockpit. Even for Joe Laval's limited imagination, the trap was crude. Whoever Laval and Tocko had sent to gun or knife him, instead of being quiet and waiting, was making himself at home, opening lockers, moving swiftly from one side of the cabin to the other.

Cade eased forward the last few feet and yanked the door of the cabin open. "All right," he said, quietly. "Let's have it. What the goddamn—"

His voice stuck like a pair of jammed landing wheels. The swimmer wasn't a man. It was a girl. Standing in the center of the cabin, her wet hair plastered to her well-shaped head and only two wisps of wet lace to keep her from being as naked as the day she'd been born. A big-eyed black-haired girl in her late teens or early twenties who was toweling vigorously with one hand while she spooned beans into her mouth with the other.

As he spoke she held the towel in front of her and began to cry without sound.

3
THE FUGITIVE

Cade leaned against the jamb of the door, studying the girl. She was exotic rather than pretty. Her cheekbones were high and pronounced, with the cheeks under them slightly hollowed. Her bare shoulders and legs were the color and texture of rich cream. Her eyes and her hair were black with red highlights glinting in her hair. She looked like classic Castilian, with perhaps a dash of the Celtic blood with which so many South American races were spiced.

"And who are you?" Cade asked.

The girl tried to speak and couldn't. She was too frightened.

Cade tried again. "Where did you come from?"

As the girl pointed toward the river, the towel slipped. She blushed and quickly retrieved it.

"Yes, I know that," Cade said. "I saw you. You live here in Bay Parish?"

She shook her wet head. "No."

The word had a faintly foreign sound to it.

"You're off a boat then?"

The girl bobbed her head.

"A ship? A steamer? The one that just dropped anchor an hour or so ago?"

"Yes," the girl said distinctly.

Cade realized that standing in the open doorway of the lighted cabin as he was, he was a perfect target for anyone on the levee. He stepped inside and closed the door behind him.

The girl clutched the towel closer to her. The well-cared for fingers of one hand caught at her throat in apprehension. Cade leaned against the door. "Why swim off? And having swum off, why pick my boat?"

The girl's hand left her throat, as she gestured in the general direction of the music still coming from Sal's place.

"You thought I would be in the cantina?"

"Yes."

Cade realized her teeth were chattering and that the portions of creamy flesh he could see were covered with cold pimples. He looked for something warm and all he could see was his uniform tunic. He picked it from the bunk and handed it to the girl. "Put this on."

She touched one of the silver maple leaves and some of her fright seemed to leave her. "Officer? You are officer?" she asked earnestly. Her intonation was definitely foreign.

"Ex," Cade said curtly.

The girl turned her back and the towel dropped to her bare feet, as she struggled into the coat. When she turned again, it was all Cade could do to keep from sweeping her into his arms. He'd never seen anything cuter. She'd done something to her wet hair. His top pockets had never been better filled. The skirt of the coat came halfway down the girl's thighs. She looked like an animated pin-up picture by Varga.

She tried to smile. *"Gracias!"*

"Colombian?" Cade asked her.

"Venezuelan," she corrected.

To keep from making a fool of himself and possibly getting his face slapped, Cade took the bottle of rum from the locker and handed it to the girl. "Here. Take a drink of this. Then maybe you can stop shivering long enough to make sense."

The girl drank without pleasure and returned the bottle. *"Gracias."*

Cade sat on the littered bunk, holding the bottle in his hand. "All right. Let's have it. You swam ashore and picked my boat to warm up in and grab some food and maybe a few clothes, because you thought I was in the cantina. Now you go on from there. Why didn't you come ashore in one of the ship's boats or in the pilot tender?"

The girl spoke distinctly, choosing her words with care. "Because they do not know I am on the ship. Because I am—" she stopped, puzzled. "How you say when you not pay the passage?"

"A stowaway?"

"Sí."

"You stowed away, where? In what port?"

"The port of La Guaira. I am from Caracas."

Cade was incredulous. "And none of the crew spotted you between there and here?"

The girl shook her head. "No." She had the charm of making everything she said sound dramatic. "For six days I am in a lifeboat, over-covered with canvas. I bribe a steward for food." She looked at the open can of beans. "Is not nice to be 'ungry. I am 'ungry now."

"I'll string along with that," Cade said. He took himself a drink of rum. "Okay. We're up to Caracas. Why did you stow away?"

The girl moved his clean clothes aside and sat on the bunk opposite him. "Because I do not have the money or the passport and I want to come to the States. I *have* to come to the United States. And when I get here, I know they will not let me in. So when the boat stopped out in the river, I slide down a rope in the dark and swim to the shore." She added earnestly, "It was a long way an' I was ver' afraid."

Cade brought himself another drink. He wished the girl would button the top button of his tunic or stop leaning forward when she talked. Wet and muddy and frightened as she was, she was one of the most attractive girls he had ever seen. That included Janice. Just looking at her excited him. He put the cork back in the rum bottle. "What's your name?"

"Mimi," she said, gravely, "Mimi Trujillo Esterpar Moran."

It was snug in the cabin with the door closed. The rum lay warm in Cade's empty stomach. He was pleased by his own sagacity. "That Moran sounds like it might be Irish."

Mimi smiled. "It is."

Cade got up and opened the cabin door. The fog was heavy now and blotted out the levee. The juke box in Sal's was still playing *Jambalaya.* As far as he could tell, there was no one watching on the pier. It could be he'd gotten his wind up over nothing. Warning him off the river and making sure he left were two entirely different things. Not even Joe Laval or Tocko could explain cut mooring lines or a dead man. Especially when the dead man was a local boy and former Army officer.

Behind him, Mimi's voice sounded worried. "Someone saw me swim ashore? Someone is looking for me?"

"No," Cade said.

He closed the door and leaned against it, staring at the girl on his bunk. She didn't look like any waterfront tramp he'd ever met. She looked like a nice kid from a good family. More, she had guts to do what she'd done. So he hadn't been with a woman in two years. He was damned if he'd force himself on her just because she had fallen into his lap. If anything should eventuate it would have to start with her, after he'd heard the rest of her story.

"I am so 'ungry," Mimi said.

Cade pumped up the pressure stove in the galley and lighted all three burners. He examined the meager ship's stores he'd purchased before putting out of Corpus Christi and decided on cream of mushroom soup, canned corned-beef hash and coffee. He put the cans on the small work table and found Mimi fingering the silver leaf on her shoulder.

"Colonel," she smiled at him.

"Ex," Cade reminded her.

She touched his wings. "And flyer."

Cade picked a clean shirt and a pair of new white duck pants from the litter of clothes on the bunk and laid them on her lap. "Put these on," he said gruffly. He opened the door of the forecabin and lighted a small lantern. "In here."

Mimi stood up dutifully.

Cade looked at a smear of levee mud on one small cheek. "You'd better wash that mud off. I'll get you a bucket of water while you peel."

Mimi was worried, "Peel?"

"While you take off your clothes," Cade explained. He picked up a bucket attached to a length of quarter-inch nylon line.

Mimi was relieved. "Oh," she smiled, "for wash."

Out in the open cockpit, Cade lowered the bucket overside. The dog on the far bank of the river was still howling. As he hauled up the filled bucket, there was a clanging of ship's bells in the channel and the steamer he'd seen drop anchor earlier, the ship Mimi must have come from, began to move up river through the fog.

The door of the forecabin was closed. He rapped on it and Mimi opened the door a crack and reached out with a bare arm and shoulder for the bucket, smiling, "*Gracias*. Thank you ver' much."

Cade was relieved when she'd closed the door. He made coffee, then added water to the canned soup and put it and the hash to warm. The rum in the bottle was gone. He sucked the last few drops and pushed the empty bottle out the open port over the sink.

The things that could happen to a man.

He set the small table, debated a moment and broke out a bottle of port and two glasses. A small glass of wine never hurt anyone—

unless the Squid worked him over afterwards. Even under the thin layer of rum, Cade could taste the orange wine he'd drunk in Sal's.

Damn the Squid. Cade felt the butt of the gun in his waistband. The Squid wanted to have a good time. The Squid didn't want him to leave. He'd do what he could to please the Squid. The next time they tangled, he'd be prepared. He'd kiss him all over his pointed head with the barrel of the .38.

The watched soup finally came to a boil. Cade turned off the burner and rapped on the forecabin door. "Okay. Come and get it."

Mimi opened the door, still smiling. She looked even more fetching than before. She'd braided her wet hair and coiled it around her head. The top two buttons of her borrowed shirt were open and she had discarded the wisp of wet lace. The white pants were tight to the point of bursting around her rounded hips. "Okay, I know," she said, "but what is this, come and get it?"

Cade forced himself to look away from her. "Just what it sounds like. Sit down. Soup's on the table."

He looked back, as she touched the adhesive tape on his cheek and nose with feather light fingertips. "Someone has hurt you. You have been in the fight."

Cade wished she hadn't touched him. "Yeah. Something like that." He sat across from her. "Okay. You said you were hungry. Eat."

The table was narrow. The benches were close together, so that their knees brushed as they ate. The cabin was small and intimate. What might happen tomorrow was a hundred years away. Cade poured two glasses of wine. It was nice sitting across the table from a pretty girl again.

He raised his glass to the girl across the table. "To strangers that met in the night."

She touched his glass with hers. *"Saludos!"*

He drank his wine. She sipped at hers and spooned her soup away from her, eating rapidly but daintily. She wasn't a tramp. Hungry as she was, her table manners were perfection.

Finished with her soup, she smiled. "You are being ver' kind and ver' gallant."

Cade tried to eat and couldn't. It wasn't food he wanted. He wanted love and companionship and someone warm and soft in his arms. He'd lived with men so long, bitter and angry men, in an alien land. "What could I do?" he asked. "Throw you off the boat? Put you back on the levee in nothing but a pair of sheer scanties and a bra?"

Mimi met his eyes. "You know what I mean."

A long moment of silence followed, relieved only by the creak of the mooring ropes and the faint swish of the water in the bilge. A new feeling, a feeling of strain, filled the cabin. Cade refilled the girl's glass. She liked him. He was affecting her just as she was affecting him. Under her calm exterior, she was as excited by the night and their mutual closeness as he was. He could tell by the beat of the pulse in her throat, the way she looked at him from time to time.

"All right. Let's go on with the story," he said. "You had no money and no passport."

"No."

"But you wanted to come to the States. You *had* to come to the States?"

"*Sí.*"

"Why?"

Mimi ran the tip of a pink tongue across her full lips.

"Why?" Cade repeated. "Let's have it. Being as pretty as you are, you could have been, well, let's say you could have had a bad six days between here and La Guaira, if one or more of the crew had happened to discover you and failed to report you to the captain. Or you might have been drowned swimming ashore. Or I might have been a heel. I still might be, for all you know."

Although the hips of the white pants fit snugly, the legs were loose. Mimi thrust out her right leg and pulled up the leg of the borrowed pants to disclose a small but efficient looking knife strapped high on the inside of her cream-colored thigh.

"So you have a knife," Cade said. "Why have you taken the chances you have?"

"To find Captain Moran."

The name meant nothing to Cade. "What's this Moran to you?"

Mimi's Latin accent was more pronounced this time. "My 'usband. We were married in Caracas almost a year ago." Her voice barely audible, she continued, "When my family find out, they were ver', how you say, *irritado*!" She found the word she wanted. "Angry. We are ver' ol' family. They did not like I should marry foreigner." Her lower lip thrust out in a sullen pout. "I am not so pleased myself."

"Why?"

"He was supposed to send for me, but he did not. That is why I stow away, to come to him."

Realizing the leg of her pants was still pulled high on her thigh,

Mimi blushed and rolled down the leg.

Cade returned his eyes to her face. Of course. She had told him her name—Mimi Trujillo Esterpar Moran, and he had kidded her about the Moran sounding Irish. For some reason the thought of any other man having had Mimi made him furious. He asked, "How long were you together?"

Mimi said, "One week. Just the week he was in Caracas."

"He hasn't been back since? That is, to Caracas?"

Mimi continued to pout. "No."

"He was Army?"

Mimi's smile was small. "A flyer. Just like you. He was on what you call mission." She accented the *on* in mission.

It was an effort for Cade to talk. "Where in the States is he stationed?"

The black-haired girl shook her head. "That I do not know. I 'ave not heard from him since he left Caracas. But I 'ave written many letters, here. To the address he gave me—Captain James Moran, Bay Parish, Louisiana, in care of one Tocko Kalavitch. That is why I stowed away in the boat that I did." She seemed to be trying to convince herself. "And in the morning I will find him."

"Yeah. Sure. Maybe." Cade said.

If there were a Moran in Bay Parish, the man was new since his time. He didn't know any Morans on the river. There were Morgans and Monroes and Moores and Mooneys. There was even a Serbian family that had changed its name to Morton, but he didn't know any Morans. Cade felt deflated, let down. He poured more wine in his glass, wishing it were rum, wishing he had a case of rum. It would seem that the wrong people always got together.

The things that could happen to a man.

First, Janice.

Then the Squid.

Now this.

"More wine?" he asked Mimi.

"No, thank you," she said, primly.

He looked at her. And now the thought he had been keeping buried within him struggled to the surface. After all, why shouldn't he just dump her in the river? Probably her whole outlandish story was a lie. Probably she was just a plant, an emissary of Tocko and Company, intending some trick to do him damage once her disarming presence had lowered his guard. Cade lighted a cigarette.

Well, he'd play along with her a while. He didn't want to believe the worst of her. But he'd keep his guard high.

It was, all things considered, Cade decided, one hell of a homecoming.

4
THE GLASS WALL

Morning dawned warm and familiar. Cade lay long moments after he'd been awakened, listening to the din of the river on one side and to the twittering of the birds on the other—thrushes, mocking birds and crested cardinals in the leafy trees rising out of the rich Delta mud back of the levee.

There had been no birds in Pyongyang. There'd been a complete lack of a lot of things in Pyongyang. As Cade lighted his first cigarette of the day, he looked at the closed door of the forecabin.

Mimi was cute. She was sweet. He liked her. But he wished the hell she had stayed in Caracas. He had enough problems of his own without having to worry about someone's abandoned bride. From where he lay, it looked like a hit-and-run to him.

Some smart punk forced down on a training mission had seen a way to spend a delightful week-end. It could be that, but Cade was fair. He could be doing Moran an injustice. If the guy were a jet pilot, and he probably was, he could be anywhere by now, all wrapped up in "Security." According to what he'd heard on the coast, the big brass was shipping the boys out of Nellis about as soon as they were able to read a cockpit panel and do a power dive on a ground target without losing their heads and pulling out so fast they caught a bad case of stick reversal and skip-hopped a Sabrejet over two miles of sand and sage to wind up "an unavoidable training fatality."

It didn't seem right that any man in his right mind, not under orders, would willingly walk out on a girl like Mimi.

Cade wished he'd bought a larger boat, a boat with two heads. No matter how big a boat a man bought, he always needed a bigger one. The head was in the prow. To reach it he would have to pass through the forecabin.

Cade swung his bare feet to the floor and cracked the forecabin door. Exhausted by her experience and the long swim, Mimi was still sleeping soundly. Her borrowed pants and shirt lay folded neatly on the starboard bunk. The sheet with which she'd covered herself had been too warm and she'd pushed it down until only her feet were covered. The small knife strapped to the creamy flesh of her thigh looked out of place, like some obscene foreign growth that had attached itself to her natural beauty.

"No man in his right mind," Cade said to himself.

He closed the door as noiselessly as he had opened it and, padding out into the open cockpit, he used the fog-dappled Mississippi for his purpose. The fog was lifting rapidly. Early as it was, smoke was emerging from the chimneys of the houses. A half-dozen white and colored fishermen were sitting on the banks of the canals and on the levee angling for their breakfasts.

Cade tried to remember how long it had been since he had eaten hard-fried bream and hot corn bread for breakfast. He looked at the useless, heavy, deep-sea rods and reels racked in their cases beside the wheel. He should have brought a cane pole, a few feet of cheap fish line and a handful of .00 hooks.

He got his sneakers and pants from the cabin aft, took the automatic pistol from under his pillow and thrust it into the right hip pocket of his dungarees. If Joe Laval and Tocko thought they were going to run him off the river, they were out of their minds. This was home. He liked it here.

As he walked down the pier, a sleek thirty-two-foot guide boat put out from a basin, new since he'd been away, not far from the pilot boat landing. Cade could see five or six more boats in the basin, all apparently guide boats, all equipped with ship-to-shore telephone antennae. He wondered if Tocko had added a fleet of charter boats to his various interests. If so, it could explain Laval's actions. He and Tocko would resent a new boat on the river, would begrudge someone else the right to make a dime. Still, that didn't seem reasonable. If Tocko Kalavitch had fifty guide boats, they'd be only a drop in the bucket compared to the earnings of his shrimp trawlers and oyster fleet.

Anyway Cade looked at it, his welcome-home beating didn't make sense. He reviewed what had happened for the twentieth time. Laval had said that Tocko wanted to see him. He'd said he didn't want to see Tocko, and Laval had turned the Squid loose. Cade looked at his watch. Five minutes of seven. Tocko should be in his office by nine. Cade meant to be there shortly after the other man arrived.

He walked down the path to the old Cain house. It wasn't as weathered-looking by daylight as it had been at dusk-dark. There were good lines to the old house. It had been built with slave labor when lumber had been cheap. There were more square feet in the open gallery under the screened second-floor balcony than there were in the average modern three-bedroom house. Someone had cut the grass and pruned the grove that his great grandfather's father had set out. For being as old as they were, the trees were in fair condition. Cade lifted the sagging gate aside and stopped as he saw the freshly painted sign nailed to one of the fluted columns. It read—

FOR SALE
Tocko Kalavitch Enterprises

Cade leaned against the fence doing a slow burn. He hadn't commissioned Kalavitch to sell the house. He hadn't commissioned anyone to sell it. The original house had been in the Cain family over one hundred years. The coach house, reputed to be built of the heart oak of the flat boat belonging to the original Cain, must be even older.

The stinker, Cade thought, when I was reported missing, Tocko figured I'd never come back.

He smoked two cigarettes, just sitting on the fence, looking at the old house, remembering the good times he'd had in it as a boy. All it needed was a clapboard replaced here and there and a couple of coats of paint and unless the river washed it away, as it nearly had on several occasions, countless more generations of Cains could live in it. The thought saddened Cade. *If* there would be more Cains. He was the last of his line. It could be he couldn't have children. At least he and Janice hadn't had any, although God knew, during the first year of their marriage, they had tried.

Cade felt baffled, frustrated. He'd never felt quite the same before. It was almost like trying to climb a glass wall. Thinking of Janice made him think of Mimi—and Mimi belonged to another man. She was Señora Trujillo Estebar James Moran. Cade hoped for a moment Moran had had a flame-out, then quickly retracted the wish. God forbid. It was bad enough just flying one of the sucker-mouthed gadget-cluttered bastards. Mimi was nothing to him. Her attraction was purely physical. He'd help her locate Moran if he could. Then he'd shake her hand and tell her goodbye. Cade felt the bulge in his hip pocket. But first he'd talk to Tocko. It should be an interesting conversation.

He climbed the levee and walked back out on the pier. Mimi was awake and up. He could see her in the cabin aft doing something in front of the stove. He jumped down into the cockpit. "Hi."

He was trying with all his might not to be suspicious of her. He didn't want to be suspicious.

Mimi cast him a hasty glance. "Good morning."

As she glanced away from the stove, the coffee she was making boiled over and the piece of forked bread she was holding over the big burner caught on fire. Mimi swore softly in Spanish, snatched the coffee-pot from the stove and extinguished the burning bread. Both were hot and she promptly put her fingers in her mouth.

Cade watched her, amused. Anyway a man looked at her, she was cute. She'd rolled up the legs of his pants to pedal-pusher length. Every time she stooped or turned he caught a tantalizing glimpse of rounded cream-colored flesh that made Marilyn Monroe's chief attractions look like she'd bought them second-hand at a war surplus sale.

"Don't you laugh," Mimi said hotly. She laid the piece of burned bread on a plate. "Because you were so ver' kind, I thought I would get the breakfast." She returned her attention to something she was stirring in a pan.

"Fine," Cade said.

He sat back of the small table, watching her, wishing she were Janice. The toast was charred. She'd used at least a half-pound of coffee to the pot. With some rare alchemic ability, she'd managed to mix and cook the powdered scrambled eggs to the same gooey consistency and shade of bilious green that countless army mess sergeants had spent years in achieving.

The black-haired girl brushed a wisp of damp curl from her perspiring forehead. "Well, as you say, come an' get it." She studied the meal she'd concocted. "I am afraid I am not so good the cook, no?"

"It's fine, just fine," Cade said. To spare her feelings he ate a forkful of the eggs and washed it down with a sip of bitter coffee. Surprisingly, when Mimi smiled, the eggs and the coffee tasted good.

Mimi explained, "Is just I am not ever do it before. In Venezuela it is different. In Venezuela no lady cooks."

Cade bit into a piece of charred toast. "Your family has money, hey?"

Mimi shrugged her shoulders. "In Venezuela ever'one has servants."

Except the Indians and mestizos, Cade thought. He asked, "What are you going to do if you can't locate Moran? Write your family for dough and go home?" He translated. "Dough, money, bolivars."

A worried look replaced Mimi's puzzled frown. "They would not send it if I did. They refused to give me money to come here." She shook her head emphatically. "No. Now I can nevair go home. My father, he is ver' proud. I am, how your say, make my bed."

And a very pretty bed, Cade thought. Aloud he said, "Then I hope you locate Moran. You're too pretty to be turned loose on your own."

Mimi was pleased. She put the fingers of one hand to the back of her head and thrust out her chest in an entirely feminine gesture. "You think I am pretty?"

Cade resisted an impulse to suck in his breath. "You get by."

When they'd finished breakfast, he dried and put away while she washed the few dishes they'd used. It was a homey, domestic moment. Cade enjoyed it. He enjoyed it very much but it deepened his resentment toward Janice. Everything could have been so wonderful.

The moment the galley had been made shipshape, Mimi wanted to go ashore. Cade explained, "But Tocko Kalavitch, the man in whose care you addressed your letters to your husband, doesn't arrive at his office until nine." He added, "Besides, try as hard as I can, I can't remember any Morans on this immediate stretch of the river."

Mimi eyed him suspiciously, "You are 'aving the fun."

"No, I mean it."

"You know this town?"

"Every inch of it. And every reef and marsh and inlet and island for a radius of fifty miles. It so happens that I was born here and lived here until I was eighteen."

"I don't believe you," Mimi said. "I mean that you don't know any Morans. You just don't want me to find Jeem."

Her lower lip thrust out in a pout, she sat in one of the fishing chairs, her small hands in her lap, looking up at Cain from time to time through quarter-inch-long black lashes.

"He *has* to be here."

"Okay. Maybe he's mayor," Cade said. "After all, I've been away twelve years."

At five minutes of nine, he examined the clip in his gun, returned the clip to the gun and fired a shot into the river to make certain the gun was working.

"Why you do that?" Mimi asked. "Why you carry a gun?"

"Just an old American custom. Especially down here in the Delta."

He walked with her up the road to town, wishing she was wearing a dress. She wobbled delightfully when she walked and the tight white pants emphasized the wobble.

"What did you do with your dress?"

Mimi told him, "I took it off, in the river. It was tight and not good for swim."

A dozen men and women he hadn't seen the night before stopped him to welcome him home. Whatever Laval and Tocko had to beef about, it was peculiar to them. Everyone else he'd met seemed genuinely pleased to see him.

Morning was hot and humid. He could smell the rich Delta mud and the green growing things sprouting in it. There was no other place in the world like it. He'd come home. He meant to stay.

As they walked up Main Street, Mimi laid a small hand on his arm.

"You have been away a long time?"

"Twelve years, I told you."

"Without once coming home?"

"That's right. You see, I stayed in the Army after the last big one, based at MacDill and Nellis and Langley jet fields. For the last two years, I've been sitting it out in a prisoner-of-war camp on the north side of the Yalu."

Mimi's fingers bit into his arm. "I'm sorry, so sorry."

It was nothing. Other folks had said they were sorry but the feel of her small fingers on his arm, the tone of the girl's voice, gave Cade a lift. If her man had been where he'd been, she would have been waiting for him, with the shades drawn and the cat put out, in her prettiest negligee, with a smile hovering between the tears on her cheeks. That was the kind of a girl she was.

Cade lighted a cigarette as he studied the outside of Tocko's new office. The one-story building was masonry and moderne, with a big picture window. The legend—*Tocko Kalavitch Enterprises*—was printed on it in gold leaf. He wasn't surprised to find the building air-conditioned. The receptionist was young and smartly dressed. The outer office was expensively furnished.

Bay Parish hadn't changed, but Tocko had. The swaggering river gunman and narcotic-and-alien runner of twelve years ago was gone. Tocko was big time now, a Delta man of distinction. His black hair had silvered at the temples. He was wearing a silk shantung suit that had cost him two hundred dollars. A heavy diamond glittered on one of his fingers. As his smartly dressed young secretary ushered Cade and Mimi into his office, he stood up behind a glass-topped desk and extended a soft white hand.

"Welcome, Cade," he smiled. "I heard you came back last night on a new cruiser—that long. And I wanted to come down and tell you how happy I was to have you home but, unfortunately, I had to fly up to New Orleans on a little business."

Cade ignored the proffered hand. Kalavitch returned it to his side, unembarrassed, still smiling, at Mimi now. "And who is the charming young person? The new Mrs. Cain?"

Cade shook his head. "No. This is Mrs. James Moran. She is attempting to locate her husband, Captain James Moran, and it seems he gave his address as Bay Parish, in care of you."

"Oh, yes. Of course," Kalavitch nodded. "Jim Moran." He continued to smile at Mimi, his soft brown eyes picking at the third button on her borrowed white shirt. "He worked for me, for some months."

Her voice small, Mimi asked, "He is here now?"

Kalavitch shook his head. "To tell you the truth, I don't know where Jim is. You see, after he got out of the Army he worked for me as my personal pilot." Kalavitch laughed. "But I guess Bay Parish was too small and dull for him, so he moved on." Kalavitch was concerned. "He didn't give you his new address?"

Mimi shook her head. "No."

Kalavitch tried to be helpful. "Maybe Miss Spence, our postmistress, can give it to you. My secretary has been turning all the letters that come for Moran over to Miss Spence."

Mimi smiled. "And the post office is where?"

Cade wanted her out of the office before he had his talk with Tocko. "Back down the same street we walked up. In the middle of the block, between a poolroom and a hardware store. I'll meet you over there."

"As you say," Mimi smiled. She transferred her smile to the man behind the desk. "An' thank you ver' much, *señor.*"

Kalavitch watched her out of the office "Nice." He looked back at Cade. "And now she's gone, what's eating on you?" He looked at his hand. "Is my hand dirty or what?"

Cade reached over the desk, caught Kalavitch by the coat lapels and smashed a hard right to the big man's mouth. "That's for last night. What's the big idea of Joe Laval turning the Squid loose on me?"

Kalavitch used his breast-pocket handkerchief to stopper the smear of blood trickling from one corner of his lip. "You're crazy. I don't know what you're talking about."

"You didn't send Laval and the Squid over to Sal's to ask me to come and see you?"

"No."

"You didn't have Laval warn me to be out of Bay Parish by noon or the Squid would really work me over?"

Kalavitch refolded his handkerchief. "No."

"I don't believe you," Cade said. "Another thing, how come you've got a 'for sale' sign on my house?"

"Your house?" Kalavitch smirked.

"You heard what I said."

Kalavitch shook his head. "But it isn't your house. It's mine. I thought, naturally, she had written you."

"Who had written me what?"

"Your wife, that is your ex-wife, the very blonde and very beautiful former Mrs. Cain."

Cade felt a hard lump form in the pit of his stomach. "Janice was here?"

Kalavitch rested the tips of his manicured fingers on top of his desk. "But of course. How else could I have bought the property? I trust it was perfectly legal? She had your power of attorney and claimed that you had given her the house and the acreage on Barataria Bay in lieu of a cash settlement in your impending divorce."

"I was in a POW camp when she divorced me."

"But she did have your power of attorney?"

"Yes. Yes, she did."

"Then it would seem that the sale was legal."

"You bought the acreage, too?"

Kalavitch shrugged. "But of course. She insisted. Why would I want any acreage in a godforsaken place like Barataria Bay?" He returned his handkerchief to his pocket. "Now I think you'd better go. Because you have been through a lot, I will forgive you this one punch." He came out from behind his desk and opened the office door. "But I wouldn't try it again. Get out."

Cade hesitated, then turned and walked through the outer office to the street. Mimi was standing under the unpainted wooden marquee of the post office. Even at that distance, Cade could tell that she was crying.

Cade had a feeling he, in turn, was being watched, and not by Tocko. The still heat was suddenly oppressive and somehow sinister. Cade wished he had asked Tocko if Janice was still on the river.

Anyway she had been here and sold him out. Judy O'Grady had been a lady compared to the colonel's wife. Tocko had an eye for beauty. It could be the old house hadn't been all that Janice had sold. He didn't like the way Tocko had said, "the very blonde and very beautiful former Mrs. Cain."

Cade realized he was breathing through his mouth to spare his swollen nose. The gun in his hip pocket rasped the flesh under it. So he'd seen Tocko. He didn't know any more than he had when he'd come to on the levee, except that Janice had been in Bay Parish, perhaps was still on the river.

Cade leaned a hand against the building to steady himself. He felt light-headed. He felt as he had while sitting on the sagging fence looking at the old house, baffled, frustrated, as if he were trying to climb an opaque glass wall—with God knew what on the far side.

5
PURSUIT OF EVIL

The sidewalk began to fill with early morning shoppers. A basket on one arm, her ample bulk corseted and encased in black bombazine, Mamma Salvatore paused on her way to market. The men in Bay Parish minded their own business. It was a fetish with them. The women weren't any different from women anywhere.

Mamma's big eyes studied Cade's nose and injured eye. "That Joe Laval. For shame what he did to your face." The fat woman was indignant. "In our place yet. He is no good, that Joe. You should take a gaff hook to him."

"I may do that," Cade said.

Mamma laid a plump hand on his arm. "For why they after you,

Cade?"

"I don't know."

Mamma patted the arm on which her plump hand was resting. "Tonight you come back. Tonight I cook for you. And eef that son-of-a-beech of a Joe he tries for make any more trouble, eef Sal don't throw heem out, I weel."

Cade lighted a cigarette. "He's sheriff."

Mamma laughed into one of the flesh folds encircling her wrists like bracelets. "Ha."

Her dark eyes concerned, she started to say more, then changing her mind, repeated, "Tonight you come back," and walked on.

Cade watched her down the street. Mamma, too, wobbled, but her wobble was different from Mimi's. It was more a side slip than a wobble. There was nothing exciting about Mamma's walk, except, perhaps, to Sal. Mamma Salvatore was built square in the stern and low to the water line, like an ocean-going tug. Cade had no doubt she could throw Joe Laval out of Sal's. If she wanted to exert herself, she could probably throw out the Squid, too. Nor was the law sacred to Mamma. There had been too many dark-of-the-moons in her life. She had helped Sal unload too many pirogues of rum and whiskey and tobacco that bore no excise stamps.

He laughed, and turned back to his own problem.

The cigarette smoke in his mouth tasted foul. His throat was constricted. So now he knew. He didn't own the old house any more. No future generations of Cains would ever live in it. Janice had been in Bay Parish and cleaned him. The hell of it was her sale of the various properties was entirely legal. Janice had been his wife at the time. She'd had his power of attorney.

The back of Cade's ears felt hot, as he wondered what Tocko had gotten for lagniappe and knew, even as he wondered. Tocko was a good businessman. He drove hard bargains. To Janice her sex was a lever, a club, a ladder. If Tocko had wanted her for lagniappe—and Tocko wanted every pretty girl he met—more than money had passed between them. That would explain the Slavonian's amused contempt and the concerned look in Mamma Salvatore's eyes. It even explained why Joe Laval had ordered him out of town by noon.

Tocko knew he would find out and Tocko didn't want any trouble with him.

His feeling of bitter frustration continued as Cade walked down the street in the shade of the wooden marquees overhanging the walk.

What of Mimi? She was still waiting patiently with the resigned and often deceptive placidity of many Latin-American women. The oyster-men, shrimpers and merchants calling for their mail all glanced at the girl admiringly as they entered the post office, then swiveled their heads on their necks and either gaped open-mouthed or sucked in their breath as their eyes patted her trim, white-duck-covered stern.

Cade had to be honest. He was no longer suspicious of Mimi, not at all. Mimi was like that. He hoped she had located her husband. He didn't want her aboard the *Sea Bird* any longer than was necessary. First there was the noon deadline. Then there was the girl herself. His own stored-up hunger was a gnawing fire and every movement the girl made added fresh fuel to the flame. He couldn't blame the men of Bay Parish for looking at her. If only he'd married a girl like Mimi instead of one like Janice.

He walked on to where Mimi was waiting. "You got Moran's address?"

Mimi nodded, bright-eyed. "He is living in a hotel in New Orleans." She consulted a piece of paper in her hand. "The postmistress was so kind as to write down the address. Royal Crescent Hotel, on Royal Street."

Cade glanced at the piece of paper. He wasn't familiar with the hotel but from the address on Royal, it was in the old French quarter, not far from the Court of the Two Sisters.

Mimi parted her lips with the tip of a pink tongue. "How far ees New Orleans?"

Cade thought he knew what was coming. "About one-hundred miles by water. A little more than sixty by air."

The tip of Mimi's pink tongue continued to explore her lips. "Oh."

The gesture excited and irritated Cade. He said crossly, "Look. Get it out of your mind."

"Get what out?"

"That I'm going to take you to New Orleans."

"Did I ask you?"

"See, I can't. I haven't the gas, for one thing. For another, I doubt very much if your husband would appreciate your showing up with some other man, especially in that outfit."

Mimi's eyes slitted. "He would be jealous?"

"Yes."

"After he hasn't even written for a year, hasn't answered my letters?"

"Then why are you so anxious to find him?"

"He ees my husband."

Cade's irritation increased. "I'm sorry, Mimi, but you're going to have to get to New Orleans some other way."

To end the pointless conversation, he entered the post office to see if any mail had been forwarded from Corpus Christi. More men welcomed him home. Miss Spence peered out through her wicket, then opened the door that led into her living quarters just behind the post office. "Would you come back here a moment, Cade?" she asked. "I want to talk to you."

Cade thought he knew what Miss Spence wanted to tell him. To the ageless maiden lady there were no shades of gray. Men and women were good or they were bad. Miss Spence intended to tell him what everybody else in Bay Parish knew.

The small living room, with its crossed Confederate battle flags on one wall, brought a nostalgic memory of childhood. The room smelled faintly of lavender. The old what-not, filled with the treasured accumulation of years, still stood in one corner.

Miss Spence closed her wicket and joined him. "Hmm. You look a little different than you did last evening."

Cade grinned at her. "Just a minor difference of opinion."

"A quarrel? With whom?"

"Joe Laval and the Squid."

Miss Spence sat on the black leather sofa and arranged her skirts so her ankles were modestly covered, "Over what?"

"They didn't bother to say." Cade realized he was still carrying the cigarette he'd lighted and snuffed it guiltily between his fingers. Miss Spence didn't approve of cigarette smoking. "But Joe did suggest that certain parties in Bay Parish would be pleased if I slipped my ropes and went back to where I came from."

"Meaning Tocko Kalavitch?"

"I presume as much."

Miss Spence looked at him over her glasses. "Don't."

"Don't what?"

"Don't go. It's time someone stood up to Tocko." The aging postmistress leaned forward. "But that isn't why I wanted to see you, Cade. I'm not worried about you. You can take care of yourself. I'm much more worried about the pretty little girl who spent last night on your boat."

Cade felt like a guilty school boy. "How did you—?"

Miss Spence said dryly, "You aren't in Los Angeles or Tokyo or even Corpus, Cade. You're back in Bay Parish." She looked over her glasses again. "What do you know about her, Cade?"

Cade evaded the question. "Not much."

"She came ashore illegally?"

"What makes you ask that?"

"I have eyes."

Cade looked at the floor and said nothing.

Miss Spence continued, "Not that I'm interested in that angle. I'd much prefer not to know. But she looks like a sweet child to me, a good girl. And if you have any influence with her, I think you'd better advise her to go back to wherever she came from without looking up James Moran."

"Why?"

"He's no good."

"In what way?"

"In any way. It's common knowledge around town that Moran used his army training to fly aliens in for Tocko. At so much a head, of course. And despite the fact that the girl thinks she's his wife, having some knowledge of the way Mr. Moran operated while he was here in Bay Parish, I would say the legality of their marriage is open to question."

"She says they were married in Caracas."

"Young women," Miss Spence said, thin-lipped, "especially young women in love, have a tendency to believe what they want to believe. But I happen to know at least four Mrs. James Morans wrote him regularly, including the young lady from Caracas."

"Oh," Cade said. There seemed to be nothing else to say.

Miss Spence laid her hand on his knee. "I know you, Cade. Outside of normal wildness, you were a good boy. You've turned into a fine man. The bitterness and bloodshed and killing to which you've been subjected haven't made you mean the way they have so many men. But if you're falsely gallant enough to help that girl locate James Moran, you won't be doing her any favor and it will only mean more heartache for you."

"How do you figure that?"

"You know your wife came to Bay Parish? That is, your former wife."

"Yes. I learned that this morning."

"And you know Tocko Kalavitch's reputation with women?"

"Yes."

Miss Spence was embarrassed. "Then I doubt if I need say more. Your former wife and Tocko were very close. In fact, she was his house guest for some weeks."

The air in the small room was suddenly hot and very humid. It was difficult for Cade to breathe.

Miss Spence continued, primly. "Of course, I have no proof, but there was talk, a lot of talk. In this instance, I believe, with good foundation." Miss Spence delicately refrained from befouling his name. "Because this young woman of whom we are speaking not only bestowed her favors on Tocko, she was, according to what the help tell me, equally generous with James Moran. Tocko and Moran quarreled over her publicly. She was the cause of the breach in their business relations. More, when Mr. Moran left Bay Parish, your former wife left with him and the only forwarding address I have for her is the same hotel in New Orleans at which Mr. Moran is now stopping."

Cade felt a hundred years old. It wasn't either right or fair that one sex machine could do the things to a man that Janice had done to him. He got heavily to his feet. "Well, thanks. Thanks a lot."

The postmistress regarded him with troubled eyes as he opened the door. "I thought you ought to know. Now I'm not so certain I did right in telling you."

Cade repeated, "Thanks. Thanks a lot, Miss Spence."

Mimi was still waiting in front of the post office. Her lower lip was thrust out in a pout. The cream-colored rounds of her breasts pushed the thin fabric of his shirt into visible peaks. Even looking at the girl excited him. He regretted he'd attempted to be a gentleman, regretted he hadn't taken her the night before, by force, if necessary. For all her pretended modesty, Mimi had probably expected him to do just that. Women loved stinkers. Both fiction and life were filled with concrete examples. The bigger a louse a man was, the more most women liked him.

Still, a man was what he was.

Cade started to cross the walk and stopped as a hand touched his shoulder from behind. His muddled eyes hopeful, his thin voice filled with sensuous anticipation, his too small head bobbing like a nodding Buddha as he talked, the Squid was smiling down at him.

"You ain't gonna leave like Joe tol' you, are you, Cade? You're still gonna be on your boat by noon." The Squid's fingers caressed Cade's shoulder. "Don't go. Please don't go."

Cade started as violently as if a snake had touched him. He shook off the Squid and, with skin goose-pimpled and flesh crawling, continued on his way.

6
DEATH ON THE DECK

The heat increased as the morning sun rose higher in the sky. Small isolated toadstools of steamy vapor hovered over the muddy pools that had formed in the low spots in the street during the night. As Cade reached the curb, Mimi laid her hand on his arm and stood looking up at him.

"How you say *dificil* in English?" she asked.

"You mean difficult?"

"*Sí*." Her big eyes searched his face. "It is *difficil* for me to beg, but—"

"But what?"

Small fingers bit into Cade's forearm. "If you would be so kind as to take me to New Orleans, I will be ver' grateful. Besides, you will be well paid."

"By whom?" Cade asked, coldly.

"By Jeem. My 'usban' will pay you."

Cade wished Mimi would take her hand off his arm. "Why ask me?"

"Because I am stranger here. Because you are only man I know. Because you have already been so kind."

The memory of his talk with Miss Spence still rankling, Cade was short with her. "You mean such a sucker."

Mimi shook her head. "Thees word I do not know."

Cade's irritation increased. "Let it go. It doesn't matter." He considered telling Mimi about the other Mrs. Morans and didn't have the heart to do so. Mimi was a good kid. It wasn't her fault that a heel like Moran had played fast with her. It could be Miss Spence was wrong. Besides, in the spot he was in, a hysterical woman was all he needed to complete the distorted nightmare through which he had been moving since his return to Bay Parish.

Mimi's fingers bit deeper into his forearm. "Please."

Conscious that the passersby on the sidewalk were watching

them, Cade palmed a cigarette into his mouth with his free hand. "How do you know, after he hasn't even written to you for a year, that Moran wants to see you?"

Mimi was truthful. "I don't."

"How do you know he'd even pay for the gas it would take me to run you up to New Orleans?"

Unshed tears formed in the corners of Mimi's eyes. "I don't know that, either."

Cade lit the cigarette in his mouth. "Look, kid. I'm afraid you've made a mistake. The best thing you can do is look up an immigration man, tell him you entered the country illegally and ask him to contact your consul. Then the worst thing that can happen to you is to be sent back to Caracas."

Mimi's under lip thrust out in a pout. "No."

"Why not?"

"I don't want to go back to Caracas. I want to go to New Orleans. Besides, I told you last night. My family would not receive me."

The heat and the scenes with Tocko and Miss Spence had made Cade's head ache. He was sorry for Mimi. They had a bond in common. She was in love with a heel. He was married, or had been married, to a tramp. But running Mimi up river to New Orleans was out of the question. He had the showdown with Laval to face. Then there was the matter of gas. Cade fingered the lone five-dollar bill in his pocket. He might raise New Orleans with what gas still remained in the tanks but he'd never get back down river again.

"I've done all I can. You'll just have to shift for yourself from here on."

"There is a road to New Orleans?"

"Of a sort, but I wouldn't advise you to hike it."

"You mean walk?"

"Yes."

"Why not?"

"It leads through some pretty rough country. Besides, you're too pretty a girl to start out through the swamps alone, especially in that outfit."

"Why?"

"You know why."

Mimi lowered her eyes and a few tears zigzagged down her cheeks. She brushed at them angrily. "Then why don't you take me to New Orleans?"

Her breasts rose and fell with her emotion until the firm young flesh straining against the fabric threatened to pop the none too securely fastened buttons of her borrowed shirt. "I've told you," Cade said. "Besides, believe it or not, I'm only human and male. I doubt if you'd be any safer with me than you would be on the road." He shook his head. "No. The best thing you can do is to contact Immigration and have them contact your consul."

Cade turned abruptly and walked up the street. He'd never felt so like a heel. Still, he had his own problems. He'd had nothing to do with Mimi stowing away in Caracas. She'd known the chances she was taking when she'd crawled under the tarp of the lifeboat on the freighter that had anchored at Pilottown the night before. He'd given her good advice. The best thing she could do was to contact the Venezuelan consul.

As an afterthought, he turned back and gave her the bill in his pocket.

Mimi eyed the bill suspiciously. "For why?"

"Because I think you're a nice kid. Because I'm sorry for you."

Mimi put the bill between her breasts. "Thank you."

This time she turned away and stood looking out over the river. Cade shrugged and walked up the street to the courthouse. The building was ancient, built of stuccoed white stone; its high-ceilinged corridors and rooms giving an illusion of coolness.

The girl back of the parish recorder's rail was new to Cade, undoubtedly one of the children who'd grown up in the twelve years he'd been away. He told her what he wanted to know and the girl located the information in the files lining one wall. Tocko had given him the truth. The sale of the house and the acreage on Barataria Bay had been duly recorded in a transfer of deed from Mrs. Cade Cain to Tocko Kalavitch. Cade asked the girl behind the desk for a piece of paper and on it wrote the dates of record, to check them against the date on the final divorce papers that had been waiting for him in Tokyo. If Janice had sold the properties before the decree became final, both sales were perfectly legal. There was nothing he could do to recover his property. If, however, she had made the sale after the decree had become final, he at least had a talking point in court. He knew nothing of the law but it seemed reasonable to assume that a divorce would invalidate a power of attorney.

Cade folded the paper on which he had written the dates and put it in his shirt pocket. He didn't care about the acreage on Barataria

Bay. It was too isolated to be of any value. The land had stood untouched and unused since his great grandfather had purchased it for some purpose lost in time. The house was another matter. The house had a sentimental as well as a cash value. He'd been born in the old house. He'd meant to raise his children in it.

The gun sagging in his hip pocket had rubbed the flesh of his thin buttock raw. Perspiration made the abrasion smart. He stood a moment on the courthouse steps wondering what to do. Well, all he could do was to go back to the *Sea Bird* and wait. It was only ten o'clock. His noon deadline was still two hours away.

He walked back toward the levee down one of the chinaberry-tree shaded streets that led through the colored section of Bay Parish. It wasn't any different from Main Street. The smiling faces were merely darker, the greetings more enthusiastic and punctuated now and then with praise to the Lord for his safe arrival home.

Cade knew fierce resentment. This was his town. He liked Bay Parish. Bay Parish liked him. If it hadn't been for Janice, Tocko and Laval, it could have been a wonderful homecoming. He turned to answer a question one of the admiring folks asked him—and saw Mimi. Pouting again, she was trailing along behind him, the black Delta mud squishing between the exquisitely formed toes of her bare feet. Even her dirty bare feet were pretty.

Cade waited for her to catch up. "Now what? Why are you following me?"

Mimi's small chin jutted, then began to quiver. "Because I don't know what else to do. I won't go back to Caracas. I won't."

Cade tried to think of something to say. He couldn't. There didn't seem to be anything for him to say. As long as the girl was so determined to have her heart broken properly, perhaps he could borrow the money from someone to buy her a dress and some shoes and pay her fare by boat, bus or plane to New Orleans.

He turned and walked on toward the levee with Mimi walking beside him.

Her voice small, she said, "I am a lot of trouble to you, am I not?"

"Yes," Cade said.

Her voice continued small. "I'm sorry. It is jus' you have been so ver' kind, that there is no one else I can trust."

Cade was annoyed. "Well, stop bawling about it."

Mimi wiped at her wet cheeks with the back of her hand. "I am not bawling. I am jus' crying a leetle."

Cade wished her voice, the sight of her small rounded body, didn't do the things to him that they did. How much was a man supposed to be able to take? He asked, crossly, "You're still determined to locate Moran?"

Mimi looked at him from the corners of her eyes without turning her face. "That is why I come to thees country."

"You won't go home?"

"I can't."

"Why not?"

"I told you. My family is—"

"Yes. I know," Cade interrupted her. He finished the sentence for Mimi. "Your family is ver' old and ver' proud. And they were ver' *irritado* when you married Moran. How long had you known the man?"

"A week."

"And you were together a week?"

"Yes."

"Living as man and wife?"

"Yes."

"You had a child by him? There's a baby back in Caracas?"

Color crept into Mimi's cheeks. "No."

"Then, after spending a week with you he left you flat and you haven't heard from him since?"

"No."

"But you're still in love with the guy?"

Mimi watched the mud squish through her toes as she walked. "I don't know."

"What do you mean you don't know?"

"I mean I don't know. I get all excited inside when I think of how it was to be married. But I am not, how you say, experienced. I am ver' strictly raised from a ver' small girl and Jeem was the first man I was evair with, alone." Mimi glanced sideways at Cade. "Until I met you."

The bastard, thought Cade. *The big Irish bastard*. Pushing Mimi over must have been as difficult as waiting for a ripe papaya to drop.

The grass-grown bank of the levee was steep and slippery. He helped Mimi up the slope, her flesh soft and warm under his fingers. He liked this girl. He'd never liked anyone so much on so short an acquaintance. She was in a bad spot but she was being a lady about it. There was nothing cheap about Mimi. One thing was certain. Easy to push or not, Cade was willing to bet the *Sea Bird* that Moran hadn't gotten what he wanted until he'd gone through a ceremony of some kind. It could be they were legally married. And now Moran had Janice.

When they reached the broad top of the levee, Mimi asked, "What are you going to do with me?"

"I don't know," Cade admitted. He walked down the levee toward the *Sea Bird* with Mimi hurrying beside him, taking three steps to his one. "I do know I'm not going to take you to New Orleans, but it may be I can borrow enough to outfit you and pay your fare."

"Outfit?"

"Buy you a dress and some shoes."

"Borrow?"

Cade combed through his meager Spanish. "*Prestado.* What you do when you haven't any money."

They were on the pier now. Mimi took the five-dollar bill from its hiding place between her breasts. Her body had perfumed it. "This is all the money you have?"

"That's right."

Her voice was as soft and small and as warm as her lovely body. "And you gave it to me."

Cade was curt with her. "So what?"

Her small fingers bit into his arm. "You are officer. You are gentleman. You are nice."

Cade was embarrassed. "Stow it. Sweet talk isn't going to get you anywhere." He jumped into the cockpit of the *Sea Bird* and helped Mimi down. "Right now, let's have a cup of coffee. I'll make it this time. But get one thing straight in that pretty little head of yours."

"*Sí?*"

"I'm not taking you to New Orleans."

Mimi's voice continued small. "That is for you to say."

Cade made certain the cruiser wasn't rubbing on the pier and that the mooring lines were fast, before opening the door of the aft cabin. At first, his eyes still blinded by the sun, he thought he'd walked into a trap, that the man on his bunk was drunk and waiting for him. He tugged his pistol hastily from his pocket.

Then Cade realized that the Cajun was dead. Laval's shirt front was stained with blood. He lay with one limp arm trailing to the deck plates. In death the gaunt Cajun sheriff looked even more like a weasel than he had in life. Cade felt the flesh of his face. It was still warm. He hadn't been dead more than a few minutes.

Cade caught at the rim of an open port to steady himself. Joe Laval was dead on his boat and he had threatened to kill him. In Sal's, the night before, in front of two dozen witnesses, during his fight with the Squid, he had panted:

"You bastards. If I had a gun I'd kill you both."

Behind him, her view of the cabin blocked by Cade's back, Mimi asked, "What is the matter? What are you looking at?"

The smell of the blood still dripping to the deck plates sickened Cade. He had smelled too much blood, lost too much of it himself. Backing out of the cabin, he closed the companionway door and leaned against it, breathing through his mouth. Perspiration beaded on his face. He felt like he wanted to be sick and couldn't.

Mimi tugged the tail of her borrowed shirt out of the waist of her borrowed pants and used it to wipe Cade's face. "What is it? Tell me. What is the matter, Cade?"

It was the first time Mimi had used his name. Cade liked the sound of it in her mouth. He tried twice before he could speak. "There's a dead man in the cabin."

"Who?"

"The local sheriff. A man by the name of Laval."

"You are certain he is dead?"

"I'm certain."

"How dead?"

"Shot. I think through the heart."

"By whom?"

"I don't know."

"But why should anyone kill him on your boat?"

He was afraid he knew the answer to Mimi's question. Tocko had always hated him, ever since they had been boys and he had refused to allow Tocko to push him around. Now, after pirating Janice, and after stripping him of property that had been in the Cain family for one hundred years, Tocko had reason to fear Cade, fear him enough to plant a dead man on his boat. A murder conviction would be much more permanent than a warning to leave town.

He had threatened Joe Laval. Now Joe was dead and his only alibi for the approximate time of the killing was that he had been walking with a pretty girl, a girl who was in the country illegally, a girl who had spent the previous night aboard his boat.

It was the sort of thing only a Tocko Kalavitch could dream up. On the other hand, Joe had been Tocko's right-hand man. Tocko would be hard put to find anyone else who would do the dirty jobs Joe had done.

"But why?" Mimi demanded.

"Put your shirt back in your pants," Cade told her.

He glanced up, then down, the levee. It dozed in the mid-morning sun. The only sounds were the jangling of a ship's bell in mid-river, the surge of the river itself and the buzz of a single-motored plane rising from the small airport on the far side of the town. The storm-pitted glass in the windows of the old house acted like so many reflectors, blinding him. The only moving object he could see were two distant men just starting up the weed-grown road that led to the business district.

Cade took his glass from its bracket over the wheel and trained it on the two men. The man in the white suit was Tocko. The face of the other man was unfamiliar but he was in the uniform of the Immigration Service. They could only be coming to one place.

Cade returned the glass to its bracket and looked at Mimi. Moran had been in Tocko's employ. Men like Moran liked to boast of their conquests. Undoubtedly, Tocko knew all the details concerning Moran's romance in Caracas—and wanted her himself. Tocko wanted every pretty girl he saw. The big Slavonian collected screams in the night as some men collected stamps.

Cold anger replaced Cade's queasiness. Tocko might or might not be able to pin Laval's death on him. A jury would decide that. But Tocko could have him held for trial, leaving Mimi unprotected.

Cade's agile mind raced on. Mimi was in the country illegally. After the "discovery" of Laval's body, Tocko's smart move would be to persuade the immigration officials to parole the girl in his custody as a material witness. Tocko was a power on the river. He was a man of property and substance. He knew whom to see. It was a fifty-fifty gamble that the immigration officials would listen to him, especially if Tocko were willing to post bond for Mimi. And Tocko would be willing. That kind of a scream from Mimi would be worth any amount of bond.

Even thinking of the girl that way excited Cade. After all, he'd been hungry for two years.

Mimi blushed at the look in his eyes and tucked more of her borrowed shirt into her already well-filled white pants. "Please, Cade," she reproved him gently. "Why are you looking at me like that?"

Cade spoke without conscious volition. "Just thinking how nice it would be."

He started the port, then the starboard motor of the cruiser. There was no strain on the aft lines. The forward line gave him more trouble. He was drenched with sweat by the time he fought it over the rusted iron and returned to the wheel of the cruiser.

Tocko and the immigration man were running now, shouting something unintelligible over the throb of the motors. Cade made a derogatory gesture and gunned the *Sea Bird* out of the slip too fast, its powerful twin screws spitting a messy wake of mangled hyacinth bulbs and churned mud.

He had to have time to think, time to get rid of Laval's body.

Her bare feet spread on the deck to maintain a precarious balance, Mimi looked from the muddy wake to the shouting men on the pier. Then holding on to the back of the wheel chair with one hand to steady herself against the slap of the river, she put the thumb of her free hand to her nose and wiggled her fingers experimentally. "What does that mean in English?"

Cade fed more gas to the boat as he swung the wheel hard, up river. "That we're going to New Orleans."

Mimi was silent a moment. Then she said, quietly, "Thank you. You are, how we say, *muy buen caballero*. It would be nice with you, too."

Cade sucked in his breath sharply as he glanced at the dark-haired girl. She was the damnedest one hundred pounds of mixed naiveté and poise he had ever seen stuffed into one feminine body. Her statement was just that, a statement, not an invitation.

To keep from making a fool of himself, Cade forced his eyes to scan the gas gauge. The tanks were still a quarter full. If he hadn't forgotten the channel, if he didn't hit a submerged object, if the immigration man didn't telephone on up the river for a Coast Guard boat to stop him, at the knots they were logging they should raise the lower harbor by early afternoon.

The more Cade thought about going to New Orleans the better he liked the idea. He wanted to meet Mimi's "husband." He wanted to talk to Janice. Perhaps one, or both, could explain why he was being pushed around.

7
THE ROYAL CRESCENT

In a sheltered cove a few miles above Buras, Cade cut his motors long enough to drag Laval's body out of the cabin. If a Coast Guard boat should stop him, he didn't want the dead man aboard. After two years in Pyongyang, he had all he could stomach of prisons and prison camps.

In this instance he had played it smart. This way he might be suspected of killing Laval but no one could prove anything.

Cade considered weighting the body but could find nothing aboard the cruiser he could spare. It had taken every penny he'd had to buy the boat and outfit it as meagerly as he had. In the back of his mind he supposed he'd reasoned that if he ran too short of cash he could always put a small mortgage on the old home place. Now the old house was gone. Tocko had bought it at his price, with Janice thrown in for lagniappe.

Mimi eyed the dead man with feminine distaste. "You knew him?"

Cade touched his swollen nose and the adhesive tape under his eye. "Very well. He gave me these last night. At least, he had his deputy do it."

"Why?"

"He didn't say. He did order me to be out of town by noon."

"I see," Mimi said with quick comprehension. "This is why you wouldn't go."

Cade heaved the body up on the transom of the boat. "Let's say one of the reasons." It was hot and still in the cove. Cade was panting just from the effort of lifting the body. He still had a long road to travel before all of his strength returned. He glanced at his watch as he rested. It was eleven o'clock. Joe had made his deadline stand up, after all. Not that it mattered to Joe. The gaunt Cajun was through taking orders from Tocko, through with throwing his weight around, finished with doing Tocko's dirty work. Cade squeegeed the sweat from his face with the side of his hand before Mimi could use the tail of her shirt. Now that he'd had time to think, Tocko sacrificing Joe Laval just to get rid of him didn't make good sense. Joe had been invaluable to Tocko.

Cade leaned against the side of the cruiser. But then, nothing made sense, nothing made sense since, lousy and dirty and half-starved, he'd called on his last ounce of strength to stagger across the line under his own power at Panmunjom.

"Rest and quiet, that's an order," one of the big-shot medics in Tokyo had told him. "I see you come from the Delta country, Colonel. When you get back to the States, buy a boat, take it easy, crawl into the bunk with your wife and a jug of rum and don't get out of the sack for two months except to eat."

Mimi watched him warily, wetting her naturally red lips with the pink tip of her tongue. "What are you thinking?"

"You might be surprised," Cade said, wryly. "Then again, you might not."

He heaved Laval's body over the edge. The splash sounded unnaturally loud in the hush of the cove. The body bobbed several times like a swimmer treading water, then was caught in an eddy and floated off down river.

Cade dropped a bucket overside and sloshed the transom and the cockpit with water. It was a minor matter to make the cockpit shipshape again. The cabin was another affair. The mattress on which Laval had been killed was sodden with clotted blood. Blood had dripped down onto the deck plates and seeped in between the cracks. Cade scrubbed the deck as best he could but there was nothing he could do with the mattress except throw it overside. When he'd finished, his trousers and shirt were sodden with sweat. Cade thought of going for a swim and thought better of the idea. The sight of Mimi in a pair of his shorts and a makeshift halter would only add to his problem. The girl liked him. She trusted him. He wasn't completely a heel, he hoped.

His sour mood stayed with him, as he started his motors again and continued up river. He hadn't been smart in running. He had acted on impulse, instead of reasoning the thing out. If the law couldn't prove he'd killed Laval, now that he'd disposed of Joe's body, he couldn't prove that he hadn't killed him. What evidence there was, was in the river. If he was suspect, and he would be, his sudden flight, the missing mattress and the blood that had seeped into the cracks would all be against him. Any half-smart lawyer, using his threat to kill Joe and the three pieces of evidence as a foundation, could build a good case against him.

Cade's resentment against Mimi grew. If it hadn't been for Mimi, if he hadn't tried to save her from Tocko, he wouldn't have run. So Laval had been shot on his boat? He hadn't shot him.

Mimi sensed his mood. "Have I done something, Cade?"

His name didn't sound so good in her mouth. "No. Nothing," Cade said, shortly. "Just leave me alone."

He sat watching the shore line fall behind the speeding cruiser, swinging wide now and then to give an outbound steamer plenty of seaway, occasionally passing a banana boat or a smartly painted tanker laboring up stream against the current.

It was two o'clock when he wove his way through the ships riding at anchor in the lower harbor and a few minutes later when he cut his motors and nosed into the private slip of a ship chandler he and his family had done business with for years, not far from the Charbonnet Street Wharf.

Mimi eyed the gear-cluttered pier with distaste. "Why are we stopping here?"

Cade told her, curtly, "To get some money. What did you think I was going to do, run the *Sea Bird* right up Royal Street and help you out in front of the hotel in that outfit?"

Mimi's eyes narrowed slightly, "I'm sorry, I am a lot of bother to you."

"Yes, you are," Cade admitted.

He made fast to the pier, then getting his papers from his strong box in the locker under his bunk, he strode down the pier to the office. The chandler was glad to see him. After a quick glance at the *Sea Bird* and its registry papers, he was glad to lend Cade a thousand dollars on the boat—at ten percent.

Cade made the arrangements to leave the cruiser where it was for the time being and returned for Mimi. She refused his offered hand and scrambled up on the pier herself. "I can manage. I don't want to be any more bother to you than I can help."

"That's fine with me," Cade said.

He told himself he would be glad to get rid of the girl. He would outfit her as best he could. He'd take her to the Royal Crescent Hotel and turn her over to Moran. From there on in, she could make out on her own, while he had a showdown with Janice.

It was almost four o'clock by the time he'd bought Mimi a dress and some hose and shoes and underthings, to replace the wisps in which she had swum ashore. The dress was white, of a waffle weave material, with a square neck cut to show the top rounds of her breasts. It looked well on her but Cade decided he'd like her better in the borrowed white pants and shirt which Mimi insisted the slightly shocked clerk put into a bag for her.

Back on crowded Barrone Street, Mimi stood so close that Cade could feel her slim body trembling. His sour mood deepened. He'd picked the girl out of the river. He'd fed her and clothed her. He'd saved her from Tocko Kalavitch. He was risking a murder rap for her. And was she grateful? No. She was so eager to get to the stud to whom she's given her virginity that she was a-tremble with anticipation.

"Cold?" Cade asked sarcastically.

Mimi shook her head and tried to smile. "No. Scared."

Cade whistled down a cab.

"The Royal Crescent Hotel. It's on Royal Street."

The cab driver looked from Cade to Mimi and grinned knowingly. "Yeah. Sure. I know where it is."

Cade didn't like his grin. It stamped the hotel. Obviously Janice wasn't as choosy as she had been when he was paying her bills. Then nothing but the best had been good enough for her.

Mimi looked straight ahead. "I haven't much time to thank you. You have been kind, ver' kind." She put her right hand to her left breast. "And I will always remember it here."

The cab stopped for the light on Canal Street.

Mimi continued quietly, "I have been beeg problem to you, I know. You are a man. I am a girl. But this I cannot help. I am also married woman. I am no longer free to give what I might like to give. And deep down inside you, you would not have wanted it to be any different than it has been. Some men are not like that. But you are that sort of man."

Even in his bitterness, Cade was amazed by the depth of her perception.

Mimi found and squeezed his hand. "Anything else but as it was would have cheapened both of us."

Cade played with her fingers. "You think Moran has been true to you?"

"That is another matter."

"What if he doesn't want you?"

"That is my problem."

"Yeah. Sure," Cade said, dryly. He leaned back against the leather seat of the cab, fighting a mild headache, wondering how Mimi was going to react when she found out that her "husband" was living with his former wife.

It could be an interesting scene.

The hotel was much as he had imagined it would be. There was a dimly lighted cocktail lounge off the foyer. The rusted ornamental wrought iron needed painting. Both the ornamental mosaic tile entrance and the glass doors looked like they could stand a good washing.

As Cade started to pay off the driver, Mimi put her hand on his arm. "Thank you. Thank you ver' much for everything. But you do not need to come in with me. After all, it has been a year and I would prefer to be alone when I meet Jeem."

Cade gave the driver a five-dollar bill and waited for his change. "Uh uh."

Mimi was puzzled. "Uh uh?"

Cade tipped the driver, put his change into his pocket, then tucked Mimi's hand under his arm. "That's American for nothing doing. How about my money?"

"Money?"

"Yeah. For the gas it took to run up here and the clothes I just bought you."

"Oh, yes." Her small chin jutted. "Jeem will be glad to pay you."

Cade tightened his hand on her arm. "Could be. Anyway, we're going in together."

Mimi glanced at him hotly from the corner of her eye but said nothing. The lobby was in keeping with the outside of the hotel. A half-dozen artificial palm trees grew out of sand pots. The chairs were covered with pastel leather and looked new. It wasn't the chairs in the Royal Crescent that took a pounding. It even smelled like the sort of a place it was.

The clerk was young and glib. He looked at Cade's white captain's cap and water-stained white shirt and pants and white top-siders, then at Mimi's ample bosom. "Yes, sir, captain. A room with a bath, I presume? Say something around eight dollars?"

Mimi blushed. "No. You have a misunderstanding. We do not weesh for a room. I am looking for my 'usban'."

The clerk's eyes turned opaque. "Oh."

"A Mister Jeem Moran. He comes here from Bay Parish."

"Oh, yes," the clerk said. "Mr. James Moran."

Mimi steadied her trembling fingers by holding on to the counter. "Would you be so kin' as to call heem and tell heem that Mimi is here."

The clerk was mildly amused. "I'm afraid that would be a little difficult, miss."

Mimi looked at the house phone on the counter. "Why would it be *dificil?*"

"Because Mr. Moran isn't stopping with us any more. He checked out a little better than two weeks ago."

She gasped. "He moved to some other hotel? Here in New Orleans?"

"That I wouldn't know, lady. Mr. Moran didn't take me into his confidence. After all, I'm only the clerk."

Mimi pounded on the counter with her small fists. "But you must know where he is. I have come all the way from Caracas."

The clerk wasn't impressed. "Look, lady. I don't care if you came all the way from St. Louis. I don't know where the guy is. Like I said. He moved out a little better than two weeks ago and he didn't leave a forwarding address." The clerk pointed to an envelope-choked slot in the key rack. "In fact, if you locate the guy, I'd appreciate it very much if you'd tell him to come pick up his mail."

Cade leaned an elbow on the counter. "How about the blonde in the adjoining room? Did she check out, too?"

Caught off balance, the clerk asked, "You mean Mrs. Cain? Yeah. She and Moran—" The clerk realized he had been trapped and stopped talking.

Mimi transferred her anger to Cade. "You knew! You knew all the time my Jeem was weeth some other woman, some she no-good. Who ees thees Mrs. Cain?"

It was an effort for Cade to speak. "My wife. That is, my former wife," he told Mimi.

8

BUSINESS PARTNERS

The barman in the cocktail lounge off the foyer refused to go on record. "Five feet four. One hundred and fifteen pounds. Blonde. Gray eyes. Very pretty. The right side of thirty." He shook his head. "No, I really couldn't say, mister. They come and go. Believe me. Good-looking blondes are thirteen to the case in here." He picked up the glass he'd been polishing and looked at Mimi. "So are big six-footers with black hair. If they drank in here, I undoubtedly seen them. But their descriptions don't ring no bell."

Mimi gnawed at her lower lip.

Cade sipped at the rum in his glass and realized that he was hungry, that he hadn't eaten since morning. "You serve food?"

The barman put the polished glass on the back bar. "The best food in town, not barring Antoine's or Arnaud's. But only in the booths, mister. The waitress will take your order."

Cade carried his double rum and Mimi's untouched brandy to one of the booths. Her eyes slitted and sullen, Mimi followed him. "You knew."

Cade waited for her to sit down. "I don't know now. But I was told that they left Bay Parish together, after a fight between Moran and Tocko."

"Over your wife?"

"My former wife."

"Your former wife then."

"So I was told."

"Tocko is the fat man who suggested the postmistress could give me Jeem's address?"

"That's right."

"The man who was running up the levee when you put out into the river?"

"That was Tocko."

"Maybe he'd just learned Jeem's new address. Why didn't you wait for heem?"

"With a dead man on my boat?"

"Even so."

"Then, let's put it this way. Did you notice a man with Tocko?"

"Yes. A man in uniform."

"The uniform of the U.S. Immigration Service."

Mimi sucked in her breath and held it for a long time. Then she exhaled slowly. "Oh, I see. Again, I have to thank you."

Cade debated telling her the obvious reason for Tocko turning informer and decided not to. The girl was keyed to the point of breaking. She had enough to worry her as it was. He said, "After all, a girl as pretty as you are can't suddenly materialize in a town as small as Bay Parish, especially a point of entry into the country, without having someone wonder where she came from."

Her eyes still sullen, her lower lip thrust out in a pout, Mimi sat toying with her glass. Cade was glad when a bored waitress spread menus in front of them. What happened from here on he didn't know, but that could wait until they had eaten.

The menu was in French. He ordered for both of them, one of the meals of which he had dreamed during his two-year diet of fish heads and rice: Pompano en Papillote. Poulet Rochambeau. Fond d'Artichaut. Glacé a la Vanille. Café au Lait.

When the waitress had gone, Mimi asked, "What are we eating, Cade?"

Cade told her. "That's easy … Fish baked in paper. Chicken. A salad. Ice cream and coffee."

Neither of them spoke again, both preoccupied with their own thoughts. The food, when it came, was good. It wasn't as good as Antoine's or Arnaud's or Mamma Salvatore's, for that matter, but it was the first meal of its kind that Cade had eaten in years and he enjoyed it.

Mimi's anger and disappointment seemed to spice her appetite. As the various courses were served, she ate everything on her plate with exquisite manners and Latin enthusiasm. Cade enjoyed watching her eat. Everything Mimi did, she did well. He thought of her as he'd seen her lying nude on the bunk of the forecabin and shook his head.

"No man in his right mind."

Mimi licked the last of the Glacé a la Vanille from her spoon. "I beg your pardon?"

"Just thinking out loud," Cade said.

He ordered a package of Turkish cigarettes and two liqueurs to finish off the meal. It had been a good meal. He'd enjoyed it.

Mimi sipped at her anisette. "It was nice, ver' nice. *Gracias.*"

Cade lighted a cigarette for her. He wished he knew what to do with Mimi. He couldn't leave her alone in New Orleans any more than he could have left her alone in Bay Parish. Mimi was a problem. Cade leaned his forearms on the table. "Look, little honey."

"*Sí?*"

"Now we've failed to locate Moran how about you changing your mind and going back to Caracas?"

Mimi blew smoke through her nose. "No."

"But Moran isn't registered here. You heard the clerk. He checked out two weeks ago."

"There is more than one hotel in New Orleans. I will go from one to the other."

"But we don't even know they are still in New Orleans."

"They?"

"You heard that, too. Seemingly, Janice checked out with him. At least, at the same time."

Mimi laid her hand on his. "Thees girl to whom you were married."

"What about her?"

"You love her?"

"At one time I thought I did."

"How long have you been divorced?"

"According to the date on the final decree, about as long as since you've seen Moran."

"You knew she was divorcing you?"

"No." Cade tried to keep the bitterness from his voice. "They didn't serve divorce papers where I was."

"Where was that?"

"North of the Yalu River in Korea."

Mimi was incredulous. "She divorced you while you were in a prison camp?"

"Yeah. I slept with the final decree on my first night back in Tokyo."

Mimi's breasts rose and fell with her anger. Cade watched them, fascinated. "I am right in what I say in the lobby. Thees woman, thees Janice, is a she no-good. Even if, how you say, I hated hees gots, eef my man had been a prisoner, eef he had been fighting for me, he would nevair have known. I would have been waiting weeth all the love in the world."

"I believe that," Cade said.

"What did you do to her to make her want thees divorce?"

"Nothing. Except perhaps not make enough money."

"You are colonel."

"Ex-colonel. But a colonel's pay was chicken feed to Janice."

"And now she ees weeth my man."

"So it would seem. Moran has money?"

Mimi's full lips twisted in wry smile. "If so, he nevair sent me some. If he had sent me money I would not have to hide under the canvas of a lifeboat."

Cade glanced casually around the bar. It was beginning to fill with early evening trade. "Not so loud," he cautioned Mimi. "You never can tell who might be listening in a joint like this."

A pleasant-faced waitress appeared in front of the booth with a silver thermos jug. "How's the coffee situation?"

"Thanks. I can use some," Cade said. He made his cup more accessible, then looked at the waitress again. "Are you the girl who served us?"

"No," the girl said. "That was Annette. I just came on shift. We change shift at five."

"I see," Cade said.

The waitress hesitated and said, "Say, Charlie, that's the day barman, said you were inquiring about a good-looking blonde and a big black-haired man who were stopping at the hotel but checked out about two weeks ago."

"That's right. James Moran and Janice Cain."

"You aren't a cop, are you?"

"Do I look like one?"

"No," the waitress admitted, "you don't. Still, a girl can never tell. You want to locate this couple, is that the idea?"

"Yes," Mimi said, "ver' much."

"How much?" the waitress asked.

Cade laid ten dollars on the table. "Say, ten dollars' worth."

"Let's say, twice ten dollars."

Cade laid a second bill on top of the first.

The waitress was fair. "First, let's make sure we are talking about the same people. She's a blonde, blue-eyed, this side of thirty, with no need of falsies? Looks and walks and dresses like she might be a model?"

"She was a model," Cade said.

"He's a big good-looking black Irishman. Curly hair, gray eyes. A cleft in his chin. A heavy drinker who laughs a lot. Has something to do with flying."

Mimi nodded. "That ees a good description."

The waitress fingered the bills on the table. "Then we're talking about the same people. The reason Charlie didn't remember them is because he never works the night shift and they always came in around this time, maybe even a little later. And always with two or three pollys in tow."

"Pollys?" Mimi puzzled.

"Politicians," the waitress explained. "You know, state representatives and senators and the like, the slickers we, the people send to Baton Rouge to raise our taxes so they can pry somebody's Uncle Benny into the poor house and build roads for the ducks. So help me. While the couple we're speaking of were here, the joint was practically an annex of the state capital."

Cade shook his head. "I don't get it."

"Neither did I," the waitress admitted. "But the tips were good while it lasted. It was almost as if Huey had come back to life and the town was running wide open again."

"But where are they now? Where did they go from here?"

The waitress continued to finger the bills on the table. "Well, don't come back and sue me if I'm wrong and I haven't the least idea how to get there, but I gathered from what snatches of conversation I overheard, that when they left here they were going to some swank resort or fishing camp that this blonde is building on a big piece of undeveloped acreage she owns on Barataria Bay."

"I see," Cade said.

The waitress picked up the bills on the table. "My money?"

"Your money."

"You're satisfied with what I could tell you?"

"I'm satisfied."

Mimi wet her lips with the tip of her tongue. "Would you tell me just one thing more? How did they act? I mean with each other. Would you say they were sweethearts?"

The waitress put the two bills in the pocket of her nylon uniform. "That's a hard thing to say, honey. They were very friendly. She occasionally called him 'dahling—' He called her 'dear.' But she also called most of the pollys 'dahling.' And from the amount of figuring and scribbling she and Moran did on the backs of menus and on the tablecloths, I got the distinct impression that if they were depressing the coils of an innerspring together, it was strictly a secondary matter. You know, more like they were business partners."

"What kind of business?" Cade asked.

The waitress shrugged. "There you have me, mister. But again I had the distinct impression it had something to do with the land on Barataria Bay."

Cade laid a bill on the tray to cover the check and a tip, then stood up and reached for his cap.

Mimi stood up with him.

"Back to the boat," Cade told her.

9
TALK OF THE TOWN

There were stars but no moon. It had been twelve years since Cade had been on the river at night. Some of the landmarks had changed. It was difficult running without lights. It was also dangerous. Once he almost rammed into a floating tree being carried out into the Gulf by the current. Once a freighter, veering from its course, for some reason known only to the man at the wheel, nearly ran them down.

After passing the cluster of lights on the west bank, which he hoped was Venice, Cade throttled the motors down until he barely had seaway and debated his best move.

He could head directly for his destination by running the little-used pass originating just south of Venice and terminating in West Bay. It would save him miles and gasoline. He could stop off in Bay Parish and attempt to refuel for the long run to Grand Isle. He might also be able to ascertain just where he stood with the law, learn what moves Tocko had made regarding Joe Laval's disappearance and his own hasty departure with Mimi aboard the *Sea Bird*.

Cade glanced through the dark at the small oval face of the girl standing beside his elbow. To save her new dress and shoes and hose, Mimi had changed back into her borrowed white pants and shirt. The black-haired girl wore them well. The more intimately Cade knew her, the better he liked her. There was no pretense about her. Mimi was for you or against you. She had been bitterly disappointed at failing to find Moran in New Orleans, but had refused to cry. She hadn't called out once or shown any outward signs of fright on the precarious trip down river. Nor had she asked any foolish questions. When he had told her he intended to head for Barataria Bay and a showdown with Janice and Moran, she had accepted his judgment without question. In the country she came from the men made the decisions. Such pants as the women wore were merely for ornamental purposes.

He said, "I'm trying to make up my mind whether I ought to stop in Bay Parish and replace what fuel we've used."

"We do not 'ave enough to get to this Barataria?"

"Plenty. If we don't run into a blow."

"A blow?"

"A storm."

"There is apt to be a storm?"

"I wouldn't know," Cade said wryly. "This is the season for them but it's a little too dark to see if the small craft warnings are flying and under the circumstances I don't think it would be smart to check with the Coast Guard."

Mimi proved she was only human by asking her first foolish question. "Why not?"

"For two reasons," Cade told her. "One, you're in the country illegally. Remember? Two, there is the little matter of the man I dropped into the river. For all I know, I may be wanted for murder."

Cade decided to stop at Bay Parish and eased his throttle forward. He'd been right about the lights. They indicated Venice on the west bank. He could see the lights of Bay Parish now. Cade felt his way inshore as far as he dared and dropped anchor. The cruiser immediately swung around and held, nosed into the current, rising and falling with a gentle motion.

"I'll swim in from here," he told Mimi. "You won't be afraid to stay on the cruiser alone?"

Mimi bobbed her head. "Yes. I 'ave been ver' afraid all the way down from New Orleans. But that does not make any difference. You are *capitan*. I will stay where you tell me to stay."

Cade patted her and wished he hadn't. Her flesh attracted his hand like a magnet. It was still a long way, a hell of a long way, to Barataria Bay. He hoped he could control himself. Only time would tell. He wrapped his gun in oiled silk and put it in his side pants pocket.

"I shouldn't be too long. I'll be back as soon as I find out where we stand and make arrangements to refuel."

The water looked dark and oily and somehow sinister. He knew how Mimi must have felt when she had swum ashore. And she had swum ashore from mid-stream. It would be nice to be loved by a girl like Mimi. As an afterthought, Cade handed her a flashlight. "If I can't locate the cruiser and have to hail, flash this down on the water, shore side, but only flash it once."

"Whatever you say," Mimi said. She raised on her tiptoes and kissed him lightly, without passion. "For good luck."

Cade held her tighter and longer than necessary. It was exquisite torture. This, too, was a part of his dream, except that in his dreams the girl had been Janice and his need had been satisfied. Mimi freed herself from his arms gently.

"I should not 'ave done that."

Cade stood, fighting himself. He wasn't afraid of her knife. He could have the knife in the river and Mimi on her back before she could say Caracas. He could take Mimi on one of the bunks, on the deck plates of the cook-pit, up against the rail. Anywhere with Mimi would give him the relief he needed. Still, it would be a breach of faith, as well as a breach of the flesh. Mimi trusted him. She liked him. He was *capitan*. It was the old army game all over. If rank had its privileges, it also had its responsibilities. There were certain things an officer and a gentleman didn't do. As long as the black-haired girl even thought she was married to Moran, it would be a hasty, meaningless meeting of two bodies. It wouldn't be the dream he'd dreamed. If flesh were all he wanted he could have stopped at any number of places in New Orleans and spent five or ten of the thousand dollars for which he had mortgaged his cruiser.

"I'm sorry. So sorry," Mimi said.

Cade stood up on the wide transom of the boat and split the water in a clean dive that carried him three-fourths of the way to shore. The cold water felt good on his body, but even this close in, the current was strong. Cade swam the few remaining feet in a powerful crawl, then, fighting his way through the inevitable tangle of hyacinth, he climbed up the side of the levee and stood panting for breath. The cruiser was lost in the darkness of the river but from where he stood he could see the business district of Bay Parish and Sal's new red neon sign. Carried faintly by the off-shore wind, the strains of the Harry Belafonte recording of *Mathilda, Mathilda* came to his ears.

Cade marked the spot where he'd come ashore. Then unwrapping his pistol, he walked toward the red sign and the juke box music. Sal could tell him where he stood with the law.

Except for the lights in the houses, the back streets of Bay Parish were as dark as the river had been. Now and then he passed or was passed by a colored man or woman. Cade walked without any attempt at concealment. His long years as a pilot, of seeing men die beside him, of kissing death daily without the union being consummated, had given him an unshakable belief in preordination. When the time came you got it. Until then, the wheel could spin like mad without anything worse than a two-timing wife and a dame you wished you could stay with, and couldn't, happening to you.

Sal's combination bar and restaurant was an isolated building with two vacant lots on one side and a sour orange grove on the other. Cade looked in one of the open windows. The familiars were bellied up to the bar. Tocko was sitting in a booth with the Squid and a bronze-faced young man in his early thirties. The heavy-set Slavonian was pounding lightly on the table with one fist but only the Squid seemed impressed. Cade decided the strange one could be either a flyer or a seaman with his master's papers. He had that look in his eyes.

Cade walked around the building to the back door. The door was open to catch what breeze there was. Through the screen he could see Mamma Salvatore busy at her stove, pausing from time to time to refresh herself from a big glass of iced orange wine.

Cade tapped on the wood of the screen softly. "Mamma. Mamma Salvatore," he whispered.

The big woman picked up her glass of wine and waddled casually toward the screen as if to get a breath of fresh air. Between sips of wine, she said softly, "Don't come in and don't talk too loud."

"Why not?"

"Tocko and the Squid are in the bar."

"I know. I saw them."

"And you are in bad trouble."

"How bad?"

"The beeg trouble. The law is looking for you. Tocko has sworn out a warrant charging you weeth keeling that dog Joe Laval."

Cade started to open his mouth and closed it for fear one of the butterflies fluttering in his stomach would fly out. When he could, he asked, "How does Tocko know Joe is dead?"

"A shark fisherman snagged his body late this afternoon." Mamma was pleased. "You keeled him, Cade?"

"No."

"Who did?"

"I imagine Tocko. Or had him killed. Anyway I found him on my boat this morning."

Mamma Salvatore shook her head. "No. Eef that was how it was, Tocko would not be so angry. No. Joe was too valuable to Tocko. Now he has no one to do his dirty work."

"He has the Squid."

Mamma was pleasantly high. "The Squid doesn't know pee from

peanuts."

"Then who killed Joe?"

The fat woman sipped at her wine. "Who can tell? Joe has needed keeling for years." She giggled. "Then there is the girl on your boat."

"What about her?"

"Tocko turned her in. Right after I saw you by the post office this morning, Tocko called Immigration and told them the foreign-born wife of one of his former employees had entered the country illegally but he would be glad to post bond eef they would parole her een his custody unteel she could locate her husband."

"I figured that when I saw Tocko and an immigration man hot-footing it up the levee."

Mamma winked salaciously. "Is good?"

Cade shook his head. "I wouldn't know."

Mamma laughed into one of her bracelets of wrinkles on her fat arms. "Ha."

"I mean it."

Mamma was serious. "Then you are fool. Is what young women are for. Is what Tocko did to your wife. Is what Moran did, too. Everyone in town was talking."

Cade realized he was sweating again. "You know this to be true, Mamma?"

The fat woman shook her head. "I did not see them in bed. But I woman. I was young once. I can tell. You do not get thee deep shadows under thee eyes from frying fish." She pressed her nose to the screen. "But what are you doing here? Papa and I hoped you were a long way by now."

All of Cade's muscles and glands ached dully. His nerve ends felt like they had been rubbed raw. Quiet and peace, the medic had told him! "I'm anchored out in the river," he told Mamma. "I'm headed for Barataria Bay and I need a little more gas."

"Wait," Mamma said, quietly. "Wait. I will get Sal."

Cade watched the fat woman waddle away across the kitchen and disappear through the swinging door. They were ignorant, sensuous, semi-illiterate, two of the last of the freebooters on the river; but Mamma and Sal were his kind of people. There were no gaps in their friendship. When they liked you they liked you.

The scuff of feet in grass attracted Cade's attention and he backed swiftly into the dark shadows beyond the light pouring out the open kitchen door. The Squid, his grotesquely small head bobbling as he peered hopefully into the dark, was padding down the side of the old wooden restaurant.

The butterflies returned to Cade's stomach as he drew his gun.

The Squid was rounding the building now, sniffing like a hound dog on the trail of a coon. Cade attempted to back still deeper into the shadows. It was a mistake. His right heel struck the bottom case of a stacked tier of empty Coca Cola cases and as he tried to catch his balance he knocked the whole tier over in a clatter of broken bottles and thudding cases.

The Squid, trotting now, came over to the sound. "You there in the dark. Who are you?"

The palm of Cade's hand was slippery with sweat. He could kill the Squid all right, but what happened then? Tocko might or might not be able to pin Joe Laval on him but there would be no doubt about the Squid. Killing the Squid in cold blood could mean only one thing.

The Squid continued to advance. Saliva drooled from the corners of his mouth as he recognized Cade. "So you came back, eh? Tocko is smart. Go see why Mamma is so excited, he tol' me, an' it's you." The Squid reached out a big hand. "You shouldn't have done it, Cade. You shouldn't have killed Joe. Tocko tol' me if I found you I could have all the fun I wanted." The big man's eyes gleamed wetly in the starlight. "Go on. Hit me with your gun. Then I'll hit you back."

Cade fought down his recurring desire to be sick as the Squid's clammy fingers caressed his face, insistent, urgent, demanding.

"Go on. Hit me," the Squid whispered.

Cade raised the pistol in his hand, then held it level with his ear, as Sal opened the screen door of the kitchen and came over to where he and the Squid were standing. As tall a man as the Squid, outweighing him by fifty pounds, the swart-faced, aging Portuguese caught the Squid by one shoulder and turned him around as easily as if he were revolving a glass under one of the beer taps of his bar.

When Sal was excited he ran his words together. His words ran together now.

"Yougoddamnsneakingsonofabitchingqueer." Sal's massive chest labored in his anger. "YouandthatlouseofaTocko." He fought for self-control. "Tocko saw Mamma whisper to me. Tocko guessed something was up and sent you to pry. Is that it?"

The Squid looked like he was going to cry. "You stay out of this, Sal."

Sal lifted his hand, made a fist of it and moved it forward, more of a push than a blow. There was a dull thud as it struck the Squid's jaw. He stood a moment weaving from side to side like the stack of a sea-going tug rolling in an offshore swell, then crumpled to the ground.

Sal apologized sadly, "Am getting old. Was time I bust his goddamn jaw."

Inside the bar, a smooth tenor was singing *Mathilda, Mathilda.* Cade could smell sweet orange blossoms spiced with the pungent scent of garlic and olive oil wafting out of the kitchen door. The starlight seemed somehow brighter. On the far bank of the river, the first white rays of the moon began to appear over the oyster camps.

Cade returned the gun to his pocket. "Thanks."

Sal shrugged. "Is nothing." His booming voice dropped to a conspiratorial whisper. "Mamma is saying you need gas. I got plenty of gas. You can have all you want for nothing." He took off his beer-spotted white apron and laid it on a tier of empty cases. "You come along with Sal. I get my boat and guide you where it is."

As an afterthought, the big Portuguese extended his other hand and pressed the full bottle of orange wine he'd been holding on Cade. "But before, up with the bottle. Mamma is saying you look like you need a drink."

The iced bottle felt cold and good in Cade's hand. He wanted to grin and laugh at the same time. It was as if an unbearable weight had been lifted from his shoulders. He uncorked the bottle and drank. "Looking at you, Sal."

"Your health," Sal said, soberly.

PART TWO
UNDERTOW

10
WATER BABY

During the morning it rained. Afternoon was hot, with only a vague suspicion of clouds in a blatantly brassy sky. Except for the distant smoke of a freighter, hull down on the horizon for Tampa, or possibly Martinique or Honduras, as far as Cade could see there was nothing but the undulating sheet of green glass being split by the prow of the cruiser and whipped into a frothy white wake by the powerful churning of the twin screws.

He'd bought a good boat. It pleased him. If he held the speed at which he was traveling, he should raise Grand Terre Island and Grand Pass by mid-afternoon and the acreage on Barataria Bay by early evening.

It had been Sal's idea that Cade ride out the night at anchor. He was glad now that he had. The Gulf was capricious, not to be dealt with lightly. A man needed all his senses. Cade had been born on the water. He had no fear of it. He did have a deep respect. The sharks and the crabs had grown fat on Sunday sailors who treated the Gulf like a salt water mill pond. Great Spanish treasure armadas had tossed like chips on its surface and spilled their stolen gold from Padre Island to the Keys and the Channel of Yucatan.

It was a few minutes of one when, her hair tied in a pony tail, Mimi thrust her head out the open companionway door and smiled, "How you say, lunch is served?"

"You just said it."

Mimi was pleased with her newly acquired phrase. "Then come and get it. Or do you wish to eat on a tray?"

Cade debated briefly. They were well out of the ship lanes. The scene with Janice and Moran was bound to be unpleasant. He had been beaten and framed and put upon. Mimi was the one bright spot in his return to Bay Parish. Instead of racing like mad to deliver her to another man, he might well enjoy her while he could. There were, it said in the book, other things in life besides sex. It said. Cade cut his motors. "No. Don't bother. I'll anchor."

Mimi's smile widened. "Good. The food on a tray, she bobbles."

"Like you, honey," Cade thought.

When the cruiser lost seaway, Cade soaped his lead and tossed his line. They were in thirty fathoms of water, over good grouper bottom. It could be, he might fish for an hour after he and Mimi had eaten. A thick filet cut from a twenty- or thirty-pound red grouper would make a tasty main dish for supper.

The anchor made fast, he rinsed his hands and ran his wet fingers through his hair. The galley looked, somehow, different. Mimi had the knack few women had of doing much with nothing. She'd managed to make the small table look attractive. The hot corned-beef hash and cold asparagus spears looked good. She'd even opened one of the untaxed bottles of tawny port that Sal had insisted on giving him.

"I am good cook, no?" Mimi asked. Her laughter filled the cabin. "All I need is the can opener."

"It looks wonderful," Cade said.

The strain he'd felt with the girl was gone. The deep V of her borrowed white shirt still exposed the cream-colored tops of her round young breasts. The white pants were amply filled. He still wanted her. He couldn't be male and not want her, but his sense of immediate need was gone. He felt as he had the first night when Mimi had stood semi-nude and dripping in the cabin of the *Sea Bird*. Mimi was a good kid. He liked her. Anything that eventuated, if anything ever did, would have to start with her. His black mood of the night before was gone. The world was still filled with good people, men who valued loyalty and friendship, women who were chaste. It was just that the few had ones like Janice and Moran and Tocko and the Squid who stood out by comparison.

The simple meal finished, Cade carried two folding canvas chairs and the partly filled bottle of wine out into the open cockpit. His vague idea of fishing left him. It was good just to sit in the sun and talk to Mimi. She wanted to know how long it would be before they reached the place they were going.

"Some time before dark," Cade told her. "I stood fairly well out from the pass but there's land right over there, just beyond the horizon. In an hour or so, I'll have to cut my speed and start feeling my way through the mud lumps."

Mimi looked out over the green sheet of glass on which the cruiser was resting. "You are anxious to see this Janice?"

Cade glanced at the girl sidewise. "Why should that interest you?"

"I am a woman and curious."

"No. Not particularly," Cade said. "Any affection I had for her is gone, I think. I'm more interested in finding out why I'm being pushed around, why she cleaned me out the way she has."

The expression puzzled Mimi. "Cleaned you out?"

"Sold my property."

"Oh. This land where we are going is ver' valuable?"

"It hasn't been for two hundred years."

"Then why does anyone want it?"

Cade slid down in his chair and shielded his eyes from the sun with the stiff brim of his cap. "That's what puzzles me. In fact I don't get any part of the deal. She is supposed to have sold it to Tocko but according to that waitress in New Orleans, she and Moran have on a big deal of some kind, a deal that has to concern the property." Cade sighed softly. "Then there's Joe Laval."

"The man killed on your boat?"

He nodded. "According to Mamma Salvatore and from what Sal told me last night while we were refueling, it wasn't Tocko who killed Joe or had him killed. Joe was too valuable a stooge."

"Stooge?"

"A cat's-paw, to pull a Slavonian monkey's chestnuts out of the fire."

Mimi clapped her hands. "I 'ave read about that. It 'appened in Mr. Aesop."

Cade's smile was wry. "Also in Bay Parish."

A nagging something in the back of his mind continued to annoy him, as it had at intervals since he'd discovered Joe's body. It was something he'd seen or heard afterward, just before he'd pushed off for New Orleans.

Mimi reached across the space that separated the two chairs and laid her hand on his. "You are so serious."

Cade looked at the small fingers resting on the back of his tanned hand. "Murder is a serious affair, especially when your name is signed to the tab." He reversed the position of their hands. "Now you've asked me a lot of questions. Let me ask you one."

Mimi eyed him suspiciously. "What?"

"You're pretty anxious to reach Moran, aren't you?"

"He is my 'usban'."

"Currently playing house with my former wife."

"Playing house?"

"Sleeping in the same bed."

"But thees we do not know. The nice girl who waited on our table in the restaurant in the hotel said they *seemed* to be business partners."

"During the hours she saw them."

Mimi looked out at the calm green water and said nothing.

Cade played with the fingers under his. "What if you find out Moran pulled a fast one?"

"How you mean?"

"What if you aren't legally married?"

Mimi's laughter filled the cockpit of the boat. "Ha. Before I let Jeem touch me," she lowered her eyes to the deck, "you know how I mean—"

"Yeah," Cade said, shortly. "I know how you mean."

Mimi continued, "At home in Caracas I am insist we go to the priest an' also the registrar, an' I have the papers to prove it."

The sun was hot and intimate. The only motion was the gentle rise and fall of the cruiser on the almost imperceptible swells. It was as if they were alone in the world, a world composed of sky and green sea water. This, too, had been one of Cade's dreams. He continued to play with Mimi's fingers. "Sure. I figured that. But that wouldn't mean a thing if Moran was already married when he married you."

Mimi clung to her faith. "Jeem would not do such a theeng."

"Then why hasn't he answered your letters?"

"Thees I do not know."

"Why didn't he send for you?"

"I do not know thees either."

"But what if I'm right? Then what are you going to do?"

"What if you are right about what?"

"About you and Moran not being legally married."

Mimi's breasts rose with her emotion until they threatened to pop the already strained top button of her borrowed shirt. "Now I 'ave come thees far I will, how you say, cross that bridge when I am come to eet."

Again Cade was tempted to tell her what Miss Spence had told him; again he resisted the temptation. The chances were Mimi wouldn't believe him. She would think he was making it up, hoping to make time on his own.

The semi-tropical sun beating down on the open cockpit was

beginning to make Cade's head ache. Sweat beaded on his face and trickled down his sides. He wished he was in, not on the water. Still, the gentle rise and fall of the cruiser gave him a pleasant feeling. At least one of his dreams had come true. He had a good boat. Perhaps that was as much as a man could expect.

Janice's sale of the old house made sense. Money was all-important to Janice. He could see that now. Janice would sell anything she owned, including herself, if the buyer met her price. But if she had sold the acreage to Tocko, where did Moran come in, and why was she building a fishing lodge on property she no longer owned?

Mimi extracted her hand from under his. "How long were you married to thees Janice?"

"About five years."

"She is pretty?"

"Very."

"Weeth nice body?"

"Very nice."

"So nice as mine?"

Cade attempted to eye the girl beside him dispassionately. "I'd say as far as curves and hollows are concerned you're very similar."

"You were colonel when you were married?"

"Yeah. I was upped from major in the South Pacific, before I was transferred to jets."

"You were happy weeth her?"

Cade wondered what Mimi was getting at. "At least, I thought I was. Yeah. Sure. We got along fine until I was sent to Korea."

"Where you were shot down?"

Cade's eyes hardened as he thought of Joe Laval's welcome. "A big-shot colonel, eh? A hero. Or maybe not such a hero. While the other men you went over with were still dog-fighting all over Mig Alley, you were sitting it out on the ground, shot down over the Yalu."

It had been a hell of a thing for Laval to say. He was glad the lean Cajun bastard was dead. Not every man could be an ace. You had to play the cards as they fell. For every big-shot jet jockey there were a hundred capable pilots who risked their lives hourly without any fanfare or newspaper publicity.

"Over the Yalu," Cade said sourly. "On my fourth mission."

"She thought you were dead?"

"Anyway, missing in action."

"And while you were prisoner, she got the divorce?"

"That's the way it happened."

All Mimi's gestures were emphatic. She shook her black curls. "No."

"No what?"

Mimi leaned forward in her chair. "Thees woman not love you. All the time you thought you were happy, she was jus' sleeping weeth the silver maple leaves on your shoulders."

Cade looked at Mimi, then away. He could smell the natural perfume of her body. Her young flesh looked soft and warm and inviting. He had been hungry for two years. "Could be," he said, sourly. "But isn't that rather dog in the manger?"

"Dog in the manger?" Mimi puzzled.

Cade's headache increased. The glare of the sun on the water hurt his eyes. He stood up abruptly. "Skip it. But if you ever get back to Caracas, look it up in your copy of Aesop."

He stood staring over the side of the boat. The green water looked inviting. "How well do you swim?" he asked Mimi.

She stopped looking puzzled and smiled. "Ver' well. *Madre mia* used to call me her water baby."

Cade's sour mood continued. He didn't care what Mimi's mother had called her. He didn't care why Janice had married him. What he wanted was a woman in his arms and a mattress under the woman. He lighted a cigarette, took two quick puffs, then tossed it overside and searched the wheel locker for the two pairs of cheap swim trunks he'd purchased in Corpus Christi. One of them was red, the other yellow. He held out the yellow pair to Mimi. "Okay. Then let's go for a swim before we start on again."

Mimi's smile turned uncertain. "I would like to, ver' much." She shook her head. "But thees I could not do."

"Why not?"

She touched her breasts with naive candor. "Because up here I would be bare. I do not have something to wear, how you say, topside."

"Wear your bra or a towel."

Still dubious, Mimi accepted the yellow trunks. Her big eyes searched Cade's face. "It—will be all right?"

"Of course," Cade said.

Mimi patted his arm. "Of course. Forgive me that I ask."

She carried the shorts to the forecabin. Cade made certain that the anchor was fast and that there was a secured rope dangling overside. Then, slipping into the red trunks, he used the transom of the cruiser for a diving board.

The water was cool, almost cold. Cade dove as deeply as he could, then fought his way even farther down. When he surfaced again, both his sense of immediate need and his headache were gone. He circled the boat in a fast crawl. The cool water and the physical exertion cleared his head. He felt good. He felt fine.

He turned on his back and floated as Mimi climbed up on the transom. She made a pretty picture. She'd knotted one of the galley dish towels and fastened it with a safety pin to form an attractive halter. The yellow trunks were much shorter and tighter on her than the red trunks were on him. Cade was proud of himself. If he got Mimi to Barataria Bay unharmed, Colonel Cade Cain could recommend civilian Cade Cain for a medal, for forebearance above and beyond the call of nature.

Mimi waved gaily, then cut the water in a perfect dive. She dove as well as she did everything else and she had no fear.

They swam for half an hour, racing, up-ending, scrambling up the rope from time to time to use the front of the cruiser as a diving board.

Cade had never felt more tranquil, more at peace. He was resting, floating on his back, when he saw the first dark cloud and realized the wind had begun to blow. There was a perceptible difference in the feel and the look of the water. He turned on his side and called, "We'd best get aboard and up anchor. It looks like we're in for some wind."

Mimi nodded. "Whatever you say."

The cruiser was swinging gently now. The rope that had been dangling to starboard was hanging over the transom. Cade scrambled aboard and leaned down to help Mimi up. As she came up over the varnished wood, the knotted towel caught on the chrome burgee standard and the safety pin opened.

The gesture was instinctive, normal, natural. Cade had taken all he could. He pulled Mimi into his arms, his free hand cupping her young loveliness, his lips pressed to hers, as they stood straining together, dripping salt water on the deck plates.

The words were a sob in Mimi's throat. "No. We must not. Thees ees wrong."

Her fingers tangled in Cade's wet hair, for a long moment she returned his frenzied kisses, every curve and contour of her young body throbbing with desire. Then she went suddenly limp in his arms. Her flesh was still firm but cold. The cheeks Cade were kissing were salty with tears. The eyes searching his face were big and black and hurt.

She had asked if it would be all right. He had told her it would. Mimi had trusted him. She had even removed her knife.

Cade forced himself to release her, recovered the knotted towel from the burgee standard. The pitch of the anchored boat was much more pronounced now. His voice was as thick as the rapidly gathering clouds.

"I'm sorry."

Mimi held the towel in front of her. "I'm sorry, too," she said, quietly. "So ver' sorry. I weesh I could tell you how sorry."

Somehow dignified and regal despite the fact that all she had on was a pair of too tight yellow swim shorts, she turned and entered the cabin, closing the door gently behind her.

Cade drained the nearly empty bottle of port he found rolling beside one of the canvas deck chairs. Then, eyeing the windblown clouds, he started his motor and up anchored, just as the first sheet of blinding rain drenched the bobbing cruiser.

The Gulf was no longer green. It was a deepening rain-pocked purple. The swells grew even more pronounced. After setting his course, Cade glanced back. The triangular dorsal fin of a curious twenty-foot shark was crisscrossing the area in which he and Mimi had been swimming.

It had been a foolish thing to do. A dozen things could have happened. It wasn't his fault they hadn't. Between lulls in the puffs of wind, he could hear Mimi crying in the cabin. Because he'd gone as far as he had? Because he hadn't gone farther?

Women.

Cade opened the motor full throttle for the run to the big south mud lump and braced himself as the twin screws bit into the water.

11
HOME TO JANICE

Cade glanced at his watch. It was twenty minutes of eight. It would be dark in a few more minutes. The rain and wind had lasted less than an hour but left a vicious chop behind them. The run from the mouth of the pass had taken longer than he had thought it would. Now he was bucking an outgoing tide.

In the deepening dusk the big south mud lump glided past to starboard. Cade cut his speed still more and swept the mud lump with his searchlight. The tide was full. Only portions of the lump were visible. The six men he had seen were gone, chum for the crabs and the fishes.

It was tricky business running the mud lumps in the dark. Cade considered anchoring for the night and decided against it. Now he was this close, he wanted to get to the showdown with Janice right away. He wanted to get Mimi out of his hair. He didn't want to spend another night aboard the boat with her.

Her eyes swollen from crying, Mimi appeared in the doorway of the cabin. She was wearing the dress and hose and high-heeled shoes he had bought her in New Orleans. Her voice was as sullen as her eyes.

"Do you want me to fix you something to eat?"

Cade shook his head. "Don't bother. We should be inside in another hour." He felt impelled to hurt her. "Besides, I might be tempted to anchor."

In the faint glow from the red and green lights on the instrument panel, Mimi looked as if she were about to cry again. "I said I was sorry."

Cade felt as if he were shouting at her. "Okay. So we're both sorry. If you're hungry, fix something to eat. But don't light any lights and stop bothering me or I'm apt to run us aground."

He cut the speed of the cruiser until he barely had seaway. The channel was narrow and tricky here, but once he was through Grand Pass he would be in open water again. Jean LaFitte, long ago, had anchored in the Bay. He had even maneuvered his barkentines and cutters through the narrow series of watercourses that helped drain the Mississippi at a point opposite New Orleans. LaFitte had used the inland route to bring his booty to the city.

Mimi gnawed at her lower lip. "Well, don't shout at me."

"I'm not shouting," Cade shouted.

He turned on his running lights, wishing to Christ he'd come into the Bay the short way. Still, if he'd cut through the series of watercourses instead of stopping at Bay Parish, he wouldn't know he was wanted for murder. Even if he couldn't do anything about it, it was always best for a man to know where he stood, especially with the law or a woman.

Mimi remained in the doorway of the cabin. "How do you know where you're going?"

Cade tried to explain and couldn't. A man could explain sailing on compass. But feeling his way through the dark was something else. It was like flying a jet. A man either could or he couldn't. It was a combination of things, of having threaded the channel a hundred times before, the sound and the feel of the screws, the color of his wake, an occasional familiar landmark.

"I've been here before," he said. "How's for breaking out another bottle of wine? As long as we're about to see our respective mates, we ought to celebrate the occasion."

"Whatever you say," Mimi said. She opened her mouth to say more, then changed her mind and disappeared into the cabin to reappear a few moments later with an opened bottle of the tawny port that Sal had given them.

As she extended her hand with the bottle the cruiser scraped over a mud bar and Cade, instinctively, held his breath. When he could speak again, he said, "You first. *Saludos*."

"No, thank you," Mimi said primly. "I nevair drink on the empty stomach."

Cade drank from the neck of the bottle. The wine tasted weak and insipid. He wished it was Jamaica rum. He wished he was roaring drunk. He wished Mimi was Janice or that he was James Moran. He could tell himself that Mimi meant nothing to him, that she was just another girl he'd met, but once she went out of this new life he was leading, he doubted if anything would ever be quite the same again. It was more than physical. He liked her.

He took a second big drink, then corked the bottle. If only he'd met Mimi before she'd met Moran. But when Mimi had met Moran, he'd still been married to Janice. Or had he? Not that it made any difference.

He was through the pass now, in deep water again. He could tell by the bite of the screws. There was no wind here, no swells, no chop. The Bay was a sheet of black glass, broken only by the white wake and the occasional phosphorescent slap of a leaping fish. Except for the purr of the motors and the throb of the underwater exhaust, the only sound was the crying of the startled birds roosting in the offshore islands.

The Bay was huge and black and mysterious and somehow sinister, much as it must have been in the days of Jean LaFitte. Its population fluctuated. People came and people left. The moon was still entangled in the trees rising from the wooded shoreline. It was too dark to see, but Cade doubted if the Bay, at least this section of it had changed. Even if it were daylight, all he would be able to see would be a few crude fishing camps, the rare cabins of muskrat and wild rice hunters squatting along the watercourses leading inland.

The thought amused Cade. It could be there were squatters on his land. Seven years of squatting established proprietary rights. If any of them cared to contest the sale the court might decide for them! It would serve Janice and Tocko right.

The moon rose from the branches of the trees and seemed to spotlight the white cruiser. The night wind was cool on his cheek, like soft black velvet threaded with silver.

As he rounded a vaguely familiar landmark, a spit of land, Mimi spoke for the first time since she had handed him the bottle. "You are ver' good sailor."

"Thank you," Cade said. He wished he hadn't drunk the wine. It hadn't helped. What he wanted didn't come in bottles.

"We are almost there?"

Cade searched the moonlit shoreline. "I'd say we're abreast of my property now, but it's been some time since I've been here." He located a pin prick of light. "That should be the camp dead ahead."

"There is a building?"

"A shack. My father and I used it maybe three or four times a year."

"How many rooms in the shack?"

"One."

Mimi wet her lips with her tongue. "Oh."

The pin prick of light brightened and became a shaded high-watt bulb outlining a substantial pier extending out into deep water. There was a fast-looking single-stack cutter tied to the pier and several smaller boats in the slips leading into it. Whatever use Janice had found for the acreage came under the head of big business.

Cade warped the boat into an empty slip. The shack he and his father had built was gone, replaced by a substantial two-story log lodge with a half-dozen small cottages flanking the main building. Back of the lodge he thought he could see a landing strip. Only the lodge was lighted.

He cut his motors and made fast.

"You said it was a shack," Mimi pouted.

"Yeah, it was," Cade said.

He started to step up on the pier and Mimi stopped him. "You are so anxious to see your Janice you are going ashore like that?"

Cade ran his hands down his sides and realized he was still wearing the red swim shorts. They and his cap were all he had on.

He put on his last clean shirt and white pants. The heavy .38 caliber pistol made an uncomfortable bulge in his hip pocket. Cade transferred it to his side pants pocket and slipped his bare feet into his sneakers. Mimi was waiting in the cockpit. He helped her up on the pier, then stepped ashore.

The pier was new. The smell of freshly milled lumber and the reek of creosote was strong. The cross planks were laid but still had to be spiked. Cade stood, his cap on the back of his head looking up at the lighted lodge.

Mimi was impatient with him. "For why are you waiting?"

"Just wondering," Cade told her.

"Wondering what?"

"If I'm walking into a trap."

He looked from the lighted lodge to the dark mat of vegetation rising back of the narrow beach. Seemingly, the pier and the beach were deserted. The only sounds he could hear were the whispering of the wind, the night noises in the swamp and the rhythmic *thud thud* of the gasoline power plant supplying the juice for the lights.

"Trap?" Mimi puzzled.

Cade didn't bother to answer. Janice had sold him out. She'd dirtied his name with Tocko. She was doing the same with Moran. She knew he had been released. She had good reason to fear him. It seemed logical to assume that she would expect him to catch up with her and she would prepare some defense against him.

The something he'd heard or seen in Bay Parish continued to nag at his mind. Suddenly he remembered what it was. Of course. He'd heard the sound of a small plane warming up. Moran was a flyer. It was only a few minutes by air from Bay Parish to where he stood. If Moran had been in Bay Parish he knew that Joe Laval was dead and that Tocko had signed a warrant charging Cade with the murder. All Janice had to do to protect herself was to have the local sheriff waiting.

Mimi swatted at a mosquito. "I am uncomfortable here. The bugs are biting me."

"Besides, you're anxious to get to Moran."

"After all, he is my 'usban'."

"Sure," Cade said. "Before you let Jeem touch you, you insisted he take you to the priest and also the registrar." He cupped one of Mimi's elbows. "Okay. Let's go see what's what."

His sneakers made no sound but the loose planks rattled under his weight. The click of Mimi's high heels sounded unnaturally loud in the moonlit silence.

Along with the other improvements, a beach had been pumped in and they had to wade through two hundred feet of loose sand to reach the wide porch of the lodge. The cypress-paneled foyer was huge, with a natural stone fireplace at each end. The furniture was new, oversized and leather. A deeply tanned youth wearing oil-stained slacks and a clean white seaman's skivy was standing behind a small hotel desk, tinkering with the star drag on a deep-sea reel. He didn't look like a hotel clerk to Cade.

The youth laid down the reel and looked at Cade's white captain's cap. "I thought I heard a boat put in. Don't tell me you came down from the city in the dark?"

Cade shook his head. "No. Up from Southwest Pass."

"That's an even tougher haul. You must know these waters."

"I do."

The youth fumbled under the desk and found a registration card. "Well, we aren't really open yet but I think we can take care of you. A room for you and the missus? Or do you want one of the private cottages?"

"Neither," Cade said. He leaned an elbow on the desk. It was an effort for him to use the name. "Mrs. Cain is here?"

"Yes, sir, she is."

"Could I see her?" It was more of a statement than a question.

"I don't see why not."

Mimi asked, almost shyly, "And Mr. James Moran? He, too, is here?"

The youth back of the desk looked puzzled. "Yeah. Sure. They're both here. They came down a few days ago to get the place ready for the grand opening next week. Who shall I say wants to see them?"

He turned as the door behind the desk opened and a striking girl wearing horn-rimmed harlequin glasses emerged carrying a handful of papers.

"These reservations, John—" she began, then used her free hand to rip off her glasses and stared at the couple in front of the desk. "Cade. Cade, darling," she screamed. "You're home!"

Cade instinctively sucked in his breath. He could feel the blood pounding in his temples. Janice hadn't changed. Her hair was still the color of ripe wheat. Her green-gray eyes were wide set and intelligent. The high, firm, peaked breasts he'd dreamed of in Pyongyang still strained against the bodice of the smartly simple cotton dress she was wearing. Neither Tocko nor Moran showed. Her deep tan was becoming. It made her face look even younger than he remembered it, almost virginal.

The papers flew one way, the glasses another, as she rushed into his arms, laughing and crying at the same time. "Oh, my darling, my darling."

Cade felt like a goddamn fool. He stood mute, motionless, embarrassed, holding the familiar body lightly. It wasn't the reception he'd expected. Janice wasn't afraid of him. She seemed genuinely glad to see him.

Janice pressed her lips to his and talked into his mouth. "Then you did get my letters and my cable."

Cade felt even more like a fool. "No," he said, flatly. He tilted the girl's saucy chin with a crooked forefinger. "Why so glad to see the returned hero? I thought you divorced me."

Janice brushed the divorce aside as immaterial. "Oh, that," she said, lightly. "I can explain that." Her lower lip quivered. Her green-gray eyes filled with tears. "Well, aren't you going to kiss me? Aren't you glad to see *me?*"

12
BED AND BLONDE

Cade decided he didn't like Moran. The big man smiled too much. He showed too many teeth when he smiled. He was too glib, too hail-fellow-well-met. And Cade didn't like the way he looked at Mimi. He'd met men like Moran before. There was nothing of which the big black Irishman wouldn't be capable.

Cade looked across the littered table at Mimi. Mimi had drunk too much wine. Her eyes were unnaturally bright. She sat looking at the face of the man beside her like a small white kitten fascinated by a big sleek tom.

Janice had finished her meal, and now was saying, "I know how it must have looked to you, Cade. But think of the spot I was in. To all intents and purposes, except legally, you were dead."

"So you divorced me."

Janice played with his fingers. "All right. So I made a mistake. But at the time, nothing mattered. I thought I'd lost you forever." She was frank. "I had myself to look out for."

"So you came back to Bay Parish and sold my property to Tocko Kalavitch."

"I sold the house."

"He lies," Moran said. "That's one of the reasons I broke up with Tocko."

"Why?"

"Because he was trying to push Janice around. His only claim to the property is pre-emption. You see, as soon as he heard you'd been shot down he moved right in and built this lodge, figuring no one would ever call him."

"For what purpose?" Cade asked. "I mean, why did he build it?"

Moran was apparently as frank as Janice had been. "As a drop for aliens." He lighted a Turkish cigarette. "Oh, not your run-of-the-deck five-hundred-dollar a head wetbacks but the big shots who had to get out of where they were. Men who could afford to pay through the nose. Big shots, for instance, who'd bucked even bigger shots behind the Iron Curtain. Men for whom the MVD were looking."

"MVD?" Mimi hiccupped.

"Russian secret police," Cade explained. "Short for Ministry of the Interior, formerly NKVD, *Narodny Kommissar Vnutrenych Del* or People's Commissariat for the Interior."

Moran laughed easily. "You seem to know."

"I just spent some time north of the Yalu," Cade replied dryly.

Moran went on, "Anyway, he started pushing Janice around. I wasn't too happy in what I was doing. So when she came up with the idea of making a swank hideaway of this place and offered me a cut if I'd help get it started, I jumped at the chance." He patted Mimi's hand. "What the hell? I'm no angel but then I'm not a complete heel and some of Tocko's business methods gagged me."

Cade drank the dregs of his highball. "Such as?"

Moran met his eyes. "Such as six guys one of his boats brought in and because a Coast Guard cutter was getting too close, he dropped them off on big south mud lump. That way the respectable shrimp fleet owner, Tocko Kalavitch, wouldn't have to take a fall." Moran added virtuously, "At least, when I was flying guys in from Martinique and Caracas, I fulfilled my contract. I set them ashore on the mainland."

Janice snuggled even closer to Cade. "Then, when I heard you'd been released, I wrote right away and I cabled. I even called Tokyo, long distance, but your old wing commander said you'd been flown to Hawaii and from there to the States." She smiled. "But I knew that sooner or later my letters or my cable would catch up with you. And all the time we were in New Orleans, at a flea bag called the Royal Crescent, arranging for publicity, and a charter for Jim to fly patrons down here, and soliciting political support, in case Tocko tried to make trouble—well, I expected the phone to ring any minute and you to say you were down in the lobby. I left a forwarding address at the post office. So did Jim."

"I see," Cade said.

It was a smooth, plausible story, the type of half-truth that Janice would concoct. He wondered if she thought he would believe her and how far she would go in her attempt to make her story stand up.

Moran tried to refill Mimi's glass. She shook her head. "No, thank you. I 'ave plenty."

He brushed her hair with his lips. "The whole thing has been a tragic mix-up but I see how it happened now, at least, as far as Mimi and I are concerned."

Mimi looked less like a little white kitten than she had. "How?" she asked flatly.

"You addressed your letters to me in care of Tocko, didn't you?"

"In care of Mr. Kalavitch, Bay Parish, Louisiana."

"And there you are. If you'll pardon the expression, the louse never turned them over to me. And that old witch of a postmistress is just as bad. Probably because Tocko paid her not to, she never sent out my letters to you."

Mimi's accent became more pronounced. "Then you deed write?"

"Every week. I even sent you passage money to join me, three hundred and twenty-five dollars." Moran lit a cigarette from the stub of the one he was smoking. "Maybe we can sue the old bag for interfering with the mail or destroying money orders."

Cade wondered if Mimi believed Moran. It was hard to tell. Her big eyes gave no clue to the way the wheels in her mind were turning.

Janice pushed her chair back from the table. "It's getting late." She stroked the back of Cade's hand with her fingers. "I know that Jim and Mimi want to be alone." She bent and kissed Cade's cheek. "And it's been more than two years since I've seen you, darling. We can talk this all out in the morning. I'm only glad it's turned out the way it has."

Moran smoothly helped Mimi to her feet. "Come on, darling. I guess we can take a hint."

Mimi stood, swaying slightly, her eyes searching Moran's face. "You are certain you wrote me? You are certain you sent me the passage?"

Moran kissed the tip of her nose. "Of course. And I can tell you I was plenty hurt when I didn't hear from you."

Janice laughed. "Hurt? The man was furious. He thought one of two things had happened. Either your family forced you to annul the marriage and wouldn't even let you answer his letters or you'd met one of your own countrymen you liked better than you did him."

"Oh," Mimi said. The word could mean anything. Her eyes still uncertain, glancing at Cade from time to time, almost as if she expected him to stop them, she allowed Moran to propel her across the floor of the dining room.

Janice linked her arm through one of Cade's and followed them. "The hell with the dishes. The full staff won't be down until Thursday but there's a girl who lives back in the swamp who comes in every day."

The wood-paneled lobby was deserted. The reel was still on the counter but the youth Cade had seen behind the desk was gone. Here the night noises of the swamp and the *thud thud* of the gasoline power plant were more pronounced than they had been in the dining room. A long, dimly lighted hall led to the rear of the building. Beside the entrance to the hall a stairway led up to a balcony and rooms on the second floor.

Moran locked the front door of the lodge, while Janice turned out most of the lights.

And so to bed, Cade thought. Both Moran and Janice had lied about one thing. They were more than business partners. They were two of a kind and they worked very well together. Smooth. Like the flesh on the inside of a woman's thigh, Cade told himself.

Finished with locking the front door, Moran took Mimi's arm again and walked her toward the hall. "Well, see you both in the morning."

"In the morning," Janice said. She stood, with one hand on the rail of the stairs leading to the upper floor. "Goodnight."

A few feet down the hall, Mimi turned. "Good night, Cade," she said, softly. "Thank you for being so kind. You are, as we say, true *caballero*."

Cade wished he could see her face.

"Sure," Moran said, soberly. "I owe you a lot, fellow. And I'll make it right with you, too." He opened one of the doors in the hall, stood aside to allow Mimi to pass him, then closed the door quietly behind them.

"My room is upstairs," Janice said.

Cade realized a lump had formed in his throat. He followed Janice up the stairs and waited while she unlocked the door of a room opening off the balcony, still wondering how far she intended to go to make her fantastic story stand up.

As Janice lighted a bed lamp made from a polished cypress knee, she smiled. "This was to have been one of the guest rooms, at twenty-five dollars a day. But now that you're home, we'll keep it for ourselves." Janice switched on another lamp, on the dressing table. "You came by boat, honey?"

"That's right."

"Your own?"

"A thirty-eight foot twin-screw job that I bought in Corpus."

"How wonderful," Janice enthused. "That gives us another guide boat." She patted his cheek. "And a good man to handle it. You should see the reservations, darling. We're booked practically solid for the season. And why shouldn't we be? This will be the only resort of its kind, the best fishing and swimming in the world, the utmost in privacy with no questions asked. And only a few minutes by air from New Orleans."

Cade continued to study the room. It was entirely feminine. The bedspread was pastel silk. So were the drapes on the windows. The open closet door revealed only dresses. If Moran had shared the room with Janice, there were no visible signs of his occupancy.

Cade walked to the screened window and looked out. Night lay dark and heavy on the Bay. The moon was waning. The stars seemed less bright. The only light was the bulb on the pier. Even at the distance, he could see the *Sea Bird* tugging at her mooring ropes and, beyond her, the dark bulk of the cutter.

"Who owns the cutter?" he asked.

"The contractor who's building the pier," Janice said. "His men are living aboard."

Cade wondered how big a fool Janice thought he was. A contractor wouldn't use a cutter. He'd use a tug and a barge. Something more than renting luxury rooms to amorous businessmen with attractive secretaries and a secondary desire to fish was being planned for the lodge. Well, he'd wanted a showdown with Janice—and here he was.

As Cade turned from the window he realized he was still carrying his cap. He hung it on the back of a chair. Janice kicked off her shoes and, sitting on the bench in front of the dressing table, began to comb her hair, smiling at him in the mirror between strokes.

The lump in Cade's throat dissolved. His knees were suddenly weak. The whole scene was fantastic. It was exactly as he had dreamed it would be, only grotesquely distorted and somehow sordid.

Janice met his eyes in the mirror and stopped smiling. "You're still angry with me, aren't you, darling?"

Cade was frank. "I don't know what to think."

"You've been listening to the nasty narrow little minds in Bay Parish."

"Among other things."

"What things?"

"After all, you did divorce me."

"I thought I explained that."

"You might have waited."

Janice nodded. "Yes. I should have known better. I see now I was wrong. But at the time it seemed the logical thing to do."

"What beats me is how you managed it," he said. "You had no real grounds, here or in any other state. And all the courts were turning thumbs down on proceedings against G.I.'s in combat abroad."

"I didn't get the divorce in this state, but it was the pollys here who fixed it for me through their connections. I told you—I'm pretty thick with them. I have been for some time."

"So is Tocko, I bet," growled Cade.

It was hot and close in the room. The gun in Cade's pocket felt too heavy.

Janice continued to study his face in the mirror. "You're very angry with me, aren't you?"

"I don't know what to think."

"Put yourself in my position."

"I'm trying to."

Finished with her hair, Janice stood up and caught the hem of her dress with both hands. "Angry enough to shoot me?"

"I don't know."

"Isn't that why you brought the gun?"

Cade breathed hard as Janice pulled her dress over her head and hung it neatly on a hanger. All she was wearing under the dress was a short white petticoat and her hose. He'd forgotten how truly lovely she was. Janice meant, obviously, to go all the way to back her claim that she still loved him, that she'd thought he was dead, that all she had really done was to look out for herself.

Janice came back to the bed, stripped off the pastel silk spread and folded it neatly. Then, sitting on the edge of the bed, she rolled down one of her hose, her blonde hair falling over her face, as Cade had dreamed a thousand times of seeing it fall.

"I can't say I blame you," she said. "From your point of view, it was a nasty, despicable thing for me to do. But any mistakes I've made have been of the head and not of the heart. So I'm an avaricious little bitch, I can't help it." She brushed her hair out of her eyes and hooked her thumbs in the elastic waistband of the petticoat. "I've seen too many wives of dead and 'missing' officers running billing machines or clerking in dime stores. And I wasn't having any."

The petticoat followed her hose to the floor and she sat looking up at Cade with her gray-green eyes slitted and sullen, reminding him somewhat of Mimi.

"Well—?" Janice asked, quietly. "Well—?"

13
THE FUTILE GUN

The night heat fondled Cade's body with little, black, moist fingers. He lay looking at the ceiling that he couldn't see, acutely conscious of Janice's breathing. He'd never felt so emotionally or physically depleted.

This was the dream he'd dreamed?

He moved slightly and Janice moved with him, as if even in her sleep she was reluctant to lose contact. Whatever else she was not, Janice definitely was a good actress. For some reason of her own, she wanted him to think she was still in love with him. She'd done her best to further the illusion. Just the same, her best hadn't been enough. Cade felt shamed and put upon and soiled—as if he'd been had. What Janice had given him held little value for her. She'd given the same to Tocko and Moran. Cade was certain of that now. Janice had been too eager to please him. There was something in the back of her greedy little mind, something for which she still needed him.

Cade eased his way to the edge of the bed and the spring, giving under his weight, made the bed sway like a boat. Over the shrilling of the cicadas and the booming of the frogs, he could hear Mimi's small, militant voice.

"Thees woman no love you. All the time you thought you were happy, she was just sleeping weeth the silver maple leaves on your shoulders."

Cade wondered what Mimi was thinking now. He felt a twinge of remorse. Still, all he had done was what she had asked him to do. She'd been determined to get to Moran. He hoped she was satisfied.

The air in the room was stifling him. Carefully, so as not to awaken Janice, Cade eased out of bed and dressed. Perhaps it would be cooler on the pier. Perhaps he could think more clearly. Janice's talk of a swank resort was a lot of foolishness. There weren't enough rooms in the lodge to make it pay. The pier had cost more than she could hope to take in in five seasons. Then there was the single-stack cutter. She and Moran were up to something, something that tied in with Janice's hectic affair with Tocko, with his being warned out of Bay Parish by Joe Laval, with Laval being murdered.

As he felt his way down the dim stairs to the lobby, Cade wondered if it were possible that Moran had shot Laval. He'd heard a light plane in Bay Parish. Moran was a flyer.

The silence in the lobby was complete. Cade turned too sharply at the foot of the stairs and the gun bulging his pocket slammed against the newel post. The silence magnified the sound. Cade stood holding his breath, looking down the hall at the door of the room into which Moran and Mimi had disappeared and realized he was jealous. After what he'd just been through with Janice!

Men, Cade decided, were complex creatures, almost as complex as women. He reached for the hook of the front screen door and found it already unhooked. Someone else had been unable to sleep. Moran? Mimi? The youth he'd seen behind the desk?

Cade waded the loose sand to the pier. The air sweeping over the dark bay was cooler and cleaner there. There was a faint slap of waves on the beach and farther out, a suggestion of whitecaps. Cade turned his attention from the water to the cutter made fast to the T-shaped pier. A white "S" enclosed in a white circle was painted on the stack. The insignia was vaguely familiar. Cade tried to place it and couldn't. One thing, however, was certain. The cutter was built for speed. It was not a contractor's boat.

He turned and looked back at the lodge. Only the lobby was lighted. There were no lights in any of the other rooms. Cade tried to put Mimi out of his mind. So Moran was a bastard. So, according to Miss Spence, he had at least three other wives. What happened to Mimi wasn't any of his affair. She'd stowed away in La Guaira to join Moran. She'd swum the river in the dark. She'd kept herself pure for the guy. Cade hoped she was happy.

He started to turn back to the pier and stopped as a faint light, feeling its way out past a drawn shade, showed in one of the cottages. So a cottage was occupied, and not by a tired businessman and his amorous secretary.

Cade raised his eyes to the tall web of steel behind the cottage. It was the first time he'd noticed the tower. It was substantial, solid. It looked like a professional two-way affair, perhaps a ship-to-shore sending outfit. Either that or a powerful ham set.

In a luxury fishing lodge?

Cade felt the butt of the gun in his pocket, as he walked out on the pier. The small cruisers he'd noticed were old work tubs with peeling paint. Sandwiched between them were several new skiffs, one a fourteen-foot job, powered with a new fifteen horsepower Sea Horse with two cruise-a-day tanks. Janice was getting money from somewhere, more, a lot more, than she could have possibly gotten from the sale of the old house.

Sweat started on his face again and trickled down his sides. He wished now he'd stayed in New Orleans. He hadn't accomplished a thing by coming to the Bay. His intended showdown with Janice had turned out to be just a show—an amorous interlude that had been all play-acting and had left him disgusted with both himself and her. He still didn't know a thing more than he'd known when he first heard Janice had been in Bay Parish and had sold his properties.

He stooped to feel the tautness of one of the lines mooring the *Sea Bird* and the sweat dribbling down his sides turned cold. There was someone behind the next piling. Cade drew his gun from his pocket and looked around the piling. Mimi was sitting on the far side, swinging her bare feet over the planking.

She looked up at him with wet eyes, "'Allo."

In the light from the bulb on the pier head, Cade could see that her face was stained with tears and that the bodice of her dress had been torn and pinned together.

He returned the gun to his pocket, lighted a cigarette and squatted down beside her. "Smoke?"

Mimi took the offered cigarette. "Thank you."

Cade had a fair idea of what had happened. He wished he could think of something to say to comfort her. It wasn't nice to see a dream dissolve. He knew.

Mimi sucked at the cigarette in silence. Then, wiping her wet cheeks with the back of one hand, she announced, "Is all right now. I weel not cry any more."

"It didn't go so good, huh?"

Mimi shook her head. "No. I 'ave been ver' *bobo*, like you say, a leetle fool."

"In what way?"

"Jeem has no affection for me."

"No?"

"No." Mimi's small chin jutted. "All he did was use me in Caracas. I was ver' pleasant way for him to spend a week. I am not even his wife."

"He admitted it?"

Mimi shook her head. "No." She put her free hand on her left breast. "It is a feeling I have here. I could tell when we were alone." Her breathing grew labored. "He has no love for me. All I am to him is a woman. All he wanted was encore. And when I wouldn't he hit me with his fist and knocked me down on the bed."

The bitterness in his voice surprised Cade. "Why didn't you use your knife?"

Mimi's bitterness matched his own. "Because he took it away from me." She studied her bare feet. "But my knife and my shoes were all he did get." She began to cry without sound. "It is funny, no, how you can want someone so badly and then not be in love at all? That is why my dress is torn. And now I do not know what to do."

"How about going back to Caracas?"

"No. My family would not receive me."

Cade sighed. "I tried to tell you. Miss Spence, that's the postmistress in Bay Parish, said the return addresses of at least three other girls writing him read—Mrs. James Moran."

"Now you tell me thees."

"Would you have believed me if I had told you before?"

Mimi thought a moment. "No." She continued to cry without sound.

"Where is Moran now?"

"I don't know. He called me bad names and tried to stop me but I ran from the room an' out here."

Cade looked back at the lodge. Janice's window was lighted. She was awake and knew he was gone. It could be Moran was with her, comparing notes.

What wind there had been had died. The bay no longer lapped at the beach. The whitecaps were gone. Cade began to sweat again. His throat contracted. The roof of his mouth was dry. He felt as if he were sitting on a cork waiting for all hell to pop.

"Rest and quiet, that's an order, Colonel" the medic in Tokyo had told him. "When you get back to the States buy a boat, take it easy. Crawl into the bunk with your wife and a jug of rum and don't get out of the sack for two months."

So he'd bought a boat. He'd drunk a few bottles of rum. He'd even been to bed with his wife; that is, his former wife. All that was missing was the rest and quiet, with a murder charge and Mimi added. The situation had all the qualities of a nightmare. Cade was almost afraid to open his mouth for fear the mounting hysteria inside him would rush out.

The squatting position cramped his legs. Cade stood up and lighted a second cigarette. Mimi stood beside him. "But what are you doing here?"

Cade told her. "I'm in the same boat you are, baby. Janice is still sleeping with my maple leaves. I still have something she wants."

"What?"

"I don't know, but she doesn't care any more for me than Moran does for you."

Mimi's Latin temper got the best of her tears. She shoved out her little jaw. "Then why did they bother to lie? Why did they not just tell us to go away?"

"I don't know," Cade said.

His feeling of attempting to climb a sheer glass wall returned. He felt unutterably tired. Nothing made sense. Nothing had made sense since his return to Bay Parish. He watched the black water lap at the hull of the *Sea Bird*, thinking that if his tanks were filled instead of empty, a partial solution of his problem would be to feel his way back up the series of inland watercourses to New Orleans and turn the whole matter over to the law. It was too big for him.

He turned his attention to the skiff with the attached outboard motor. The small port of Grand Isle was only a few miles away. He and Mimi could easily make it in the skiff but running away wouldn't solve anything. Besides, he had no reason to run. He hadn't killed Laval. All he'd done was come home.

Mimi followed his eyes and sniffed. "I 'ad outboard like that in Caracas harbor. At La Guaira."

Cade knew a moment of irritation. He had enough problems of his own without worrying about Mimi. He wished she were back in Caracas. Or did he? He'd never known any girl he'd liked so much in so short a time. Mimi was everything Janice wasn't.

He lifted his eyes from the skiff to the sky as he heard a familiar drone. There was only one sound like it. He waited for the lights on the landing strip to come on. They didn't. Instead, all the lights in the lodge winked out and the door of the radio shack opened briefly to spill an indeterminate number of men into the night. Then all was dark again.

Mimi tried to locate the sound. "Is plane."

Cade continued to study the clouds. "A helicopter," he corrected her. "And from the sound, a big one." He slipped the gun from his pocket. "You wait here."

"No," Mimi said determinedly. "No. Wherever you go, I am going."

There was the pad of bare feet on the deck of the cutter. The crew men, roused from their sleep, wearing only their shorts, leaned on the aft rail, studying the night sky, as if they were watching a show.

Cade looked from the yawning men to the dark lodge, then walked back down the pier to the stretch of pumped-in beach. From the sound of the revolving planes, the 'copter was having trouble locating the strip.

Drop a flare, you fool, Cade thought.

Then the depth of the nightmare increased. From somewhere back of the lodge a voice that could only be Tocko's called, "Okay. Show your lights, boys, so Charlie can come in."

Closer at hand, Moran's voice answered profanely, "I'll shoot the first bastard who does. I might have known you'd try to foul up the deal by pulling something like this?"

A flashlight beam stabbed the sky, followed by a shot.

"I warned you," Moran said.

Cade walked around the unlighted lodge with Mimi panting beside him. Its huge planes revolving slowly, the helicopter was hovering over the landing strip now. Then a second and a third and a forth flashlight beam pierced the sky and the pilot set it down. As he did, a dozen shots thudded into the metal and from the far side of the strip. Tocko called:

"Find Moran, Squid."

The Squid's thin voice answered, "I'll find him."

A second burst of scattered shots evoked an echoing chorus of frightened foreign voices from the plane. No one else seemed excited. It was business with them and this was their business. Cade watched, fascinated, as a searchlight moved across the field and pinpointed the landed plane. The bronze-faced youth he'd seen in a booth at Sal's with Tocko and the Squid was at the controls. He brushed at the light on his face, more annoyed than worried, as he urged the frantic passengers in the cabin to descend the ladder. Then someone on the far side of the landing strip shot out the light with a rifle.

Cade rounded the corner of the lodge and was forcibly stopped by a muscular arm. "You!" Moran said. "As the saying goes, you should have stood in bed."

Cade caught a glint of blued steel in Moran's hand and raised his own gun. "For God's sake, someone make sense before I put in for

Section Eight. What's this all about?"

Moran was amused. "Now he's going to shoot me. Some of you boys keep that pain-queer pinhead off me while I take care of the colonel. The little bastard couldn't be a good sport and die in Pyongyang. He would have to come back."

"Make sense," Cade repeated. "What's this all about?"

"Money," Moran laughed. "A hell of a lot of money." His bulk huge in the dark, the big man moved toward Cade slowly until the buckle of his belt was almost flush with the muzzle of Cade's gun. "Go ahead. Shoot."

Cade lowered his gun in sudden tardy suspicion and triggered a shot at the ground. There was only a sharp click of metal on metal. Cade wondered how he could have been such a fool! He wouldn't have been if it hadn't been for the dream. In the back of his mind, knowing better, he'd still hoped to make it come true.

He knew now why Janice had been so eager to resume her marital obligations. It hadn't been love. It hadn't even been passion. It had been cold calculation. She and Moran could see he was armed and had good reason to kill them both and neither she nor Moran had any intention of being sporting about it. They'd wanted him set up like a sitting duck on a pond. So sometime during the frenzied interlude in her bedroom, while his attention had been elsewhere, Janice had extracted the bullets from his gun.

Cade attempted to reverse the weapon and use it as a club but the barrel of Moran's gun sliced viciously through the dark and knocked him to his knees.

Moran continued to be amused. "Try that for size, little man. I've always wanted to slug a colonel."

Through his blur of pain Cade could hear Mimi screaming. Farther away there were shots and blows and the Squid's excited squealing.

Moran singled out two men. "You, Fred and Roy. You know what to do with him. Don't mark him any more than he is. And remember, I want him to have some water in his lungs if he should wash ashore."

"You're running the show," a man said.

It sounded like the voice of the youth Cade had seen behind the desk. Mimi was still screaming. The confusion around him continued. At a distance, the Squid bleated, "Goddamn. You let me by. You heard what Tocko said."

Cade attempted to get to his feet and Moran drew back his foot and kicked him in the face. His voice was almost gentle. "Lie down, little man. You've had it You're out of all this now."

A second sharper wedge of pain seemed to split Cade's head in two. He mentally damned the armor and head rest on an F-86. He'd always known it would happen and it had, on his first mission. A flight of Migs had jumped him at six o'clock and he hadn't even seen them come in. He pulled back to stop the falling sensation and the whole gadget-loaded cockpit exploded and propelled him into space.

14
TIME TO KILL

It was a pleasant sensation. Cade, still fogged with pain, thought briefly that he was riding the moss-filled sack swinging at the end of the long rope tied to one of the upper branches of the huge sweet bay tree behind the old house. If he swung high enough he would be able to see the oyster camps on the far bank of the river.

His mild glow faded and he was cold again. He wasn't on the swing. He couldn't be. The swing had been gone for years. Besides, someone was holding his hands and feet. Somewhere a man was counting.

"One. Two. Three."

The impact of his falling body on the water knocked the air from Cade's lungs and shocked him back to partial consciousness. Then, at a small distance and going away, the man who had counted said:

"Well, that takes care of that."

"Better circle to make sure," a second voice said. "Some of these small wiry guys are tough."

Cade's sinking sensation resumed, but now he was unable to breathe. An irresistible force was exerting increasing pressure on his body. He sank listlessly, revolving slowly, until his instinctive will to live forced his hands and feet into motion. He broke water, gasped air and sank again, with the churn of the screw of a fast-moving cruiser threatening to puncture his eardrums. As instinctive as the will to live, he dove as deep as he could. When he surfaced the second time, he was riding the frothy white wake of the boat whose running lights were now fifty yards away.

The man who had counted asked, "What's Jim going to do with his cruiser?"

"That's up to Jim."

"And the girl?"

The man who had counted laughed. "That's up to Jim, too. But first he's got to catch her."

The laughter and voices and lights disappeared in the deep morning fog. Fully conscious, Cade lay on his back, looking up at the dimming stars, barely moving his hands and legs enough to stay afloat. He'd never been so tired. The cold water felt soft and good on his fevered body. Rest, the medic had told him. Well, why not? What had he left to live for? Deep in his subconscious mind Cade was tempted to lie still and let the water take him.

But there was something he had to do.

Cade tried to remember what it was. First it eluded him. Then he remembered. Of course. *He had to kill Moran.*

He continued to float, conserving his strength, reorienting his mind. Strangely, he felt no resentment toward the men who had dropped him from the boat. All they had done was to follow orders. He was nothing to them. They were nothing to him. It was Moran who'd kicked him in the face and laughed:

"Lie down, little man. You've had it. You're out of all this now."

Moran was his oyster. Moran was the man he wanted.

The planes of Cade's face changed. His cheekbones grew more pronounced, as his lean cheeks firmed. His black eyes became even blacker. The wisp of a mustache became an affectation.

He named Moran in Portuguese, Serbian and French, then turned on his belly and swam with an easy overhand stroke he could keep up for hours, if need be. His top-siders weighted his feet. He trod water and unlaced them and twelve years fell away with the sneakers. The silver maple leaves were gone from his shoulders. He was no longer former Lieutenant Colonel Cain. He was all river Cajun, as much at home in the water as he was on land. He was old man Cade Cain's boy, a direct descendant of a cold-eyed Kaintucky flatboat man who had mated with an olive-skinned Baratarian flame who was kin to Jean LaFitte.

Cade shook his head to clear it. He wouldn't die. He couldn't die. It was inconceivable for him to die until he'd stuck a knife in Moran and twisted it sufficiently to do what he'd come to do.

The scene at the lodge, the mysterious plane, the babble of foreign voices and the gun fight between Tocko's and Moran's men didn't matter. They were of no consequence. He could figure them out later.

Right now he had to stay alive. Moran was the oyster he wanted.

Cade swam blindly for a long time. Then reason asserted itself. Moran had wanted water in his lungs in case his body should wash ashore. It was logical to assume that Moran wouldn't want him to wash ashore in the Bay. Embarrassing questions might be asked. Both Mamma Salvatore and Sal had known that he and Mimi had been headed for the lodge. That probably meant that he'd been dropped in the Gulf, possibly near big south mud lump where he'd seen the six dead men. It seemed to be a favorite drop, undoubtedly because a body left on the lump would eventually wash out into the Gulf.

Still, big south mud lump was a long run from the lodge. It had been early morning when he'd left Janice. He had no way of knowing how much time had lapsed. Cade stopped swimming and trod water while he searched for the north star. It was so faint he could barely see it. Full morning wasn't far away. One by one, the stars were fading from the sky. The fog rising wraithlike from the water was veined with the deep red of false dawn. One of the old-world superstitions he'd learned in his youth from an aged Dalmatian fisherman occurred to Cade. The fog was veined with red, which didn't happen very often. When it did it meant that the Lamb of the Lord was crying tears of blood for his lost sheep.

Orientated, Cade swam on. He had no way of knowing how far away it was but by swimming east, he had to reach land.

Fifteen minutes, a half-hour passed. Twice, large, slowly moving bodies passed him in the water. The sky was almost bright now but the gathering fog had deepened. Swimming through it was like flying blind through an endless bank of clouds, except that he had to furnish the motive power.

Cade's arms grew heavier with every stroke. It was an effort to kick. The overhand crawl that had been so easy when he had left Bay Parish was rapidly becoming torture. Two years of fish heads and rice and garbage soup had drained him of his strength. He still had a long way to go before he would be the man the youth had been who impulsively had left Bay Parish to enlist in the Air Force.

Cade swam on doggedly. He wouldn't die. A Cain always paid his debts. He couldn't die until he'd killed Moran. His head was as light as his arms were heavy. He was hearing things now. He thought he could hear the twittering of birds and there were no birds on the mud lumps. His light-headedness increased as his strength failed. Now he even thought he could hear Mimi calling him.

"Cade," she called guardedly, "Cade."

Cade tried to answer her and gulped water. He'd swum as far as he could. He couldn't take another stroke. He took one. He took two, then three and his thrashing hand struck sand. His fogged mind tried to analyze the hard granules between his fingers. There was no sand on the mud lumps. He wasn't in the Gulf. He was still in the Bay. The birds and perhaps Mimi were real.

"Here," he called weakly. "Here."

Flat in the shallow water, like a swimming frog, he worried his way across the sand and tried to rest his cheek on one arm but the water was still too deep. He worked his way farther up on the beach and felt dry sand under his hands. Then, a great roaring filling his ears and the black water lapping at his bare feet, he turned on his back with the last of his strength and passed out....

The sun had risen. He could feel it on his face. His head was cradled on something soft and yielding. He thought he could smell feminine flesh. Cade opened his eyes and saw a fourteen-foot skiff bobbing at anchor with the attached outboard motor tilted at the right angle to allow the salt water to drain out. Beyond the skiff was a solid wall of fog.

He opened his eyes and looked up into Mimi's face and beyond her face into a tangle of green leaves. On one of the lower branches of the tree, a vivid splash of crimson became a crested cardinal, puffing its small throat in strident song.

Mimi touched his face with her fingertips. "Rest."

It was an effort for Cade to talk. His throat felt like it was encrusted with salt. "How did you get here?"

Mimi continued to fondle his face. "I followed the lights of the men in the boat." She nodded at the anchored skiff. "I tol' you I 'ad boat in Caracas."

Cade snuggled down in the lap on which his head was resting. "I'm glad you're not in Caracas."

Mimi smiled. She closed his eyes with her fingertips.

When Cade opened his eyes again the sun had begun to climb. The bank of fog was gone but his head still reposed in Mimi's lap and the skiff still bobbed at anchor.

It was easier now for him to talk. "I didn't dream it, then."

Mimi shook her head. "No."

"How long have I been asleep?"

"Not long. Perhaps an hour."

"And there have been no boats?"

"No boats."

"No one looking for me?"

"No. They think you are dead," Mimi said.

"And you?"

"What about me?"

"Aren't they looking for you?"

She shrugged. "Maybe."

"You followed the men who dropped me, is that it, Mimi?"

"I tol' you. As soon as I could get to the *Sea Bird* an' put on some clothes."

Cade realized that Mimi was wearing his white shirt and pants again. "What happened to your dress?"

"Mister Moran tore the rest of it from me when I tried to keep heem from keeking you." Her lips twisted in a wry smile. "I 'ope he enjoys it as much as he does my shoes an' my knife." She sighed. "Such a nice dress."

Still incredulous, Cade asked still another time, "You followed the men who dropped me?"

"Yes."

"Weren't you frightened?"

"Ver' frightened." Mimi's big eyes seemed to grow larger. "An' I am even more frightened when I call an' call an' call an' you do not answer. I am theenk maybe I am come to the wrong place or you do not become conscious again when they are put you een the water." She pressed one hand to the bulge on the left side of her borrowed shirt. "I am nevair so relieved as when I hear one ver' faint 'here'."

"No one tried to stop you when you started the kicker?"

Mimi shrugged and the yielding substance on which Cade's head was cradled was more delightful as she moved. "No," she said, scornfully. "They were all too busy fighting an' shooting an' calling each other the bad names." Mimi reported with satisfaction, "Is something about a lot of money an' both that Tocko an' Jeem wanting to be the only one to enjoy the favors of thees yellow-haired old woman to whom you were married. While they were still fighting an' shooting at each other she screamed at them to stop an' Tocko called her a hot-panzed leetle beetch an' said unless she would come back to heem, he would foul up the deal, if it was the last thing he evair deed." Mimi blushed.

"How did you know where the men in the boat were taking me?"

Mimi shrugged again. "I did not. I followed their lights until they disappeared, then I kept on a few miles farther. Then I shut off the motor and waited until they came back again. And when they had passed me sitting in the dark, I went on in the direction from which they came an' began to call."

Cade pressed the fingers stroking his face. "You're okay."

Mimi was pleased. "You like?"

"I like very much."

Cade attempted to digest what Mimi had just told him. They were, obviously, on one of the smaller islands in the mouth of the Bay. Pressed for time the two men following Moran's orders hadn't bothered to take him out into the Gulf. They'd dropped him in one of the passes, East Pass probably, hoping the suck of the tide would complete their work for them. That was why he'd reached land as soon as he had.

The abortive landing of the helicopter and the fight at the lodge made less sense. Moran had admitted openly that until he and Janice had broken with Tocko, the latter had *intended* to use the lodge he'd built on land he didn't own as a drop for smuggled aliens. Aliens willing to pay any price Tocko named to be put ashore on the mainland. The men the 'copter pilot had landed or had tried to land were undoubtedly aliens.

But to whom did the cutter belong? It came under the head of big business. Who had advanced the money to build the expensive pier and pump in the beach and equip the radio shack? What was worth so much money? Why had Moran and Janice spent two months in New Orleans currying favor with city and state politicians? What was the deal Tocko intended to foul up if Janice didn't come back to him?

Only one thing was clear. He, Cade, was a fly in everybody's ointment. Janice wanted him dead badly enough to give herself to him, merely to get at the shells in his gun. Either Tocko or Moran had tried to frame him by killing Joe Laval. When he'd asked Moran to make sense at the beginning of the fight on the landing strip, Moran had been amused. He'd said:

"The little bastard couldn't be a good sport and die in Pyongyang. He would have to come back."

For one reason or another all three of them wanted him dead. The dryness returned to Cade's throat. He wished he had a drink of water. He wished he had a cigarette. He wished he was smart. The hell of it was he'd never pretended to be smart. All he was was a guy by the name of Cain.

He did know Mimi's legs must be cramped. He knew he should be up and on his way if he intended to kill Moran, and he did intend to. But he liked being where he was. It was the closest he'd come to his dream, the closest he'd come to following the medic's orders. It was quiet and peaceful on the island. He liked the sun on his face. He liked the song the cardinal was singing. He liked lying with his head on Mimi's lap. It was like being returned from the dead, like walking across the line at Panmunjom.

Cade had never been more content or comfortable. There was something more than the normal biological attraction of the sexes between himself and Mimi. They were, as Latin-speaking people said, *sympatico*, in accord on all things, at least all things that mattered.

"I'm tiring you?" he asked her.

She shook her head and smiled. "I like."

Cade lay looking up into her face, almost afraid of pushing a miracle too far. "You wouldn't happen to have a cigarette?"

Mimi nodded brightly and dug down into her borrowed shirt. "I 'ave just one and two matches. I knew maybe you might want."

She put the crumpled cigarette between his lips. It was perfumed like a cigarette carried loose in a woman's purse, daintily fragrant, tasting more of her flesh than of tobacco. Cade was a little sorry when she lit it.

He sucked smoke into his lungs and offered the cigarette to her. "We'll smoke this and be on our way."

Mimi bent over him. "Where?"

Cade wished Mimi would learn to button more than the bottom two buttons of his shirt.

"Where?" Mimi repeated.

"Back to the lodge."

"Why?"

"I'm going to kill Moran."

"How?"

"I don't know."

Mimi leaned down to blow smoke in his face. "It is for you to say. You are the man."

A thought suddenly struck Cade. "You remember that cutter

docked at the pier?"

"Of course."

"Did the men aboard it take any part in the fight?"

Mimi shook her head emphatically. "No. All they did was watch. And while I was starting the keeker I could hear bells aboard and seamen began to haul in the lines."

Cade wondered how he could have been so dumb. Of course. It had been so simple all the time. The big boys seldom interfered, openly, in inter-family quarrels. It wasn't politic. They preferred a policy of watchful waiting, but now the bitterly contested states' tide bill had passed, vesting all off-shore sovereignty in the states involved, there were a good many firms which might be vitally interested in certain types of waterfront acreage.

Cade could think of five off-hand, all internationally known, all in the same line of business.

15
MANY A SLIP

Its long immersion in water had stopped Cade's watch but from the position of the sun he judged the time to be close to four o'clock. It had seemed so simple while he'd been swimming through the fog. He would return to the lodge and kill Moran.

How?

He had no weapon but his hands. There was a chance that now, thinking he was dead, Moran and Tocko and Janice had worked out some sort of truce. In that case, he would have not only Moran but Tocko and the Squid to deal with.

Cade parted the drooping branches of the water oak behind which he'd poled the skiff and looked out. He was not surprised to see the *Sea Bird* cruising fitfully off-shore. One of the two men in the cockpit was sweeping the irregular shoreline with a pair of glasses. As Cade watched, the cruiser moved on slowly. Cade followed it with his eyes.

"Buy a boat," the medic had told him.

Mimi exhaled softly. "They saw us?"

Cade shook his head. "No. At least, they're moving on."

He debated waiting until dark before poling on again. It was one thing to beat his way back up the Bay with the throttle of a fifteen-horsepower kicker wide open. It was something else to pole his way along the shore line, following the contours of the land, moving from one point of cover to another. He hadn't dared to use the kicker since they'd started. Its high-pitched whine was audible for miles and while Moran might think he was dead, the men in the boats combing the Bay were looking for a very alive girl in a fourteen-foot skiff powered by an outboard motor.

Mimi had trouble swallowing. "I am thirsty."

"Yeah," Cade said. "So am I."

He started to pole out from under the tree and stopped to look at the tilted motor attached to the metal transplate. His mind still wasn't working clearly. Between the two tanks and the motor he had poled an unnecessary one hundred pounds all day. He detached the gas tank. It was empty enough to float. He threw it on to a tangle of exposed roots, then unscrewed the motor and the extra tank and dropped them overboard.

Mimi looked at him, puzzled.

"They're no good to us," Cade told her. "We don't dare use them." He looked out through the screen of leaves, trying to locate some familiar landmark. "We can't be more than four or five miles from the lodge. I'll pole a few miles closer if I can. About a mile from the lodge there used to be a spring. If it's still there, we'll have a drink. After that, I think we'd better go on by foot."

"Whatever you say."

Cade poled out from under the tree and on up the shore line. Without the motor and the tanks, the boat was easier to handle. But the pole he'd broken off a dead tree wasn't entirely straight. On a hard push it twisted in his hands. During the morning, blisters had formed on his palms. Shortly after noon, the blisters had broken and now it was torture to grip the pole. It had been a long time since he'd poled a boat and that had been a pirogue, not a skiff.

He'd been right about this portion of the Bay remaining unchanged. During the long hot day they'd passed four fishing camps but all of them were deserted. Animal life was abundant. There were 'gators on the mud slides in the bayous, snakes lying sunning themselves on partly submerged roots and sand bars. The muskrat population had increased since the days when he'd come to the Bay with his father. Twice he'd seen swimming otters. Several times, deer had peered out of tangles of brambles.

Blood from the raw flesh on his palms began to stain the pole. Cain went on doggedly. The sun sank still lower in the sky. As it touched on the water and seemed to bounce, Mimi wet her lips with her tongue. "There will be trouble when we reach the lodge, perhaps shooting?"

"Undoubtedly."

"And you have no gun."

"No."

She spoke, as always, dramatically, as if imparting a great secret, "Then instead of going to the lodge, why don't we go to the *policia?*"

Cade was hot and tired. His injured head and his swollen jaw ached. His pole caught in a submerged root and when he pulled it free, an angry cottonmouth came with it and tried to climb into the boat. Cade used the pole to throw the snake up on shore, and poled on. It was the first foolish question she'd asked. Even so, it was an effort for him not to be curt with her.

"Where do you think you are?" he asked her. "In Times Square or on the corner of Canal and Royal? The nearest local law, if any, is on Grand Isle. Moran's men would pick us up before we got two miles across the Bay. The only real law down here is the Coast Guard and we've no way of contacting them. Besides, you're in the country illegally. Remember?"

The sun had burned a deep V on Mimi's chest. In the morning her nose was going to peel. She looked down at her bare feet. "After you kill Moran, if you can do it, what are you going to do with me?"

"I don't know," Cade admitted.

Once it touched the water, the sun sank rapidly. Cade hoped he was as close to the lodge as he thought he was.

The next spit of land looked familiar. As Cade recalled, there had been a huge water oak near the spring. The tree was still there, only shattered. A storm blowing in off the Gulf had split and partially uprooted it and lightning had completed its destruction.

Cade beached the boat on the shelf of sand in front of the tree. "This is it. I mean the spring. We're not more than a mile from the lodge."

He led the way inland through the trees, with Mimi following closely behind him. The spring was where he remembered it, but also changed. Some fisherman or squatter had bricked it in and built a crude cabin in the clearing. The cabin, as the others he had seen, was empty.

Cade lay on the moist ground with Mimi beside him and showed her how to make a crude cup of her hands. When she had drunk what he considered enough, he stopped her.

Mimi's eyes turned sullen. "But I am still thirsty."

"Even so," Cade said.

He drank sparingly, then sat with his back against a tree. Now that he was almost to the lodge, the impossibility of what he hoped to do appalled him. Cade wondered if he were turning chicken. He doubted it. It was just that he was one man against perhaps a dozen and the other twelve men would be armed.

"Why can not I drink?" Mimi asked.

"It might make you sick," Cade told her. "Wait. After we've rested a few minutes we can drink some more."

While he waited he searched the shack. There was a crude bunk, a wood-burning stove, a few shelves to hold provisions. On a hunch, Cade felt along the shelves. On the top shelf, pushed back and forgotten, were a rusted can of beans and a small tin of sardines. The rust didn't seem to have eaten through the can. The sardines were easy to open. There was a key on the can. The beans were another matter. Cade kept up his search of the cabin and the small clearing around it and near what had been a woodpile, he found a dull axe with a broken handle. He used the blade of the axe to open the beans. He divided them and the sardines equally on two leaves from a wild mango tree.

They ate beside the spring, Cade watching Mimi, feeling as he had during their first meal together aboard the *Sea Bird*. A dozen times during the day they'd had to climb out and push the boat over ankle-deep grass flats. Her bare feet were cut and torn by shells. The sun had tortured her flesh. She'd been through hell all day without one word of complaint. Now, as during their first meal together, she was starved. Still, hungry and frightened as she was, squatted beside a wilderness spring in the deepening dusk, she managed somehow to look as if she were eating Huitres en Coquille a la Rockefeller at Antoine's. There was no doubt about it. She was people.

"Is good," Mimi smiled at him. "Now may I drink again?"

Cade nodded. "Yes."

His own hunger left him as he looked from the drinking girl to the faint trail barely distinguishable in the darkening mat of vegetation. He had no right to risk Mimi's life, especially after she'd saved his. So he would manage to kill Moran. There were still Tocko and the Squid. There were Harry and Fred and the bronze-faced 'copter pilot, all living outside the law. With the exception of the Squid, any one of them would be very pleased to get their hands on Mimi.

Cade was sorry now he had jettisoned the motor and the tanks. The girl had been right. He should run for Grand Isle and turn Mimi over to the local authorities. Even being sent back to Caracas couldn't possibly be as bad as what would happen to her if she fell into the hands of any of the men at the lodge. They might even share her. To men of their type a woman had only one purpose. She was a vessel to be filled. And when they had finished with Mimi the light would be gone from her eyes. If she didn't use a knife on herself, she would be just another waterfront jade perched on a bar stool somewhere, willing to sell, for food and lodging and drink, that on which she no longer placed any value.

Mimi was concerned. "You are not eating."

"No," Cade said, shortly.

He'd been mad. He could see that now. He couldn't go back to the lodge. He couldn't attempt to kill Moran. His revenge would have to wait. He wasn't all river Cajun, after all. He'd carried rank on his shoulders too long. If rank carried privileges, it also carried responsibilities. And the succession of gold and silver bars and maple leaves had burned into the flesh of his shoulders. His first duty was to Mimi. Once he got her to a place of safety, he could think of himself.

He drank from the spring and stood up.

Mimi stood up with him. "Now we are going to the lodge?"

Cade nodded. "Yes. But not to kill Moran."

"No?"

"No. I'm going to try to steal a boat and get you to Grand Isle."

"But you said Jeem's men would catch us before we 'ave gone two miles."

"Possibly not at night."

Cade led the way back to the shore. It was completely dark now and the water was slightly phosphorescent wherever it was broken. The power plant at the lodge had resumed its monotonous *thud thud*. The high-watt bulb on the pier head was lighted. He could see it through the trees on the next spit of land. Whatever he did he would have to do before the moon rose.

Mimi's fingers bit into Cade's forearm in sudden comprehension. "You are doing this for me."

"Let's say for both of us."

"You are afraid something bad will happen to me."

"Moran hasn't had his men searching the Bay all day because he wants to hold your hand."

"No," Mimi agreed with him. "I should nevair 'ave come to the States. I should nevair 'ave stowed away in La Guaira."

Cade squeezed the hand on his arm. "If you hadn't, I'd still be back on that island, possibly snake bit or 'gator bait by now."

Mimi shook her head. "No. You would still be in Bay Parish an' everything would be fine for you. The law would know by now that you deed not keel Señor Laval. It was because I insisted on finding Jeem, insisted you take me to New Orleans, that you are in all thees trouble."

Cade studied the pole he'd left lying across the stern thwarts of the boat. "That's water over the dam."

"Water over the dam?"

"Spilled milk."

"Thees I do not know."

Cade continued to study the pole. It would be useless in the basin in front of the lodge. The water in the basin was at least six fathoms deep almost all the way to the shore, another reason why the big firms might be interested in the land. "Over and done with," he told Mimi. "You got mixed up with a heel. I married a sex-propelled cash register. The best we can do is forget the whole affair and get out of this with as much skin as we can."

"But ees your property."

"I'll live. That is, if I'm not executed for killing Joe Laval."

Cade walked back the way they had come, tore a four-foot piece of twelve-inch clapboard off the shack and shaped a rough paddle with the dull axe-head.

There were luminous eyes around the spring now, as the night things of the swamp and hammock began to stir. As he worked, he heard a thrashing in the underbrush as some wild thing made its kill and once a dry slithering whisper as a snake crawled through the grass.

There were things to be said for flying an F-86. The worst that could happen to you was for a Gook to lob a .37 shell into your cockpit, or forget to turn off the emergency fuel system after you took off and have the pump accidentally kick on and the excess fuel pouring into the engine literally burn you alive. Either way was quick. The Delta and the creatures in it, human and otherwise, worried a man to death.

Mimi was sullen-eyed when he returned. "No," she said.

"No what?" Cade asked her.

"You 'ave your pride," she said. "You are doing thees as you 'ave done everything else, for me."

Cade lost his temper. "Goddamn it, get into the boat."

Mimi's lower lip trembled. For a moment Cade thought she was going to cry. She didn't. "Whatever you say," she said, with simple dignity. "You are the man."

Cade poled along the shore and out to the extremity of the next spit of land. The basin lay just beyond it. The pier looked the same as it had the night before but the cutter was gone. The three work boats and the *Sea Bird* were still in their slips. The men who had used the *Sea Bird* to look for Mimi had had to gas the boat. If he and Mimi could get aboard the cruiser undetected, what he hoped to do would not only be feasible, it would be relatively simple. The *Sea Bird* could run away from any of the other three boats.

Cade looked from the pier to the lodge. However the fight had ended, it was over. The helicopter was gone from the landing strip. A half-dozen of the rooms on the first floor of the lodge, as well as the dining room and the lobby were brightly lighted. He could see no one on the pier or on the beach. As on the night before, the only sounds in the basin were the lapping of water on the shore, the shrilling of the cicadas, the booming of frogs and the *thud thud* of the plant powering the lights.

"What are you going to do?" Mimi whispered.

Cade told her. "Steal my own boat, if I can."

He poled away from the shore and was almost immediately in deep water. Cade let the pole slip from his bleeding palms and picked up the crude paddle he'd hewn. The wind was off-shore and brisk. It was as difficult to paddle the flat-bottomed skiff as it had been to pole it. No matter on which side he paddled it yawed off course. The distance from the point of land at which he'd started to the end of the pier was less than half a mile. Cade was breathless and drenched with sweat. Over an hour passed before he could reach out and catch a breather by holding on to the creosoted pilings. As new as it was, barnacles had already begun to form. The fresh creosote burned his raw palms. The skiff thudding against the pilings was even more difficult to handle in the chop under the pier than it had been in open water.

Laboriously, Cade made his way inshore until he could grasp one of the sagging ropes that moored the *Sea Bird*.

The men who had used it hadn't bothered to put out the fenders and there was a nasty scar to starboard where the cruiser had rubbed against the lee aft piling.

He pulled the skiff under the transom and held it as steady as he could while Mimi scrambled aboard. Then he followed her, casting the skiff adrift.

The skiff drifted out into the bay. From time to time the off-shore wind carried a burst of laughter from the screened dining-room windows of the lodge. Once Cade thought he heard Janice laughing. He stood a moment panting in the dark, squeegeeing the sweat from his face and chest, then checked the controls by feel. Everything seemed to be in order.

He cast off the slack aft line and hauled it in, then waited for the cruiser to yaw and cast off the line to lee.

"What can I do?" Mimi whispered.

"Nothing," Cade whispered tersely. "I'm going to play it out between the pilings if I can and let the tide and the wind carry us out into the bay before I cut in the motors. Because the minute I do, all hell is apt to pop."

He scrambled up on the catwalk and moved forward, wishing it weren't quite so dark. It was like trying to see through a solid black wall.

The tide was out and the cruiser was riding three feet lower than the pier. Cade reached up through the dark to locate the bight making it fast and a strong hand grasped his arm and lifted him up onto the pier as easily as he might have lifted a bottle.

His pinhead bobbling, his thin voice shrill with excitement, the Squid said, "It's you. It's you I bin watchin' for an hour. They said you was dead but you ain't. You come back, didn't you, Cade? Back to the Squid."

Cade stood limp, depleted, beaten. He'd come to the end of his stick and there was no silk to hit.

Mimi scrambled up on the pier beside them and beat at the Squid with her small fists. "You leave him alone."

The Squid used his free hand to hold her. "An' you're the girl who ran away." The Squid was well pleased with the Squid. "Tocko is goin' t' like this. Maybe now Joe is gone he'll even make me sheriff."

Mimi bit the hand holding her and the Squid squealed shrilly. "Do it again, huh?" he pleaded. "I like that."

The big man walked Cade and Mimi down the pier. It was useless to try to hold back. It was like being towed by a drag-line. Mimi continued to scream and fight. Cade walked stiff-kneed, beaten. He'd done his best and it hadn't been good enough.

As they reached the patch of loose sand the screen door of the lodge opened and a man called, "What the hell's going on down there?"

"I got the girl who run away," the Squid called back. "Her an' Cade come sneaking back, a-paddlin' in a skiff. Tried to steal his boat."

The wind whipped away most of his words.

"Who?" the man called. "Who did you say came back?"

"Cade," the Squid shouted. "You know. The guy Moran said was dead. Cade Cain. The guy who killed Joe Laval."

16
THE BIG DEAL

The dining room seemed filled with men. There were at least a dozen at three tables shoved together in the center of the room. A half-dozen more were grouped at a table in the corner. These glanced up apprehensively as the Squid pushed Cade and Mimi into the room ahead of him.

The big room was fogged with smoke. The tables were littered with scraps of food and empty dishes and partially filled bottles. All of the men were in their shirt sleeves. Most were wearing guns. All of them turned and looked at him and Mimi. Two of the men stood up.

They would be Fred and Roy, Cade decided. He looked for Janice and found her. She and Tocko and Moran were sitting at the same table that she and he and Moran and Mimi had occupied the night before. From the look on Moran's face and the way Janice was fondling Tocko's over-plump white hand, his former wife had changed sides and beds again.

The Squid pushed him up to the table and looked accusingly at Moran. "Ya didn't tell us the truth. Cade ain't dead at all. Him an' the girl come paddling up t' the pier jist as alive as could be, usin' a piece of board for a paddle. They was atryin' t' steal his boat when I caught 'em."

Tocko got to his feet and looked across the table at Moran. "I thought you said Cade was dead."

One of the two men standing at the other table said, "Goddamn, he has to be. He was out cold when we dropped him in the mouth of the pass. He should be thirty miles out in the Gulf by now."

Tocko continued to look at Moran.

Moran spread his hands. "You heard what Roy just said."

Janice brushed the ash from the tip of her cigarette. There was begrudged admiration in her voice. "You're a hard man to kill, Cade."

His feeling of weakness and depletion passed, Cade rested his hands on the back of an unoccupied chair. "You might try loving me to death. You did a pretty good job last night."

"You seemed to like it."

"A man who's just spent two years in a Commie prison isn't exactly a connoisseur."

Janice flushed angrily but made no answer.

Cade studied the deeply tanned faces watching him. "Just what is this, a love feast?"

"I guess you could call it that," Moran said. "Although I can't say I enjoyed my food."

"It would seem you lost."

Moran sipped at the drink in front of him. "So it would seem."

Tocko sat back in his chair and looked at the Squid. "Is there anyone on the pier?"

The Squid shook his head. "Naw."

Tocko glanced at the six men sitting by themselves.

"Then you'd better get back. Right at the moment it could be very embarrassing if Lieutenant Peyton or one of the other Coast Guard officers should take a notion to drop in unexpectedly to see how Mrs. Cain is getting along with her new resort."

"Sure," the Squid said. "Sure. But I done good, didn't I, Mr. Kalavitch?"

"You did fine," Tocko assured him.

Janice watched the Squid leave the room. "Ugh. He gives me the creeps. Why do you keep that thing on your payroll?"

"He's useful," Tocko said. "Just as Joe Laval was useful." He looked reproachfully at Cade. "You shouldn't have shot Joe, Cade."

Cade shook his head. "I didn't."

Tocko studied his face for a long time. "I believe you." He looked from Cade to Moran. "So shooting Joe was more of your work."

Moran palmed a cigarette into his mouth and lit it. "Prove it."

Tocko shrugged. "It doesn't matter. But the picture is beginning to clear. Joe was taking money from both of us. It was you who told him to order Cade off the river. For that I got a punch in the jaw. Then when Cade didn't frighten, you were afraid he might look up Janice and interrupt your ill-advised idyll, so you killed Joe aboard Cade's boat, hoping the law would relieve you of one of your minor problems."

"Prove it," Moran repeated.

The fat man shrugged. "As I said, it is immaterial." He asked one of the men at the big table to bring over another chair and offered it to Mimi. "Do sit down, my dear. I tried my best to help you. I didn't want you involved in this. You see, I happen to know Moran wasn't legally married to you. That is why I reported you to Immigration, hoping they would deport you before you became mixed up in this mess."

Mimi sat looking at Janice. Her eyes were sullen and slitted. *"Gracias."*

Tocko returned his attention to Cade. "And you, Cade. You look like you've had a rough time of it. I'm afraid you're in for an even rougher one. But there is no need for us to be ungentlemanly about it. Sit down. Have a drink."

Cade paid Tocko the same begrudged admiration Janice had shown him. Tocko had grown. He was no longer that Kalavitch boy. He'd parlayed guts and shrewdness and an utter contempt for the law into big business.

The fat man poured four fingers of whiskey into a clean glass. "Your chief failing, as I see it, is in not being a good judge of wives." He patted Janice's hand. "She is smart, this one. As our Greek friends would say, she can nail a horseshoe on a fly. Her selling me the acreage after her power of attorney had been nullified by the final decree of divorce was very shrewd."

Cade tasted the whiskey in his glass. It tasted good. "Then I still legally own the land?"

"That would seem to be the crux of the matter." Tocko smiled. "But there is also the will you entrusted to Janice, leaving everything 'of which I die possessed, real and personal, to my beloved wife, Janice Cain'."

"The divorce also nullified that."

"True, but as there are no other heirs and as several prominent local politicians have already been promised a cut of the spoils, I doubt if there will be any official investigation into just when you died. Officially you never reached Bay Parish."

"You can't make it stick."

"I think I can."

Cade felt cold sweat start on his spine. "But I don't give a damn about the land. I'd almost forgotten I owned it."

Tocko shrugged. "Unfortunately for you, we are not concerned with your feelings. Alive, you are a very serious obstacle in the wheels of progress."

"With who turning the wheel, Sun, Shell, Sinclair, Standard Oil, Sunoco?"

"You're shrewd."

"I saw the cutter at the pier."

Janice sucked in her breath and exhaled slowly. "Gee-Sus. I never knew there was so much money in the world."

Tocko continued to beam. "The amount of money involved at the same time complicates and simplifies things for us all." He looked across the table at Moran. "To give Jim credit, he was the first to see the possibilities, once the new state's tide law had passed. He also saw the advisability of interesting certain local politicians so there wouldn't be any legal complications to hurdle."

Moran poured himself another drink. "So here I am."

"Wrapped in cotton," Tocko assured him. "As I have been telling you since morning, as long as we agree I am the head man and certain domestic problems are resolved, there is plenty for us all. You are a good man. I admit it. If you hadn't been I wouldn't have engaged you in the first place."

Moran gulped the drink he'd poured. "Thanks."

Cade looked at the larger table. None of the men at it were paying any attention to the conversation. All they were interested in was the individual sums they had been promised. He asked, "And the landing of the 'copter and the gun fight on the strip this morning?"

Tocko's smile returned. "Was merely a successful attempt on my part to resume a pleasant and profitable business and physical association. Also, shall we say, a club."

Cade's sunburned face felt uncomfortably warm. His cut feet and raw palms pained him. The whiskey failed to ease the constriction in his throat. He said, "Just as a matter of curiosity, let's see if I have this right."

"By all means," Tocko smiled.

"You met Moran shortly after his discharge from the Army. Still posing as an officer, he spent some months flying in aliens your boats had collected in La Guaira. It was for that purpose, as a drop, that you built this lodge."

"That is correct."

"While in Caracas, Moran met Mimi. We know that angle."

Mimi's eyes grew more sullen.

Cade continued. "Shortly after that, Janice showed up in Bay Parish and you bought or thought you bought the old Cain house and the acreage here on the Bay. As lagniappe, you insisted on certain favors from Janice—and grew to like them."

"Very much," Tocko admitted. He ran a plump hand down the small of Janice's back and patted her. The thought seemed to amuse him. "I might even marry her. Because outside of these favors of which you speak, she is the most unscrupulous woman I have ever met. We should go far together."

"Is that a nice thing to say?" Janice asked, but she was smiling.

There was an open package of Camels on the table. Cade offered the package to Mimi, put one in his mouth and lighted both cigarettes. "Meanwhile," Cade waved out the flame of the match, "Moran returned to Bay Parish and used the possibilities in the recently passed tide law to pry Janice out of your arms."

"It wasn't difficult," Moran said, thickly.

Janice scowled at him over her glass. "You keep your dirty tongue off of me."

Moran began an obscene reply and thought better of it. Cade looked from one flushed face to the other and realized both of them were drunk, that they had probably been drinking since morning. The chances were, the same was true of the men at the big table. It was a love feast, but an armed one. Janice and Tocko were sitting with their backs to the wall. Cade looked over Janice's shoulder at the open screened window behind her and the big veins in his temple throbbed visibly.

If he could create a diversion, if he could get them to quarreling among themselves, if he could get out of the room for five minutes, it might just be he could do what he had hoped to accomplish in the first place—with Janice and Tocko thrown in for *his* lagniappe. It was at least worth trying. He and Mimi had nothing to lose.

Tocko suggested suavely, "Suppose we leave personalities out of this."

Cade shook his head. "We can't. After leaving Bay Parish, Janice and Moran went to New Orleans together and spent several months getting to know and greasing state and city politicians who might be useful to them. As a cover they talked about a swank fishing lodge, a cheater's paradise in an unspoiled wilderness; but Janice also let it be known in the right places that she was sole owner of several thousand acres of tideland on a deep-water basin in the Bay. A basin with a deep ship's channel leading to the river and the city—a perfect spot for a storage dock or a refinery, not to mention the submerged potential oil land that went with the acreage. One of the larger oil firms was interested; interested enough to advance her sufficient money against possible future royalties to complete and furnish the lodge; to build a pier; to build and equip a radio shack with which they could keep in touch with their mobile test outfits working the Bay and Gulf."

"You son-of-a-bitch," Janice said. "You should have been a fortune teller instead of a flyer. You'd have gone a lot farther with a crystal ball than you did with a Sabrejet."

The men at the big table were listening to the conversation now. Cade glanced over his shoulder at them, then snuffed his cigarette and looked at Tocko. "This morning you crashed back into the picture," Cade said, "by making Moran an unwilling accomplice to the illegal landing of six aliens. This gave you the bluff of calling in the law, with the certainty you'd all go to jail if Janice didn't return to you and you weren't permitted to resume your rightful position as head man."

Tocko was amused. Moran said, "You're good, guy. That was just what happened. And with my record I don't dare call his bluff. So there it stands. I'm damned if I do and the same if I don't."

"Why?" Cade asked flatly. "Why not play it smart?"

"How do you mean?"

"Why not dump Tocko and play along with me? The land is legally mine. If you let Tocko take over, all you'll get is crumbs. I'll cut you in for a full half."

"Shut up, Cade," Janice said thickly. "You're trying to make trouble."

"How?" said Moran.

"By having him indicted for conspiracy in the murder of the six aliens he had one of his boats maroon on big south mud lump when a Coast Guard boat got too close." Cade added, "I saw the bodies. You must know the details."

"And Janice?"

"Janice isn't mine to offer, but with Tocko out of the way I don't imagine you'd have any trouble with her."

Tocko got to his feet slowly. His plump face was pink with anger. "Words, words words. Use your head, Jim. Let's not have any more trouble. We have everything ironed out."

Cade laughed. "Sure. With you taking both Janice and nine-tenths of the money and Moran being kissed out of the picture because of his past record."

Janice stood up beside Tocko. "Don't be a fool, Jim. All Cade is doing is trying to save his neck." She laid her hand on Moran's arm. "Can't you see? He *wants* us to fight among ourselves."

Moran slapped her. "Shut up. No. I can't see."

"You can't see what?"

"Why I should let you and Tocko make a chump out of me. Why I should take the short end of the deal. I figured this thing out. I made the original contacts. I arranged for the advance. What Cain says makes sense to me." Moran looked at the men milling restlessly around the big table. "What do you think, fellows?"

The silence broke as the men voiced their views. Tocko shouted, in vain, to be heard. The men moved up in arguing knots.

Tocko struck one in the face. "Shut up and keep out of this or you'll wind up on a mud lump." He resumed his effort to be heard. "Men. Listen to me—"

Cade hit the window screen hard. For a sickening moment he thought the copper wire was going to hold, then his body catapulted into space. The dry sand under the window seemed to rise to meet him.

Behind him he heard Janice scream. The flat slap of a fired pistol followed. A second, a third, a fourth report followed the first shot.

His nerves tensed against the expected impact of the bullets, Cade zigzagged desperately, but there was no familiar pacing whine of lead as he ran on.

The moon had risen. He was a perfect target, but whoever had fired the pistol hadn't been shooting at him.

The radio shack was the last in the row of separate cottages. Cade paused in the shadow of the tower to pant for breath. The lack of pursuit worried him. Tocko couldn't permit him to live. Even Moran's men, realizing they had been tricked, should be boiling out of the window by now.

Through the lighted windows he could see figures moving around in the lodge but the wind whipped away their voices before they could reach him. The only sounds were the slap of the water on the beach, the *thud thud* of the power plant and the chirp and thunking of the night things in the swamp.

Cade rounded the radio shack cautiously. There was a small angle iron leaning against one of the concrete piers. It wasn't much of a weapon. It was something. Cade picked it up and turned the knob of the closed door. The door seemed to be unlocked. Cade gripped the angle iron and walked in.

His upturned white monkey hat cocked low over one eye a gum-chewing youth in blue dungarees and white skivy was covering the radio operator with a .45 caliber service automatic. He included Cade in the coverage.

"Come in," the youth said. "Who are you?"

17

THE SCATTERED SCUM

A bead of sweat dripped from Cade's nose to plop inaudibly on the floor of the shack. After all he had been through, this was an anti-climax. He knew who the youth was, at least whom he represented. He'd seen similar gum chewing youths in blue dungarees and web gun belts before—a lot of them.

The youth noticed the iron. "Put it down, fellow."

Cade put the angle iron down carefully.

"Okay. Now I ast you a question."

"My name is Cain," Cade told him.

"The former Air Force colonel who's been kiting all over the Delta with that skirt from Venezuela?"

"Anyway my name is Cain."

The youth was still skeptical. "I betcha. You don't look like no colonel to me. Anyway, we can find out. The lieutenant says he is acquainted with you personal."

A second youth stuck his head in the doorway. "You have any trouble with the sparks, Chuck?"

"Naw," Chuck said scornfully. He looked at the sallow-faced radio operator. "I point the thing at him and he almost heaves his Hershey bars."

"Who's the other guy?"

"He says his name is Cain. You'd better take him up to the lodge and let the lieutenant look him over."

"Sure thing."

"You guys have any trouble?"

The second youth grinned. "Naw. They were so busy fighting among themselves they didn't even know we were there until the lieutenant blew his whistle." He covered Cain with the gun in his hand. "Let's take a walk, fellow. And don't give me no trouble."

As a precaution against the seaman's youth, Cade held his palms shoulder high as he waded the loose sand along the beach. There was no big boat made fast to the T of the pier. "Where's the cutter?" he asked.

"We didn't come in a cutter," the seaman said. "We came down fast, in a crash boat. And just so you guys wouldn't scatter we heaved-to around the next bend and walked down along the beach."

"I see," Cade said. He wished his knees would stiffen. He felt as if he were walking on rubber legs.

The cypress-paneled lobby was filled with men, most with their hands in the air. An alert and armed Coast Guardsman was posted at every exit. As Cade and the youth guarding him entered the room a grizzled chief whose bare arms boasted a colorful gallery of anchors and entwined hearts and lush beauties in scant bathing suits looked up from the collection of pistols and knives and revolvers he was making.

"Who you got there, Hanson?"

"Chuck says he told him his name is Cain."

The Coast Guard lieutenant who was questioning Moran turned and grinned at Cade. "Hi, Colonel. Remember me?"

Cade couldn't be certain after the years but the lieutenant looked like one of the Mitrovica boys of the family which had changed its name to Morton. He had the same friendly white-toothed smile. "You wouldn't be Skip Morton, would you?"

Lieutenant Morton was pleased. "You do remember me. And I was just a squirt when you went away." He offered his hand. "Glad to see you, man. I'm glad you're back in Bay Parish. Welcome home."

Cade shook hands, wondering how long his knees would continue to hold him. He felt as he had on his first night back in Bay Parish, suddenly humble and shy. The lieutenant meant what he said, just as Miss Spence and old man Dobraviche and Mamma Salvatore and all the others had meant it.

Some strength returned to his knees as he accepted a cigarette from the package Morton offered him. "And am I glad to see you. But how come the raid right now. Who tipped you?"

Lieutenant Morton grinned. "Who didn't? We've been keeping our eyes on this place and laying for both Tocko and Moran for a long time, see? Then about fifteen hundred this afternoon the tips began to pour in. Mamma Salvatore was worried because you'd come down to the Bay and hadn't shown up again. Immigration was raising hell because you were supposed to have a girl stowaway on your boat. About the same time the crashed 'copter pilot the boys on the cutter fished out of the drink this morning loosened up enough to tell how he got all the bullet holes in his plane."

Lieutenant Morton continued. "It wasn't any one thing." He nodded at a small knot of men still huddled together in one corner of the lodge. "Then there were our alien friends there. We've had undercover agents in Havana tailing them for quite some time, waiting for them to make a break. We knew they'd made a contact. We suspected it was with one of Tocko's captains and when they disappeared last night an all-out alert was sounded." Lieutenant Morton's grin grew even more expansive. "Then just to make it official one of the seamen off a converted cutter one of the big oil companies is using to smell around these waters got drunk in a Royal Street bar. He sounded off about a big gun fight that had taken place between Moran and Kalavitch's boys down here last A.M. So the brass put it all together, I got the nod—and here we are."

The chief dumped his assortment of confiscated weapons on one of the tables. "All clear, sir."

"Good," Morton said crisply. "Now you and Jack go back and get the boat and bring it down to the pier."

"Aye, sir."

"As soon as you make fast we'll start loading."

"Aye, sir."

Moran's voice was bitter as he suddenly spoke up. "Sure. You'll tell the truth, Cain. You'll swear it in any court. The hell of it is, from what the lieutenant tells me, some pair of punks in Bay Parish saw me shoot Joe Laval. I'd have done better to have strung along with Tocko." Moran's mouth twitched in a nervous tic. "Well, no, not exactly."

Cade tried to hate the man. He couldn't. He felt drained of all emotion. He didn't hate anyone. All he wanted to do was rest. He looked for Mimi and found her sitting with her bare feet curled under her in one of the oversized leather chairs. Cade sat on the arm of the chair. "You're all right? You weren't hurt?"

Mimi shook her head. "No. Just frightened. That was all."

Her voice sounded strained. It was almost as if they were strangers.

Cade glanced around the room. "Where's Tocko?"

"Dead," Lieutenant Morton told him. He nodded at one of the men. "As I get it, Kalavitch slapped that man and got four slugs in his guts just as we came in the door." Morton shook his head. "Tocko made a mistake when he tried to climb into the big time as far as aliens are concerned."

Two seamen came out of the dining room carrying a canvas-wrapped bundle between them.

"Take him out on the pier," Lieutenant Morton ordered. "The chief's gone to get the boat."

"Aye, sir."

Lieutenant Morton snuffed his cigarette in one of the clam shells serving as ash trays. "Do you notice anyone else missing, Colonel?"

Cade looked at the faces in the lobby. "My former wife."

"That would be the blonde who went out the window on your heels."

"And the Squid."

"I forgot the pinhead," Lieutenant Morton admitted. He nodded to the seamen guarding the prisoners. "All right. Let's take them down to the pier, boys."

Morton opened the front screen door to permit the men to file through. As he did, somewhere out on the moonlit bay a balky motor coughed as if reluctant to start. "How many cruisers were there in the slips, Cade?" Morton asked.

"Three," Cade told him. "And mine."

"One of them is gone," Morton said. He swore softly. "Of course. The girl and the Squid. They must have cut loose and let the wind and the tide drift them out into the Bay."

The balky motor caught and turned over. There was the throb of an underwater exhaust. Cade joined Morton on the front steps of the lodge. A quarter-mile out in the Bay one of the three fishing boats were silhouetted briefly against the moon. Cade glimpsed, or thought he glimpsed, Janice's wheat-colored hair, then a huge bulk intervened.

One of the seamen asked, "Shall we try to get them, Lieutenant?"

Lieutenant Morton shook his head. "No. Let them go for now. Neither are very important. We'll put out a pickup on them, but I doubt if they'll get very far in that tub. If they do manage to get through the pass they'll probably hang up on one of the lumps."

Cade watched the fishing boat blend with the moonlight. His stomach felt slightly queasy. It was, he thought, ironic that Janice, whose specialty had been giving pleasure for gain, should escape with the Squid. Of all people. He hoped they had fun.

As the last of the men filed past him, Morton asked, "Now about this other girl, Colonel?"

"You mean Miss Esterpar?"

"If that's the name of the girl who jumped ship."

Cade looked at Mimi. She hadn't moved. She was still sitting white-faced and frightened in the big leather chair. "What about her?"

"Well, Immigration has alerted us to pick her up."

"What happens then?"

"The usual, I imagine. There'll be a hearing. Then they'll hold her for deportation."

"They'll send her back to Caracas."

"If that's where she came from."

"What if she can't go back? What if her family won't receive her?"

"Immigration isn't concerned with that."

"No," Cade said, "I don't suppose so." He tried to imagine what it would be like without Mimi and his imagination wouldn't stretch that far. He asked, "What if she was to marry an American citizen?"

"Who?"

"Me."

The situation was new to the lieutenant. "There you have me. I never came up against one quite like this before."

"I'll marry her in Grand Isle, now, tonight, in the morning, whenever we can find a priest."

Lieutenant Morton was dubious. "Now, look. I don't know about this, Cade. My orders are to pick her up."

Cade continued earnestly. "I'll be responsible for her appearance at any hearing that may be held. I'll sell my boat for whatever I can get and post bond if necessary."

"You must think a lot of her."

"Let's say I'm sorry for her."

"And you'll bring her to Bay Parish as soon as possible?"

"On my word of honor."

Morton watched the nose of the crash boat round the point of land above the pier and mentally computed the meager deck and cabin space aboard the boat.

"Well, in that case," he said. "I suppose it will do until we can get a ruling from Immigration. We're going to be pretty full up going back and I hate to crowd a nice kid—and she must be nice if you feel the way you do about her—in with the scum we're carrying."

18
COME AND GET IT

The day as a wedding day, left much to be desired. Morning was hot, as only the Delta can be hot. Then there was the matter of the priest. The priest in Grand Isle was visiting a colleague in Golden Meadow and Cade had been forced to rent a car to drive the thirty-one rutted miles separating the two towns. En route he'd had a puncture and a blow-out. Then when they had reached Golden Meadow there had been the matter of a license and the aged priest's natural reluctance to marry a couple dressed as they were dressed.

Despite the fact they were of a size, Mimi had flatly refused to wear any of the dozens of dresses Janice had left behind her. Nor had she been willing to move from the chair until dawn. She'd sat most of the night crying softly while Cade, his feeling of trying to climb a glass wall returned, had drunk too much rum.

Now, with night falling again, Cade still had a sour taste in his mouth. He sat in the dinghy on the shore of the small bayou in which he'd anchored the *Sea Bird*, trying to catch fish he didn't want, wishing despite the lateness of the hour that when he had concluded his business in Golden Meadow and Grand Isle he had pushed on for Bay Parish. At least Mamma Salvatore and Miss Spence and old man Dobraviche liked him. There would have been music and lights in Sal's and endless bottles of chilled orange wine.

Cade was bitter. He was no better off emotionally or financially than he had been when he'd first returned. He was still hungry and his hunger wasn't for food. He wanted love, friendship, tenderness, all the things he'd gone without during his time north of the Yalung.

With Tocko dead and Janice gone and his property recorded in Tocko's name, not forgetting the advance against possible royalties the oil company had made to Moran, the situation was typical Army. His property was so fouled up it would take seven chicken colonels from the Provost Marshal General's office and the same number from the C.I.D. to unscramble it. When the various lawyers were finished fighting it would probably turn out that Jean LaFitte still owned the land.

"Rest and quiet," the medic had told him. "Buy a boat."

Cade scowled through the purple shadows settling on the bayou at the ugly scar plainly visible on the rail of the *Sea Bird*. Mimi was supposed to be cooking supper. Not that he was hungry. He and Mimi had eaten in Grand Isle and also in Golden Meadow. Once the fatherly old priest had gotten over the shock of marrying a bare-footed couple, the man with assorted bruises and a black eye and the girl dressed in a pair of much too tight men's pants and shirt, he had insisted he and Mimi stay for lunch. He had even wished them numerous progeny. And that was a laugh. A real laugh!

Cade jerked the bait from the mouth of an eager two-pound grunt that was attempting to hook itself and pulled in his line wondering if Mimi held Janice against him, wondering just why she had agreed to marry him.

To stay in the country? It seemed the most logical reason. Was it that important to her? Was it the only reason?

With the deepening dusk the mosquitoes droned out of the marshes. Cade was relieved when he heard a jangling of ship's bells from the *Sea Bird*. He rode toward it slowly. His position hadn't changed. He still felt the same way about Mimi that he had when he had found her almost nude and dripping in the cabin of the *Sea Bird*. Mimi was a nice kid. She was people. She had guts. Anything that eventuated, if anything ever did, would have to originate with her.

She was leaning with her arms on the scarred rail of the cruiser. Her eyes were still slightly slitted and sullen. As Cade started to make fast, she said, "Could I ask you some questions before you come aboard?"

Cade looked up at her, puzzled. "Ask away."

"Why did you marry me?"

"That's a hell of a question."

"I have to know. Was it because you feel sorry for me? Because I would have to go back to Caracas?"

Cade started to say "partly" and thought better of it. He sat in the bobbing dinghy looking up at her. *Why had he married Mimi?*

Still leaning on her elbows, Mimi asked, "Was it just because I am a woman! Because I am young? Because I have the pretty body?"

The cool and deep peace of early evening spread slowly over the bayou. The night wind began to blow. Cade looked from Mimi to a great white heron winging its way through the deepening dusk back to its nest and all of his bitterness left him. It was good just to be home. He knew why he had married Mimi.

"No," he said. "I don't think so. That is, not entirely."

"Then why did you marry me?"

Cade told her. "Because you're the girl I thought I was marrying when I married Janice. Because I love you."

Cade realized, shocked, it was the first time he'd told Mimi he loved her.

Her eyes no longer slitted and sullen but big and black and luminous, Mimi smiled down at him. "Then, how you say, come an' get it." She added softly. "This you not 'ave to ask how to say. I love you, too."

Her face disappeared from the rail. Cade made the dinghy fast. Of course. Every woman had a right to know she was loved. He pulled himself over the side of the cruiser into the cockpit.

The table was set but there was no light in the galley.

The only light came from the open door of the forecabin. Her borrowed white shirt and pants, folded neatly on one of the bunks, Mimi was sitting on the other bunk, waiting, smiling, combing her hair, making her sweet self beautiful—for him.

Cade took a deep breath and held it. He'd been right after all.

From here on in he had it made.

THE END

DAY KEENE BIBLIOGRAPHY
(1903-1969)

This is Murder, Mr. Herbert and Other Stories (1948)

Framed in Guilt (1949; published in UK as Evidence Most Blind, 1949)

Farewell to Passion (1951; reprinted as The Passion Murders, 1951)

Love Me—and Die (1951; as by Keene, collaboration with Gil Brewer)

My Flesh is Sweet (1951)

To Kiss, or Kill (1951)

About Doctor Ferrel (1952)

Home is the Sailor (1952)

Hunt the Killer (1952)

If the Coffin Fits (1952)

Naked Fury (1952)

Wake Up to Murder (1952)

Mrs. Homicide (1953)

Strange Witness (1953)

The Big Kiss-Off (1954)

Death House Doll (1954)

His Father's Wife (1954; reprinted as by "Daniel White," 1970)

Homicidal Lady (1954)

Joy House (1954)

Notorious (1954)

Sleep With the Devil (1954; reprinted in Australia as Sin With the Devil, 1955)

There Was a Crooked Man (1954; revised 1963)

The Dangling Carrot (1955)

Who Has Wilma Lathrop? (1955)

Bring Him Back Dead (1956; revised 1963)

Flight by Night (1956)

Murder on the Side (1956)

It's a Sin to Kill (1958; reprint of Dead Man's Tide, 1953, as by William Richards)

Passage to Samoa (1958)

Dead Dolls Don't Talk (1959)

Dead in Bed (1959; Johnny Aloha series)

Moran's Woman (1959)

So Dead My Lovely (1959)

Take a Step to Murder (1959)

Too Black for Heaven (1959)

Too Hot to Hold (1959)

The Brimstone Bed (1960)

Chautauqua (1960; with Dwight Vincent)

Miami 59 (1960)

Payola (1960; Johnny Aloha series)

World Without Women (1960; with Leonard Pruyn)

Seed of Doubt (1961)

Bye, Bye Bunting (1963)

L.A. 46 (1964; published in UK as City of Angels, 1964)

Carnival of Death (1965)

Chicago 11 (1966)

Acapulco G.P.O. (1967)

Guns Along the Brazos (1967)
Wild Girl (1969; reprint of 1952
  edition as by Lewis Dixon)
Live Again, Love Again (1970)
League of the Grateful Dead
  and Other Stories: Vol. 1
  (2010)
We Are the Dead and Other
  Stories: Vol. 2 (2010)
Death March of the Dancing
  Dolls and Other Stories: Vol.
  3 (2011)
The Case of the Bearded Bride
  and Other Stories: Vol. 4
  (2013)
A Corpse Walks in Brooklyn
  and Other Stories: Vol. 5
  (2014)
Homicide House and Other
  Stories: Vol. 6 (2015)

As Lewis Dixon

Wild Girl (1952; reprinted 1969
  as by Keene)

As William Richards

Dead Man's Tide (1953;
  reprinted as It's a Sin to Kill
  as by Keene, 1958)

As Daniel White

Southern Daughter (1954;
  reprinted as by Keene, 1967)
His Father's Wife (1970;
  originally published as by
  Day Keene, 1954)

Rediscover the hard-hitting, character-driven fiction of

Lorenz Heller

The Savage Chase
written as Frederick Lorenz
978-1-944520-75-5 $19.95
Combined with *Tall, Dark and Dead* by
Kermit Jaediker and *Run the Wild River*
by D. L. Champion, three noir thrillers
originally published by Lion Books in
the 1950s.
"…a sexually frank, violence packed
thriller with vividly crisp dialogue."
—*GoodReads.*

A Rage at Sea / A Party Every Night
978-1-944520-99-1 $19.95
"In both novels the dialogue is crisp,
the story edgy and populated by
eccentric, volatile characters who just
can't get a grip on life."
—Paul Burke, *CrimeTime.*
"Lorenz's characters are what keep the
pages turning."—Alan Cranis, *Bookgasm.*

Dead Wrong
978-1-951473-03-7 $9.99
Black Gat Books #26.
"These interesting, well-developed
characters propel this rather standard
crime-noir plot into something special
and unusual. The prose is smooth and
there's no confusion in the storytelling
despite many clever twists and turns
leading to the tidy ending."
—*Paperback Warrior.*

Hide-Out / I Get What I Want
978-1-951473-15-0 $15.95
"Tough, gutsy novel of passion and
corruption in a small town. Sure-fire!"
—*Real Magazine.*
"In Lorenz's fiction, it feels like he
moulds the plot from organic character
confrontations, his writing is electric and
alive with unpredictability."
—Paul Burke, *CrimeTime.*

"[One of] the real pros of suspense." — Anthony Boucher, *New York Times*

**"He can put a story together that will have you on the edge of your chair.
[Heller] writes in a hard, fast, crisp style and he has a feel for colorful
language and characters that makes the story sing."** — *Mammoth Mystery.*

Stark House Press
1315 H Street, Eureka, CA 95501
griffinskye3@sbcglobal.net / www.StarkHousePress.com
Available from your local bookstore, or order direct via our website.

www.ingramcontent.com/pod-product-compliance
Lightning Source LLC
Chambersburg PA
CBHW070744190726
48292CB00002B/403

* 9 7 8 1 9 5 1 4 7 3 1 9 8 *